Janet Evanovich's novels are:

"Suspenseful."
—*Los Angeles Times*

"Terrific."
—*San Francisco Chronicle*

"Irresistible."
—*Kirkus Reviews*

"Thrilling."
—*The Midwest Book Review*

"Hilariously funny."
—*USA Today*

"A blast of fresh air."
—*The Washington Post*

"Inventive and fast-paced."
—*San Diego Union-Tribune*

"Superb."
—*Detroit Free Press*

TWO FOR THE ROAD

TWO BOOKS IN ONE

FULL TILT
and
FULL SPEED

JANET EVANOVICH
and
CHARLOTTE HUGHES

St. Martin's Paperbacks

This is a work of fiction. All of the characters, organizations, and events portrayed in this novel are either products of the author's imagination or are used fictitiously.

Published in the United States by St. Martin's Paperbacks, an imprint of St. Martin's Publishing Group.

TWO FOR THE ROAD: FULL TILT copyright © 2003 by Evanovich, Inc. and FULL SPEED copyright © 2003 by Evanovich, Inc.

For information, address St. Martin's Publishing Group, 120 Broadway, New York, NY 10271.

www.stmartins.com

ISBN: 978-1-250-21348-8

Our books may be purchased in bulk for promotional, educational, or business use. Please contact your local bookseller or the Macmillan Corporate and Premium Sales Department at 1-800-221-7945, ext. 5442, or by e-mail at MacmillanSpecialMarkets@macmillan.com.

Printed in the United States of America

St. Martin's Paperbacks edition / August 2019

10 9 8 7 6 5 4 3 2 1

Chapter
ONE

"Our relationship has grown stale."

"Give me a break, Max."

"You're shallow, Muffin."

"Shallow?" She gave a snort of disgust. "This coming from a man who was married to a gold digger named Bunny for three years? Now, there's a relationship with depth."

He grinned. "There's something to be said for gold diggers. A man always knows where he stands. In the end, both parties get what they want."

"And we both know you always get what you want. But let me remind you, Maximillian Holt, I'm the best thing that has ever happened to you. You need me. I listen to your problems, I feed that enormous ego of yours, and I can match wits with you any day. With both hands tied behind my back, I might add."

"Don't forget I made you what you are today, sweetheart. Without me you'd be nothing."

"And don't *you* forget, I'm the one who bails you out every time you get your ass in a sling. Speaking of which, you're out of fuel. You're running on fumes."

"How far to the nearest gas station?"

"A good ten miles."

"You could have told me sooner."

"Yes, I could have."

"I've created a monster."

Max guided the radically customized car down the narrow mountain road, taking each twist and turn with the precision of a professional driver. A Pink Floyd CD played from a cutting-edge sound system that would not be available to consumers for at least another year.

Max took a great deal of pride in his automobile, the same one his friends laughingly referred to as his Maxmobile. The car had been designed from the chassis up by former NASA scientists. The body and frame were composed of titanium and a newly identified polymer that offered the lightness of fiberglass and the durability of the strongest steel. The end result resembled a Porsche, but Max's version was bigger, better, and could do things that car manufacturers would not find on their drawing boards for years to come. Nothing was indestructible, but the Maxmobile came close.

The dashboard was more complicated than the cockpit of a Learjet. A team of first-rate computer whizzes, hired away from top government contractors, had created the car's instrumentation using state-of-the-art equipment. Spread out among luxury automotive goodies like a tachometer, an altimeter, and a global positioning satellite system were a highly enhanced PDA, a keyboard, a digital speech recognition module, a photo-quality printer, a fax, a satellite phone, an HDTV display screen, and a full video-conferencing suite, all operated by a high-powered computer that was smaller than an ashtray. Thanks to all these modifications, Max, if he wanted to, could run his vast business empire without ever getting out of his car.

Only a man like Max Holt would have laid out the kind of money it had taken to build such a machine; and only a man like Max would have created computer intelligence with voice recognition technology and a sassy personality to match. Just for the fun of it, he had named her Muffin and programmed her with a sexy voice that one employee claimed gave him a stiffie every time he heard it.

There were those who'd said it couldn't be done. Max had proved them wrong. He insisted on the best. He drove himself and his employees hard. If he exuded confidence it was because he always succeeded in what he set out to do. Always. Not a difficult task for a man with an off-the-charts IQ, and business acumen that put fear in the hearts of his toughest competitors. He'd created two companies, simply to put a scare into AOL and Microsoft. The television network he'd purchased ten years ago had grown far beyond even his own imagination. He had recently sold all three companies for a king's ransom, simply because they no longer offered the challenges he craved.

The New York Times, Newsweek, and *Money* magazine were clamoring for interviews, but Maximillian Holt did not give interviews. He maintained a low profile at all costs. Sure, photographers had grainy pictures of him slipping into buildings wearing expensive Italian suits, or ducking into stretch limos with a gorgeous model or actress on his arm, but he was clever at keeping his image out of the media. Most people wouldn't recognize him, even if they did know his name.

And that's the way Max liked it.

He had homes all over the world, but he preferred his horse farm in Virginia, not far from his cousin Nick, who'd instilled in Max a love of horses. His farmhouse offered sanctuary from his hectic lifestyle, and he maintained his privacy with cameras, an alarm system he'd personally created, and enough security personnel to guard the White House.

People called him eccentric and egotistical, but Max had never cared what others thought. He made his own rules, especially when it came to women. He didn't like entanglements. Commitment was a four-letter word that spurred him to move on the minute a woman mentioned it. As a result, he had a reputation for being a ladies' man, but he was generous to a fault and did his best to end relationships on a positive note that often created close friends out of once-intimate relationships. This included his ex-wife, Bunny, who, with his help, had launched a new line of bath and body products that competed heavily with the likes of Crabtree and Evelyn. Max liked to think women benefited from knowing him because he believed he was a better man from having been in their company.

"I want a complete printout on Jamie Swift. See if you can find a photo."

"What do you mean see if I can find a photo? Of course I can find a photo. I can get everything on anybody at any time, including where they purchase their lingerie."

By the time Max stopped for gas and filled his tank, Muffin had a complete dossier and recent photo of Jamie Swift. "Not bad," he said. "You know how I like blondes."

Muffin gave a snort. "Not to mention brunettes and redheads. But you can forget this one, stud. She's engaged to one Phillip Ravenal Standish, a well-respected tax attorney, and the most eligible bachelor in Beaumont, South Carolina."

"Your point being?"

"Hands off. You're going to Beaumont because your sister Deedee needs you."

Max smiled. "Deedee needs more help than I'm capable of giving her. Besides, there's no sin in checking on my investment with the *Beaumont Gazette* while I'm in town. And having the pleasure of meeting Miss Swift. After all, I'm her partner."

"*Silent* partner. And when she finds out Deedee asked you to help her financially—"

"She's not going to find out."

"The woman isn't stupid, Max. As soon as she discovers you're Deedee's brother, she'll put two and two together. She and Deedee might be close friends, but I'm willing to bet she won't appreciate people discussing her financial problems. She's struggled for years to keep her newspaper afloat."

"She was looking for an investor, and I have a fondness for the newspaper business. Don't forget I cut my teeth on my cousin's newspaper. There isn't much I don't know about it."

"Just don't lose sight of why we're really going to Beaumont," Muffin said. "Sounds like Frankie's in trouble."

"I still can't believe it," Max said. "Who would have thought my brother-in-law would run for mayor?"

"He's not the first wrestler to run for political office."

"I wonder if people still refer to him as Frankie-the-Assassin?"

"I'm sure he's maintained a following, despite having retired. By the way, it doesn't sound like Deedee is thrilled about his decision to join the political arena. Her last e-mail wasn't good."

"You should realize by now that although my sister is about as sweet as they come, her life is one crisis after another. Just like our mother," he added.

"You don't sound especially fond of your sister."

"Oh, I'm crazy about Deedee, although we've never had much in common. She's ten years older than me. Not to mention a little flaky at times," he added.

"Your brother-in-law doesn't seem at all concerned about what's going on," Muffin said.

"Frankie knew what he was getting into when he decided to go into politics, and he's not the first politician to receive hate mail." Max paused and smiled. "You know, Muffin, you're supposed to read my mail and report to me, not make judgments or offer advice. And then pout when I don't agree," he added. "One would think you were capable of emotion." The pride in his voice went unchecked. "And they said it couldn't be done. Guess I proved them wrong."

"You're gloating, Max. It's not flattering. Somebody needs to teach you a little humility."

"A good woman could do that."

"She'd have to be armed and dangerous."

"Send a fax to Miss Swift and tell her I'll drop by after lunch tomorrow. That'll give her time to have her hair done and buy a new dress for the occasion."

"Oh, puh-lease."

"Then take a nap. You're getting moody on me."

"You know I don't nap. That genius mind of yours couldn't find its way out of a paper sack without my assistance, much less make it all the way to Beaumont, South Carolina. Face it, Max. I'm indispensable."

"Double damn!" Jamie Swift dropped the fax as though it were hot to the touch. It fluttered to the top of her desk, face up, as though openly defying her to ignore it.

Her secretary, Vera Bankhead, drew herself up sharply. "You'd better be glad your father isn't alive to hear you, young lady. I warned you about using foul language in this office, what with me being a God-fearing Baptist and all. You owe the kitty one quarter for cursing."

Without taking her eyes off the fax, Jamie reached into a side drawer of her desk where she kept a stash of change. She pulled out a quarter and handed it to Vera. Sixty years old and the closest thing Jamie had ever had to a mother, Vera Bankhead was a woman to be reckoned with, and the only thing Jamie feared.

"Mr. Holt is coming *here*? *Tomorrow?*"

"That's what it says."

"This must be some kind of joke."

"Looks serious as an open grave to me, but then I'm just a lowly secretary who hasn't had a raise since they did away with garter belts."

"We have to stop him."

"I keep a .38 in my purse. It'll stop a Brahma bull at one hundred paces."

"We can't *kill* him, Vera. Besides, he owns a sizable portion of this newspaper. We simply have to find a way to detain him. I mean, would you look at this place!"

Both women paused and glanced around the office, or what there was left of it.

Vera nodded. "Yeah, well, I told you not to sell all the furniture."

"You knew you needed the money."

Jamie's managing editor, Mike Henderson, raced into her office, light brown hair uncombed, shirt badly wrinkled, and his coat askew. His briefcase reflected his personality; the fake leather pouches were stuffed with papers and newsworthy articles that he planned to follow up one day but never got around to. The tie he kept on hand in case he needed it peeked out from the side pocket of his jacket.

"Wonder whose bed he just crawled out of?" Vera muttered.

"Sorry I'm late," he said.

Jamie pressed her lips together in irritation. Mike was a good editor, but his poor time-management skills and his sexual prowess kept him from doing the job he was capable of. She attributed it to immaturity; after all, he was only a year out of college. But he worked cheap.

"Do you know what time it is?" Jamie asked.

He paused and checked his wristwatch. "Oh, man, I'm later than I thought."

Vera gave a snort of disgust. "Long night?"

He looked slightly offended. "Okay, so I have a reputation for, well, never mind, but I actually worked most of the night and morning because of our deadline. I must've drifted off to sleep at some point because next thing I knew—"

"Well, Miss Swift has enough to worry about without you showing up this time of day."

He looked at Jamie. "Did another piece of equipment break down?"

"Worse," Vera said. "Mr. M. Holt is coming tomorrow, and this place is pitiful."

Mike looked around. "Yeah, we could use some furniture. Not to mention a few desks. I'm working on a damn card table. By the way, who the hell is M. Holt?"

There were no secrets in the office. Everyone knew Jamie struggled to keep the newspaper afloat. "Mr. Holt is the investor who prevented the bank from foreclosing on this place," Jamie said. She looked at Vera. "Why does he get to curse, and I don't?"

"'Cause I didn't practically raise him and teach him good Christian manners like I did you. Besides, he's going to hell anyway for his tomcattin' ways."

Mike sighed. "I have trouble committing."

"You need to learn to keep your britches zipped, mister, and you need to be on time for work."

Mike's face reddened, but he, like the rest of the staff, knew better than to talk back to Vera. "What does the *M* stand for?" he asked as though desperately wanting to change the subject.

Jamie shrugged. "Who knows? I was just so glad to get the money I didn't care." She pulled out the center drawer of her battered desk and fumbled through it for a pack of unopened cigarettes.

Vera planted her hands on her hips. "Don't you *dare* light that cigarette, missy, or I'm going to quit on the spot, and then you're going to have to pay someone *real* money to run this office. Have you forgotten how hard it was for you to give up smoking in the first place? The only reason you started to begin with was because your daddy smoked."

"I'm not going to light the darn thing, Vera." Jamie tore into the pack and stuck one of the cigarettes between her lips. Oh, how she craved one. If ever there was a time to light up it was now. "We've got to do something about this place."

"Why are you looking at me?" Vera asked. "I don't have any say-so around here. I just keep my mouth shut and do what I'm told *when* I'm told. But let something go wrong and everybody comes running to Vera. Yessirree." She sank into the old leather chair facing Jamie's desk. "Somebody get me a cup of coffee. It helps me think better."

Jamie hurried down the hall and into the small kitchenette or what had once been a kitchenette before she had been forced to sell the refrigerator, microwave, table and chairs, and everything else that had not been nailed down. Thankfully, the cabinet and small stainless steel sink remained, which meant the coffeepot had a resting place and running water to rinse and fill it. Jamie returned to her office and handed Vera a cup of coffee that looked as though it had been brewed the day before. "It's hot," she warned.

Vera sipped cautiously. "Okay, I hate to do this, but I guess I have no choice. We can't allow Mr. Holt to see this place as is." She glanced around. "Lawd, I don't remember when these walls were last painted. We need to do something about that, too."

"You have an idea?" Jamie asked hopefully.

"A few people in this town owe me favors."

Jamie noted the thoughtful look on Vera's face. Baptist or not, the woman could be downright devious at times. "I'm listening."

"You know Herman Bates who owns Bates's Furniture? His son has been busted twice for DUI. Just so happens I was a nice person and kept it out of our arrest section. And then there was that messy scene between Tom Brown and his wife—"

"Tom Brown who owns the paint store?" Mike asked.

"Uh-huh. Seems he told his wife, Lorraine, he had to work late one night so he could finish painting the VFW Hall, and Lorraine decided to check it out. Found him and Beth Toomey doing the nasty on a sofa in the back office. I heard Lorraine went after both of them with a letter opener. Beth managed to call nine-one-one, and Lorraine was hauled in and thrown into the slammer."

"Oh, Jeez," Jamie mumbled.

"Yeah, and Tom refused to bail her out until she signed an agreement stating she wouldn't do him bodily harm. Didn't matter 'cause there was some serious butt-kicking when he got home."

"How come I don't know about this?" Jamie asked.

"I decided to keep it out of the newspaper, as well, because both families belong to my church."

Jamie shook her head. There were times she wondered who was in charge. Obviously it was a silly question. "So what's the point?"

Vera took another sip of her coffee as though trying to build the tension until she reached the climax of her idea. "We need this place painted, and we need furniture. Simple as that. Tom and Herman either do it my way or pay the price."

"Isn't blackmail a crime in this state?" Mike asked.

Vera set her coffee cup down and crossed her arms over her chest. "Not when it's for a good cause."

He and Jamie nodded as though it made perfect sense.

Vera rose from her chair in a queenly fashion. "Have either of you ever known me to fail when I set my mind to it? You can rest assured that it's as good as done. Vera Bankhead always comes through, and she doesn't mind getting her hands dirty in the process. Nosirree."

Deedee Holt Fontana sat at her French provincial dressing table and gazed into the mirror, frowning.

Her Maltese, Choo-Choo, licked the last of Deedee's Frappuccino from a dainty white cup.

The man fussing with her hair paused. He wore his own coal-black hair in a buzz cut, with the exception of a few wispy bangs that he claimed were necessary because he felt his forehead was too tall. "What's wrong, sweetie pie?" He had a French accent mixed with a Louisiana drawl that was sometimes difficult to understand.

"Oh, Beenie, I need another face-lift," Deedee said in her Betty Boop voice. Despite having recently celebrated her forty-sixth birthday, Deedee had never lost the childlike quality that gave her an air of innocence. Even though she often appeared quite savvy and astute, her voice and air of innocence made Frankie, her husband of twenty years, want to take care of and protect her.

"You most certainly do not need a face-lift! You have one more face-lift, and your eyes are going to be at the back of your head, and you'll have to enter rooms butt first. You'll give new meaning to the words 'grand entrance.'" Beenie waved his comb from side to side as he spoke, as though conducting an orchestra. "Besides, how many women do you know who have an entire room devoted to their beauty queen trophies?"

"That was a long time ago, Beenie."

"Well, you're still a beauty queen as far as the rest of us are concerned but *especially* to that hunk of man you married. Why, the way he looks at you—" Beenie paused and shivered. "I get all goose-pimply every time I see it."

Deedee obviously wasn't listening because she seemed to take little delight in his words. "It's a wonder Frankie hasn't left me for a younger woman," she said. She picked up her magnifying mirror and looked into it. "Eeyeuuw!" she screeched so loudly that Beenie's hand flew to his chest as though he feared his heart might take flight.

"Yikes, where did you get that mirror?" Beenie wrestled it from her. "How many times have I told you *not* to look into that mirror? Lord, girl, Britney Spears would look like a stray dog with mange in that mirror."

"Look at me, Beenie. I've turned into a frumpy housewife."

"You are definitely *not* frumpy."

"I have dark circles beneath my eyes."

"That's because you're not sleeping at night, sugar-plum." Beenie patted her on the shoulder. "You spend too much time worrying about your husband and every-body else you can think of. You're the only rich person I know who worries about leaving a bathtub ring when you have a perfectly healthy housekeeper, who is over-paid in my opinion, to see to it. And if Frankie knew how much you were fretting over him he'd put you over his knee and give you a good spanking."

Deedee seemed to consider it. "That's not a bad idea, Beenie. Frankie and I could use some variety in our sex life."

Beenie's hands fluttered about his face like butter-flies, something he often did when he became anxious. "I do not believe what I'm hearing. Mr. F worships the marble floors you walk on. His eyes light up when you enter a room. It's obvious he thinks you're the sexiest woman alive."

Deedee wasn't listening. She covered her face with her hands. Her long slim fingers flashed with dia-monds, as did her dainty wrists and earlobes. She was still as slender as a college girl, and as much as she'd sworn off exercising in her youth, she now worked out with a personal trainer three days a week. Of course it was up to Beenie to drag Deedee out of bed, kicking and screaming, and coax her downstairs to Frankie's gym each time her trainer arrived for their appointment. He claimed he was just doing his job, but it was obvious Beenie had a thing for the muscle-bound jock because he always wore his favorite silk Armani shirt when the man was expected. Today, Beenie was dressed in Gucci.

But Beenie was like a pit bull when it came to Deedee, seeing she ate right, that her hair and makeup were perfect and her clothes neatly pressed. Deedee had stolen her "personal assistant" some three years prior from an exclusive spa, doubling his salary in order to get him. It had paid off. Beenie had transformed her, tossing aside Deedee's tight-fitting, rhinestone-laden outfits for linen and silk ones designed especially for her in Milan and Paris.

"I never thought I'd be this old," Deedee cried. "I thought getting older was for everyone but me. I should have married a cosmetic surgeon instead of a wrestler. I tell you, Beenie, the stress is killing me. I don't know what Frankie is thinking. We should have stayed in Scottsdale where it was safe."

"Honey, you know Mr. Fontana loves this little town and the people who live here. He wants to make a difference."

"So why is Frankie receiving all those nasty letters?"

"People can be jerks."

"Max had better get his behind here fast. Heaven only knows where he is. He's as bad as our father. Just can't stay in one place long enough."

"Now, now," Beenie said. "That's not fair. From what I understand, Max is a very important man with a lot to do. Frankly, your parents have always sounded a wee bit selfish to me, what with traveling all over the world without a second thought to their children. I would never do that to my children."

All at once, Deedee cried out. "Eeyeuuw, I'm perspiring! Quick, Beenie, turn down the air before I melt."

"The air is already as low as it can go, honeycomb. You're going to cause the units to freeze up like last time if you don't leave the thermostats alone. You're just having another hot flash."

Deedee met the man's gaze in the mirror. The look in her eyes would have wilted a head of lettuce on the spot. "I am *not* having a hot flash. I am *not* going through menopause or premenopause, as you call it, and that's final!"

Beenie slapped his hand over his mouth as though suddenly realizing his mistake. "What was I thinking?" he said. "Of course you're hot. It's the middle of June, and we're having a record heat wave. Look at me, I'm glistening myself." He pulled the lid off her most expensive talcum powder and made a production of powdering her neck and his. "There, now. Feel better?"

"I'm having a nervous breakdown, Beenie, that's what it is. I'm going to have to go on tranquilizers. I'll probably become addicted and have to spend time at the Betty Ford Center. It'll look bad for Frankie. He'll lose the election and blame me, *then* he'll get a mistress."

"Lord, girl, are you having a mood swing or what?" Beenie said, then winced and raised a fist to his mouth at the look she shot him. "Oh, my, I should cut my tongue out, chop it into little pieces and feed it to an alley cat."

"I need to be alone," Deedee said tiredly.

Beenie sighed his immense relief. "That's a good idea." He helped her into a satin Christian Dior bathrobe. "You need to rest now. Tonight is a big night for Mr. Fontana, and you want to be at your best."

"I want to be awake when Max arrives."

"I'll wake you the minute he gets here." Beenie paused and shot her a coy look. "What does he look like?"

"Oh, he's very handsome and polished, and don't think he doesn't know it. He's also a freakin' supergenius. Used to blow up everything in sight when he was a kid."

Beenie's eyes widened. "Like in bombs?"

"Not real bombs, just stuff he found around the house. Kid's stuff, really. He had his own laboratory. Fortunately, our cousin and his wife took him in and turned Max around."

Beenie tapped a forefinger against his top lip. "And a genius, huh. I love brainy men."

Frankie grinned and pumped Max's hand enthusiastically the minute the butler led him inside a living room that was the size of a bowling alley. "It's good to see you again, Max. Deedee will be thrilled."

"Have you grown?" Max asked, looking straight up in order to meet the man's gaze.

Frankie laughed. "Actually, I shrank an inch. I'm six foot seven now." He slapped his massive chest. "Still fit as a fiddle, though. I work out every day."

Suddenly, Max shivered. "Why is it so cold in here? Your butler is wearing an overcoat."

"Shoot, that's nothing," Frankie said. "The chef has a fire going in the kitchen fireplace." He glanced about as if to make sure they were alone. "It's Deedee," he whispered. "She's going through, uh, *the change*."

"You mean menopause?"

"Shhh, not so loud. She's in denial. Claims she's too young for that sort of thing, but it started about six months ago. You know how Deedee is about maintaining her youth. But don't worry, the housekeeper put an electric blanket on your bed so you won't freeze at night."

There was a squeal of delight that caused both men to turn. Deedee raced down the long, freestanding staircase, her robe swirling about her long legs. She ran right into Max's waiting arms. "Oh, little brother, it's so good to see you!"

Max hugged her. "Let me have a look at you," he said, stepping back for a full view. "You haven't changed a bit. How do you stay so young looking?"

"She has a face-lift once a year," Frankie said, earning a dark look from his wife. As if sensing he'd said the wrong thing, he added, "Not that she needs it, of course."

"It's just a teeny-weeny procedure," Deedee said quickly. "Dr. Mitchell says I'm much too young for the real thing. Frankie, honey, why don't you fix Max a drink."

"What'll it be?" Frankie asked, heading for a cabinet that opened up into a wet bar. "We have everything."

"A soft drink will do."

"Sit down, Max," Deedee said, leading him to a group of sofas that were covered in a bamboo print that were placed on a leopardskin rug. Tall wooden giraffes peeked through leafy banana trees, and brass elephants supported glass cocktail tables.

"Do you like what I did to the room?" she asked. "I was going for a jungle look."

Max took in the room. "You succeeded very well," he said. "I noticed you chose to paint the house pink."

"Salmon," she corrected. "It's the *in* color these days."

"It looks pink to me, too," Frankie said, handing Max a cola. "Good thing I'm not still wrestling. The guys would think I had grown soft."

Max toasted his brother-in-law with his drink. "Congratulations on winning the primary, Frankie. You'll make a great mayor."

Frankie beamed with pleasure. "I still have a lot to do and Election Day is just around the corner, but I have a good campaign manager so it's going okay. The present mayor has been in office for ten years, and his father spent almost twice that time in office. I say it's time we get new blood." He leaned closer and gave Max a conspiratorial wink. "What I say in my speech tonight should win me the election."

Deedee covered her face. "Oh, Lord, he's going to make somebody else mad, and they're going to run us out of town." Suddenly, she cried out. "Beenie, come quickly!"

There was the sound of footsteps overhead. Beenie raced down the stairs. "What, what? Did your eyelash fall in your drink?" He came to a screeching halt at the sight of Max. He sucked in his stomach. "You must be Deedee's brother."

Max glanced from him to an amused Frankie.

"I'm Deedee's personal assistant, of course," Beenie said. He held out his hand. "Charmed, I'm sure."

Max nodded. "Yeah, so am I."

"Stop socializing, Beenie, and pack my jewelry," Deedee said loudly. "Sew it into the hem of my dresses like they did in the Civil War when the Yankees came. And all my makeup and moisturizing creams," she added.

"But I don't know how to sew," he whined.

She ignored him. "And tell the housekeeper to start packing the china and silver. We'll have to bury it in the backyard."

Beenie planted his hands on his hips. "I hope you don't expect *me* to dig holes."

Max watched silently, one corner of his lip turned up. He was obviously enjoying himself.

"Deedee, what on earth are you planning?" Frankie said, his black brows drawn together so that they touched and made him look stern, a look that was normally completely foreign to him.

She began wringing her hands. "That's what people do when they're getting ready to flee their homes."

He immediately softened and took her hands in his large beefy ones. "We're not going to be forced from our home, sweetheart. Whatever gave you that idea?"

"Frankie, it's obvious somebody doesn't want you elected; otherwise, why would you be getting all that hate mail?"

"How do you know about that?"

She hitched her chin high. "I'm your wife. I make it my business to know what's going on around here."

Frankie looked hurt. "Do you think I'd let anything happen to you? Deedee, I'd risk my own life for you."

"Listen, Frankie, I've watched you in the ring, and I dealt with it better than most wives, but this time I'm scared."

"I thought you trusted me."

"I *do* trust you, but I still worry."

"That's for sure," Beenie said. "Why do you think she's got those god-awful bags under her eyes? Lord, I couldn't conceal them with white enamel paint." Beenie seemed to catch his mistake the minute he said it because his hands fluttered about his face and he turned three shades of red. Deedee glared at him. "Could we forget I said that?" he asked. "I would agree to forgo this year's Christmas bonus if we could just pretend I'd never uttered those words."

"I want you to stop this nonsense," Frankie told his wife. "We are not going anywhere. I am going to protect you. Besides, all your jewelry is insured. If somebody takes it I'll just buy you more."

"Oh, Frankie. What would I do without you?"

He leaned over and gave his wife a long kiss.

Max chuckled. "When are the two of you going to stop acting like newlyweds?"

"When you find the right person, it just keeps getting better and better," Deedee said dreamily. "You should try it sometime, little brother."

Frankie checked his Rolex. "It's getting late. We have to get ready for the fund-raiser at the country club."

Deedee looked proud. "Frankie's trying to raise money for the park he's planning. He's going to put it right smack in the center of town, and dedicate it to the founding fathers."

"Yeah," Frankie said. "It's going to have this big

fountain, and in the center a raised statue of two bronze wrestlers, one of them caught in a body scissor."

"Like one of those Michelangelo statues," Deedee said.

"I figure the kids will get a kick out of it," Frankie added. "Oh, and there's going to be a playground for the little ones."

"Sounds like you thought of everything but a wrestling ring," Max said.

"Oh, Frankie has already had one built at the YMCA," Deedee said, "and he gives lessons once a week."

"He's very devoted to this town," Beenie said, still eyeballing Max.

"Doesn't sound like you're taking retirement very seriously," Max said.

Frankie shrugged. "I like staying busy, and it's for a good cause."

Finally, Max stood. "Guess I'd better clean up."

"I'll show you to your room," Beenie offered, already moving toward the stairs gracefully. "I'll even see that your bags are carried up for you."

"By the way, there's a tux in your closet," Deedee called out once Max was halfway up the stairs.

He turned and scowled down at her. "You did that on purpose. You know how much I hate to dress up."

Max stood beside Frankie, shaking hands and making small talk, but the look on his face suggested how bored he was. Deedee had simply introduced him as Max, her little brother, and nobody had made the connection. After an hour, Max slipped through a pair of French doors leading to a large balcony that overlooked a perfectly manicured golf course.

He gazed at the woman on the balcony for a full minute, a smile playing on his mouth. It would have been impossible not to recognize her. Jamie Swift was even better looking in person.

Jamie Swift was one irritated woman, and she didn't notice the stranger at first. Her mood had only worsened since she'd learned her investor was coming to town, and the last thing she wanted to do was mingle with the crowd inside. Frankie must have invited close to two hundred people, most of them couples, and she was without a date.

Where the heck was Phillip? Here she was, dressed in her navy silk cocktail dress, the one Phillip claimed showed off the best legs he'd ever laid eyes on and brought out the highlights in her blond hair. Oh, what she'd give to be wearing her comfortable jeans and loose-fitting T-shirt and sprawled on her sofa reading a good book.

And what was with these high heels? The saleslady at the discount shoe store had talked her into buying them. Dumb idea. She preferred sneakers. The spiked heels added a good three inches to Jamie's five feet seven and made her feel as though she should have strapped herself into a parachute before putting them on. If she fell she would break every bone in her body.

Not that it would be the worst thing that had happened to her that day. She took a sip of her wine, her second glass.

"Darn you, Phillip," she muttered. "Of all times to be late." He was probably sitting in his private club right now, sipping a Dewar's and talking about tax law. *Tax law,* for Pete's sake! Who cared? The subject held as much interest to her as a hernia operation. "Oh, double damn," she said.

Jamie caught movement and turned quickly, almost spilling her wine. Her mouth flew open, and her cheeks burned with embarrassment as she found herself gazing at one of the best-looking men she'd ever seen. And, he had caught her talking to herself.

Chapter TWO

"Excuse me," Max said. "Is this a private conversation?" When the woman winced, he smiled. "I'll bet he's a rabbit and his name is Harvey."

Jamie was tempted to dive from her high heels and end it all right there. "How much did you hear?"

"Something about a guy named Phillip who's really late." Max cocked his head to one side. "He must not be very smart."

"Phillip is my fiancé. And very late. Who are you?"

"Max."

"Jamie Swift." She offered her hand.

He took it and they shook. "Nice to meet you, Miss Swift." Max reluctantly let go of her hand.

Jamie studied him. "You're not from around here, are you?"

"Just visiting."

Jamie wasn't surprised. She would have noticed him, what with those broad shoulders and olive complexion that was even more attractive against his white shirt. He did wonderful things to a tux. His face was striking, interesting to look at. She didn't know if it was the wine or the man, but one of them was making her light-headed. Be just her luck to do something stupid and swoon. And her engaged and all. That would certainly start tongues wagging in Beaumont.

"Nice to meet you, uh, Max." Dang, her voice suddenly sounded as though a bullfrog were giving birth in her throat. She cleared it. "Welcome to Beaumont."

"I came out for some fresh air. The view out here is great."

Jamie noticed he was staring at her and not the scenery. Smooth guy, she thought. Very smooth.

"So, is your fiancé the jealous type? Should I disappear in case he shows up and finds you standing out here alone with a strange man?"

Jamie chuckled. "Maybe that's exactly what he deserves. I think he's beginning to take me for granted." She checked her wristwatch. "But he's more than an hour late. I seriously doubt he's going to make it at this point."

"I'll bet he has a very good reason."

"Men always stick together."

"If you were my date I would have been here early, and I would have brought you a dozen roses. But that's just me. I'm the sensitive type."

Jamie saw the teasing look in his eyes. "Yeah, right. The minute I laid eyes on you I said to myself, "Jamie, there stands one sensitive, touchy-feely guy."

Max grinned. "Could I get you another drink?"

"Uh, no, thanks. I've had my limit."

"And I'll bet you never go over that limit, do you? I'll bet you've never once thrown caution to the wind and said, "Oh, what the hell, I'm going to slam down another tequila shooter whether anyone likes it or not."

She laughed. "Hey, I've written on bathroom walls."

"No way."

Jamie nodded proudly. "In seventh grade I carved Davey Callaway's initials with mine and drew a heart around it."

Max pretended to look shocked. "I would never have thought it of you."

"I can be quite brazen at times."

"Oh, yeah? I'm beginning to hope your fiancé doesn't show up after all."

Jamie realized the wine had gone straight to her head. She tried to pull herself together. "So, Mr., uh, Max. What do you think of our little town?"

"I've only been here a couple of hours so I haven't had a chance to see it."

"You should take a complete tour sometime when you have an extra ten minutes on your hands."

"It can't be that bad. What do people do for fun?"

"Mostly they go to church. Folks are big on church socials. You know, potluck dinners and all that. You want a good meal in this town you have to join a church. We have a theater we're very proud of, stadium seating and eight different movies from which to choose. Not to mention a skating rink and arcade for the kids."

"Yes, but what do the wilder, more sophisticated people like yourself do for fun?"

"We have a steak house and a seafood restaurant. Not to mention a hamburger joint where the onion rings are so greasy they almost slide off your plate. They insist on checking your cholesterol before you're allowed to order them."

"Sounds like my kind of place."

"Oh, and we've got this roadhouse on the outskirts that serves the coldest beer in town and plays music on Friday night. The Baptists pretend it doesn't exist so everyone gets along just fine."

"And here I thought I'd seen and done it all," Max replied. "I'll bet you can tear up a dance floor."

Jamie's smile faded slightly. "I'm afraid I don't go out much. I own the newspaper so I spend most of my time there." Jamie realized she was enjoying talking to the man.

"I used to work for my cousin's newspaper," Max told her after a moment.

"Then you know what it's like."

"Stressful at times."

"You should try finding news in a town this size. *That's* the stressful part. Not much action around here, you know?"

Max chuckled. "Perhaps you could pay someone to commit a crime."

"I can't afford it," she confessed. "If you saw my circulation you'd laugh."

"Why do you stay?"

"I guess it's in my blood." She smiled. "Maybe I need a transfusion." She drained her glass. "So tell me something interesting about yourself. Anything. Something I can print."

He shrugged. "I'm afraid you'd find my life rather boring. I live on a farm in Virginia. My house is old and falling apart. I'm in the process of renovating it. When I have time," he added.

"You're doing the work yourself?"

"Uh-huh."

Jamie looked at his hands. They were nice and brown and strong looking. "I should hire you to renovate the newspaper building. It's falling apart, too. I never really noticed how bad it was until today. I've got this big-shot investor visiting tomorrow. I'm sure he'll get a huge laugh when he takes a look at the place."

"It can't be all that bad."

"Trust me on this one. The man will take one look at the place and wish he'd never put any of his money in my little newspaper." She sighed heavily. "I'm sorry. I don't know why I'm telling you all this. I guess I just needed to talk to someone. I've had a crummy day."

"You know what you need?"

"Yeah, a sword to fall on."

"No, seriously. I know what will cheer you up."

Jamie's eyes narrowed. He was so easy to talk to she'd forgotten he was drop-dead gorgeous and a little on the flirtatious side. "I'll just bet you do."

"I've got this cool car. My friends call it my Max-mobile. We could take a ride."

"I'm engaged."

"Hey, listen, if I were trying to pick you up I would have used a better line than that."

"I bet you've got a lot of lines."

"I don't need them. Most women come on to *me*."

Jamie laughed out loud. "You know, I wouldn't want to pay your grocery bill. I'll bet it takes a lot to feed your ego."

"That's just a front I put on to hide my shyness."

He gave her a smile that would melt a woman's bones. She might be engaged, but she wasn't blind.

"Yeah, I was just noticing what an introvert you are."

"I'm serious about my car," he said. "I have a computer inside that talks to me. She's a real pistol."

"A computer that talks to you. Now, *there's* a line I've never heard. And after that we'd want to go by your place to see your etchings. No, thanks. Wouldn't want to miss out on the delicious overdone roast beef they're serving tonight." Probably she would be dining alone.

Well, what did it matter? She was a new-millennium woman and all that, and she was on business. Phillip could stuff his tax law business up his behind because she was quite capable of mingling with the best of them, including his mother, Annabelle Standish, Beaumont's Queen Bee of high society.

"Before you go, would you give me the name of that hamburger joint you mentioned a few minutes ago?" Max asked. "As much as I hate to eat alone, it sounds a lot tastier than this evening's fare."

Jamie's mouth watered at the thought of Harry's famous burgers and onion rings. And milkshakes so thick it felt as though you would suck your guts out getting them through the straw. She sighed.

"You're dying for a burger," Max said. "You're practically drooling."

"Yeah, but I can't. I have to take notes on Frankie's speech so I'll have something to print tomorrow—my newspaper is endorsing his campaign."

"We'll be back before the speech. Come on."

Jamie was sorely tempted. It would serve Phillip right. "Okay," she said at last. "We'll grab a burger and come right back. Let's go this way so nobody sees us leaving."

"Coward."

"Hey, I have to live in this town."

Max led her down the back steps and across the parking lot to his car. He pushed a button on his key ring, and the doors unlocked.

Jamie arched one brow. "Nice wheels." She climbed in, and a padded bar came down, locking into place. "What the—"

"I tend to drive fast," Max said. "The car is designed for speed, but it's equipped with more safety gadgets than a jetliner." He closed the door, joined her on the other side, and waited for the bar to lock him in, as well.

"Get a load of this dashboard," Jamie said.

"I have everything I could possibly need at my disposal. Muffin runs it all."

"Muffin?"

"My computer. You'll love her. She's somewhat of a smart aleck when she gets in a snit, but other than that—"

Jamie frowned. "What do you mean she gets into a snit? Computers don't get into a snit."

Max started the engine and shot out of the parking lot like a silver arrow. "On the contrary, Muffin can be moody."

Jamie's look was deadpan. "Moody, huh?"

"She wants me to change her name to Lee or Hannah because she claims it sounds stronger. She also doesn't like that I gave her a voice that sounds like Marilyn Monroe. It was all in fun."

"I see."

Max pulled onto the main road. "Muffin, I want you to meet Miss Jamie Swift from the newspaper office. I'm taking her for a ride."

Silence.

Jamie looked at the man. Not only had she just climbed into a car with a stranger, he was obviously unstable as well. And she was locked inside a metal bar. Damn.

"Muffin, you're being rude. Now, say hello to Miss Swift." Max looked at Jamie. "I knew it. She's in a mood."

Jamie's smile was forced. "That's okay. She doesn't

have to talk if she doesn't want to." Jamie tested the
bar that covered her. It didn't budge. It reminded her
of the bars they closed over people during one of those
crazy roller-coaster rides. She fidgeted with her hands,
shifted in her seat. She felt trapped. She didn't like it.
Not one bit.

And this Max person was talking crazy.

"Okay, Muffin, *don't* talk," Max said.

Jamie looked at him. Maybe he was playing a joke
on her. He looked the type who would enjoy practical
jokes. Either that or he was a nutcase.

"Um, I was just thinking, I really should be mingling with the crowd at the country club," Jamie finally
said. "You know, to sort of get their take on our new
candidate and all. I understand Frankie is going to
have a big surprise. At least that's what I heard."

"You'll have plenty of time for that," Max replied.
Suddenly, the car died. "Dammit, Muffin, that's not a
bit funny! You're making a fool of me in front of Miss
Swift. Now, restart the engine."

Nothing.

Max looked at Jamie. "I'm sorry." He turned the
key and the engine came to life. All at once, the radio
blared a country-western song that had something to
do with a broken heart, an old dog, and a pickup truck.
Max gritted his teeth and switched it off. "That's not
funny, Muffin."

Jamie glanced out her window as he accelerated.
She ought to have her head examined for coming with
him in the first place. Once again, she'd let her temper get the best of her. Probably Phillip had a perfectly
good reason for not showing up. Or maybe he was just
running unusually late. A client could have come in

at the last minute. Some of his clients could be long-winded. No doubt, Phillip had lost track of time. He sometimes did that when he talked tax law.

Or maybe, just maybe, she'd forgotten to tell him about the dinner. She rolled her eyes. It had happened before. She hadn't thought to touch base with him before she'd left her house because, as usual, she'd been running behind.

Whatever the reason for his not showing up, she had to learn to be more tolerant. Phillip certainly tried to work around her crazy schedule, and he seldom complained. She, on the other hand, was too impatient and always in a hurry. She let stress get to her until she just snapped and took it out on Phillip. She would start taking anger-control classes at the mental health center, that's what she'd do. Or start going to church with Vera. Most Baptists seemed sort of laid-back. They spent a lot of time sitting in lawn chairs in their backyards talking to friends and neighbors. She made a mental note to buy a lawn chair the next chance she got.

First she had to get out from behind this blasted bar.

Max sped up. Jamie balled her fists at her sides but tried to remain calm despite the fact they were going way too fast for her comfort. Why was the man in such a hurry, for Pete's sake? She wasn't wounded or missing a body part that had to be sewn back on in the emergency room. Not that she could do anything about it. If she did manage to raise the steel bar and jump out, she would be road kill.

"Why are you driving so fast?" she asked Max.

Max looked at her. "I like speed. But don't worry, I'm a good driver."

She was riding in a car with a madman. Where were the darn cops when people needed them? The little town of Beaumont passed by her in a blur, the square where the old courthouse had stood for more than eighty years, and the bandstand where the townspeople often gathered on summer evenings to listen to music or watch free movies on a large screen, all provided by the local arts association. She and her father had sat on those same benches feeding pigeons when she was a little girl.

Max slowed the car and rounded the square. "So, this is town, huh?"

Jamie nodded, thankful they were moving at a slower pace. Her pulse slowed as well. She tested the bar once more as they passed Lowery's Hardware, Susie-Q's Cut and Curl, and Maynard's Sandwich Shop, places Jamie visited on a regular basis. Bates's Furniture took up half a city block. Jamie wondered if Vera had managed to talk Herman Bates into lending them furniture. Her earlier problems seemed insignificant at the moment when all she wanted to do was get the heck out of Max's car and his imaginary talking computer.

"Nice town." Max sped off again.

"I need to get back now," Jamie said.

"We've got plenty of time."

"No, really, I—"

"Would you relax?" Max said.

Jamie took a deep breath. Okay, so he wasn't going to take her back. She was pinned inside his car with no way of escaping. How many times had Vera warned her against getting into a car with a strange man, the kind of man who did terrible things to people, especially women. As far as Vera was concerned, the whole world was dangerous. Men lurked in alleys and parking lots, just waiting to pounce on the first unsuspecting female. Vera knew every gruesome detail of every crime ever committed, thanks to a detective show she watched each night in bed while eating caramel corn.

Maybe Vera was right. Maybe Max was really a deranged maniac out to rape and kill. They'd probably find her body tomorrow in a Dumpster, and Vera would say, "By golly, I tried to warn her about how dangerous this old world is getting to be." Jamie shivered at the thought.

"Cold?" Max asked.

"Huh?" She looked his way. He appeared normal, but then so did most serial killers, as Vera had mentioned many times. "I'm fine. The hamburger place is just up the street. Take a right at the next light."

"I thought we'd ride a bit first," Max said. "Maybe I can coax Muffin into saying something. Did I tell you she's equipped with a global positioning system? This car has enhanced PDA, with keyboard, printer, fax, and e-mail capabilities."

Jamie wanted to tell him she didn't give a hoot in hell what the car could do, she just wanted to get back to the country club. Besides, she didn't believe him. What she *did* believe was that he was delusional. Not that she had any intention of telling him as much. Vera would have told her to play along, pretend to be interested in everything he was saying. Keep him talking, Jamie thought.

"I'm impressed," she said. "I happen to know a few things about cars myself."

"Oh, yeah?" Max looked interested.

"My dad used to rebuild old cars in our garage. I helped him rebuild the vintage Mustang I drive now. As a matter of fact, it was one of the first to roll off the showroom floor. They referred to it as the nineteen sixty-four and a half edition. Back then it was only

available in the coupe and convertible models. I have
the convertible."

Max studied her closely as he stopped at a red light.
"You know, I'd like to continue this conversation. Is
there somewhere we can talk? Alone?" He smiled.
"I'm not about to let you get away. I'm surprised you
didn't suspect as much when you climbed into my car."

Jamie took a shaky breath. Holy cow, the man had just
admitted he wasn't going to let her go, that he'd planned
the whole thing. He probably already knew where he
was going to leave her poor body. Vera was right. She
was as good as dead. Oh, damn. Double damn.

Fear shot through Jamie's veins, sending such an
adrenaline rush that she thought her heart would burst
in her chest. She felt dizzy, out of breath, her entire
body shook uncontrollably. She could hear Max talking
but couldn't make out the words, only that his voice
suddenly sounded very loud and irritating

"Hey, are you okay?" Max asked.

All she could do was stare and try to catch her
breath.

Max hit the brakes, and the car skidded to a halt.

"Jesus Christ!" Muffin shouted. "Would somebody
please tell me what's going on?"

Jamie was only vaguely aware of a woman's voice.
A hallucination, she thought, because the voice sounded
like Marilyn Monroe. She felt a sense of impending
doom as the colors around her became muted and dark,
closing in on her.

There was no escape.

Suddenly, her door was flung open, and the metal
bar lifted. "Jamie, what's wrong?" Max demanded.

"My chest," she said in a strangled voice.

"What's she doing?" Muffin asked.

"Holding her chest and gasping for breath."

"Do you think she's having a heart attack?" Muffin asked. "Should I call nine-one-one?"

Jamie looked into Max's face. "Who is that?"

"Muffin."

Jamie sucked in a deep breath. "Y-your computer? You were serious about that?"

"Yes! Do you need an ambulance?"

"You're not going to rape and butcher me and—"

Max looked incredulous. "What the hell are you talking about?"

"She doesn't need an ambulance, Max," Muffin said. "She needs a psycho ward."

Jamie blinked rapidly. The colors around her brightened, and the sounds weren't as loud anymore. She could breathe again. "But I thought—"

"That I planned to kill you?" Suddenly, Max laughed. "You're kidding, right?"

Jamie's face burned. The heat crawled to the tips of her ears, and she was certain they were flashing like neon lights. She almost preferred having a heart attack to the look on Max's face. She had made a fool of herself. Max and his friends would probably have a good laugh over it later. "What's so funny?" she demanded.

Max made an attempt to wipe the smile from his face and failed.

"Is she okay?" Muffin asked.

"I think so," Max said. "I think she was having a panic attack or something."

"I most certainly was *not* having a panic attack." It sounded plausible, though, Jamie had to admit. She had been awfully scared and half-afraid she would go crazy. She was going to wring Vera's neck, that's what she was going to do. Vera, who filled her head with all kinds of nonsense about serial killers and men who climbed into women's windows at night and— She shuddered.

"You're not going to have another one, are you?" Max asked.

Jamie wished she could wave a magic wand and disappear from those laughing dark eyes. Here she was, mortified to death, and the man was laughing at her. She straightened her shoulders, trying to scrape up what little pride she had left. "Would you kindly drive me back to the country club?"

"What about the burger and onion rings?"

"I'm not very hungry right now."

"Well, then, maybe another time." Max closed the door and joined her on the other side. He started the car, and the bars closed over them once more. "I hate this thing," she muttered.

Max drove in silence, as though he suspected she needed time to gather her wits, but he glanced her way now and then in concern. "Are you sure you're going to be all right?"

"Uh-huh." Jamie figured it was best to keep her mouth shut.

"Ask her if she has considered therapy," Muffin said.

"I don't need therapy," Jamie replied, then realized she was talking to a computer. Maybe she *did* need a little counseling after all. She laced her fingers together in her lap, trying to appear as normal as she could after having convinced them she wasn't. Okay, she was obviously more stressed than she'd thought. "You know, I wouldn't have freaked out if your computer had made herself known a little earlier. I thought you were nutso."

Muffin spoke. "I didn't approve of Max inviting an engaged woman to take a ride with him. It's not proper. Instead of saying anything I decided to keep quiet."

"Sounds like you've been reading Miss Manners again, Muf," Max said.

Jamie looked at him. "Um, Max, could we just forget this ride and conversation ever took place?"

"Aw, Jamie, don't be embarrassed. It happens to the best of us."

"I'll bet you've never had a panic attack."

"Are you kidding?" Muffin said. "The man thrives on stress."

Max patted Jamie's hand. "Don't worry, I won't say anything."

Max pulled into the parking lot of the country club some minutes later and parked close to the front door. The bars lifted. "Thank you for an, um, interesting evening," he said. "I hope to have the pleasure again real soon."

Jamie couldn't get away quickly enough. Without another word, she climbed from the car and raced toward the building, almost running into Phillip inside as he was coming out of the men's room. Safe, predictable Phillip. He hadn't stood her up after all.

"Jamie, I'm so sorry I'm late. Both of my tuxes were at the cleaners. I completely forgot. I had to call the owner and ask him to reopen so I could get them. I tried to call."

She buried her face against his chest, no longer annoyed with him for being late. She smoothed his reddish-blond hair into place. The man had obviously rushed to get there.

"Honey, are you okay?"

"I am now."

". . . and one more thing," Frankie said, standing at the podium before a crowd that took up four dining rooms. "I promise not only to lower the sales tax, I'm going to make significant cuts to what I see as outrageous property taxes."

The group applauded heartily.

"The people in this town pay far too much in taxes. And for what?" He paused. "What happened to the new sewage treatment facility we were promised?

"Our government offices are overcrowded. We probably have more committees and task forces than New York City. We've even got a committee that oversees the rest of the committees. Why?" Several in the crowd chuckled. "I, for one, am sick of all the bureaucracy. Hell's bells, I had to go through ten different departments to get my name on the ballot." More laughter.

Max, having arrived just as they were serving dinner, glanced at Deedee. She met his gaze and frowned. "What's wrong?" he whispered.

"I saw you on the balcony with Jamie Swift earlier. Shortly before the two of you disappeared. What's with that?"

Max shrugged. "She and I both share an interest in cars. Did you know she and her father rebuilt the Mustang she's driving?"

Deedee nodded. "That's how we met. Frankie tried to buy it from her a couple of years back. She wouldn't part with it, but we've been friends ever since." Deedee paused. "You didn't mention the fact I asked you to help her out?"

"Of course not. But she's a smart woman. She'll figure it out sooner or later."

Deedee looked thoughtful. "So, what do you think of her?"

"I think she's a fine person."

"You know she's engaged."

Max looked across the room, not for the first time, and noticed the man sitting next to Jamie. "He's a lucky man."

Frankie continued his speech. "I promise, if I'm elected, I'll start a full investigation into our missing tax dollars. I'm going to find out once and for all what happened to that money."

Max leaned close to Deedee. "Smile, big sister. You should be very proud of your husband for wanting to make this town a better place."

"Frankie's made a lot of promises to these people. I just hope he lives long enough to keep them."

An hour later, a man stepped inside a telephone booth, dropped two quarters into the slot and dialed. He waited for the person on the other end to answer. "Fontana just won the hearts of everybody in this town with his speech tonight. He's planning an investigation into the missing tax dollars."

There was a slight pause. "That's bad news."

"I don't know how seriously we can take him. He's an ex-wrestler, for God's sake. He's not smart enough."

"Oh, he's smarter than you think. He also has his brother-in-law by his side now. Max Holt has the brains and the wherewithal to get anything he needs."

"So what's the plan?"

"We get rid of them. And I know just the person who will do it."

Chapter
THREE

Jamie parked her Mustang in her personal slot near the front of the building and sat there for a moment, collecting her thoughts. She felt crummy for sending Phillip home last night, but she had been in no mood for lovemaking. After he'd left, she'd lain awake most of the night thinking about how she'd made such a fool of herself in front of Max whatever-his-last-name-was and worrying about what today would bring.

She ran her hand along the dashboard and was surprised to find it dusty. Normally, she kept her car spotless. She lovingly washed it once a week and hand-waxed it when necessary, taking comfort in the task because of the comfortable feelings it evoked, as well as the memories. It frightened her sometimes to think how close she'd come to selling it. Her father had given it to her as a college graduation gift, and she tended to it as one would a well-loved family member. She often wished she had a brother or sister, but she had no one, no aunts and uncles, no cousins. She had lost her grandmother years before, a soft-spoken, white-haired woman with crystal-blue eyes and a kindly face who had once offered to take Jamie in because she feared her son was incapable of handling the responsibilities of fatherhood.

Jamie had balked at the idea. She and her father could handle anything as long as they were together. She would simply have to try harder to be a better daughter, she'd told herself. She would cook his favorite foods and keep the house just as her mother had left it. She would keep the woman's framed pictures dusted and sitting just so on her father's night table. And she would pretend, just as he had, that her mother would come back and everything would be fine. A normal family.

Sometimes, Jamie imagined she smelled her father's Aqua Velva aftershave in the upholstery, and then she would get tears in her eyes because she felt so very much alone now that he was gone. Then she would think of Phillip, and the knot in her stomach would melt like soft candy. Phillip, who loved her deeply and wanted to share his life with her. They'd met at a fundraising dance where the men had to pay to dance with the woman of their choice. Phillip had paid five hundred dollars to dance with Jamie.

He offered the stability she'd craved as a child. His family loved her, brothers and sisters, aunts and uncles, cousins and second cousins. And Phillip's mother, Annabelle, who treated her like the daughter she'd always wanted and planned to give them a wedding to end all weddings.

Jamie knew she was blessed. Finally, she would have the family she had always longed for. She imagined holidays with fat turkeys and brown-sugar-coated hams and relatives rushing in and out bearing Christmas gifts and shopping with Phillip for nieces and nephews. The scenes in her head were like Norman

Rockwell paintings. They represented everything that was sane and normal and real.

Jamie and Annabelle had settled on an outdoor wedding in September, hoping the heat and humidity would be more tolerable. She and Phillip would say their vows beneath the massive moss-draped live oaks that had graced the family estate for more than two hundred years and were as deeply rooted in the history of Beaumont as the Standishes themselves.

Jamie felt more optimistic as she climbed from the car. She was marrying the man of her dreams, and she faced a rock-solid future with him. Although she had never experienced the maternal instincts her friends had, she suspected it wouldn't be long before she and Phillip started a family. Annabelle loved her grandchildren more than anything in the world, and Jamie knew the woman would be eagerly awaiting her son's firstborn. As scary as it was sometimes to imagine actually walking down an aisle and becoming Mrs. Phillip Standish, Jamie knew she was making the right decision.

She hitched her chin high as she started for the building. Even though the day held a lot of uncertainty, what with her silent partner paying a surprise visit, Jamie was determined not to let it stress her. She had sacrificed almost everything she owned to keep the newspaper going, and she was a darn good publisher. In her mind, that was enough. If she was a little short on furniture and desks, M. Holt would simply have to understand.

Jamie rounded the building and headed toward the double glass doors. She found Vera standing outside, as if she were guarding the place. "Good morning, Vera."

"You don't want to go in there."

Jamie came to a halt, feeling a sense of dread wash over her. "Why not?"

"It, uh, needs a little more work."

"What do you mean?"

"Tom and Herman are going to pay for this. I'm on my way to their places right now. I plan to shoot holes into their tires."

"Are you out of your mind?"

"Once you see the place you'll want to be the trigger person, but it's my gun and I insist on being the shooter. You can drive the getaway car."

"You *have* lost your mind. Now, get a grip, we have work to do." Jamie tried to sidestep her, but the woman refused to budge. "Would you please move out of my way, Vera? Jeez, how bad can it be?"

She found out as soon as she pushed through the doors. "Oh, double damn."

"I told you it was bad. I'm not even going to charge you for cussing this time."

Several employees stood around the water cooler whispering. They scurried away like squirrels when they spied Jamie. "Is this some kind of joke?" Jamie asked.

"Danged if I know. I've been trying to reach Tom and Herman all morning, but they aren't answering their phones. They're probably having a good laugh over it right now."

Jamie planted her hands on her hips in obvious annoyance. "Why would anyone in their right mind paint an entire office battleship gray? It looks like a dungeon in here."

"I tried to warn you. Tom's crew recently painted the armory building. This was probably left over from that job."

Jamie took in the furniture. Herman Bates had obviously thought it would be fun to decorate the reception area in what looked like cowhide. The sofa and matching chair were a furry tan with white splotches that made Jamie think of a Guernsey dairy cow. Bullhorns hung from the wall. "I don't believe this." She looked at Vera. "I would be scared to sit on it in case it has fleas or mad cow disease."

"I don't think it's real cowhide, hon." Vera patted her shoulder. "The good thing is the furniture doesn't have to be returned. Herman left a note that we can keep it. Which is a good thing for him considering where I'd planned to stick it after we finished with it."

Mike Henderson came through the front doors and stopped dead in his tracks. "Wow! Cool furniture."

Jamie and Vera glared at him.

He shrugged. "Okay, so it's a little different, but that's not always a bad thing."

Jamie turned and started for her office. "I wouldn't go in there," Vera warned.

"It can't be as bad as this room." Jamie opened the door. Her heart sank to her toes. "Oh, God, it's Graceland."

"I've never seen a desk made of shellacked tree trunks," Mike said. "Is that a velvet painting of Elvis?"

Jamie crossed her arms and tapped one foot impatiently. "This is not a darn bit funny. I know Herman and Tom are a couple of pranksters, but this is way over the line. I have half a mind to—"

"Shoot 'em?" Vera said hopefully.

"I wouldn't waste the bullets." Jamie pressed her hand against her forehead, where a headache was starting to form. "There's nothing we can do about it now. Mr. Holt will be here in a few hours, and we're on deadline." Jamie reached into her desk drawer for her pack of cigarettes and pulled out one.

"You're not going to light that," Vera said.

"I just want to hold it. And be alone for a while," she added. She turned and faced the window. "Mike, give me fifteen minutes to calm down, and then we'll get started."

"Sure, Jamie." He paused. "By the way, you look very pretty and professional today. I wouldn't worry about the way this place looks. Mr. Holt will be so impressed with you he won't even notice the décor."

Jamie didn't respond. She knew Mike was simply trying to make her feel better, but it didn't work. She heard the door close behind her, and she sank into her chair.

The morning dragged for Jamie, who kept glancing at her watch. The knot in her stomach grew with each passing hour, but she tried to ignore it, concentrating instead on the job at hand. Mike worked beside her tirelessly. Although he had a tendency to get distracted by a pretty face, he was good at his job and buckled down like the best of them when the heat was on. Some people, including Jamie, worked better under pressure. She wondered if she should delegate more authority to Mike so he would feel challenged.

Shortly before lunch, Vera announced Mike had a telephone call. He didn't look up from his work as he grabbed the phone. "Is she going to be okay?" he asked after listening quietly.

Jamie looked up. Mike's face was pale, all the color gone. "What is it?" she said once he hung up.

"My mom fainted in the grocery store. She's in the emergency room."

"You have to go," Jamie said, knowing Mike was an only child. His parents were older and required a lot of attention.

"What about the newspaper?"

"It will be here when you get back."

He stood and fumbled in his pocket for his car keys and started for the door.

Jamie stood as well. "Are you okay to drive?"

"Yeah."

"Call me when you know something," she said. He hurried out, almost slamming into Vera.

"Where does he think he's going?"

Jamie explained the situation. "I'm going to be rushed for the rest of the afternoon. Please hold my calls."

"Did you remember to return Phillip's call?"

"No, but I will."

"That's what you said an hour ago. He's going to think I didn't give you the message. He'll blame me. Word will get around that I'm not a good administrative assistant, and I won't be able to find a new job."

"You're not going anywhere, Vera."

"That's what you think. Just so happens I'm updating my résumé. Not only is the pay bad, but there are no opportunities for advancement."

"Do we have to discuss this *now*?" Jamie asked wearily.

"Oh, yeah, this *is* a bad time. Just forget I said anything."

Five minutes later Jamie's phone rang. It was Phillip. "I'm sorry I haven't called you back," she said quickly. "You know how it is around here during deadline, and I'm short a person."

"I wouldn't have bothered you, but my mother

has called my office three times and wants to know if we've settled on that platinum-leaf china pattern from Starlings, Ltd. She says it has to be soon because people will have to special order it once they receive the wedding invitations. Also, she's threatening to take you over her knee personally if you don't decide on your gown."

Jamie groaned. "Oh, Phillip."

"I know, I know. She's driving me up the wall, too. Don't think you're in this alone." He chuckled. "That's what we get for agreeing to let her plan this whole thing."

"I need to get this newspaper out first," Jamie said, knowing Annabelle would keep her on the phone for hours if she called.

Jamie's headache had worsened. Too much stress in her life, she thought. The newspaper consumed every waking moment. She was annoyed with Phillip the night before for being late, but how many times had she been forced to break a date at the last minute? And poor Annabelle. She had taken on all the responsibility of planning the wedding, talking to caterers, dressmakers, florists, and Jamie couldn't even decide on a china pattern. September had seemed so far away. Jamie hadn't realized the work and planning that went into a wedding, especially the kind of wedding Annabelle planned.

Right now, though, Jamie had a newspaper to publish. She had struggled too hard to keep it going. Not only had she sold most of her office furniture, she'd sold her grandmother's jewelry and antiques and everything else she could think of in order to keep the bills paid. She couldn't afford to drop the ball now.

Jamie glanced at the clock. Still no sign of Mr. Holt.

She was beginning to feel desperate and panicky, just as she had the night before in Max's car. Max and his talking computer. She wondered where he was now, wondered if he was already on his way back to Virginia. She hoped that was the case. She never wanted to lay eyes on him again and remember how she literally flipped out.

Dang, her palms were wet. Jamie swiped them across her skirt. What was wrong with her? She had always been the calm one, the one who took charge when the pressure was on. She wished she could cancel the appointment with Mr. Holt. Of all times to have to face her partner.

"Hey, dude, I think we passed it."

Vito Puccini finished off a slice of cold pizza, wiped his mouth on his arm, and looked at the man in the passenger seat. "What the hell you mean we passed it? You said we were supposed to take exit eighty-eight. The last exit was eighty-three."

"I think I misread it."

In the backseat, Vito's wife, Mitzi, moaned aloud. "Lenny, you're such a dumbass."

Vito gave his head a small shake. "Mitzi, how many times have I told you not to use that language? You sound like some kind of cheap slut when you talk like that." He looked at Lenny. "You can take a stripper out of a sleazy bar, but you can't take the sleazy bar out of the stripper."

Mitzi smacked him on the head with her open palm. "Watch your mouth, Vito. I was an entertainer, and a damn good one. Which beats the hell out of having a rap sheet the length of the Jersey Turnpike like some people I know."

"I've had just about enough of you," Vito said. "I knew I shouldn't have brought you along."

"She gave you no choice, man," Lenny said.

"Damn right," Mitzi snapped. "Vito has already screwed every woman from Maine to Spain. You think I'm about to let him go off on his own and spend the night humping somebody else?"

Vito sighed. "Mitzi, I told you I made a mistake. Are you going to nag me over it for the rest of your life?"

"That's the plan, Vito. You're going to regret the day you cheated on me."

He shook his head. "A marriage made in hell, that's what this is. Lenny, hold the wheel so I can read the map."

Mitzi laughed out loud. "Oh, that's a good one, Vito. Lenny probably snorted a yard of coke back there at the truck stop. You're going to let him steer the car?"

"Shut up, Mitzi." He studied the map as Lenny tried to steer the car. "Shit, I guess we got to turn around," he said, slowing at the next exit.

"Stop at a gas station while you're at it," Mitzi said. "I have to pee."

Vito glanced at her from the rearview mirror. "You just peed, for Christ's sake."

"Just do it, okay? It's bad enough I have to ride in this crap car with no air conditioner. I'm sticking to the seat, and I think I'm getting a heat rash on top of it. Or maybe it's hives. I'm getting a bad case of nerves sitting in this car."

"Hey, I got something that'll calm you down," Lenny said.

"Forget it. I'm not about to take anything from a low-life druggie. Besides, it's probably illegal as hell."

Vito grunted. "This coming from an ex-stripper who used to give lap dances." Vito exited and pulled into a gas station, and Mitzi raced to the bathroom. Lenny pumped while Vito talked quietly. "I should have my head examined for marrying that woman. All she does is bitch. I'm beginning to miss prison."

Lenny nodded. "Me too, dude. At least we had some peace and quiet. I haven't seen *General Hospital* since we got out. Hey, I could slip a couple of downers in Mitzi's soft drink. Knock her out cold."

"Just what the hell are you carrying?" Vito demanded.

"Dude, you name it and I got it. Uppers, downers, a couple of pounds of good Jamaican weed, a little coke."

Vito glared at him. "You're carrying all that shit? What are you, crazy? We get stopped and we're both going back to the slammer."

"You're worried about drugs when we've got an arsenal in the trunk?"

"That can't be helped. You expect me to do a hit with a slingshot?"

"Just drive the speed limit, dude, and we won't get stopped. We look respectable enough."

"Yeah, right. I got an ex-stripper in the backseat who looks like she's been hustling on some street corner, and a guy in the passenger seat who hasn't bathed in a week. I could fry eggs in your hair, Lenny."

"My hair has always been oily. I could wash it three times a day, and it would look this way."

"You could have gotten a haircut, you know. I told you we were supposed to look like businessmen. How else are we going to get close to Holt?"

Mitzi returned to the car and climbed into the backseat. "You feeling any better?" Vito asked, obviously trying to be nice. She muttered something under her breath, stretched out on the seat, and closed her eyes. Before long she was snoring. Vito and Lenny exchanged looks of relief.

"I want to do the job tonight and get out of town right away," Vito whispered.

"When do we collect?" Lenny asked.

"Soon as Holt's obit shows up in the newspaper."

Max pulled into the parking lot of the *Beaumont Gazette* and cut the engine. He just sat there staring at the building.

"Afraid to go in?" Muffin asked.

"I'm thinking I should wear a bulletproof vest."

"A vest won't do you any good. Jamie Swift is going to kill you with her bare hands when she realizes you kept your true identity a secret."

"It seemed a good idea at the time. I figured she'd be uncomfortable if I'd told her who I was, and I really wanted to get to know her first."

"That sounds real good, Max, but this is me you're talking to, remember? You wanted to nail her."

"I don't *nail* women, and I certainly wouldn't have tried it with an engaged woman. I just wanted to spend some time with her." He sighed. "Wish me luck." He climbed from the car and started toward the front of the building, hesitating only a moment before going through the double doors.

Max took one look at the room, and his jaw dropped open.

Vera looked up from her work. Pens and pencils jutted from her beehive hairdo in every direction because she had a tendency to tuck them in and forget them when she got busy.

Max stepped up to her desk. "I'm here to see Miss Swift."

"Are you Mr. Holt?"

He nodded. "And you are?"

"Vera Bankhead. Miss Swift's administrative assistant. I sort of run the place."

Max smiled. "I'll bet you're good at it, too."

"Let's put it this way. I know everything that goes on around here."

Max glanced around. "I smell fresh paint."

"Yes, Miss Swift recently redecorated the place." She leaned closer and whispered. "I had nothing to do with it." She picked up the telephone. "I'll tell her you're here."

"Thank you."

Vera hung up the phone a moment later. "She'll be right with you."

Max turned at the sound of a door opening. Jamie Swift stepped out, took one look, and gasped at the sight of him. "What are *you* doing here?"

"Hello, Jamie."

She simply stared back at him.

Still wearing her most professional smile, Vera cut her eyes from Jamie to Max then back to Jamie. "Uh, Miss Swift, this is Mr. Holt. As in M. Holt."

"Max Holt," he said, stepping forward and offering his hand.

Jamie experienced a moment of total disorientation. "*The* Max Holt?"

"Yeah."

"Oh, Lordy," Vera said. "I don't believe it. We've got a celebrity in our office."

Jamie stared at the man. "You can't be serious. Is this some kind of joke?"

"Afraid not."

Jamie's look turned from stunned disbelief to pure annoyance. "I don't believe it," she said. "You have some nerve coming into this office after lying to me about your true identity last night and allowing me to make a complete fool of myself. Just who do you think you are?"

Vera gawked.

"I'm sorry," Max said. "I should have told you the truth."

"*Sorry?* That's *it*?"

"I don't know what more I can do than apologize. I never meant for it to turn out the way it did."

"What in heaven's name is going on?" Vera asked.

"This man is a dirty rotten liar, Vera. If I were a violent woman I'd—"

"The least we can do is act civilized here," Max said. "After all, we have business to conduct."

"I refuse to conduct business with you."

"Jamie, have you lost your mind?" Vera said.

Jamie realized she was trembling. "This man is an imposter. He tried to pass himself off as somebody else last night. He abducted me—"

"You came with me of your own free will," Max reminded.

"He scared me to death, then he made a fool of me."

Vera tossed him a dark look. "You did all that?" When Max nodded sheepishly, she reached for her purse. "Let me shoot him, Jamie."

Max put his hands over Vera's before she could reach inside her purse for her gun. "Before you shoot me, at least give me the chance to make it up to Miss Swift."

Vera paused. "Okay, but this had better be good

because I am definitely not having a good day and you just made it worse."

Max looked at Jamie. "I really am sorry, Jamie. I had no right to do what I did."

Vera waited. "That's the best you can do?"

"I wanted to get to know you on a personal level," Max continued. "I knew you'd feel uncomfortable if I told you who I really was, what with me being an investor and all."

Jamie refused to listen. Instead, she turned and strode into her office, slamming the door behind her.

"I don't think she likes you," Vera said. "I think you'd better leave."

"You have to help me," Max said.

"And why should I do that?"

"Jamie overreacted, Vera. For some reason she thought I had abducted her and was out to rape and kill her. I don't know if she's been watching too many cop shows or what, but she clearly panicked for no reason."

Vera averted her eyes and shifted in her chair. It was obvious she felt guilty for having filled Jamie's head with so many terrible stories.

"Well, Jamie *has* been under a lot of stress lately, but when push comes to shove I'm going to take her side. Besides, you had no right to pass yourself off as somebody else. I'm afraid I can't help you."

"Tell you what, Vera. If you'll just help me this once, I promise I'll make it up to Jamie. Not only that, I'll have this place redecorated inside and out at my expense." He reached into his jacket for his wallet and pulled out a credit card. He offered it to her.

"Do you think you can just buy your way out of everything, Mr. Holt?"

"Not everything."

Vera eyed him suspiciously. "Do I get a new desk?"

"Everybody can have a new desk."

"How about the computers? They're old."

"Whatever you need. I don't care if you rebuild this place from the ground up."

"What's the limit on this card?"

"There is none."

Vera stared at the card like a hungry mongrel would a large steak. "Well, in that case." She snatched the card from him and tucked it inside the bodice of her dress.

Max arched one brow.

"Don't worry, your credit card is safe." She patted her breast. "Nobody ever goes here." She stood and made for Jamie's office. "You'll have to give me a few minutes. This isn't going to be easy. Have a seat."

Max glanced at the sofa. "I'll stand."

When Vera came out of Jamie's office five minutes later, she nodded. "You can go in now. She's calm."

"You're sure?"

"I told you I run the show. I know how to talk to Miss Swift."

Max took a deep breath, opened the door to Jamie's office, and walked in.

Jamie had a lit cigarette in her mouth. "Close the door."

"Sit," she said after the door shut.

"I think I ought to stand in case I have to make a quick getaway."

Jamie had no desire to talk to him, and the only reason she'd agreed to do it was because Vera had given her permission to smoke one cigarette. Just one. "What you did was bad."

"Despicable," he said.

"Worse. It was appalling, contemptible, loathsome, and vile."

"Wow, you even managed to alphabetize the list. I'm impressed."

"Truly, there are no words."

"Sounds like you found pretty good substitutes."

Jamie's phone rang. She snatched it up. "Mike? How's your mother?" She paused and listened. "A stroke? How bad is she?"

Max took a chair in front of her desk and waited.

"I told you not to worry about the newspaper," Jamie finally said. "You need to be with your family. I'll make the deadline." She tried to reassure him several times before she hung up.

"I really don't have time to meet with you today, Mr. Holt," she said. "My managing editor had an emergency, and the paper has to go to print this evening. Perhaps some other time."

"I can help you, Jamie," he said. "Don't forget, I know the newspaper business inside and out."

"This is a weekly newspaper. Small potatoes compared to what you're used to."

Max reached for her phone and dialed. "May I speak to Deedee?" He waited. "Hi, big sister. I just wanted to tell you not to wait dinner on me. I'm going to be tied up with business for a while."

Jamie's eyes widened, but she waited until he hung up before saying anything. "Deedee, as in Deedee Fontana?"

"Uh-huh."

"She's your sister?"

Max nodded.

"So that explains how you got involved with my

newspaper to begin with. Deedee told you all about my financial woes so you decided to take me on as a charity case."

"I bought into the paper because I believe in the value of local press."

Jamie stubbed her cigarette out in a potted plant. "I don't like people butting into my affairs, business or otherwise."

"Face it, kiddo, you need me."

He smiled that knockout smile, and Jamie knew she couldn't turn him down. "Okay, but just this once because I'm shorthanded. I'll show you what I have so far, and we can go from there."

Vito held the door open for Mitzi as she stepped into the cramped motel room. The double beds were draped in faded spreads that looked as though they'd seen far too many washdays, and the carpet was badly stained. Mitzi turned and planted her hands on her hips.

"You're kidding, right? You don't really expect me to sleep in this room."

"It's the best we could afford right now," he said. "It's not like we're going to find a Hyatt Regency in a town this size."

"I am *not* believing this," she almost shouted. "I spend hours riding in a hot car, thinking how great it's going to be when I get to the hotel and I can take a nice long bubble bath." She peeked inside the bathroom and muttered a four-letter word. "I wouldn't bathe my dog in that nasty-looking tub."

"So take a shower."

"I need to soak in hot water. I have a bad back."

"Probably from spending so many years working on it."

"Bastard."

"I did the best I could," Vito said. "It's either sleep here or in the backseat of the car."

She pointed at Lenny. "Where is *he* supposed to sleep?"

"On the other bed."

"You're shittin' me, right? You expect me to share a room with a dirty druggie who would sell his own sister for a fix?"

"I don't have a sister," Lenny said, "so you're safe with me."

Mitzi and Vito just looked at him. Finally, Vito checked his wristwatch. "Listen, Mitzi, Lenny and me have to get some work done. We're here on business, remember?"

"And that's another thing. I want to know what the hell you two are up to. I've asked you at least fifty times, and now I'm demanding an answer."

Vito shrugged. "We're hit men, Mitzi. We're here to kill someone."

"Oh, very funny. You're just a barrel of laughs, Vito. But I'm sure whatever it is, it's illegal, and if you end up in the slammer again, I'm outta here. You got that?"

He looked at Lenny. "Almost makes it worth it, huh?"

"I just wish the two of you would stop arguing," Lenny said.

"Tell you what, Mitzi," Vito said. "I'll call the maid and have her scrub out the tub for you. You can take your bubble bath and read one of those magazines you bought for the trip. After that, you can watch TV."

"They don't have HBO," she said between gritted teeth. She turned for the bathroom and slammed the door so hard it knocked a picture from the wall.

Vito looked at Lenny. "I think I'm about to shoot the wrong person."

It was after midnight by the time the newspaper was ready to go to print. Jamie had to admit Max knew his stuff; he'd arranged the actual page layouts in half the time it usually took her. "I added some last-minute advertising Vera gave me," he told Jamie, once they'd handed everything over to the pressroom staff.

"Good. We can always use advertising." Her eyes ached from all the copy-editing and final proofing she'd done. She was bone tired and looked forward to some shut-eye. Max, on the other hand, looked fresh and ready to put in another day.

"I'm pleased with the results," Max said, "but next time we'll do even better."

"There's not going to be a next time, Max. You helped me out of a bind, and I appreciate it, but—"

"What's the problem, Jamie? We worked very well together today."

"I have an editor, Max."

He looked amused. "You don't like me very much, do you, Swifty?"

She looked at him. *"Swifty?"*

"I thought it sounded like a cute nickname."

Jamie rolled her eyes.

"Back to my question."

"I like you fine, Max, but it doesn't matter one way or the other. We're business partners, we don't have to be best friends."

"But you're a little distant, don't you think?"

"Meaning I don't fawn all over you like most women?"

He smiled. "Well, that, too."

"Do the words 'happily engaged' mean anything to you?"

"Of course."

"Even if I weren't engaged I would never get involved with a man like you."

"A man like me?"

"I've got your number, Max Holt. I read the newspapers. You go through women like a horse goes through oats, and you have an ego the size of Texas."

"Other than that what do you think of me?"

"Can't you be serious for five minutes?"

"I am being serious. Okay, so I'm not perfect, but that doesn't mean I can't help you. You want this paper to succeed or you wouldn't push yourself so hard."

Jamie felt uncomfortable with his dark eyes boring into hers. "Listen, you've seen what you came to see. My accountant will continue to send financial reports and whatever else you need, but our business is finished."

"What's he like?"

"Who?"

"The man you're going to marry."

"You're getting a little personal, aren't you?"

"I'm curious."

"Phillip is a very nice man. He's kind and loving, and he will make a wonderful husband and father. Now, if you don't mind, I'd like to go home and—"

Max caught movement out of the corner of his eye and realized a car had passed by the front of the building where a large, plate-glass window looked out on Main Street. The blinds were partially closed, so he only caught a glimpse of headlights and nothing more. He turned back to Jamie but before he could say anything, he heard the rapid repetitive bursts of an automatic weapon. The plate-glass window exploded.

Jamie screamed as Max dove for her, pulling her down onto the floor. Together they rolled against the wall and lay there while the shots continued and everything shattered around them.

Jamie tried not to move as the firing continued, the noise so loud she feared her eardrums would burst. Suddenly, something painful pierced her leg, and she winced. "Oh, crap," she said. "And I didn't think this day could get worse."

Max held her fast, covering her with his own body. "What is it?"

"I've been shot," she said.

Chapter

FOUR

The firing stopped as quickly as it had begun, followed by the sound of screeching tires as a car sped away. Max rolled off Jamie and winced at the sight of her leg. An ugly shard of glass protruded from her calf. Quickly, he searched for other wounds. Thankfully, there were none.

Jamie sat up, took one look at her leg and gave a sigh of absolute disgust. "Would you look at that? I've gone all day without getting a run in these pantyhose. Now I wish I'd gone ahead and bought the store brand instead of spending four dollars more for a name brand." She sighed. "Oh, double damn."

Max just looked at her.

"Well, are you going to pull the blasted thing out or do I have to sit here and bleed to death?"

Max reached for the knot in his tie, undid it and pulled it from his neck. He jerked the glass shard from her leg.

Jamie sucked in her breath sharply. "Ouch!"

"I never promised it would feel good," he said as he wrapped the tie around her, binding the wound tight to keep it from bleeding worse. "This should do until we can get help. Call nine-one-one. I need to check outside." He hurried from the room and almost bumped into one of the men from production. They did a little dance as Max tried to get past him, and the other man didn't seem to know which way to move. Finally, Max pushed him out of the way and ran.

Jamie was already on the telephone, explaining the situation to the police dispatcher. With assurances that help was on the way, she hung up and found Lyle, her production manager, staring at her leg in concern.

"Miss Swift, are you okay?" he asked. "I came in from the back to go to the bathroom and I heard the noise." He glanced around the shot-up office in disbelief.

"I'm okay," Jamie replied. "I'll probably have a scar on my leg the size of our parking lot. There goes my dream of competing in the Miss South Carolina beauty pageant. Is everyone in back okay, Lyle?"

He nodded. "I'm sure nobody back there heard the shots, what with the printing press going at full speed. Do you need me to do something?"

"The police are on their way."

The police arrived ten minutes later, followed by an ambulance. As a paramedic treated Jamie's wound, the police chief, Lamar Tevis, a slightly overweight, sandy-haired man in baggy khakis and a badly wrinkled cotton shirt, issued orders to his men. "Call Bud from the crime lab, and tell him to get over here right now."

"Yes, Chief."

Lamar turned to Jamie and Max. "Did either of you see anything?"

Max shook his head. "They got away before I could get a look."

"Who are you?" Lamar bluntly asked.

Jamie introduced Max. Lamar looked impressed. "I've read about you in the newspaper."

Max handed him a metal casing he'd found in the street. "Looks like it came from a high-powered automatic."

Lamar turned the casing over several times as though he might find a clue. "We don't see this kind of action down here. Somebody is mighty serious about killing somebody." He studied Max. "Do you have any enemies? Anybody who might want you dead?"

"I try to conduct business fairly," Max said, "although I'm sure I've made a few people angry in my dealings. I can't think of anyone who'd actually want to kill me."

Lamar turned to Jamie. "Have you been printing anything controversial in your newspaper?"

She rolled her eyes. "Well, I did accidentally print that Peggy Block won a blue ribbon for her Wedding Ring quilt, when it was actually Jane Barker."

Lamar frowned. "Did you print a retraction?" When Jamie nodded, he went on. "Well, then, we know that's not it." At Max's incredulous look Lamar added, "These ladies take their quilts seriously."

"Obviously," Max said, his voice controlled as though he were trying to practice patience. "But one possibility we might consider is that Jamie is covering the mayoral campaign and has already endorsed Frankie Fontana. Since she owns the only newspaper in town, it won't sit well with his opponent. I'm sure you're aware of the threatening mail Frankie has received."

Jamie looked surprised. "He's getting threatening mail? I didn't know that."

Lamar nodded. "Yeah, we're looking into it, but I don't see how the two are connected." He looked at Jamie. "Are you sure you printed a retraction?"

"Yes, Lamar!"

"How about your employees? Anybody holding any grudges against you?"

"Just Vera. She's mad at me because I haven't given her a raise in a long time."

"She carries a .38, doesn't she?"

"How do you know that?"

"My cousin's wife goes to the same beauty parlor. The gun fell out of Vera's purse once." He looked concerned. "Guess I'll have to wake Judge Dobbert so I can get a search warrant. He's not going to like it."

"You're not going to search Vera's house! Jeez, Lamar, Vera wouldn't lay a hand on me. She loves me like a daughter."

"Well, that's true." He sighed. "Doesn't look like this is going to be an easy case. Doesn't look like I'm going to be able to take time off for my annual fishing trip, either."

"Perhaps this was politically motivated," Max said.

Lamar's expression went blank. "Are you thinking of running for office, too?"

Max and Jamie exchanged looks. "No, but the attempted hit might have been a ploy to scare off Frankie," Max said. "Nobody can get to him because his place has more security than Fort Knox. Since I'm his brother-in-law they might try to get to him by hurting me. Or Miss Swift since she's a close friend."

"Well, he did threaten to look into those missing tax dollars," Lamar said. "You might be on to something."

"And who better to help Frankie with the investigation than his brother-in-law Max Holt?" Jamie said.

"Man, this puts a whole new light on things," Lamar said.

Bud from the crime lab arrived. "Holy smoke, Lamar!" he said the minute he stepped into Jamie's office. "What happened here?"

"Somebody shot holes through Jamie's window."

"Hell's bells, I figured that out for myself. Does anyone know *why*?"

"We're working on it. I want you to run this metal casing through ballistics and see if we can get an exact make on the weapon."

Bud took the casing and looked at it closely. "Man oh man, this here puppy is bad." He looked at Jamie. "I hope you cleared up matters between the quilting-bee ladies. My wife is part of the group, and she was mad as a hornet that somebody else got credit."

Max turned and looked out the window.

Jamie suspected Max was growing impatient with the local law enforcement personnel. "Lamar, can we go?"

"Give me just a sec," he said. "I need to write up a quick report and have y'all sign it. And I'll have my men board up the front window for you," he added.

"Would you mind leaving one of the deputies here until my production crew finishes up?"

"Sure thing. Do you want me to post someone outside your house?"

"I'm taking Miss Swift to the Fontana place," Max said. When Jamie looked like she might argue, he went on. "Frankie's house is the safest place in town right now."

Jamie relented. She was bone tired, and she suspected she wouldn't get much sleep if she was home alone.

"I may as well tell you there's someone from the local TV station outside," Bud said. "I tried to get rid of him, but he's looking for a story."

"I'll go out with you," Lamar said.

As soon as they finished the report Jamie followed Max and Lamar outside. Sure enough, a reporter stood outside the door, another man taping them as they tried to pass.

A man shoved a microphone in Jamie's face. "Miss Swift, can you tell me what happened here tonight?"

"I have no comment," she said.

"Go ahead," Lamar said quietly. "I'll talk to them."

The reporter faced him and raised the microphone to him. "We're ready, Chief."

Max and Jamie hurried away. His car was parked on the other side of her Mustang convertible. As Jamie started around her car, she paused.

"Oh, my God!"

Max whipped around. "What is it?"

"They shot a hole through my passenger door!" Jamie knelt on the ground beside her car so she could get a closer look. She felt her throat close up. "I don't believe it."

Max knelt beside her. "Probably ricocheted off the building. That's too bad."

Jamie's eyes stung. "You don't understand. I love this car. It's—" She almost choked on the words. She looked up at Max. "You wouldn't understand."

"Help me."

"My father gave me this car as a graduation present, it's really all I have left," she added mournfully.

"I'm really sorry, Jamie. The good news is it can be fixed."

She swiped her eyes, determined not to burst into

tears. To a man like Max Holt, who'd probably spent millions having others design his automobile, her car was just an old Mustang convertible. "It's just a car," she muttered. "Don't worry about it."

"You think we got 'em, dude?" Lenny asked, as Vito parked behind the motel and cut the engine.

"I don't know how we could have missed, but we can't leave town until we know for sure. We don't get paid until it's a done deal." He grunted. "I wanted to get out of here tonight. The cops are probably combing the area as we speak."

"Nobody knows we're here, man. The motel manager thinks Mitzi is alone."

Vito nodded. "Yeah, but the sooner we blow this town the better. I've got a bad feeling. Now, be quiet going in, okay? If Mitzi's asleep I don't want to wake her. She'll ask questions."

Frankie and Deedee were awakened at two A.M. by the telephone. Frankie picked it up. "Yeah?" He rubbed his eyes and listened. "Let them in."

"Who is it?" Deedee asked, reaching for the lamp. She turned it on, and the two blinked at one another sleepily.

"Max and Jamie. What in the world are *they* doing together?"

Deedee wrinkled her brow in thought. "Oh, I wish I wouldn't do that," she whined. "One day I'm going to frown, and the wrinkles are going to permanently lock into place." She smoothed her forehead as though checking to make sure they were gone. "Max is sort of her business partner," she finally said.

Frankie just looked at her. "Why didn't I know that?"

"Sweetie, I try not to bother you with every little thing. You know Jamie's had financial losses with her newspaper. I asked Max to help."

Frankie's look softened. "Why am I not surprised? My little Deedee, who always wants to make things easier for people. What I don't understand is why he would bring her here at this hour."

"I hope he's not planning to nail her. I hope I didn't screw up by asking him to help her."

"Your intentions were good." Frankie climbed from the bed, shivering from the cold. He reached for his terry-cloth bathrobe. Deedee, wearing a tight-fitting gossamer teddy, got up as well.

"Go back to bed, kitten," Frankie said, his warm breath creating a vapor in the cold air as he spoke. "I'll take care of it."

"I can't just lie here. Something must be wrong for them to show up here in the middle of the night." Deedee checked her reflection in the mirror over the vanity. "*Eeyeuuw,* my hair looks terrible. I should wake Beenie."

"Let him sleep, honey. Your hair looks fine. Besides, Beenie will pitch a tantrum and throw all your hairbrushes in the toilet like he did last time he got angry."

Deedee slipped on her own bathrobe. "I know he's temperamental, but it's part of his creative nature."

Frankie shrugged and opened the door, letting her pass through first. "If you're happy with him, that's all that matters. We can afford to buy hairbrushes."

The housekeeper was in the process of making coffee and preparing sandwiches for Max and Jamie when Frankie and Deedee joined them. Deedee took one look at Jamie's bandaged leg.

"Oh, no!" she cried. "What happened to *you*?"

"It's just a small cut," Jamie said. "I'm more annoyed than anything."

"There was a shooting at the newspaper office," Max said. "Just some drunk with a gun, no doubt. The glass from Jamie's window shattered, and a piece of it hit her leg. The paramedic put a couple of butterfly stitches on it, no big deal."

Deedee's hand flew to her breasts. "You could have been killed!"

Jamie knew Max was trying to play it down so as not to frighten Deedee. Frankie was hell-bent on protecting her. There was no way they could pretend it hadn't happened because the local TV station would broadcast news like that for the next six months. Deedee would find out eventually. "Yeah, I figure it was probably a redneck with his grandpa's deer rifle trying to show off. Or maybe the quilting club."

"You called the police, right?" Frankie said.

Max nodded. "They're investigating now. I brought Jamie here because I wanted to make sure her leg was okay."

Jamie nodded. "In case it starts bleeding," she said. "I don't have any Band-Aids at home, and all the stores are closed."

"That was a good idea," Deedee said, taking Jamie's hand in hers. "I know all about first aid. I took a course. And you don't have to worry about a thing because we'll take good care of you. This place is crawling with security." Deedee looked adoringly at her husband, then at Max. "And we have two big strong men in the house."

The housekeeper set a plate of sandwiches in front of Max and Jamie. "Would anyone like coffee?"

All four nodded.

"So you think the shooting was random," Frankie said.

"I can't imagine why anyone would want to hurt either of us," Max replied, his eyes making contact with Frankie. The two exchanged silent messages. Frankie seemed to get it, but remained poker-faced.

"That has to be it," Deedee said. "We read about this sort of thing all the time. I can't believe we have so many psychos running loose."

Jamie took a bite of her sandwich. She was not the least bit hungry, but she was trying her best to act calm. "Great chicken salad," she told the housekeeper. "You must've known Max and I were starving to death." The woman smiled at her.

Jamie looked from Frankie to Deedee. "My managing editor's mother was sent to the ER today. Max was kind enough to help me get the newspaper out on time."

"Besides," Deedee continued as though she weren't listening to the conversation. "Why would anyone try to hurt Jamie?"

Jamie shrugged. "The only person who dislikes me right now is Vera. I can't afford to give her a raise."

"Sweetheart, why don't you go back to bed?" Frankie suggested to his wife. "I'll make sure Max and Jamie get settled in."

"Frankie's right," Max said. "You look exhausted."

Deedee glanced around the table. "Why is everyone trying to get rid of me?" When they didn't respond right away, she looked suspicious. "Something's going on, isn't it? Something none of you want me to find out about. What is it?" She didn't wait for anyone to answer. "This has something to do with Frankie's campaign, doesn't it? Oh, Lord, I knew it."

"I certainly don't see a connection," Max said.

"Oh, yeah? First we get threatening letters, now someone is trying to kill you and Jamie. Why are you keeping it from me?"

"Now, honey." Frankie reached for her hand and squeezed it. "One has nothing to do with the other."

"You're getting upset over nothing, big sister," Max said. "Jamie and I just happened to be in the wrong place at the wrong time."

"Max is right," Jamie said. "We were working in my office, which overlooks Main Street. We were easy targets."

"Lamar will find the person responsible," Frankie said.

Deedee didn't look convinced. "Well, I don't think Jamie should go back to work until they find this person. What if he returns?"

Jamie shook her head. "I'm not the least bit worried. Vera keeps a gun with her at all times, and she's mean enough to use it."

"You're shivering, Jamie," Max said.

"Oh, my," Deedee said. "She's probably in shock, poor thing."

Jamie knew Deedee kept the air-conditioning just above freezing because of her hot flashes, but she wasn't about to bring it up, knowing how sensitive her friend was on the subject. She had never been so damn cold in her life. She would have wrestled a bear for his hide right now. "I'm fine," she insisted.

"Honey, let me take you upstairs and tuck you into bed," Deedee offered. "You can sleep as late as you want."

Frankie waited until he and Max were alone before he spoke. "Thank you."

"Don't mention it," Max said.

The big man settled back in his chair. "Now tell me what really happened."

Max waited until the housekeeper refilled their coffee cups and went off to bed. "Do you know anyone besides the mayor who doesn't want you to win?"

"Could be a bunch of his cronies don't want to lose their jobs. They got this good-old-boy system. The people running this town are all either related by blood or marriage. Maybe they're hoping to scare me off."

"The person responsible for the shooting was trying to do more than scare someone off, Frankie. We're talking attempted murder here." Max described the type of gun that had been used.

"Don't tell Deedee," Frankie said.

"I know how protective you are where my sister's concerned," Max said, "but she's bound to find out sooner or later, and she's not going to appreciate your keeping it from her." He chuckled. "It would be just like her to insist on taking shooting lessons."

"That's what I'm afraid of."

Max grinned. "She's still a handful. Anyway, in the meantime, I'll help you look into it, if you like. Truth is, it smells like rotten money, and I think the fact that you threatened to investigate the missing tax dollars stirred up a hornet's nest. If someone is willing to kill over it, you can bet it's serious."

"But why go after you and Jamie?"

"Because it's impossible to get to you, what with all the security you've got. And the powers that be will suspect I'm going to help you look into it, which I have every intention of doing. They know I have the resources to do it right."

"This is nothing like wrestling," Frankie said. "At

least I could look across the ring and see my opponent." He shook his head sadly. "What can I do to help?"

Jamie felt somebody watching her. She opened her eyes and bolted upright in the bed. "What the hell?"

Beenie screamed and almost tripped on his own two feet jumping back. "Oh, Lordy, you scared me half to death!" he cried. "My heart is going pitter-patter, pitter-patter. I almost weeweed on myself."

"Beenie, don't you ever slip up on me like that," Jamie said, pulling a baseball bat from beneath the covers. "You're lucky I didn't bash your brains."

He eyed the bat and cocked one slender hip, planting his hand on it as though miffed. "*Wherever* did you get that weapon?"

"Deedee gave it to me. Do you have a specific reason for slipping into my room without knocking?"

"Mr. Fontana asked me to check and see if you were awake."

"I am now. What's going on?"

"You know I don't delve into other people's business."

"I'm waiting, Beenie."

"Okay, okay, your fiancé is here."

"Phillip? Here?"

"Yes, and he's looking very dapper this morning, dressed in a navy pin-striped suit and crisp white dress shirt that shows off his tan. Of course, the man doesn't know the first thing about choosing ties. It's burgundy, for heaven's sake." Bennie sighed. "But what can I do? I've certainly dropped enough hints. Anyway, he looks worried."

"What time is it?"

"Seven."

Jamie climbed from the bed, unabashed in her thin nightgown. "Tell him I'll be right down."

"Okay, but it's not my job, and I'm not getting paid for it. The housekeeper in this place is a lazy slut, if you ask me."

Jamie ignored him and reached for a bathrobe as Beenie hurried away. Donning the robe, she checked her hair and general appearance in the mirror. Not great, but it would have to do. Downstairs, she found Phillip sipping coffee at the dining room table, deep in conversation with Max and Frankie. This time his strawberry-blond hair was perfectly combed.

"Jamie!" Phillip stood and reached for her, hugging her tightly against him. "I came as soon as I heard the news. Are you okay?"

"Just a minor cut, Phillip," she said, loving the feel of his clean-shaven jaw against her cheek. His gray eyes looked concerned. "It's no big deal, really. How did you find out?"

"Vera called me. She went in early this morning and saw the crime-scene tape. She tried to reach you at home. When you didn't answer she called me, and I called Lamar. He explained the situation, told me you were staying here."

Jamie had planned to call Vera as soon as she'd had a cup of coffee. She knew how the woman fretted over her. "Vera knows I'm okay, right?"

"Yes. I called her back and promised her I'd come right over. My mother is frantic, too. She said to pack you up and bring you home immediately. You'll be safe there."

That was the last thing Jamie needed at the moment. Annabelle would make such a fuss over her that Jamie wouldn't get a minute's peace. The woman would insist on keeping her locked inside the house. Jamie would be forced to eat stuff like liver pâté and those tiny cucumber sandwiches she hated and Annabelle would discuss every minute detail of the wedding plans. Jamie shot Frankie a pleading look.

"Jamie is welcome to stay here as long as she likes," he said. "The grounds are crawling with security, and I'm hiring more. Under the circumstances, I think it's the safest place for her."

Jamie silently thanked him.

"It's up to you, honey," Phillip said, "but you know you're welcome anytime." He paused. "You'll be living there soon anyway. We'll have an entire wing to ourselves."

Jamie had misgivings about living on the Standish estate, but she figured she'd give it a shot since the family employed a cleaning staff and Jamie didn't have time for that sort of thing. She also wasn't crazy about having to dress up for dinner, but it didn't seem like much of a sacrifice when somebody else was doing the cooking and cleaning up afterward.

The housekeeper offered Jamie a cup of coffee, and she accepted it. "Would you like something to eat?" Frankie asked, motioning to a large platter of fresh-cut fruit on the table, beside which sat a basket of sweet rolls and bagels. "The cook can fix you eggs and bacon if you like."

Jamie shook her head. "I'm not a breakfast person."

Frankie chuckled. "Neither is Deedee. But that's because she sleeps till lunchtime."

Jamie took a seat next to Phillip. She glanced across

the table and found Max watching her curiously. "Phillip, I assume you've met Frankie's brother-in-law, Max Holt."

Phillip smiled. "Yes. He tells me he was helping out at the paper last night when the incident occurred. I'm glad you weren't alone at the time of the shooting."

"I'll bet he didn't tell you he saved my life."

Phillip looked surprised. "No."

"If he hadn't pushed me down on the floor when the shooting started, I would be riddled with bullets this morning."

"I guess I owe you a world of thanks," Phillip told Max.

Max wasn't looking at Phillip. He was staring at Jamie, an amused look on his face. "My pleasure."

"Does anyone have any thoughts as to why the shooting occurred?" Phillip asked. "Do you think it's politically motivated?"

"That's what we're trying to find out," Max told him.

Frankie looked at Jamie. "I wish you hadn't endorsed me. Not that I don't appreciate it, but you may have put yourself at risk. It might be better if you remained neutral from here on out."

"I've never had a neutral thought in my life," she said. "I'm not about to start now."

Frankie sighed heavily. "Or maybe this person is after Max," he said. "I threatened to look into missing tax dollars. People will assume Max is here to help me, and anybody who has heard of him knows he's capable of getting the information. Could be I put both of you in danger," he added, shaking his head.

"I'll see that you get all the cooperation you need with regard to looking into the matter," Phillip told

Max. "It's the least I can do for the man who risked his own life to save my fiancée."

A tired-looking Deedee appeared on the stairs looking like a princess. Beenie followed, holding her little Maltese dog, and helping Deedee down slowly, as though he feared she might fall. He was dressed casually in white slacks with razor-sharp creases, and a navy Ralph Lauren oxford shirt.

"What's going on?" Deedee asked. "How come you people are up so early? You're not eating at this hour, are you?" She shuddered.

Frankie jumped from the table and put his arm around his wife. "You didn't have to get up, sweetheart."

"I heard voices. I was afraid something else had happened."

"Our Jamie is safe as a bug in a rug," Frankie said, pulling out her chair. "Look, honey, Phillip is here."

Deedee smiled wearily. "I guess you heard, huh?"

Phillip nodded. "First thing this morning."

Beenie hurried into the kitchen with Choo-Choo. When he came out he was carrying a cup of Deedee's favorite Frappuccino. "I'm taking Choo-Choo out for his morning potty."

"It's been a while since we've seen you, Phillip," Deedee said. "You and Jamie never come to dinner anymore."

"I would come more often, but Jamie is always busy with the newspaper. One of the drawbacks of being engaged to a workaholic," he added with a smile. He reached across the table and squeezed Jamie's hand. "Try scheduling a honeymoon around her work schedule."

"You should talk," Jamie said.

"I hope the two of you slow down once you're married," Frankie said. "Take a little time to stop and smell the roses."

Phillip chuckled. "I'm going to insist Jamie quit work immediately so she can join the garden club and attend teas and luncheons with my mother." He looked at Jamie. "Naturally you'll want to get involved with her charity work."

"Yeah, right, Phillip," Jamie muttered, even though she knew he was teasing. "How about I invite the garden club over to my place and see how good I am at growing weeds?"

She happened to glance in Max's direction. He gave her a private smile. She suspected he knew she would never be satisfied sitting home playing hostess or heading up garden committees.

"Jamie is very driven," Deedee said. "I respect that about her."

"I'm very proud of her," Phillip said, "but I'd like to see her have more fun in life. I plan to spoil her."

Once again, Jamie felt Max's eyes on her. "That's just it, Phillip. I love having my own newspaper."

He patted her hand. "I know." He checked his wristwatch. "Uh-oh, I have a client in half an hour. Are you sure you're okay?" he asked Jamie.

"I'm perfectly fine. Now go to work and stop worrying about me."

"Are you planning to go into the office today?" he asked.

"I probably need to talk to Lamar first."

"Just call me on my cell phone." Phillip kissed her lightly. "Frankie, Deedee, thanks for coffee. Max, it was a pleasure meeting you. Call me and we can have a drink at my club."

Max nodded.

Frankie walked Phillip out. When he returned he held the newspaper. "Neither rain nor hail nor a drive-by shooting prevents our newspaper from getting out."

Jamie accepted another cup of coffee as Frankie perused the paper. She dreaded calling Vera, knowing the woman would somehow blame her for the shooting incident.

"Are there any sales, sweetie?" Deedee said.

Frankie looked. "Aw, Bates's Furniture is having a liquidation sale. Everything in the store is half price. I don't know if they have French provincial furniture, though."

Jamie looked up from her coffee cup. "What did you say?"

"And Beaumont Paints is having a going-out-of-business sale," Frankie added. "I didn't know they were going out of business. This might be a good time to repaint the house, Deedee." He winked at Max.

"Let me see that," Jamie said, reaching for the newspaper. The two ads together took up a full page. "Oh, no!"

"What is it?" Max said.

"I never saw these advertisements."

He got up, rounded the table and glanced over her shoulder. "Those are the two ads I told you I put in at the last minute. Vera handed them to me on her way out."

The color drained from Jamie's face. "Double damn!"

"What's wrong, honey?" Deedee asked.

"I can't believe she did this to me," Jamie said. "I'm going to kill her. I'll kill her with her own gun, that's what I'll do. That way it'll look like suicide."

"Do I sense a problem?" Max asked.

Jamie briefly filled them in.

Max stared at her in disbelief. "You had the place painted and furnished for my visit? Why?"

"I didn't want you to see how bad it looked."

"You mean it looked worse before it was redecorated?"

She shot him a death look but went on to explain. "Vera asked Tom and Herman, well, actually, she threatened them, to give the place a little face-lift, and that's how they responded."

"Oh, Jamie," Deedee cooed, patting her hand. "I would have decorated it for you."

Jamie could only imagine the results had Deedee been in charge, and she immediately felt ashamed. "Tom and Herman are going to sue my pants off. I need to call my lawyer."

"Let me see if I can talk to these guys first," Max said.

Beenie rushed through the swinging door with Choo-Choo. "Here's your mama," he told the small dog, placing him in Deedee's outstretched arms.

"Did he go?" she asked.

"Oh, yes! Choo-Choo is a very good boy. I gave him his treat, brushed his teeth and coat, and then I sprayed him with doggie deodorant."

"Mama is very proud of her little boy," Deedee exclaimed, kissing the pooch on his nose.

She suddenly yawned. "I'm going back to bed. I can't handle a crisis this early in the morning. Besides, I feel bags growing beneath my eyes."

"I'll get you an eye mask from the freezer," Beenie said, hurrying through the swinging door once more.

Deedee turned to Jamie with a look of determination on her face. "Honey, I insist you stay with us for a while. At least until we find the guy who shot out your window last night."

"I'll be fine," Jamie said.

Deedee looked at her husband. "Frankie, make her stay."

"You have to stay," Frankie said. "Deedee will worry."

"We can run by your place later so you can pick up some clothes," Max offered. "I'm going into town anyway."

Jamie debated whether or not to remain in the Fontana household. She had been scared the night before, but the sun shining through the dining room window made her feel as though everything were going to be okay. Besides, she liked being in her own place. "I'm not afraid of being alone," she said.

Deedee leaned closer. "You know Phillip will have a hissy fit if you stay at your place," she said in a conspiratorial manner. "He and Annabelle will march right up to your doorstep and drag you home with them. You won't be able to wear jeans because you won't blend. You'll have to wear dresses."

"Eeyeuuw!" Jamie said.

"Yeah, I figured that would settle it. Besides, you've got a baseball bat under your bed, and I've got a rolling pin on my night table. Ain't nobody going to mess with us, sister."

Jamie looked at Max. The smile on his face told her he was glad she was staying. She was definitely going to have to put Max Holt in his place.

Chapter
FIVE

Jamie tried not to worry about a possible lawsuit as she dialed the city police. She was put through to Lamar, who told her it would be okay to go back into the building.

"My deputies are over there now looking around in case we missed anything last night. They'll keep an eye on the place for a few days. Also, I'm going to have to question your employees, if that's okay."

"That's fine." Jamie hung up and dialed Vera, who answered on the first ring.

"You must've really made someone mad this time," Vera said, before Jamie spoke. "What in the world did you do?"

"Vera Bankhead, don't you *dare* start on me. Have you lost your mind? You've opened me up for a lawsuit from Tom and Herman."

"Oh, that," Vera said, as though it were no big deal. "Tom and Herman wouldn't dare sue us."

She didn't sound very confident.

"You're going to print a retraction, and an apology. But first, you're going over to Tom's and Herman's stores and apologizing to them personally."

"And if I refuse?"

Jamie paused abruptly. She loved Vera like a mother, but the woman had crossed the line and left the newspaper vulnerable to legal problems. Still, she couldn't fire her. She took a deep breath. "You won't get the raise I was planning to give you with your new job title."

"You never said anything about a raise *or* a promotion."

"I wanted to surprise you."

The woman on the other end was quiet for a moment. "What's my new title?"

Jamie sighed. "Assistant editor. I want you to work more closely with Mike and me. Mostly Mike."

Vera seemed to ponder it. "I'll think about it."

"And I might put you in charge of selling advertisements if that part-time guy doesn't start doing a better job."

"How much of a raise are we talking about?"

"I'll let you know as soon as I look at our budget. But first you need to tell Tom and Herman you're sorry."

Vera grumbled under her breath. "I'll work on it."

Jamie came downstairs wearing a pair of Deedee's jeans that were a bit on the snug side, and a cotton pullover that molded nicely to her breasts.

Max smiled at the sight. "You ready to go?"

Jamie nodded and followed him out to his car. "I spoke with Lamar," she said, once they were on their way. "He's going to have deputies watching the place."

Max nodded. "Muffin, rise and shine. We've got work to do."

"And a hearty good morning to you, Max," Muffin replied. "I'm fine, how are you?"

Jamie couldn't hide her amazement. "She's being sarcastic."

"Good morning, Miss Swift," Muffin said. "I hope you rested well considering all the turmoil last night. Is your leg better?"

Jamie stared, dumbfounded. "I'm, uh, fine, thank you." She covered her face. "I'm talking to a computer."

"At least she's being nice to you," Max said. "Okay, Muffin, now that we've exchanged pleasantries, would you mind looking up the number to Bates's Furniture? I want to talk to Herman Bates."

"Yeah, yeah, yeah."

"What are you doing?" Jamie asked Max.

"I'm trying to kill two birds with one stone. We need new furniture, and we need to suck up to Herman Bates and the other fellow."

"Tom Brown."

"Right."

"I can't afford to redecorate."

"But I can. Besides, I need the tax write-off."

Jamie shook her head. "You know, between you and Vera I don't stand a chance."

"I've got Herman Bates on hold, Max," Muffin said. "The Bates brothers seem to have this town tied up. There's a Bates's Computer and Office Supply store, a Bates's Furniture, and a Bates's Builder's Supply."

"Muffin is right," Jamie said. "The Bates family owns half the town. They've got the power and the resources to wipe me from the face of the earth."

"Now we have to find out how greedy they are. Muffin, put Mr. Bates through."

A gruff voice answered.

"Good morning, Mr. Bates," Max said. "I appreciate your holding."

"Is this Maximillian Holt?" he asked. "The guy who makes all those big business deals that I read about in *Fortune*?"

"Yep, that's me."

"Man oh man. What can I do for you?"

"Well, Herman, I'd like to do some business with you and your family while I'm in town."

"You're talking to the right guy."

"I'm completely renovating a business. A large building with offices. I'll need the name of a good contractor and interior decorator to begin with. The place needs carpentry work, painting inside and out, actually a number of things before we put in new rugs and furniture. Oh, and I'll need new computers. Top-of-the-line stuff, mind you. I may need some specialized office equipment, as well."

"Between my brothers and me, we can handle all your needs," the man said proudly. "Which building are we talking about?"

"The *Beaumont Gazette*." Max waited.

"The *Gazette*, huh? I'm afraid I don't do business with those folks anymore. They're a bunch of crazies. In fact, I've got an appointment to see my lawyer this morning concerning a little problem I'm having with them."

Jamie winced. She would be forced to close down the newspaper.

"Gee, that's too bad, Herman. I was counting on your help. Perhaps you could give me the name of someone else who could assist me."

Herman was silent for a moment. "Tell you what. I don't know how you're connected to the newspaper, but you sound nice enough. Why don't you meet me at the store before I open today? I'm going to have a lot of pissed-off customers coming in so I won't be able to talk to you once I open up."

"Yeah, I know about the advertisement," Max said. "I'm afraid it was a practical joke, but I can assure you Miss Swift had nothing to do with it."

"That's no excuse," Herman said. "She's responsible for what's printed in her newspaper." He paused and his voice was softer when he spoke. "'Course I heard what happened over there last night. Sorry to hear it."

"Thanks, Herman. I've got an idea how you can avoid a crowd of angry customers."

"I'm listening."

"Put a wreath on your door."

"Come again?"

"No sin in closing if someone in the family has passed away," Max said, earning a dark look from Jamie.

Herman chuckled. "Now, that's a new one."

"Surely you have some long-lost aunt or uncle you could mourn."

"We're going to take a loss."

"You'll more than make it up with my business. Trust me."

"It's eight-thirty now. Why don't you come on over, and we can talk."

"Give me twenty minutes."

Muffin disconnected the call. "Well, that proves two of my theories," she said. "Everybody has a price."

"What's the other one?"

"You have no soul. Put a wreath on the door. That really stinks, Max."

Jamie nodded. "She's right."

"Okay, so I can be unscrupulous at times, but this way we avoid a lawsuit, get the newspaper building fixed up and new equipment installed. It's a win-win situation. Oh, and, Muffin. I want a couple of security guards stationed inside the *Gazette* building pronto. Unless Frankie has already hired everyone in town," he added. "By the way, how are you coming along with that job I gave you? Almost finished?"

Muffin sighed. "I'm working on it, Max, but it's going to take me a little while. This is no small task, and I've got technicians feeding me information twenty-four/seven. It's 'Muffin, do this; Muffin, do that.' I can't be expected to do everything. I need an assistant. Preferably a male one, with an English accent."

Jamie glanced from Max to Muffin and back to Max. "What did you ask her to do?"

"She's checking bank accounts and portfolios, both here and overseas, on half the people in this town."

"And I'm supposed to have the information lickety-split," Muffin said. "I'm good, in fact, I'm damn good, but what he's asking is impossible."

"Whose accounts are you looking into?" Jamie asked.

"Mostly city officials," Max said. "You can't misappropriate tax dollars without involving people in high places."

"Are you going to share the information with me when you get it?"

"I don't know if you can be trusted."

"You can just go jump in a lake, Holt." She noted the amused look on his face, but Jamie didn't think it was a bit funny. "You are *really* beginning to annoy me."

"Welcome to *my* world," Muffin said. "I have to deal with him on a daily basis."

"Now, Muffin," Max said. "You're going to make Jamie think badly of me, and I'll never win her over, despite her strong attraction to me."

Muffin snorted.

Jamie simply looked at him. "Has anybody ever told you that you have an ego the size of planet Earth? Darned if I've ever seen anything like it."

"Think about it, Jamie. You and me, white sand, crystal-blue water, and—"

"When pigs fly."

Max laughed out loud. "I like a woman who plays hard to get. More of a challenge."

Jamie shook her head in disbelief and looked out the side window.

"So, what do you think?" he asked. "Think maybe we could be more than friends?"

"You're being presumptuous," she replied. "I never agreed to be your friend. Besides, isn't it enough that you can have any woman you want? Do you have to have *every* woman you want?"

"You're not every woman, Jamie. Far from it."

"You don't know me."

"I know enough. I know you're a tough, no-nonsense woman who gets the job done no matter what."

"I'm flattered, Max, but I'm not interested. I believe in love and monogamy, words that haven't found their way into your vocabulary."

"You've got me pegged all wrong."

"I read *People* magazine."

"You can't believe everything you read, darlin'. I'll admit I've had a few affairs, but I'm really a nice guy."

"This is a pointless conversation, Max. I'm engaged."

"I just can't imagine you married to someone like Phillip Standish."

"What's wrong with Phillip?"

"He lives with his mother, for one thing."

"He lives on the family estate which he will inherit one day."

"He seems too—" Max paused. "Predictable."

"I like predictability."

"You're a risk-taker like me. You mortgaged your family home to the hilt in order to save your newspaper from foreclosure. That takes guts."

She looked at him. "How do you know about that?"

"Are you surprised I would take the time to look into your financial dealings before investing in your company?"

"What else do you know?"

"I know you attended one of the best journalism schools in the country and graduated in the top five percent of your class. I also know you were offered a job with the *Atlanta Journal–Constitution,* but you chose to come back to Beaumont."

"I belong here. It's my home. It took me a while to realize it, but it's true."

He turned into the parking lot of the *Beaumont Gazette* and pulled into an empty slot.

Jamie went on. "I can certainly understand your checking the solvency of my company. I would have done the same thing. But I draw the line at delving into my personal life."

"I would never do that," Max replied.

"Thank you."

"Max, may I have a word with you?" Muffin asked.

"Later," he said.

Jamie climbed from the car and closed the door behind her. She passed a patrol car. Inside, the deputy leaned against his seat, his cap over his face. Jamie banged on the window, and the man jumped and reached for his gun.

"Jesus Christ, Jamie, you trying to get yourself shot?"

"Wake up, Fred. You're supposed to be guarding this place. If you're going to sleep you may as well be sitting in the booth at Coot Hathaway's doughnut shop."

"Give me a break," he said. "I've been out here all night."

"Yeah, well, I didn't get much sleep, either."

Max followed Jamie inside the building. Several employees had already arrived and were taking note of the damage. Vera was busy with the phones and handed Jamie a stack of messages. She put her hand over the mouthpiece. "Dang thing hasn't stopped ringing all morning. I've tried to play down the shooting. I'm telling everybody it was an escaped convict who was trying to break into the place for food."

Jamie slumped. "Great idea, Vera. Next time I get a craving for a burger and fries I'll know right where to come."

"Don't get fresh with me, young lady. I had to think of something fast. Lamar will like the escaped-convict story. Makes him sound more important."

Jamie looked at her messages. She wished she had a Valium. "How are the others taking it?"

"They're confused."

"So am I." Nevertheless, Jamie knew they needed her reassurance.

Max pulled her aside. "Look, I know things seem hopeless right now, but we can get through this."

"We?"

"I'm not going to just walk away when I can help."

"I'm perfectly capable of handling my own problems."

"Which is why I'm on my way to suck up to Herman Bates," he said. "Well, got to go." He winked at her and headed for the door.

"What was that all about?" Vera asked as soon as Max left.

"Max Holt thinks he's hot stuff."

"He *is* hot stuff."

"Well, he can be hot stuff someplace else because I've got work to do. I need to talk to the staff. Would you ask them to meet me in the conference room in ten minutes?" She went into her office. Shards of glass still covered the floor, but Lamar had seen to boarding up her window as he'd promised.

Mike sailed through the front and into Jamie's office. He skidded to a stop. "What happened in here?"

Jamie searched for the notepad she kept on hand. "I'm holding a meeting in the conference room in a few minutes. I'll explain everything then."

Jamie walked into the conference room and found her employees waiting. She quickly filled the group in on the previous evening's events. "I don't know why this person or persons targeted the newspaper office, but it happened. Chief Tevis has assigned several deputies to watch the place."

"Do you think we're in danger?" Jamie's accountant asked.

"I don't know, Helen, but everyone has a choice as to whether they want to stay or take a leave of absence until we get to the bottom of this."

"Is Mr. Holt in on the investigation?"

"Mr. Holt is my partner. I would assume most of you have heard of Maximillian Holt." They looked impressed. "As you know, he's quite successful in his business dealings, and we're lucky to have his financial backing, as well as his expertise. He's had a great deal of newspaper experience so I hope you'll cooperate with him." She paused so everyone could take it in. She was thankful Max wasn't around to hear her brag about him.

"He's also going to update some of our equipment, including our computers. Much of what we have is obsolete."

"You can say that again," Vera replied, earning a dark look from Jamie.

"Mr. Holt has also generously offered to renovate this building and have the office painted and refurnished. With tasteful pieces," she added.

The small crowd clapped.

"That's not funny," Jamie said, although she broke into a smile. "Now, if you have any questions, please feel free to ask."

Mike raised his hand. "Jamie, do you think the shooting had anything to do with the mayoral campaign? I understand Frankie Fontana has received threatening letters."

"I don't know, Mike. Chief Tevis is looking into it. Like I said, if anyone feels uncomfortable working here after what happened, you're free to take leave until the investigation is over. I also want you to know that the paper will be reporting on the matter and we'll be continuing our own investigation."

"I'm not going anywhere," Vera said.

"Me, neither," Mike replied.

Helen hesitated. "Count me in."

Jamie was not surprised when the entire group agreed to see it through. They had remained loyal, even when it looked as if the newspaper wouldn't survive. "I want all of you to exercise caution." Jamie paused when she heard the bell over the door in the reception area ring several times, indicating a visitor. Vera bolted from her seat, reached inside the back of her slacks and pulled out a gun. Everyone in the room ducked.

"Vera!" Jamie cried. "Put that gun away this instant!"

Vera grunted but did as she was told.

Jamie spied two security guards waiting in the reception area and her knees suddenly took on the consistency of banana pudding. She hated to think what would have happened had Vera rushed out of the room waving her pistol.

When Max arrived at Bates's Furniture shortly before ten, he found a wreath of flowers on the door. Herman, Tom, and Herman's brother George met him at the door, all wearing black and looking somber.

"Sorry for your loss," Max said.

"Yeah, well, Daisy was a good barn cat," Herman replied. "Lived to be fourteen years old."

"When did she die?" Max asked.

"Last Christmas. We're just now getting around to mourning her."

"God rest her soul," George said respectfully.

Tom Brown nodded. "I didn't know Daisy personally, but I'm a friend of the family so I closed my paint store in order to be with Herman and George in this most trying time."

"Let's go into my office," Herman said. He waited until everyone was seated before he spoke. "You'd better make this worth our while, Holt," he said, leaning back in his chair, hands propped behind his head. "Jamie had no right to run that advertisement."

"I don't think she was real happy with the decorating job you guys did."

"That's what she gets for letting Vera threaten us," Tom said. "Hell, we would have done Jamie right had she come to us personally. I used to have a thing for Jamie Swift way back in high school." He glanced at the other men. "Don't, uh, mention this to the wife. You know how jealous Lorraine is."

"I say we let bygones be bygones," Max said. "Now, let's get down to business."

"Dude, would you get a load of that shit? He didn't even get a bruise."

Vito muttered a string of expletives under his breath as he spotted Max going into Bates's Furniture. "The boss ain't gonna like it."

"So, we don't call him, man. We wait till the job is done, then call."

"Lenny, you stupid shit. You don't know the kind of person we're dealing with. We screw up this job, and the two of us are going to end up in body bags."

"You should have told me, dude. I mean, what do we know about offing someone anyway? I ain't never killed nobody, have you? I never even run over a raccoon."

"There's good money to be made in this line of work," Vito said. "If you don't have the stomach for it you need to get out now."

Lenny looked thoughtful. "I don't want to run out on you, man."

"Okay, so stop complaining. What we have to do now is figure out a way to get close to Holt without a bunch of people around. We need to know his whereabouts at all times. If he's staying at his brother-in-law's place, we've gotta figure a way to get past all those security guards. We can't get close to the newspaper, there are cops crawling around like cockroaches."

"Yeah, dude, we need a plan."

"Let's walk," Vito said. "We can't be seen hanging around, even in these disguises. I need to think."

Lenny nodded. "Yeah, we gotta stay one step ahead of him."

Vito stopped and looked at him. "You know, you're right. Damn, Lenny, just when I think you've fried your brain huffing Sterno, you come up and say something smart."

"Yeah?"

"So, where do you figure Max will go next?"

"Well, let me think." Lenny looked up suddenly. "There's only a few places I can think of, and we can't get close to two of them, meaning the newspaper and Fontana's place."

"Where else?"

"You've seen Jamie Swift. Where would *you* go?"

"Straight to the nearest motel," Vito replied. He suddenly brightened. "But why rent a motel when she's got her own place?"

They gave each other a high five.

Max followed Jamie home at the end of the day. She parked her Mustang convertible in the garage as Max parked his car in the driveway. He followed her toward the front door of a sprawling frame house that sat on a lawn in dire need of cutting.

"I don't have time for yard work," Jamie said, "in case you didn't notice. The only saving grace is the fact the grass next door is twice as high."

Max glanced at the house beside hers where a For

Sale sign sat near the mailbox. "Looks like your neighbors are moving."

"They're already gone. Which explains why the yard hasn't been cut."

Max followed her inside the house. "I like your place. It looks comfortable."

Jamie glanced about the living room. Her dark beige sofa and matching chair were old, but they had been well cared for, as had the antique library table and desk her grandmother had left her. Jamie had not been able to part with them when she'd sold off other items in order to put money into the newspaper. Two Andrew Wyeth prints adorned one wall. It was simple and uncluttered, the way she preferred it, but she couldn't think why a man with Max's wealth would appreciate it. "I'll bet your place is a lot nicer."

"Right now it's a mess from all the renovations I'm doing."

"Why would you do it yourself when you can afford to pay someone?"

He shrugged. "Why not? I enjoy it." He glanced around once more. "So you grew up in this house?"

"Yes. Come with me, I want to show you something."

He followed Jamie out the back door. "Nice yard."

She smiled. "The flower beds need weeding, but I don't have time for that, either." She pointed. "See that tire swing? My daddy put that up when I was a little girl. It's lasted all these years."

"The two of you were very close?"

"Yeah." She felt Max's eyes on her. "My mother left while I was still in diapers. I don't think my dad ever got over it."

"How about you? Did you ever get over it?"

She gave him a strange look. "I had no choice."

"You haven't seen her since?"

"No. This probably sounds cold, but I don't think I'd want to. Would you like a cup of coffee?" she asked, changing the subject.

"Sure." Max followed her back inside.

"This is my favorite room," Jamie said. "I have fond memories of my dad and me playing cards at this table. He was a big gin rummy fan. We had some marathon games." She smiled at the memory. "I usually won, but I think he let me." She motioned toward a chair. "Have a seat."

Max sat down at a round oak table while she made the coffee. "Will Phillip be angry that you've chosen not to stay at his place?" he asked.

"He's pretty laid-back. I'm the one with the temper." She smiled. "You might say he has his hands full with me."

Max watched her pull out cups and saucers. Neither of them said anything for a moment. "What's his mother like?"

Jamie heard the sound of a lawn mower and wished it were her yard being cut. "Annabelle can be a little flighty at times. Sort of like Deedee. But she has done a lot for this town." Jamie reached into the refrigerator for the cream, grabbed the sugar dish and set them on the table. "Annabelle is responsible for organizing the building of our women's shelter, the Help Center, and now she's fighting to build a nursing home."

"Busy woman."

"I can't help but respect all she's done for this town, even if she tends to get on my nerves now and then with her constant chatter." Jamie joined him at the table and filled the cups with fresh coffee. Max asked her about growing up in Beaumont, and she told him what it had been like.

"We had our usual hangouts in high school," she said. "The bowling alley was the place to be because we all played pinball and air hockey and soft drinks were cheap. That was before they built the arcade, of course. And there was the drive-in." She chuckled. "I can't tell you how many monster movies I've seen or how many boys tried to get me into the backseat of their cars."

"Smart guys."

She ignored him. "It has been closed for years now. Oh, and I used to roller-skate."

"I'll bet you were good at it."

Jamie was surprised what a good listener Max was. Perhaps that's why he was so successful. When you talked to Max Holt he gave his undivided attention. "It was a puny little town then," she added, "compared to the booming metropolis it is now."

Max smiled. "There's something to be said for small towns."

Jamie was quiet for a moment. "I've been afraid to ask, but I was wondering how it went with Tom and Herman."

"They're happier than a pig in mud right now because I gave them a lot of business. Of course, they're still mourning the death of Daisy the cat."

Jamie rolled her eyes heavenward. "I think I'm better off not asking about poor Daisy, but at least Tom and Herman aren't going to sue me. What a relief!"

"Hey, I'm good."

"Oh, brother."

"Admit it."

Jamie knew if she agreed it would only serve to

raise his already mammoth ego another notch. "You do okay."

"It's nice to hear that you're developing respect for me. I think that's important in a relationship."

Jamie's look was deadpan. "Let me remind you, Holt, we don't have a relationship, except for maybe the one that exists in your own mind."

"You're a hard woman, Swifty."

"Meaning I'm not putty in your hands. And don't call me Swifty."

"I'm pretty good with my hands."

"All men think they're good, Max. It's a woman's job to convince them of it even when they really aren't."

"Are you speaking from experience?"

Jamie's face flushed a bright red. "I was just making idle chitchat."

"Yeah, whatever, but some of us really are good."

Jamie had to laugh. "You're hopeless."

"Yeah, but what can I do?"

She saw that he was joking, and she couldn't help but enjoy the camaraderie. Life had been far too serious lately. She became thoughtful. "You're really not a bad guy even if you can be intolerable at times."

"There it is, I knew I could win you over. Won't be long before I have you eating out of my hand."

She muttered a sound of disgust. "See how you are?"

He looked amused. "Work with me, Jamie. Humility doesn't come easy for me."

She was quiet for a moment. "You know, I'm not the shrew you think I am. It's not always easy for me to warm up to new people, and I sometimes have trouble getting close."

"Tell me something I don't already know."

Jamie hitched her chin high. "You see how you are, Holt? I tell you something personal about me, and you have to be a smart aleck about it. Just when I start thinking you're a decent guy."

"I am a decent guy."

"And I was close to saying something really nice about you."

"Oh, yeah? Like what?"

"I'm not going to tell you now, for Pete's sake."

"Come on, Jamie. Say something nice. I won't hold you to it."

"You can be so exasperating."

He frowned. "That's supposed to be nice?"

"I was trying to tell you that I've noticed how easy it is for you to warm up to people. You seem to fit in wherever you go. You always seem to do and say the right thing."

"I don't see you as someone who has problems fitting in, and you don't seem to have trouble getting close to people. You and Deedee act like sisters."

"That's a no-brainer. How can you *not* love Deedee? She's so unpredictable."

"I thought you like predictability."

"Okay, so Deedee is unpredictable in a predictable way." Jamie went on. "What I like most about her is, despite her money and flamboyance, she's really honest and down-to-earth. At least with me," Jamie added. "She doesn't put on airs. What you see is what you get."

"Sort of like you," he said, his tone softer. He'd barely gotten the words out of his mouth before an ear-splitting alarm went off.

Jamie jumped. "What was *that*?"

"My car!" Max bolted from his chair and raced out the front door, almost slamming into a bearded, heavyset man in work clothes.

"What's going on?" Max demanded.

"Your car alarm just went off, but I guess you already know that."

"Did you see anyone go near it?"

The man wiped his forehead with a dirty bandana. "Me and my partner were round back when we heard it."

Max was only vaguely aware of a tall skinny man in the background as he raced toward his car. He jerked open the door.

Muffin spoke immediately. "Max?"

"What happened?"

"Get away from the car. Somebody has tampered with it."

He ignored her and began checking beneath the seats. Nothing. He popped the trunk. "Dammit!" he shouted.

"What's wrong?" Jamie asked, peering over his shoulder. What she saw made her freeze. "Holy cow, is that what I think it is?"

"It's dynamite," Max said. "Get away from the car. It's timed to go off in forty seconds."

Chapter
SIX

"Oh, damn!" Jamie cried. "Double damn!" She almost tripped over her own two feet as she backed farther away, ticking off the seconds in her head. "Get away, Max!" she cried. "Please!"

"Clear the area, Max," Muffin repeated loudly. "I'm phoning the bomb squad."

"No time!" he yelled. Max grabbed the small tool-box he kept in the trunk and flipped open the lid. He reached for a pair of wire cutters, and studied the wires leading from the clock to the sticks of dynamite. Twenty-five seconds.

A giant fist seemed to grab Jamie's stomach and squeeze so tightly she feared she'd be sick. "Max, for God's sake, please move away from the car." She suddenly realized she was crying.

Max leaned in for a closer look. "I can do this, Jamie."

"Okay, Max," Muffin said. "Forget the bomb squad, I'm calling the county coroner. Not that I expect him to find much."

Ten seconds. Max very gently pulled the wires away

from one another, put the wire cutters to one of them and snipped. He grinned and punched the air with his fist. "Like taking candy from a baby. And only two seconds left." He glanced in Jamie's direction. "Am I good or what?"

Very calmly, and without taking her eyes off him, Jamie marched toward him, eyes menacing, fists balled at her sides. "I ought to punch you right in the face for that," she said.

"Go ahead," Muffin said. "I'll cheer you on."

Max looked surprised. "What'd I do?"

"You stupid idiot!" she shouted. "You imbecile!"

Max cocked his head to one side. "I'm going out on a limb here, but something tells me you're not happy."

Jamie feared her knees would fold beneath her. "I wish I were a man. A *big* man," she added, "because I would kick your butt from here to the moon. Are you crazy?" she yelled at the top of her voice.

"Crazy as hell," Muffin said. "Welcome to Max's world."

"Jamie, now calm down."

"Don't talk to me! Don't even speak my name."

"But, Jamie—"

"Who do you think you are, Holt? Superman? Or do you have some kind of death wish?"

"I know about bombs, Jamie. I've trained with the best. I wouldn't have taken the chance if I hadn't known what I was doing."

"You love this sort of thing, Max. Probably it gives you some kind of sick thrill. Well, guess what? I don't want to be a part of it. I don't want to be the one who has to scrape you off the pavement when your luck runs out."

Country music blared from the car. Max winced. "Now look what you've done. You've upset Muffin." He walked over to the car. "Shut it off, Muffin," he ordered.

"To hell with you," Muffin replied. "You deliberately ignored my warning."

Max sighed as the music turned to disco. "Where do you find that stuff?"

"I am trained to protect you, Max. I am fed information around the clock by some of the brightest people in the world. What good is it if you refuse to cooperate? I'm telling you, this job sucks."

Max reached in and turned off the radio. He stood there for a moment, his mind searching for answers. "It's over," he said. "Everything is okay." Max very carefully picked up the dynamite. He carried it to the side of the house, found Jamie's metal garbage can and placed it inside. He then reached for the garden hose, turned on the spigot and filled the can with water.

Having followed him, Jamie watched, hands on hips. "Trying to blow up my garbage can now?"

"I've disabled the bomb. I'm simply taking extra precautions." He stepped back. "That should do it. We won't get any action out of this sucker now."

A few minutes later, Max rounded the house with Jamie on his heels. He suddenly looked up. "What happened to the guys cutting the grass next door?"

"How should I know? I was counting off the seconds until I'd have to watch you blown to smithereens."

"That's strange," he said, noting the lawn mower sitting in the middle of the yard.

Jamie was still fighting her anger. "Maybe they're taking a lunch break. Or maybe they heard the word 'dynamite' and decided to get the heck out of here. Sane people run from that sort of thing, Holt."

Max gazed thoughtfully at the still overgrown grass. "Did you happen to see if they were in a vehicle?"

Jamie wondered why he was so interested in the yardmen. Probably trying to get her mind off the fact he needed a padded cell. "No, why?" It suddenly hit her. "Do you think they put the dynamite in the trunk of your car?"

"That's what I'm thinking. They certainly had the opportunity, and it's odd they left so quickly. Wonder if your neighbors saw anything."

Jamie glanced around. "Doesn't look like anyone has gotten home from work yet. The only person who would have been around to see anything is Mrs. Chadwick, but she's old and senile and spends most of her time in bed watching TV. I think it would scare her if we started asking questions, and we wouldn't get any information anyway."

Max nodded. "Why don't you go ahead and pack a bag?"

Jamie swallowed, and it felt like a chicken egg going down her throat. She wasn't used to guns and bombs and crazy men. She turned for the front door, and then paused. "The only reason I'm being civil right now is because we've got a dangerous situation on our hands. I want you to know I'm still mad and never want to speak to you again as long as I live."

As Jamie packed her bag, she wondered if life would ever return to normal. Max Holt had literally roared into her life and turned everything upside down and inside out, and he seemed determined to keep it up.

She needed to hurry up and marry Phillip, she

thought. Phillip was safe and normal. Max Holt was anything but. He was dangerous. Probably more dangerous than the person who was after them.

Jamie and Max arrived at the Fontana house with plenty of time to spare before dinner. Jamie soaked in a hot tub with lavender bath salts Deedee provided, dried with a thick towel, and coated her body with a special lotion that Deedee swore no woman should be without. Instead of reaching for one of her nightshirts, Jamie grabbed a satin guest robe. Deedee believed in pampering everyone.

Finally, she settled into an overstuffed club chair and leafed through several magazines with beauty tips, none of which she'd ever tried. Heck, she didn't even pluck her eyebrows, and she wore minimal makeup. There simply wasn't time to go through a lot of fuss getting ready for work. The last time she'd used a curling iron had been at her father's funeral, and she would be hard-pressed to find it now. Her hair, like most of her clothes, was wash-and-wear, and that was good enough for her.

Jamie dozed, only to wake an hour later and discover cocktail hour was only twenty minutes away. She dressed in record time, stepping into the only linen slacks she owned, and a cotton blouse, knowing she would curse herself later when it came time to iron them again. She arrived downstairs and found Deedee looking like she'd stepped out of the pages of *Vogue* in a Kelly-green silk evening dress that hugged every curve she owned.

"I didn't know we were supposed to dress for dinner," Jamie said, wondering how her friend managed to look like a million bucks all the time. Deedee obviously had good genes, which meant Max probably had them as well.

"Oh, you're fine," Deedee said. "It's just something Frankie and I do to sort of keep the romance alive in our relationship."

Frankie and his campaign manager stepped out of the library and made for the front door. Frankie returned a moment later wearing a black tux that, while it added an air of sophistication, looked out of place on his massive body. He bowed respectfully toward the women. "I'm one lucky man," he said, "to be dining with the loveliest women in town."

"I was wondering if you fellows were going to talk shop all night," Deedee said. "Once this election is over, I'm going to expect preferential treatment."

Frankie walked up to his wife, pulled her from the sofa and kissed her hard on the lips. "How's that, baby-cakes?" He winked at Jamie. "Have to keep the little woman happy or she'll make me take her to the jewelry store. You don't want to go into a jewelry store with Deedee."

"It's an investment, Frankie," she said. "Diamonds never lose their value."

"So you've told me," he said, goosing her.

"We have guests, darling, or have you forgotten." But her green eyes sparkled in delight at the attention. "By the way, where is Max?"

As if on cue, Max called out from the stairs. "I'm on my way down."

"We were waiting for you to grace us with your presence, brother dear."

"The wait is over." He dropped a kiss on her forehead.

Frankie turned to Jamie. "Did Deedee tell you Phillip was having dinner with us?"

"I haven't had a chance to mention it," Deedee said.

She looked at Jamie. "Phillip called while you were in the tub to see if you'd made it home yet. I asked him to join us."

Jamie was touched they'd included her fiancé, but she hoped Phillip wouldn't spend the evening asking questions for which she had no answers. She felt Max's gaze on her but avoided eye contact. "That was nice of you. Thanks."

"He said to go ahead with cocktails because he had a late appointment. Sounds like you're marrying a workaholic. Not that you aren't a bit of one yourself," Deedee added. "You and I should take a week and go to that nice spa in Atlanta. It would do us a world of good, and we could shop at some of the finest stores."

Jamie smiled, but she wasn't a spa kind of person, even if she could afford it, which she couldn't. She often wondered why Deedee had agreed to move to Beaumont in the first place, even though she had to admit it was a charming, quaint little town where folks knew one another by name and were quick to smile. She knew Frankie and Deedee had lived in Scottsdale, Arizona, for a number of years before moving here, and although Deedee had liked Scottsdale, Frankie had felt the desert wasn't his thing.

They'd accidentally found Beaumont while Frankie was touring for a charitable organization, and their private plane had experienced engine problems. The two had been forced to stay in a local bed-and-breakfast for several days while awaiting a special part, and Frankie had fallen in love with the area.

"Frankie, be a sweetie and pour our guests a glass of wine," Deedee said.

"Gladly."

Beenie appeared at the foot of the stairs carrying

Deedee's dog. He was impeccably dressed as usual. "Choo-Choo needs to say night-night to his mama," he said. "I gave him a couple of tablespoons of yogurt so he would sleep through the night."

Deedee took the furry white dog from Beenie and nuzzled him close. "He smells like baby powder."

"I sprinkled a little of it on him before I brushed him. He's ready to be tucked in. Give Mama a kiss-kiss," Beenie told the animal. "She has dinner guests."

Deedee kissed her pooch on the nose, and Beenie carried him upstairs.

The chef sent hors d'oeuvres from the kitchen, Frankie's favorite, pickled eggs and Vienna sausage, and a wedge of Brie surrounded by apricots and gourmet crackers.

Frankie finished pouring the wine and was about to hand Jamie a glass when the window behind them shattered.

Deedee screamed. Jamie automatically ducked but not before she caught sight of what appeared to be some kind of fireball. It hit the floor, shattering the bottle in which a burning rag had been stuffed. Liquid spewed from the bottle, and the fire flared high and followed what smelled like kerosene across the rug and up the draperies.

Max wasted no time. "Get down!" he ordered Deedee, shoving her so hard she toppled from the sofa. "Frankie, grab a fire extinguisher. Jamie, dial nine-one-one."

Jamie automatically reached for the telephone and dialed. As she quickly explained the emergency, Max jerked the drapes from the rod and tossed them into the fire. He grabbed several large potted plants and dumped the dirt on the flames as Frankie rushed in with the extinguisher. Smoke alarms blared through the house, drawing the staff like flies. The chef appeared from out of nowhere and dumped a fifty-pound bag of flour on the fire.

"Jesus Christ!" Phillip called from the doorway as he and several security guards rushed through the door and joined the frantic group, stomping small flames that threatened to spread.

Max waited until the fire was under control before he took off toward the window. He literally jumped through it and landed hard on the ground outside. He quickly scanned the yard. Putting out the fire had only taken a few minutes, but it had given the intruder time to flee.

Acres of land were lit up like a baseball field. Lights shone from trees and poles and fence posts. Security men raced past him, some with bloodhounds yelping loudly. The men swapped information on walkie-talkies as they shone flashlights in every direction. Grabbing a spare from one of the guards, Max skirted the property where tall red-tipped hedges concealed an electric fence.

Finally, Max stopped running. He stood there for a moment trying to catch his breath. In the distance he heard sirens.

Tim Duncan, head of security, hurried over. "Did you see anything?"

Max shook his head. "I think we lost him."

"We're not giving up yet."

"I need to check back at the house," Max said. "The fire department is on its way." He turned and started back toward the house as the men continued to search. As he walked, Max shone his light toward the bushes. He stopped short when he spied something that had been caught in the brush. "Over here!" he shouted.

All at once, he was surrounded by security men and

dogs. A gloved hand yanked a yellow and blue bandana from a bush and pressed it against the dogs' noses. They cried out, as though in agonizing pain. The man lifted the bandana to his nose and winced, even as the dogs continued to wheeze. "Ammonia. Shit."

Max and Duncan parted the bushes and shined their lights. "The fence has been cut," Max said dully. "He's gone."

Duncan got on his walkie-talkie once more. "I want every vehicle we got circling the property," he said. "The guy is probably on foot, but he has to have driven out here somehow. Find him."

The sirens closed in, fire trucks and police cars with flashing lights turning onto the property and pulling in front of the house. A few seconds later, Wrangler Jeeps and pickup trucks combed the road outside the property line, lights pointed in every direction.

An hour later they were still searching. Frankie and Lamar Tevis joined Max. "How the hell did he get away so fast?" Frankie asked.

Max sighed his disgust. "He tricked us, that's how. He set us up."

"What do you mean?" Lamar asked.

"I think whoever did this was here earlier. He cut the fence and purposely left the rag behind where we'd be sure to find it. Tonight, he entered and exited the property from another location." Max paused. "Unless he's still here."

Lamar glanced around quickly. "You thinking what I'm thinking? That maybe the person responsible is pretending to be on our side?"

"It's possible."

"Well, if that's true, it's going to make my job a whole lot harder." Lamar shook his head and walked away.

"How's everybody inside?" Max asked Frankie.

"Jamie, Beenie, and Phillip are trying to reassure Deedee who, in turn, is trying to reassure the staff. The fire marshal is inspecting the house for damage, but at least we kept it from spreading. I'm thinking we should tell Deedee it was a prank."

"That's not going to fly. Not even with Deedee."

"I don't want to worry her."

"She should be worried. You've received threatening letters, Jamie and I have been shot at, someone put dynamite in my car today, and somebody else just threw a Molotov cocktail through your window. Hell, even I'm worried."

"Back up," Frankie said. "What's this dynamite business? You didn't mention it."

"This is the first chance I've had."

"Damn, Max. You and Jamie could have been killed."

"I think that was the plan."

Frankie wiped his hand down his face. "I don't know what to make of it."

"Doesn't make sense to me, either," Max said. "Think about it. Bombs and high-powered automatics are designed to kill. If the person who threw the burning bottle through the window wanted to kill one of us, he was certainly close enough to use a gun."

"He would have come closer to killing us if he'd thrown the bottle of kerosene through the window after we'd all gone to bed. It would have been less risky for him as well."

"The smoke alarms would have awakened us," Max said, "and we still would have had time to get out. As for risk, if this person is somebody we're accustomed to having on the property, the guards wouldn't pay attention to him."

"The only person who came on and off the property was my campaign manager. And Phillip, of course."

"Who just happened to arrive only minutes after the fire started."

Frankie shook his head. "Phillip is like family. Besides, he would never do anything that might endanger Jamie."

Deedee jerked her head back so hard it would have given an older woman whiplash. "Beenie, would you get that nasty stuff away from me!" she cried, wheezing, eyes watering. "What *is* that!"

"It's smelling salts, sweet pea. All Southern women use it when they get the vapors."

"Someone almost burned down my house. I *deserve* to have the vapors if I want them. What the heck is a vapor?"

"I don't know, but it sounds dangerous to me."

"You're the one who's going to be in danger if you put that stuff near my nose again."

Jamie decided it was time to cut in. They had moved into the library so the fire marshal could investigate, but the acrid smell of smoke lingered through the house. "Women in the South are more sophisticated today," she said. "They don't get the vapors anymore. If they get upset they have a couple of tequila shooters."

"Sounds good to me," Deedee said.

"And they call it something like a Magnolia Blossom tonic so it doesn't look bad," Phillip added with a smile.

Deedee's face was flushed a bright red. "Lord, I'm so hot I could die. Could someone turn on the air conditioner before I spontaneously combust?"

Phillip hurried toward the thermostat. "It's already on sixty. If I turn it any lower it'll freeze."

"That's what I need. Ice."

"Is there anything else I can do?" Phillip asked. When Deedee shook her head, he started from the room. "I'm going to see what's happening out back."

"Oh, God, I hope Frankie and Max are safe," Deedee cried.

"Take this, Deedee," Beenie offered.

"What is it?"

"Just a little nerve pill. It'll calm you down."

Jamie stepped closer. "Wait a minute, Beenie. Let me see that."

"It's Xanax, honey. I take them when I get anxious."

"Aren't they habit-forming?"

"I'm only giving her one, love. She's not likely to end up on some street corner selling sex for another fix. It'll take the edge off."

Deedee pushed his hand away. "I don't need a tranquilizer, Beenie. I need you to get out of my face so I can breathe. Why don't you check on Choo-Choo? The poor thing is probably hiding because of all the commotion."

"I'll get him for you, and then I'll make you a Frappuccino. That'll cool you off."

"Are you okay?" Jamie asked her, once Beenie hurried away.

"I feel like a train wreck right now. I never thought something like this would happen just because Frankie decided to go into politics. Now, we're not safe in our own beds. I can't even leave the house. How am I supposed to shop? Not that there's any place to shop in this godforsaken town. I'll be reduced to shopping from catalogs. What fun is that?"

"You can shop over the Internet."

"It's not the same, Jamie. I enjoy sitting on those

dainty little sofas drinking champagne while women model the latest fashion. I like the smell of designer clothes. Sometimes, I wish Frankie had never laid eyes on this town."

Jamie tried to reassure her, but the fire had left her shaken as well. She wondered if Max was okay. Had he not acted so quickly when the fire had started, the house would have very likely burned down over their heads.

"I hope Max didn't hurt himself jumping out that window," Deedee said as though reading Jamie's mind. "I've never seen anyone do that except on TV, and it's usually a stuntman."

"Some actors don't use stuntmen," Beenie said, coming through the door with the Frappuccino in one hand, Choo-Choo running behind him. "I don't think Clint Eastwood ever used a stuntman."

"Does Harrison Ford?" Deedee asked, scooping up her dog. "No, don't tell me, I'd be too disappointed if he did."

Jamie wasn't listening. She wondered how someone had managed to get onto the property and so close to the house with all the security surrounding it. Of course, the estate was huge, and the men couldn't patrol every inch of it, but they were obviously dealing with someone cunning enough to slip on and off the property unnoticed. Unless it was one of the servants; but she couldn't imagine anyone on the staff trying to hurt Frankie or Deedee. They were kind and generous to a fault when it came to their employees.

"I'm willing to bet half my salary that Brad Pitt uses a stuntman," Beenie said. "Not that I'd blame him, what with his looks. That Jennifer Aniston is one lucky lady." Beenie sighed, raised his forefinger to his lip and tapped it. "What a man."

The housekeeper appeared at the door. She looked shaken. "Would anyone care for something since dinner has been held up?"

"I couldn't eat if someone put a gun to my head," Deedee said, then winced. "Gee, with the way things are going that might be a distinct possibility. Jamie, would you like something?"

Jamie didn't have much of an appetite, either. "I'm fine."

Phillip stepped into the room. "They're still looking," he said, "but I'm willing to bet the culprit is long gone."

"I wish they'd come back inside," Deedee said. "What if that deranged person was trying to lure Frankie outside so he could—" She paused and shuddered.

"Frankie and Max are perfectly capable of taking care of themselves," Jamie told her. She suspected Max could hold his own in any situation. She had seen how fast his mind worked, and despite being irritated with him much of the time, she had to respect him for taking control of matters as quickly as he did.

"Jamie's right," Phillip said. "They seem to have everything under control. Try to relax."

Frankie entered the room, his eyes going directly to his wife. "Are you okay, sweetheart?"

Deedee leapt to her feet. "Did you find him?"

Frankie hesitated. "They're still looking."

Deedee gazed at her husband, her eyes bright with fear. She turned away. "I can't live like this, Frankie. I know how much this election means to you, but I can't stand the thought of you getting hurt—" She paused and swallowed. "Or worse."

Frankie stepped closer and took his wife's hand in his. "Do you want me to pull out of the race, Deedee? I will if that's what you want."

She met his gaze. "I just want my husband and friends to be safe, that's all."

Max joined them a few minutes later. "I spoke with the fire marshal. He and the others are getting ready to leave. He said he'd call you tomorrow."

The chef appeared at the door. "I'd like to go ahead and serve dinner now before it's ruined."

"Yeah, sure," Frankie said, offering Deedee his hand. She gave her guests a brave smile, but it didn't quite reach her green eyes.

Everyone was quiet as they entered the impressive dining room. Jamie wondered why they even bothered. Food was the last thing on her mind. As if sensing her unease, Phillip patted her hand but waited until they'd been served bowls of lobster bisque before speaking.

"In all the commotion, I forgot to ask you how things were at work today," he said.

"A little tense at first, but I think everything is going to be okay."

"I tried to reach you a couple of times at the end of the day, but you'd already left."

"Max and I had to run by my place so I could grab some clothes."

Phillip turned to Max. "I appreciate your keeping an eye on my fiancée," he said. "I'm trying to reschedule my workload so I can be available at all times."

"There's no need, Phillip," she said. "I don't need you or Max baby-sitting me. I can take care of myself." Jamie realized all eyes were on her, and she wished she hadn't used such a curt tone with him. "I'm sorry," she said, looking from Phillip to Max. "I guess I'm a little anxious after what happened."

"You know it's all over the news," Phillip said. "The TV station has interviewed Lamar several times.

Mother was shocked when she found out the kind of weapon that was used."

Jamie and Max exchanged looks. Frankie shifted uneasily in his chair.

"It was a deer rifle," Deedee said.

Phillip laughed. "Hardly."

"Let's change the subject," Frankie suggested.

"What kind of gun was it, Phillip?" Deedee asked.

Phillip glanced around the table as if sensing he'd said something he shouldn't. "You don't know?"

"What kind of weapon *was* it?" Deedee repeated, this time firmly.

Phillip hesitated. "Some kind of automatic weapon," he said. "The police aren't releasing anything else on it at the moment."

Deedee gasped. "Are you sure?"

Phillip looked at Jamie as if hoping she could somehow fix his mistake. "That's just what I heard, Deedee," he said. "You know how the media is. They tend to blow things out of proportion."

Deedee whirled around in her chair and looked at Frankie. "Why didn't you tell me?" she cried. "Deer hunters don't use those kinds of weapons and you know it."

"I didn't want to worry you."

"*Worry* me? How could you keep something like that from me, Frankie? You've always been honest with me."

"Calm down, big sister," Max said. "The truth is, nobody knows anything yet, not even Chief Tevis, so we're wasting our time speculating." He glanced around the table. "Surely we can come up with better dinner conversation than this." He smiled at Jamie. "Why don't you tell us how your wedding plans are going?"

Jamie shot him a look that could have killed a raging bull. "I'm afraid you'd have to ask Phillip's mother. She's handling most of it."

"Are you planning to wear white?" Max asked, a teasing lilt in his eyes.

Phillip glanced at him curiously. "Why wouldn't she?"

"Max is just being funny, darling," Jamie said. "Ignore him and maybe he'll go away."

Phillip relaxed. "You should come to the wedding, Max. I'll see that you get an invitation."

"Hey, I wouldn't miss it for the world. I'd like to see Jamie all gussied up. I may even spring for a wedding gift."

"Deedee, I'd really like your opinion on my wedding gown," Jamie said, hoping to get her friend's mind off her worries.

"Of course," Deedee said, but she didn't sound as enthusiastic as she usually did when it came to discussing clothes.

Tension was thick throughout the rest of the meal, and nobody seemed particularly interested in food. Deedee didn't touch hers, despite Frankie's coaxing. Finally, she stood. "I don't wish to appear rude," she said, "but I need to go to bed. I have a splitting headache."

Chapter
SEVEN

Frankie slumped on the sofa, looking at Max. "What do you think I should do?"

"I've already given you my opinion. You pull out now and you're going to let a lot of people down, the same people who are counting on you to make a difference in this town."

He sighed. "I know. I talk to people all the time who are struggling to make ends meet because there are no jobs to be found in this town. Some of them are living on unemployment, and these are proud people who are accustomed to supporting themselves." He shook his head sadly. "This town needs more industry so we can put people to work."

"I don't know what I'd do in your predicament," Phillip said. "I wouldn't want to jeopardize my family's safety either, but I know you're devoted to this town."

"I couldn't go on without Deedee," Frankie said miserably. "She's my whole life."

Jamie was touched by his words. She had never met a couple so close, and she wondered if she and Phillip would ever reach that level. "That's so sweet, Frankie."

Phillip looked at Jamie. "Are you planning to stay here tonight?"

She nodded. "I want to be here for Deedee."

"I understand." He checked his wristwatch. "It's getting late so I'll run and let you folks get to bed. Frankie, thanks for a great meal."

"I'll walk you out," Jamie said. She followed him to the door.

"Now, you be careful," Phillip warned. "I don't want anything happening to you." He kissed her softly and headed for his car.

Jamie returned to the living room. "Do you want me to look in on Deedee?" she asked Frankie.

"No, I'll check on her," he said.

Max waited until he and Jamie were alone before saying anything. "Are you okay?"

"Yeah."

"He slipped right through our fingers, Jamie."

"Do you think it could have been one of the security guards?"

"Anything is possible."

Jamie shivered.

"Are you cold?"

"Well, that's pretty much a given in this house, but I'm okay. It frightens me that someone was able to get that close unseen."

Max studied her. "I didn't mean to scare you. I probably said too much."

"I'm not Deedee. I don't want information held back from me. I'm in this, too."

As if to comfort her, Max put his hand on her knee. Jamie felt his warmth seep into her skin. She shifted on the sofa. Max hesitated a moment before pulling his hand away. "We should talk."

His voice was low and intimate, making the hairs on the back of her neck prickle.

"We are talking," Jamie said, trying to shift the direction in which he was traveling. "We have to figure out this thing."

"Which thing? There is more than one thing going on here at the moment."

"I'm perfectly aware of that." She stood and crossed the room, but she could still feel his touch. She didn't have to look at him to know how handsome he was in the white shirt and brown linen slacks he wore, how his dark eyes seemed to take in everything at once, even though he seemed entirely focused on her.

There was no denying the attraction she felt for him, and she only had to look into his dark eyes to know it was mutual. Lately, she found herself gazing at his handsome face when she thought he wouldn't notice. She wished she could touch his hair because she could only imagine what it would feel like. She also wondered what it would be like to feel his arms around her, and she immediately felt guilty. She had promised herself to Phillip, and she had no right to think about another man.

All at once Max came up behind her. She'd not heard him get up or cross the room. She'd simply felt a shift in the air, the sudden involuntary tensing of her body, and she knew he was close. He placed his hands on her shoulders, and her body reacted immediately.

"Jamie?"

"Leave it alone, Max," she said, stepping away. She knew she didn't have to clarify her statement.

"And if I refuse?"

She turned and faced him. "I'm not giving you a choice. I've made myself clear all along. I'm not interested."

He studied her. "Are you really that much in love with Phillip?"

"Of course I am."

"The kind of love Frankie and Deedee share?"

It was ironic that Max should ask the same question she'd asked herself earlier. "Why are you so concerned about my relationship with Phillip?"

"Because I know what it's like to marry the wrong person."

"And that's what you think I'm doing?"

He shrugged. "I don't see a whole lot of passion between you and your fiancé."

"I'm content with Phillip. We might not share this great passion you speak of, but we share the things that count. We love each other, and we have a lot in common. We're comfortable together, and I enjoy his family. I've always wanted to be part of a large family, Max."

"What happened to you, Jamie?"

His voice was soft, coaxing, inspiring a feeling of confidence. Jamie fought it, but he was so sincere that she felt compelled to answer. She sighed heavily. "I don't like to rehash my past, but if I tell you will you promise to leave me alone?"

"Okay."

"My dad wasn't well, Max. He wasn't emotionally fit, so to speak. I guess he never got over losing my mother. Or maybe he'd always had problems, I don't know. Maybe that's why my mother left him. He and I never discussed it, but he was seriously depressed most of the time."

"That's why you came home instead of going with a bigger newspaper, isn't it?"

"He needed me. Wouldn't you have done the same if a family member was desperately ill?"

He looked thoughtful. "I'm glad I've never been faced with that kind of decision. Had I been in your predicament I would have tried to find a way to make it work for both of us, but that's easy for me to say because I didn't live it."

"I like knowing from one day to the next what to expect, because I never really felt secure growing up." Jamie paused. "I don't regret the past, Max, but I know it has affected a lot of decisions that I make today."

He looked confused. "So you're marrying for financial security?"

"No. Security doesn't come from having a lot of money." She shrugged. "Look, I don't expect you to understand."

"I want you to be happy, Jamie, that's all."

The next morning, Max and Jamie climbed into his car and headed for town.

"I've been thinking," Jamie said.

"About us?" He grinned.

Jamie made an effort not to smile. "Not."

"What's on your mind?"

"This is just a possibility, but I know someone, or rather, I know *of* someone who is probably capable of skulking around other people's property and not being found."

"I'm all ears."

"They call him Swamp Dog. I don't know his real name, but he's scary as all get-out. Someone once told me if anybody needed any dirty work done, they could count on Swamp Dog."

"Have you ever met him?"

"No. I don't even know if he's still alive, but I know

where he used to live. It's an old ramshackle houseboat in the middle of—"

"The swamp?"

"You catch on fast, Holt. Anyway, I had trouble falling asleep last night—"

"You did?" Max looked at her. "Because I had the same problem. I thought about you a lot."

"Actually, I was on edge."

"You know the reason for that, of course."

She looked at him. "I'm sure you're going to tell me it had something to do with you."

He merely grinned.

Jamie did an eye-roll. "Now, how about we get down to business?"

"If you insist."

"Someone got close enough to the house to throw a Molotov cocktail through the window. That's quite a feat considering the property is crawling with security. So, I got to thinking, who would be capable of doing something like that without getting caught?"

"And you came up with this Swamp Dog person."

"Right. And he has the background for it. He was in Special Forces in the military. Word has it he lost it over there."

"Define 'lost it.'"

"Went off the deep end."

"Crazy as a bedbug, huh? Tell me more."

"He's a poacher. He tosses dynamite into the river. It goes off and stuns the fish. They float to the top and he scoops them up with a net. Rumor has it there was an accident, and he lost an eye."

"That would certainly make him easy to find in a crowd. How do you know where he lives?"

"Back in high school, a few of us decided to find out if he even existed. We took a boat out there. We were able to find the houseboat, but the minute we got close somebody started firing shots at us, so we hauled butt."

"You didn't see anybody?"

"No, but the game warden caught word of the poaching and decided to look into it. Somebody found him a few days later in his boat with a bullet between his eyes. Nobody could prove anything, although they suspected Swamp Dog."

"I'm already looking forward to meeting him." Max paused. "I don't know, Jamie. It sounds farfetched. Why would he be after us?"

"Maybe he's being paid to come after us by someone who doesn't want you and Frankie looking into the missing tax dollars but doesn't want to get their own hands dirty. I think it's worth checking out. He's actually the only dangerous sort of guy in the area."

"Okay, we'll pay him a visit."

Jamie laughed. "I don't think Swamp Dog accepts visitors."

"You're saying he's not going to serve us tea and crumpets."

"He may shoot us."

"Maybe I should go alone."

"You'd never find the place."

Muffin came on. "You know, I don't like to tell people what to do, but I'm going to make an exception. This whole thing sounds dangerous."

"How else are we going to find out if Swamp Dog is involved?" Jamie asked.

"I wish you could give me his real name," Muffin replied, "so I could get some information on him."

"I'm not sure anybody knows his real name." Jamie looked at Max. "We'll need a boat to get there. Lucky for us I know someone who has one. I'll try to wrap things up quickly at the office, and we can head out around lunchtime."

"I don't like this," Muffin replied. "Not one bit. You're both asking for trouble."

"You call this a boat?" Max asked some four hours later, as he gazed down at a small skiff that was to carry them down the river.

"You were expecting a yacht, maybe? I don't think the river can accommodate the kind of boat you're accustomed to." Jamie was a bit embarrassed about the boat; she didn't remember it being so rough looking. The color had long ago faded, one seat was broken, and she wasn't sure the motor was powerful enough to get them away from the dock.

"This thing doesn't look as though it should be floating in a bathtub," Max said.

"Tell you what, Holt. Next time *you* get the boat."

"Next time? Sounds like you're looking for a long-term relationship."

"I'm really glad you're bringing your ego on board." It was going to be a long ride, Jamie told herself, and they could very well be on a wild-goose chase. For all she knew, Swamp Dog could be long dead and buried. "So, are you with me or not?"

"Hey, I wouldn't miss it."

Hitching the straps of her handbag on one shoulder and grabbing the canvas bag containing supplies Max had purchased—snacks, flashlights, first-aid kit, insect repellent, and hiking up the rubber knee-length wading boots she wore—Jamie carefully stepped into the boat.

It rocked back and forth. She gripped the map Muffin had printed out so they could study the river closely beforehand. She was glad she'd taken the time to change into jeans and a long-sleeved shirt. Although the sleeves were now rolled up to her elbows, the added clothing would protect her from insects. That, and the mosquito repellent, she reminded herself.

A bemused Max watched as Jamie struggled to keep her balance. Finally, she grabbed a seat and held on, her behind perched high, waiting for the boat to stop rocking. Max arched one brow. "You don't do a lot of boating, do you?" he asked.

Jamie sat down. "Okay, so I'm not a boat person. Just get in the darn thing so we can be on our way."

"Let's get something straight, Swifty," Max said, trying to affect a stern look and doing a poor job of it. "The one operating the motor is the captain. That makes you the first mate. You don't have the authority to talk to me like that."

"Oh, so this is about power," Jamie said. "You forget, Holt. I'm the one who found the boat, and I know how to get to Swamp Dog's place. Face it, you need me." Even as she said it she knew better. Jamie suspected Max Holt could do anything he set his mind to.

"You're right," he said. "I'm helpless without you." He climbed into the boat and reached for the small Styrofoam ice chest filled with soft drinks, as well as the two gas tanks he had purchased and filled for the trip. He'd even thought to bring flashlights. "Go ahead and untie us," he said, once he'd settled in.

Jamie did as she was told. Once she'd pulled the rope in she shoved them away from the dock.

Max reached for the small handle that was attached to the cord on the motor and yanked it. It took several attempts to start the motor, but it finally chugged to life. He steered the boat down the river. "Am I going the right way?"

"Very funny. It's obvious there is only one way in and one way out."

"Just checking since you're supposed to be our guide."

They rode for close to an hour before Jamie pointed toward a thin tributary. She grabbed one of the oars and stuck it in the water. "Stay in the center," she warned. "The water is shallow here."

"Good thing you brought that sophisticated depth finder," Max said. "I wouldn't want to run aground." Finally, he cut the motor, tilted it so the propeller was out of the water, and paddled the rest of the way. The boat nudged against the bank.

Jamie gazed at the green scum that covered the water like a filmy curtain, hiding only heaven knew what that waited just beneath the surface. She suppressed a shudder.

"Now what?" Max asked.

"We walk."

Max tied off the boat. Jamie grabbed her purse, slipped the long strap over her shoulder and waited until Max climbed out. He turned and helped her out. They rolled down their shirtsleeves and sprayed insect repellent on their necks and hands.

"Let's go," he said.

Jamie was already feeling irritable from the heat. There'd been little breeze on the river. It was hot, and her blouse was sweat-soaked and plastered to her back. She found a sturdy tree limb to use as a stick. Hopefully it would offer protection in case she ran into some undesirable creature. Max did the same. "These boots aren't going to mean crap if we meet up with an alligator," she said.

"Then I suggest we avoid them at all cost. Besides, they're more afraid of us than we are them."

"Yeah. That would explain why we're the ones carrying sticks and wearing rubber boots instead of them."

"You're getting testy on me," Max said, "and I may as well tell you it's not attractive."

Jamie bit back her reply. She was determined to show Max Holt she was made of tough stuff.

They started up the bank. It wasn't long before they found themselves in shallow water. Jamie became even more anxious as the murky water climbed to her ankles.

"Are you okay?" Max asked, noting how she hesitated before taking every step.

"I can think of other things I'd rather be doing right now if that's what you mean."

"This was your idea."

"Do you see anyone else beating a path to investigate the situation? You won't find Lamar Tevis and his deputies combing the swamp looking for a madman."

"I've been meaning to ask you about Lamar," Max said. "He doesn't really seem qualified for the job."

"His daddy was sheriff for a while. He was very popular. Lamar got in on his coattails, so to speak. He does okay for the most part."

"Sounds like the jobs in this town run in families."

"Doesn't take a genius to figure that one out." Jamie jumped at the sight of a thin stick. She could have sworn it was a snake. The thought of looking for Swamp Dog had seemed exciting when she'd first mentioned it. Now she was beginning to regret it.

Jamie tried to concentrate on the scenery, the bald cypress, tupelo, and sweet gum trees. A canopy of vegetation shrouded the area, giving the swamp an eerie feel that sent goose pimples along her arms.

"I wish I had Vera's gun."

"You'd probably only end up shooting yourself in the foot," Max said.

"Hell's bells, I'm going to die anyway." Jamie took a step, felt the mud give beneath her feet, creating a suction noise each time she walked. "Oh, Jeez," she said. "This is so gross. Do you see any snakes? Water moccasins, maybe?"

Max chuckled. "You're acting like a girl, you know."

"I am a girl. Deal with it."

Max grinned. "It's not like I haven't tried. Are you sure we're going in the right direction?"

"I'm not even sure I'm going to live to see night-fall." Jamie paused and looked at her map. "I thought it was around that last bend." The water had risen almost to her knees. "We've had more rainfall than usual the past few months. That can change things."

Max stopped walking and regarded her. "Are you hinting that we might be lost?"

"I'm saying that's a strong possibility."

He sighed. "I should have known better than to agree to this harebrained idea. I'm beginning to think this Swamp Dog business is a crock."

"So why'd you come?"

"Because I knew you were hell-bent on finding this guy, and you'd probably go alone. Somebody has to look after you. You wouldn't last five minutes out here without me. Admit it."

Jamie froze. Something long and black was heading

straight for her, and this time it wasn't a stick. "Oh, double damn."

"It's just a simple water snake," Max said.

Jamie didn't so much as breathe as the snake slithered along the water and swam right between her legs. She turned her head as he continued past her. "I can't believe I'm doing this," she said. "It's all your fault. You shouldn't have let me talk you into it."

Max was only vaguely aware of her words as his eye caught something. "Quiet," he said. "There's the houseboat."

Jamie looked up. Sure enough, she saw the rugged outlines of a wooden structure through the trees. "That's it," she whispered.

"Maybe you should stay back and let me investigate."

She shook her head. "I've come this far, I'm not backing out now."

They moved soundlessly through the water, although Jamie feared Swamp Dog would hear the steady drumming of her heart and ragged breathing. Finally, they hit dry land. The boat was less than one hundred yards away, rocking gently in the river, less than twenty feet from the shoreline. They circled around and approached it with caution, taking care to stay behind the trees and shrubs. Jamie tried to avoid stepping on sticks, fearing one would snap and attract attention.

"There he is," Jamie whispered so low she could barely hear her own voice. She stared at the roughhewn man with shoulder-length iron-gray hair and a black patch over one eye. He was bathing in the river beside his boat. They continued walking, taking greater care with every step. Jamie jumped when she heard gunshot. She gasped as a snake flew into the air and fell into the water with a splash. Swamp Dog grabbed it and tossed it on the side of the boat. Then, without warning, he turned and aimed his pistol in their direction. "Out from behind that bush," he said. "Hands in the air."

Chapter
EIGHT

"We're dead," Jamie said.

"Better do as he says," Max replied.

They raised their hands above their heads and stepped out from behind the bush. "We're not armed," Max said.

"That don't mean jackshit to me," Swamp Dog replied. "You're trespassing. That's enough for me to put a bullet in your head."

"We need help," Jamie said once they'd come within fifty feet of him. "The motor on our boat quit on us. We're stranded."

Swamp Dog didn't lower his gun as he climbed from the water naked as the day he was born. "You picked the wrong guy."

Jamie tried to keep her eyes above his shoulders, but not before she caught sight of his leathery skin and sinewy body. A multitude of purplish scars zigzagged across his chest and abdomen. The left side of his face was disfigured, obviously from the same accident in which he'd lost an eye. The menacing look on his face told her he'd sooner shoot them than not.

"Well, then," Jamie said lightly, "I guess we'll be going. Sorry to have bothered you."

"Make one move and you're dead."

Max turned to Jamie. "Perhaps we should tell him why we're really here."

Jamie nodded. What the heck was he talking about? "Uh, why don't *you* tell him?"

"Miss Swift owns the *Beaumont Gazette*," Max said. "She'd like to interview you."

"Is that supposed to excite me?" Swamp Dog reached for a towel and wrapped it around his waist.

Jamie just looked at Max. If that was the only plan he had then they were in big trouble. "Uh, yeah," Jamie agreed, thinking anything was better than sudden death. "I was wondering if you'd be willing to let me do a piece on you as a human-interest story."

Swamp Dog lowered his gun, but his gaze never left Jamie's face. "That's bullshit."

"Trust me," Jamie said. "If we were trying to bullshit you we'd have come up with something better. You'll have to admit you're somewhat of a legend in these parts."

It was obvious the man didn't believe a word she said. He waved the gun. "Inside."

"Probably we picked a bad time," Jamie said. "I could try to set something up when it's more convenient. Get my photographer out here and do it up right."

"Do I look like someone who would agree to have his picture taken?" Swamp Dog said.

Jamie shrugged. "Why not?"

"Stop messing with me, lady, and go inside."

Max and Jamie walked a rickety plank that led from the riverbank to his boat.

"This way," Swamp Dog ordered.

They both headed toward the door leading to the cabin. The room was dirty and smelled of dirty clothes and rotted food.

"Sit." He motioned toward a sofa.

Jamie was almost afraid to sit on the rumpled sofa, but she was more afraid of the gun. Max joined her. She looked around. "Uh, nice place."

"Yeah, I was going for a Martha Stewart look." Swamp Dog took a chair opposite them and reached for a pad and pencil from a rickety table. He tossed them to Jamie, whose hands were trembling so badly she missed. Max picked them up and handed them to her.

"So, what do you want to know?" the man said. "Think carefully 'cause I'm gonna get pissed if you ask the wrong question."

Jamie straightened on the sofa, trying to appear professional as she tried to think of what to ask him that wouldn't make him angry. He looked ominous with the black patch over his eye, and she avoided looking into his face. "Okay, let's start at the beginning," she said, sounding more confident than she felt. "Could I get your real name?"

Swamp Dog fired a shot two inches from her head. Jamie dove toward Max.

"What the hell?" Max said. "Why'd you do that?"

"I don't like answering personal questions."

Jamie tried to swallow. "Okay, okay, I understand the rules now," she said, trying to think of something that wouldn't send him over the edge. Rumor was right; the man had definitely lost it. She would keep the interview light and superficial.

"Perhaps we could discuss your hobbies. Do you garden?"

"What?" he and Max asked in unison.

"That's the stupidest question anyone has ever asked me," Swamp Dog said. "Do I *look* like a gardener?"

"Jesus, Jamie," Max said under his breath.

She looked from one to the other. "Well, excuse the heck out of me," she snapped, "but it's not easy conducting an interview at gunpoint. I'm trying to do a job here, and I don't appreciate rudeness. I'm hot and tired and hungry. I traveled all this way just to ask this, this, *person* a few questions, and this is how I'm treated? Forget the interview." She tossed the pad of paper aside and reached for her purse.

"Hold it right there," Swamp Dog said.

"I'm getting a cigarette, okay?" She reached for her pack and lighter. In the distance she heard a small-engine airplane and suspected they were spraying for mosquitoes. She wished she were on it.

"I don't permit smoking in my place."

Jamie glanced around at the filth. "You're kidding, right?" At the same time, she noted he was becoming more agitated. Swamp Dog obviously didn't like the sound of small planes. Maybe it made him think of other things he wanted to forget.

"You're really starting to piss me off," he said. "I don't like mouthy broads." He raised his gun slowly.

"I'm not a broad, and I don't appreciate—"

"Shut up!" Swamp Dog seemed to have difficulty breathing, and his eyes took on a wild look as the plane closed in on them. He looked disoriented; nevertheless, he pulled back the hammer and aimed his gun. The plane swooped low.

Max glanced toward the window. "Everybody down," he yelled.

Swamp Dog automatically swung around and trained

the gun on the plane as it bore down on the water, causing the houseboat to vibrate as a cloud of insect spray
filled the air. "Those bastards," he muttered.

In one fluid move, Max was off the sofa. He kicked
the gun from Swamp Dog's hand. It hit the floor and
fired. Swamp Dog, still dazed, dove for it, but Max
was faster. He grabbed the pistol, put a chokehold on
the older man and held the gun to his head. The plane
went on.

"Okay, you rude son of a bitch. I'm about to teach
you some manners."

"Screw you, Holt."

Max blinked. "You know who I am?"

Swamp Dog smiled, showing a mouthful of yellow
teeth. "Surprised?"

"Who are you working for?"

"I don't have to tell you anything, man. And I'm not
afraid of being shot, so go for it."

"Go ahead and kill him," Jamie said. "We can say it
was self-defense."

"I'm more interested in getting answers out of him
at the moment," Max told her, not taking his eyes off
the man. "Somebody is paying you to go after my
brother-in-law. You tried to kill Jamie and me. Why?"

He looked smug. "If I wanted to kill you, you'd already be dead."

Max sat back on his heels but kept the gun aimed at
Swamp Dog's head. "I like confidence in a man."

"I guess that makes us best friends."

"We don't have to be friends, pal, but I'm prepared
to offer you a job with a nice paycheck. I want you to
be part of what I call my special projects team. Immediately," he added. "Your first job would consist of
protecting a friend of mine."

"Frankie Fontana. He already has a security team in place."

"Yeah, and they aren't doing a very good job. I need someone I can count on to keep Frankie and his wife safe. If you accept the job I'll deposit a nice chunk of money into an account in your name."

"And if I refuse?"

Max shrugged. "Then you're not as smart as I thought you were." He tossed the gun aside and got up.

Swamp Dog came to his feet and grabbed the gun. "You just signed your death warrant, Holt."

"Some genius you are, Max," Jamie muttered. "If he wasn't going to kill us before, he'll certainly do it now. And what do you think he'll do with our bodies? Throw them to the alligators, of course. Have you ever seen what a gator can do to a man?"

He shook his head. "Have you?"

"No, but I've heard. They drag the victim beneath the water and drown him. They don't eat the body for a few days."

Swamp Dog laughed. "It's worse than that, Miss Swift. I've seen it firsthand. And enjoyed every moment of it if I might say so."

They both stared at him.

"Relax," Max said finally. "He's not going to shoot us. He would have already done it by now." He reached into his shirt pocket, pulled out a business card, and placed it on the table beside the chair where Swamp Dog had been sitting. "Call me when you're ready to make a deal."

Jamie held her breath as Max led her from the boat. Swamp Dog was probably a good enough shot that he would kill her instantly. She wouldn't have to suffer or die slowly while copperheads and God-knows-what slithered across her body. She wouldn't have to live under the same roof as Annabelle Standish.

They crossed the plank leading off the boat. Nothing. She could feel Swamp Dog's eyes on her.

"Keep walking," Max said.

The swamp was bathed in shadow as they made their way back. A bullfrog croaked nearby, birds called out to one another. Jamie waded through the water, keeping an eye out for anything that moved.

"Are you okay?" Max asked.

"Fine, except for the fact you almost got us killed."

"Me? You're the one who mouthed off."

"He's a sick man, shooting just over my head if I asked the wrong question. It reminded me of an old western, where the bad guy shoots bullets at someone's feet in order to make them dance. I refuse to be treated like that. I'd rather they just shoot me and get it over with. You wouldn't have put up with it, either, Max."

He was quiet.

"Would you?"

"It depends. If I were the only one involved, then no. If I were trying to protect someone I cared about, I'd probably go along with it until I could think of a way out."

Jamie was thoughtful as they walked on. "Do you think he's the one after us?"

Max shrugged. "He knew who we were. And he's cagey enough to outsmart Frankie's security men."

Jamie looked at him. "I don't understand. Why didn't he kill us back there? He had the perfect opportunity."

"It would have been too easy. The man is a hunter. A predator. We were easy targets; there was no challenge. He's also been in the military, and like you said, probably served in a special unit."

"I don't actually know that for a fact. I don't even know if he was in the military. Probably just another rumor."

"Did you notice the table beside his chair? It was partially covered with oilcloth, but it was a footlocker. There was a name on it. J. Hodges."

"Finally, we have a name."

"Swamp Dog, I mean Hodges, is just the trigger-man. He's cunning and mean, but he's not exactly an Einstein. I'm more interested in finding the one who hired him."

"You weren't serious about offering him a job."

"Dead serious."

"Why, for Pete's sake?"

"I can't keep an eye on the man way out here. I want him close enough so I can watch him."

"Dang, Max, you'll put us all in danger."

"Trust me on this one, okay? Swamp Dog is just a player in a much bigger game that obviously involves a lot of money. The person behind him is smarter and more dangerous."

"You're keeping something from me. What is it?"

"Muffin and I are still looking. I'll let you know when I have something."

Jamie had so many unanswered questions. She grew up in Beaumont, went to school with a number of people who now ran the city. She attended weddings and funerals, watched her friends have babies, and she didn't want to think any of them were thieves.

"You're awfully quiet," Max said.

"I have a lot to think about."

They arrived at the boat. Jamie climbed in and Max shoved it away from the shore. He paddled a short distance and tested the water with his oar to make certain it was safe to drop the motor. He reached for the cord and pulled. Nothing happened. He tried again without success.

Jamie glanced back. "What's wrong?"

He shrugged. "Damned if I know. We aren't out of gas, I switched to a new tank shortly before we got here. I don't think the gas is getting to the motor." He looked closer. "What the hell?"

"What is it?"

Max held up a black hose leading to the motor. "It has been cut."

Jamie gaped at him. "Who would do that?"

"Obviously somebody who didn't want us to extend our visit to Swamp Dog."

She glanced around frantically, but all she could see were trees and brush. "They could be watching us," she said quietly.

Max followed her gaze. "I don't see anybody, but that doesn't mean they aren't there." He reached for the oars. "The sooner we get out of here the better."

"Don't tell me you're going to row all the way back."

"What choice do we have?"

Jamie tried to think. "It's going to take forever."

Max continued to row, his eyes cautiously taking in the wooded area. "Check inside the seats and see if there is any tape I can use to repair the hose."

Jamie did as she was told. She lifted the lid on one seat and found a tackle box filled with lures and rusty hooks. The next seat held a couple of blankets that looked as though they hadn't been washed in years. "Oh, Jeez, there's a dead fish in here. No wonder the boat smells." She found a rusted ice pick, speared the fish and tossed it into the water.

Max, in the process of looking beneath his own seat, glanced up. "I wish you hadn't done that," he said, as the fish floated to the surface.

"It's disgusting."

"There are worse things."

"Yeah, like these nasty blankets. I can't believe my friend let this boat go to pot like he did. I'm surprised it still floats." She sighed. "Sorry, no tape." She continued to glance around uneasily as she talked. "Do you think Swamp Dog cut the hose? He would know shortcuts through the swamp. He could have found the boat, cut the hose and been out of here by the time we arrived back."

"That's a possibility," Max said.

"That would explain why he didn't kill us. He'd rather watch us die out here in the swamp."

"We're not going to die. You're with me, kiddo, and it just so happens I know a few survival skills."

"Oh, yeah, right. Like carrying your Visa Gold in case the restaurant doesn't accept American Express."

"You underestimate me."

Suddenly, something slammed against the boat. Jamie gasped and bolted to her feet. The boat rocked hard to one side.

"Sit down!" Max yelled. "It's a damn alligator."

Jamie tried to catch her balance but overcorrected. The boat veered to one side, dumping her into the river. She screamed.

Max saw the gator go for her. No time to pull her from the water. "Be still and shut up," he said, bringing the oar high in the air. The alligator was less than three feet from Jamie when Max brought it down on his wide snout. Jamie screamed again as the animal thrashed about. Max slammed the oar harder, aiming for the creature's eyes. The gator became still and sank beneath the surface.

Fear robbed Jamie of all logic. She was certain the alligator was right beside her; she could only imagine the horror of having him sink his teeth into her leg and pull her under. Frantically, she tried to pull herself up into the boat. "Let me help you," Max yelled. "You're going to—"

Too late. The small vessel flipped to its side and immediately began to fill with water. Max jumped into the river. It came to his shoulders. "Calm down," he ordered, reaching for Jamie. "We have to get to shore." He literally dragged her the short distance to the riverbank. She plopped onto the grass and gulped back the tears she felt forming behind her eyes.

"Jesus H. Christ, did you see the size of that thing?"

Max could see she was on the verge of hysteria, but he had to get the supplies from the boat before it went under. "Stay put." He grabbed a short but thick stick and started into the water. If the alligator or one of his relatives showed up, he might stand a fighting chance.

Jamie jumped to her feet. "Max, don't go back out there!" she cried. "He'll kill you." When he continued toward the boat, she stamped one foot. "Dammit, Max, are you going to *force* me to stand here and *watch* you get eaten alive by that damn gator? This is the most selfish thing you've ever done next to almost getting blown up by dynamite. Would you please try to keep my purse from getting wet? My cigarettes are inside."

Jamie watched the water closely for signs of movement as Max waded toward the boat. Hopefully, he had done enough physical damage to the alligator to drive it away. She knew that, for the most part, alligators avoided humans unless they were accustomed to being fed by them. But there were rogue gators who feared nothing and would sooner snap a man's head off than look at him. She spied a turtle sunning on a log nearby and wondered if she should try to catch it. They might have to cook it if they became stranded for any length of time. As though it had read her mind, the turtle slipped into the water and disappeared.

Max reached the boat. Jamie watched him grab as much as he could before hurrying back to shore, holding the items high to keep them from getting wet. Back on shore, he dumped everything out of the ice chest.

"What are you doing?" Jamie demanded.

"Trying to save the boat from sinking."

"You're not going back out there! Tell me you're not—" But he was already gone, and once again, she stood there feeling helpless. She watched him scoop water from the boat, using the ice chest like a bucket. He'd only managed to dip out a small amount before Jamie spied what looked to be a huge log floating in his direction. She knew better.

"Get out of the water, Max!"

Max looked in the direction in which she pointed.

Jamie knew he was trying to gauge the distance between himself and the alligator, see how much water he could dip out of the boat before it got close enough. The man was either an idiot or on a suicide mission.

"Get out of the water, Max! It's coming straight after you. He's big!" She suspected Max had seriously injured the other alligator and this one smelled fresh blood, just as the dead fish had brought on the first one.

"I swear to God!" Jamie cried. "If you don't get out of that river I'm coming in after you." Her heart was pounding in her chest like war drums. She glanced around for a stick or a rock. She remembered her metal fingernail file. She dumped everything from her purse and plucked the file from her personal stash. She started into the river.

Max glanced her way, found her waist high in water, and muttered a line of expletives. "Get back to shore!" he ordered. "I'm coming in." He swam away from the boat and caught up with her on the riverbank. "Are you crazy?" he yelled.

"Not as crazy as you."

"What's that?" he asked, checking her hand. "A fingernail file?" He looked incredulous. "You were going to kill a ten-foot alligator with a fingernail file?"

"I had to do something since you were too stupid to get out of the damn water."

"I was trying to save the boat. How do you think we're going to get out of here without a boat?"

"I've had nothing but trouble since the day you hit town. People try to kill me every time I turn around." She was so angry she didn't feel the tears roll down her cheeks.

"You're crying."

"I am *not* crying! I'm releasing stress. This is the only way I know how to do it without taking off your head."

One side of his mouth twitched.

"You know, you're damn cute with your wet hair slicked back, and your clothes plastered to you. This might not be a bad thing, the two of us stranded out here like this. We can finally explore our feelings for each other."

Jamie gaped at him. It was hard to know if he was serious because of the teasing glint in his dark eyes.

"I don't believe this," she said. She pressed her hands against her temple, half afraid she would lose her mind if he said another word.

"Face it, Jamie, you're stuck with me. At least until we get out of this place. You could do worse, you know. You could be stuck out here with Phillip."

"That's not one bit funny. Phillip would manage perfectly in a situation like this." Jamie paused. "Oh, no."

"What?"

They both stared. In the few minutes they'd spent arguing, the boat had filled with water and was barely visible. Beside it, the alligator waited.

"We're screwed," Max said.

Chapter
NINE

Deedee squealed in delight as Frankie led three over-sized ex-wrestlers through the front door and into the living room. "Oh, my goodness," she said, dwarfed beside the men who averaged six feet six in height, "we haven't seen you guys in years." She rushed up to Snakeman, who gave her a bone-crunching hug. "Where's your boa?" she asked.

"He died of old age. I was going to replace him, but now that I'm retired I enjoy traveling. The airlines wouldn't let me take him on the plane, even when I offered to pay for an entire row of seats in first class."

Snakeman's blond hair had dulled slightly, gray creeping in at his temples, but he was still in excellent physical shape.

Deedee hugged Big John and Choker, who'd earned his nickname by perfecting the headlocks once used by the world-renowned Ed "Strangler" Lewis, who'd begun his wrestling career in the early 1900s and was touted the greatest wrestler ever.

"It's just like old times, isn't it?" Frankie said, putting his arm around Deedee's shoulders.

"Why didn't you boys tell me you were coming?" Deedee asked.

Snakeman exchanged looks with Frankie. "We heard you've been having a little trouble so we're here to help. You don't think we'd just sit by twiddlin' our thumbs when you and Frankie need us."

"That's so sweet of you," Deedee said, looking from one to the other. "But I don't know what any of you can do about it."

"Frankie has men guarding the outside of the house. We're here to guard the inside." He paused. "And we wouldn't miss Frankie's election for anything."

Deedee's smile faded slightly. "We're so glad to have you," she said in an obvious attempt to sound like a gracious hostess. "How about I order some grub and let you gentlemen have some time to yourselves? I need to make a few phone calls."

"Did you hear from Max or Jamie?" Frankie asked before she left the room.

"No." She hurried away without another word.

"Your wife has gotten prettier," Snakeman said, "but she looks troubled. Maybe I shouldn't have told her why we're here."

"She'd figure it out," Frankie said.

"I wish you'd called us earlier," Big John told him.

Frankie shrugged. "I know you guys are busy."

Choker gave a grunt. "Never too busy to come to the aid of an old buddy."

Beenie came into the room with Choo-Choo and did a double take. "Well, smack my jaw, Scarlett," he said, patting his hair into place. "I didn't know we had company."

Frankie introduced the wrestlers. "This is Beenie, Deedee's personal assistant."

The three wrestlers nodded mutely.

"Sorry to interrupt, gentlemen. I'm looking for Deedee."

"She said she had to make some calls," Frankie said.

"Oh, well, I'll find her." Beenie paused and studied the wrestlers one by one, then turned for the door. He almost bumped into the butler, who carried a silver tray containing icy glasses and various designer beers. The housekeeper followed with the food.

"Oh, man, Vienna sausage," Snakeman said. "And pickled eggs. What a treat."

"I thought you guys might enjoy them. Deedee always insists on fixing all this fancy stuff when we have guests."

Once everyone was seated, Frankie became serious. "I called all of you because I don't know what else to do. Deedee's scared to death with all that's going on. I try to keep as much from her as I can."

"Have there been any new developments since we talked?" Big John asked.

"Not since the fire." He clasped his big hands together. "I'm worried about Deedee. I was hoping you guys would provide a distraction and make her feel safer at the same time."

Snakeman cracked his knuckles. His hands resembled small hams. "You just tell us what to do, and it's as good as done. Somebody tries to get past me, and he's a dead man."

"You two look like a couple of idiots," Mitzi said. "And Vito, you need to suck in your fat gut before you pop the buttons on that shirt."

"Would you just shut your trap?" he snapped. "They didn't have a uniform in my size."

"You should have asked for a large tent. What are you guys supposed to be anyway?"

"Security men," Lenny said.

"Oh, Jesus. How did you two thugs get a job like that?"

Vito gave her a smug look. "Because I happen to have friends in high places, Mitzi. Did that thought ever occur to you?"

She laughed out loud. "Which explains why we're driving a twenty-year-old car and keep getting our electricity cut off."

"I need something to hold in my stomach," Vito told Lenny.

Mitzi grunted. "I'd suggest liposuction, only they're going to need a fire hose to suck out all that flubber."

Vito wiped sweat from his brow. "Keep your fat mouth shut, Mitzi, you got that? I'm sick of listening to you."

"Fine. Go like that. You look like a fool, but that's never stopped you before. I'm taking a bath." She strode into the bathroom and slammed the door.

"Jesus, that woman is driving me right up the wall," Vito said.

"You could try being nicer to her," Lenny replied, "instead of mouthing off every time she says something."

"What the hell do you know about marriage? You should try living with the grand bitch of hell."

"Mitzi is still an attractive woman, dude. Why don't you stop chasing women and concentrate on your wife. Buy her some flowers or something."

"Just shut up, okay? I don't have time to discuss

my marriage woes; we got a job to do." He wiped his brow once more. "Damn woman is going to cause me to have a heart attack. Now, listen up. We won't have a lot of time for messing around once we get on the property tomorrow."

"Which reminds me. How did you manage to get us this job in the first place?"

"The guy we're working for took care of the paperwork. He's got connections, and he moves fast." Vito opened the top drawer of a battered dresser and pulled out a folder. "You need to study this in case Fontana's security chief asks questions."

Lenny opened it and read through it. "Man, this is awesome. I could get a job guarding the White House with this résumé. That's what it's called, right? A résumé?"

"Yeah. And look, we each got a letter of recommendation. We're good to go, pal. Now, like I was saying, we need to find Holt as soon as we get on the property. Whoever gets to him first does the hit, you got that?"

Lenny frowned. "What if I miss?"

Vito grabbed him by the collar. "You ain't gonna miss, asshole, because if you do I'm going to shoot *you*. Max Holt is not going to live to see the sun go down tomorrow night."

"Okay, don't panic," Max said, as Jamie, cigarette in hand, paced the riverbank. "This is *not* the end of the world."

She stopped and looked at him. "You don't realize the seriousness of this," she said. "Nobody, I mean *nobody*, ever comes down this part of the river. We're miles from civilization. Even if I *did* know how to get back, it would be impossible to get through this thicket. We'd need a machete."

"You worry too much, darlin'. The minute we turn up missing Frankie is going to call the police. Depending on how adept Lamar Tevis is, they'll eventually find my car back at the dock."

She crossed her arms and tapped one foot impatiently. "What are we supposed to do in the meantime?"

"We need to set up camp."

"You mean we're going to spend the night out here?"

"Think, Jamie. Deedee won't start worrying until we don't show up for dinner. By then it'll be dark. Even if they do find my car, they won't be able to send out a search party till daybreak."

"Oh, double damn."

"I say we look through our supplies, then start gathering wood." He pulled two flashlights and a package of batteries from the canvas sack and handed them to Jamie. "Would you do the honors?"

By the time Jamie put batteries into the flashlights and tested them, Max had finished his inventory. "We're not too bad off. The blankets could use a good washing, but they'll keep us warm during the night."

Jamie tried not to think about the night that lay ahead.

"We still have several hours of daylight left," Max said. "Better start gathering wood."

They went to work. Max found a stand of cane and broke off one, tying fishing string to the skinny end to use as a fishing pole. As Jamie gathered wood, he dug through the black dirt for worms. He baited the fishing pole. "You fish while I finish gathering wood," he said.

Jamie did as she was told. If they were to survive through the night, which wasn't likely, they would have to work together. Max had stripped off his shirt and begun digging a broad hole near the riverbank using sticks and pieces of rock as a shovel. He placed several larger rocks at the bottom of the hole. Jamie tried not to stare as the muscles in his arms and back flexed and contracted while he worked, but it was hard to concentrate on her task when he looked so darn good.

Max caught her looking. He sat back on the heels of his boots and held his arms out in offering. "Take a good look, Jamie. This could all be yours."

Her look was deadpan. Suddenly, her line jerked. "I've got one!" she cried.

"Go for it," Max said.

"This sucker is big. I can tell by the way he's tugging."

Max watched her, a smile playing across his lips. "I want mine filleted and marinated in papaya juice and served with Caesar salad and fresh asparagus."

Jamie struggled with the pole. She gave one hard jerk and pulled in a medium-sized bass. Her eyes popped open at the sight. "Look at the size of that sucker!"

Max was still looking at Jamie as she stood there, pole in both hands, grinning from ear to ear. The fish flipped about in protest. "Nice-looking fish," he said. "Where's yours?"

"There's more where this one came from, Holt."

Jamie managed to catch two more fish in the next half hour, during which time Max cleared a dry area of limbs and brush where they could later sleep. The blankets were still hanging from tree limbs, airing out.

Jamie presented her three fish. "Dinnuh is served," she said.

Max looked up from his work. "How are you at cleaning them?"

Jamie tossed her head. "I don't clean fish, Bubba." She gave him a speculative glance. "And I'll bet you don't know how. I'll bet you've never cleaned a fish in your life. Probably, the only time you've ever seen one is on a dinner plate with lemon slices on the side."

Max just smiled.

The sun was low in the sky by the time Max began cooking the fish he'd expertly cleaned while Jamie shared a soft drink with him. They only had a couple of bottled waters and had agreed to ration them.

When the fish were done, Max laid them on the lid of the ice chest. They'd watched the ice chest itself float down the river.

He and Jamie waited until the fish had cooled before tasting it.

"It could use a little seasoning," Jamie said.

"Next time have Emeril do your cooking."

"I wasn't complaining," she said. "Actually, it's very good."

"Thank you," Max said. "Coming from you, I consider that a high compliment."

Jamie looked at him. "What do you mean, coming from me?"

"You're not always easy to get along with. Some women would be happy to be in your shoes right now." He grinned.

Jamie knew he was goading her. Max Holt enjoyed getting her riled. "I'm sure that's the case," she said matter-of-factly. "No doubt they would have cleaned the fish *and* chewed it for you, but I'm not that desperate for a man's attention."

They stared at each other over the campfire. Night had settled in, cooling the temperature. The air felt good on Jamie's skin. As she looked at Max, taking in the dark hair and eyes in the soft firelight, she could easily understand why women flocked to him.

"You look mighty fine sitting by a campfire, Miss Swift, with your hair shining like gold in the firelight. I'll bet it feels like silk."

Jamie dropped her gaze, but she could feel Max's eyes on her. She felt self-conscious, knowing he missed nothing. "You're staring," she said, still refusing to look up.

His voice was soft. "How do you know?"

"I feel your eyes on me."

"I'm looking at your neck, and I'm thinking—"

"Stop it, Max." She turned and looked toward the water, which was too black to see.

"Know what else I'm thinking? You have a nice profile. Strong stubborn chin, dainty little upturned nose, high cheekbones. A perfect face, Jamie."

Jamie felt her throat tighten. For some reason she felt very sad. She felt bereft, as though something very important was missing in her life, and she'd only just realized it.

She had planned her future down to the last detail, and Max Holt had stepped into her life and made her question it for the first time. Max Holt, who thrived on taking chances and lived life on the very edge; Max, who would think nothing of picking up and leaving for a new adventure at the drop of a hat. Like her mother.

Jamie blinked back a tear and stared up at the night sky where stars winked back at her, bringing back memories of her youth. "This reminds me of when I was a Girl Scout," she said, trying to hide the emotion in her voice.

"You were a Girl Scout?"

"Does that surprise you?"

"Not really. I can see you going door to door threatening people to buy cookies."

She smiled while her eyes sought out the different constellations her father had taught her long ago. "Hey, I was a sweet little Girl Scout. Naïve, too. I was probably the last Girl Scout to find out how babies are made." She paused. "I'm still pretty naïve, I guess. Either that or I'm just plain dumb."

"What do you mean?"

Finally, she looked at him. And wished she hadn't. Max Holt was even more handsome with the fire casting shadows across his face and turning his hair an inky black. She could almost sense his desire, and it would be so easy to give in to it. But then what? She shoved the thought aside. "This whole business about missing tax dollars has me thinking," she said.

"Yeah?"

"I thought it was all a bunch of malarkey, even though people speculated about it now and then. I realize I didn't *want* to believe it because I was afraid people I grew up with and cared about were involved."

"We always want to think the best of people."

Jamie was quiet for a moment. Finally, she looked at him. "What was your family like?" she asked, realizing she was suddenly curious about him. She smiled. "I would imagine there was never a dull moment with Deedee around."

"Deedee and I weren't close because of our age difference. I was an accident, so to speak. A mistake, as far as my parents were concerned."

"Oh."

"Don't worry, I don't feel like a mistake. My enormous ego, as you refer to it, has convinced me I have too much to give to this world. But there was a time when I believed they were right.

"I was very fortunate. My cousin and his wife took me in when I was sixteen so I was raised in a loving home and given every opportunity to succeed. I had a lot more than most kids. There are times I miss the normalcy of that life."

"I would imagine it's hard for you to live a normal life under the circumstances. I mean you're so well-known."

"I try to maintain a low profile. That's why I keep my place in Virginia. It's fairly private."

"Max?"

"Yeah?"

"What's it like being so damn rich?"

He laughed. "I don't know, Jamie. I've never been poor so I have nothing to compare it to."

"Then you'll never be able to say you've lived a full life," she said laughingly. "You'll never know the humiliation of bouncing a check or having your credit card denied in front of your friends. What kind of life is that?"

"I'm lucky that somebody else pays my bills," he said, "but what you have to realize is, I don't think about money."

"Because you have so much of it?"

"No. Because rich people can get as obsessive about money as those who don't have a lot of it. If I sat around and worried about where every dime of my money went or whether I was investing it wisely, I wouldn't have time to enjoy my life. I just don't think about it."

Jamie couldn't imagine living without money problems because she'd always raked and scraped to keep her head above water, even when her father was alive.

"I try to do the best I can," Max went on. "I try to concentrate on doing the next right thing. Sometimes it works and sometimes it doesn't."

Jamie enjoyed hearing him talk. His voice was nice. It lulled her into a sense of well-being. A splash sounded near shore. Jamie shone her light in that direction.

"It's just a fish," Max said. "If you're feeling anxious you could always sit closer."

"I'm not afraid of a silly old fish."

"What *are* you afraid of?"

She looked at him, brow wrinkled.

"Let me guess," he said. "You are afraid of not knowing what tomorrow will bring. Am I right?"

It was uncanny the way he was able to read her. "I suppose you never worry."

"I'd be a liar if I told you I wasn't concerned about what's been going on, but I usually let tomorrow take care of itself."

Jamie yawned. "I'm beat. This has been a long day."

"Why don't you rest?"

She hesitated. "Yeah, right."

"I'm not sleepy. I'll let you know if the boogeyman shows up."

A few minutes later, Jamie settled herself on top of the blanket Max had laid on the ground, and she covered herself with the other one. Surprisingly enough, she was able to relax. She peered out at Max who continued to sit quietly by the fire. Even though he'd claimed he wasn't tired, she could see the fatigue around his eyes and mouth, and she realized he was staying awake and keeping watch. Once again, she felt a lump in her throat.

Was she making a mistake by marrying Phillip? Could it be that love offered more than security, companionship, and a warm body beside her at night? She had thought herself in love before, but it wasn't until Phillip came along that she began to take it seriously.

Phillip picked fresh flowers and brought them to her door because he'd read somewhere it was supposed to be more romantic than store bought. Phillip always saw that Jamie sat at her favorite table in the restaurant they frequented, sang in her ear when they danced close, and had offered to bail her out financially when he'd discovered how hard she was struggling to make ends meet.

But as Jamie drifted off to sleep, her last thoughts were not of Phillip but of Max.

Sometime during the night, Jamie awoke. "Max, are you asleep?"

He was lying beside her. "Just resting. Are you cold?"

"A little."

"Scoot closer. I'll share some body heat."

Jamie was only too happy to comply. She curled against him, seeking his warmth. It felt safe, even in a place filled with danger. She tried to soak in the feeling because it was the first time she could remember experiencing it full force. It amazed her that Max, the man who made her crazy by taking so many chances, provoked such feelings of comfort and security.

Suddenly, Max shivered.

"Are you cold, too?" she asked.

"No, I'm shivering for a different reason."

Oh, God, he was obviously feeling sexy, she thought. What to do, what to do? Jamie had to admit she was feeling sexy as well. Damn, she was lusting after Max Holt. Okay, that did not necessarily make her a bad person. She suspected every red-blooded female under the age of ninety would experience a feeling of desire lying next to a man like Max. She was no different, only that she had a good man who wanted to make her his wife and give her a normal home, emphasis on normal. What would Phillip think if he knew she was snuggled up against Max in the woods beside a gator-infested swamp?

She tried to pull back. "I don't think—"

"Try not to think right now, Jamie," he said.

She turned her face away.

Max rose up on one elbow. "I wish you'd stop running from me."

"I'm not—" She paused.

He put a finger beneath her chin and gently lifted her face to his. "I'm going to kiss you, Jamie. You can punch me in the jaw afterward if you like, but I think it'll be worth it."

She opened her mouth to reply, but it was too late. Max covered her mouth with his. All thinking ceased. It was as if someone had just reached inside her head, snatched her brain and tossed it aside, as if to say, "You won't be needing this right now." Her body went wacko, nerve endings jangling as loudly as the old pots and pans the junkman tied to his pickup truck as he bounced along the road looking through people's garbage piles. And what the heck was going on with her stomach? It felt like there were eight lords a-leaping inside, all of them wearing cleats with pointy toes. And that wasn't the worst of it. The worst of it was she was enjoying every minute of it.

Max slipped his tongue inside her mouth, and

Jamie knew she was a goner. Instead of using her common sense, as she should have, Jamie pressed herself against his solid body, seeking more. If somebody had come along at that moment and told her she was engaged to another man she would have called them a liar because the last thing on her mind right then was Phillip Standish.

She pulled him closer.

He was hard as granite.

And she was hotter than a barbecue grill on the Fourth of July.

He slipped his knee between her thighs. She gasped and held her breath. Oh, double damn. She didn't try to stop him when he reached for the buttons on her blouse and undid them slowly. He pushed her bra away and touched her nipple with his tongue. It felt hot against the night air. She sighed as he tugged on it with his lips, and the sensation ran the full length of her and settled low in her belly. Even as he twirled his tongue around the nipple, his free hand massaged her other breast.

She opened her mouth to speak, but Max cut her off, planting his lips firmly on hers. He nibbled her bottom lip before slipping his tongue inside. Jamie felt as though she were sinking into the fragrant earth. She wrapped her arms around him and kissed him back, loving the taste and texture of his mouth. She ran her fingers through his hair as she had wanted to many times before, and it was just as thick and silky as she had suspected.

Jamie moaned and arched against him, even as Max raised his head and dropped soft kisses across her cheeks and forehead and finally her closed eyes. He moved over her, pressing himself against her intimately. Jamie sucked in her breath.

Max pulled his head back after a moment. "Are you okay? You're not breathing."

"Huh?" She opened her eyes, blinked several times. "Am I too heavy?"

"Uh, no."

"I want to make love to you, Jamie," he said, his face a fraction of an inch from hers. "I want to kiss you all over and bury myself deep inside of you."

"Then what?"

He looked confused. "Well, then I want to hold you warm and naked against me through the night."

Jamie searched his face, saw the passion. "But then what?" she repeated.

He shook his head as if to clear it. "I'm confused. I don't know how to answer that."

Of course he didn't know the answer. He didn't even understand the question. Common sense returned with the force of a bucket of cold water in the face.

"I'm telling you, something is very wrong," Deedee said, pacing the living room as Frankie and the other wrestlers sat quietly, each seemingly lost in thought. Tears welled in her eyes. "Max and Jamie could be seriously injured or worse for all we know."

"Calm down, sweetheart," Frankie said, reaching for her hand and squeezing it. "Lamar has every one of his men looking for Max's car. I'm sure he'll call soon."

"It's three o'clock in the morning!" Deedee said. "Lamar has been searching for four hours. This is not a big town."

Frankie's campaign manager, Aaron, handed her a handkerchief. He'd come for dinner and stayed when Max and Jamie hadn't shown up. "Your brother is smart," he said. "He can hold his own in any situation. Besides, as soon as Frankie's withdrawal from the mayoral race is announced, this should all die down."

"You're withdrawing from the race?" Deedee asked in disbelief.

"Isn't that what you wanted?"

She glanced away.

"I don't like this sitting around waiting," Snakeman said. "Me and the boys could go out on our own and look for them. We have cell phones so we can stay in contact."

Big John stood. "I'm ready when you are."

"I'm sorry you have to go through this," Frankie said to Deedee. "I would never have run for mayor if I'd known this sort of thing would happen."

"You should have talked to me before you made the decision to drop out," she replied. "I don't like that you're doing it for me, and I don't want people to see you as a quitter. If you believe you can do something about the corruption in this town, stay in the race. We need to know who's been trying to hurt us, Frankie."

Frankie and his manager exchanged looks. Aaron scooted toward the edge of his chair. "Mrs. Fontana, I would like to see Frankie stay in the race myself, but you're going to have to be prepared to go all the way with this. Things are probably going to get much worse before they get better."

Deedee hitched her chin high. "Frankie and me aren't quitters. Besides, my husband is good and honest, and he will clean up this town. *We* will work together."

Frankie took her hand, and the look on his face was filled with love. "I don't know what to say, Deedee."

"You're going to make a fine mayor, Frankie," she

said, "and I'm going to be the best mayor's wife I can.
If you care that much about this little town, so do I."

The portable phone on the coffee table rang, causing Deedee to jump. "Jeez!" She snatched it up and
listened. "Are you sure?" she asked after a moment.
"Okay, we're on our way." She hung up. "They've
found Max's car. It's at the boat landing."

"Let's go," Frankie said.

Frankie, Deedee, and Aaron made the drive in record time. Lamar Tevis was on his car radio, and several
deputies scouted the area. A few minutes later, Snakeman pulled up, followed by Big John and the Choker.
Frankie filled them in.

Deedee climbed into Max's car while her husband
and the others looked on. "Talk to me, Muffin," she
said. "It's Deedee."

Snakeman looked at Frankie. "What's she doing?"

"Max created a computer with voice recognition,"
he said. "She keeps up with his every move."

Deedee waited for Muffin's response, but there was
none. "Look, Muffin, Max has already told me how
stubborn you are, but this is an emergency. Max is
missing. I think he's in trouble."

"Deedee Fontana?" a voice said from an unseen
speaker.

"Yeah, it's me."

Big John and Choker stepped closer to the car.

"I have a question for you, Deedee," Muffin said.
"You once broke into Nick's house looking for a piece
of jewelry. What was it called?"

"You mean my Stargio?"

"What exactly is a Stargio?"

Deedee looked at Frankie and shrugged her shoulders as if confused.

"I think Muffin wants to make sure it's really you," Frankie whispered.

"Oh." Deedee looked at the dashboard. "The Stargio was a piece of jewelry specifically designed for a dress I'd planned to wear to the ambassador's ball. I broke into Nick's house and set off all his alarms. I'm lucky I wasn't tossed into the slammer, but the cops were used to me setting off Max's alarms."

"Nice to meet you, Deedee," Muffin said. "Tell me about Max."

"He's been missing since this afternoon."

"Miss Swift is with him," Muffin said. It was more a statement than a question.

"Yeah."

"Oh, damn."

Big John nudged Snakeman. "It cusses. I've never heard a computer cuss."

"I specifically warned Max not to go through with it," Muffin said. "He has put himself and Miss Swift in serious danger."

"Where is he?" Deedee asked.

"They borrowed a boat so they could visit a man called Swamp Dog."

"Swamp Dog!" Deedee shrieked. "You can't be serious. He's supposed to be some kind of murdering sleazebag lunatic."

"Have you contacted the police department?"

"Yes. They're here now."

"I can arrange a rescue team," Muffin said.

She was quiet for a few minutes. "I've lined up a chopper, but they can't start searching until daybreak."

Deedee sounded surprised. "You did it that fast?"

"I *have* to work fast when it comes to your brother. The minute you see Max, tell him I have the information he asked for. By the way, are you still having hot flashes?"

Deedee blinked. "As a matter of fact, I am. Everybody thinks I'm menopausal."

"You're too young for that."

Deedee shot a look at Frankie. "Yeah, I know."

"Still, I might be able to help you."

Deedee glanced in the direction of the men. "Excuse me, gentlemen, this is a private conversation." She closed the door and locked it. "Okay, Muffin, I'm listening."

A regal Annabelle Standish stood at the wet bar in the study of her Georgian mansion and poured her best brandy into two snifters. She wore a satin dressing gown and bedroom slippers, but her hair and makeup looked as fresh as it had when she'd walked out of the house that morning. At fifty-seven, her face was as smooth as a thirty-year-old's, thanks to the daily beauty regimen she followed, which included a brisk walk each morning after her first cup of coffee. Her husband had been dead a good ten years now, but she had never remarried. She filled her days with luncheons and dinner parties and, of course, her charity work.

She handed one of the brandy snifters to Phillip. "Are you okay?"

He didn't respond. Instead, he raised his glass to his lips and drained it.

"That's an insult to good brandy, Phillip. You're supposed to sip it slowly. One would think you'd been raised on Wild Turkey."

"What time is it?" he asked, obviously ignoring her.

"It's only ten minutes later than the last time you asked." Annabelle's look softened. "Why don't you try to rest? I'll listen for the telephone."

"I should have made Jamie stay here. I should have insisted."

"It wouldn't have done any good, Phillip. That girl has a mind of her own, and there's no budging her once she makes a decision. I can't complain, though, because I'm just like her. What I don't understand is why she spends so much time with that Fontana woman."

"They're best friends."

Annabelle sniffed. "Well, once I introduce her into nice society, Jamie will make new friends, Lord help us."

"Stop acting like a snob, Mother. Frankie and Deedee Fontana are fine people."

"Well, I know that, son, but they aren't—" She paused.

"Up to snuff?" Phillip said.

"That's not at all what I meant."

"You know what your problem is, Mother?" he said. "You do everything you can to help the less fortunate, but your standards are way up there when it comes to choosing your friends and acquaintances."

"You're being unfair to me, Phillip. I care just as much about this town as your friend Frankie Fontana. The only difference is I was making progress long before he showed up with his redheaded wife and built that god-awful house that I don't mind telling you is an embarrassment to this town. Wouldn't surprise me if that wife of his wallpapered it in red satin. That's what happens when people have more money than they do common sense. I only hope she'll try to tone down that hair before the wedding." Annabelle took a sip of her drink. "Speaking of that family, what do you know about this Max Holt person other than what we've read in the newspaper?"

Phillip stood and walked toward the wet bar where he poured another drink. "I'm having trouble getting a fix on the guy. He's very private. I know he's assisting Frankie in the tax-fund investigation, but that's about all I know."

"Well, he spends entirely too much time with Jamie, if you ask me. It doesn't look good for an engaged woman to be in the company of another man. Won't be long before the rumors start flying." She sniffed. "The fact they're both missing is certain to start tongues wagging."

"I'm more concerned about Jamie's safety right now than I am local gossip," Phillip said. "Besides, I trust Jamie."

"Well, of course you do. It's not Jamie I'm worried about. Mr. Holt has quite a reputation with the ladies from what I understand. I fear he'll take advantage of her.

"I hope she settles down after your marriage," Annabelle continued. "Perhaps I can get her involved in my work."

"Jamie will never give up that newspaper," Phillip replied. "She's determined to make it what it was when her grandfather ran it. Before her father made a mess of everything."

Annabelle looked thoughtful. "She might sell if somebody offered her enough money."

"I see the gears turning in your head already, Mother. You need to stay out of it and let Jamie do what she likes best."

"You don't understand, son. There is nothing more satisfying than helping someone in need. The Standish women have never worked for a paycheck. We don't need the money, and it won't look right for your wife to be working sixty hours a week. Folks will think you can't take care of her. Of course that will be an unnecessary consideration if she decides to take up with this Max fellow."

Phillip gave a weary sigh. "Go to bed, Mother, before you give yourself a migraine. I'll worry about Jamie."

Jamie was awakened by a sound far off in the distance. A helicopter. No doubt, it was searching for them. She sat up. Max was in the process of covering the fire with dirt. He looked pensive.

The chopper grew closer. Without a word, Jamie stood and tried to brush the wrinkles from her clothes. She shook her blanket and folded it. They were being rescued. So why was she feeling sad?

"Uh, Max?"

He looked up. "Yeah?"

It was impossible to read his expression. Jamie wondered what he was thinking. "About last night."

"You didn't do anything wrong, Jamie. I started the whole thing. Forget it."

"Forget it? Is that all you have to say?"

He stood and walked closer. "You've got your entire life mapped out to the nth degree. You've obviously thought it through carefully, and I respect that." He sighed and wiped his hand down his face. "I need to finish the job I started and go home."

Jamie nodded. Max was being noble. It was the right thing to do, and he was doing it. No doubt he'd spent much of the night thinking about it, just as she had. "Yes," she agreed. "It *is* the right thing to do."

Chapter
TEN

The pilot set the chopper down near the boat landing. Max and Jamie waited until the blades stopped turning before they climbed out. Deedee was the first to greet them.

"I've been worried sick," she said, hugging Jamie, then Max. "Eeyeuuw, you guys smell like swamp water."

Jamie saw Phillip, waiting, the relief in his eyes palpable. She went to him. He hugged her tightly against him. "I haven't slept all night for worrying about you," he said. "You don't know what a relief it was when Lamar called and said you were okay. But why in God's name would you go out to Swamp Dog's place?"

Jamie knew he was still upset over the fact she'd been missing. "Two attempts were made on my life, Phillip. Deedee and Frankie's house was set on fire. You were there to witness it. What do you expect me to do, just look the other way and end up with a bullet in my back?"

"That's why we have the law, Jamie. You have absolutely no business getting involved in an investigation. When did you become a cop?"

She touched his cheek. "I'm safe, Phillip. Let's talk about it later."

"I'm sorry. You look exhausted. I'll bet you didn't sleep a wink last night."

"Actually, I slept better than I thought I would. Max kept watch so I could rest."

"Let's go home," Deedee said. "We're all exhausted. I don't know about the rest of you, but I need a nap, and Max and Jamie are probably starving."

"Actually, Jamie caught enough fish for a small army," Max said.

Phillip looked from one to the other. "Sounds like a scene straight out of *Robinson Crusoe*. I never knew my bride-to-be was so adventuresome."

Jamie gave him an odd look. "What's wrong with you?" she whispered.

Phillip pulled her aside. "What's going on with you two? How's it going to look to everybody that you spent the night with Max Holt? I understand he's quite the legend when it comes to women."

"We had no choice," Jamie said. "Our boat capsized. I was more concerned about staying alive than I was what the gossipmongers might say."

"I swear, Jamie, you do the strangest things."

She was losing her patience with him. "Someone tried to *kill* me, Phillip. Don't you *get* it? Does it seem so odd to you that I might want to find out who that person is?" She realized she was shouting.

"That's Lamar's job."

"I could be dead and buried before Lamar finds anything."

"I'm going to be your husband. It's up to me to see that you're safe."

"Then work with me instead of against me."

He wiped his brow. "This is not a good time for us to talk," he said. "I haven't slept all night, and for all I knew you were dead. I need time to calm down, I guess. I'll call you later." He climbed into his Mercedes and pulled away.

Jamie watched the car disappear around the bend. When she looked up she found Max standing there. "Looks like you need a ride," he said.

They climbed into Max's car after agreeing to meet the others back at the house.

"Good morning, Muffin," Max said as soon as the bars had closed over them. "Did you miss me?"

"It's about time you got back," she said in a terse voice. "I was so worried I almost rebooted my system. Did you meet Swamp Dog?"

"Yeah. I'm thinking of fixing you up with him."

"I'm not in the mood for your jokes, Max. Besides, I'm involved with a laptop at MIT, but every time we get into a really good chat you beep me, and I have to brush him off. Which proves I'm not supposed to have any sort of personal life. Your staff is worried about you. They think I'm not doing my job. That doesn't look good for me."

"Tell them I'm okay, and there's nothing to worry about."

"I'm doing so as we speak. I have to tell you, Max, there's too much stress in this job. I should give my notice. I want to work for someone who lives a normal life."

"Nobody is normal, Muffin. Besides, you'd get bored. What do you have for me?"

"So it's business as usual," she said.

"Okay, I'm sorry I caused you to worry."

She sighed. "From now on I'm keeping my personal

feelings to myself. I don't care if you want to roller-skate naked down Mount Everest, you got that? Just don't tell me about it ahead of time."

"The information, Muffin."

"Does the name Harlan Rawlins mean anything to you?"

"Sounds familiar."

"He's a big-time tent revivalist from Tennessee."

"I don't attend many tent revivals, but now that I think of it, I've read about him."

"Harlan was one of several who put in a bid for your television network."

"My broker handled the sale."

"Harlan has a huge following, and from what I gather he's a fanatic. Crazy, too."

"Aren't most fanatics?"

"Anyway, seems he wasn't happy that you chose to sell the network to someone else. He was counting on using it for his ministry so he could spread the good word."

"He has that kind of money?"

"Like I said, he put in a bid, but your broker sold it to an educational company instead so Rawlins lost out. I hear some of his followers are big on grudges."

"Just how big *is* this ministry?"

"We're talking hundreds of thousands of people. He comes off as this small-town minister who's barely making ends meet. He uses fear tactics on his congregation. You know, fire and brimstone and all that. He's got a radio spot three days a week, including Sunday. I listened to one of his so-called sermons yesterday. It would give children nightmares."

"Other than that, why is he scary?"

"He's got friends in bad places."

"How bad?"

"Mob connections. And that means professional hit men."

Max was thoughtful. "If that's the case it would explain the type of weapon used at the *Gazette,* but it doesn't explain Frankie's threats."

"These guys could be playing mind games. There's another possibility. Maybe they're using Frankie's political aspirations to throw off suspicion."

Max and Jamie exchanged looks. "Have you found anything out about the missing tax funds?"

"Max, the people who run this town are shady. It's a good-old-boy system, as we suspected. Before city council approves a contract for a new building or park, they set requirements so that only one or two people can possibly meet their standards."

"You're saying it doesn't matter if a bid is overpriced because they're going to give the job to someone in the loop."

"Precisely."

"Have you been able to find out who's on the take?"

"I've checked bank accounts. Everything looks normal. I don't know where the money is going, but it's going somewhere."

"Out of the country probably."

"Deedee mentioned there are three wrestlers staying with them," Muffin said. "How well do you know them and what are they doing there?"

"I've known them since I was a kid. I think they are mostly there for emotional support, but I wouldn't be surprised if they decided to offer their own brand of security."

"We have to consider every possibility," Muffin said.

"Listen, I need a favor—"

"Yeah, yeah, yeah," she grumbled. "What is it this time?"

"What's wrong with you?"

"What's wrong with me? Did it ever occur to you to say thank you for what I've done thus far? My job isn't easy, you know. You get to sleep at night, I don't. I have to work double time to keep up with you. I'm tired, Max."

"Not to mention irritable."

"You should try sitting in this hot car all day. The least you could do—" She paused and sniffed. "Is park it in the shade."

Max and Jamie exchanged looks. "Are you crying, for Pete's sake?" he asked.

"No." Her voice broke.

"Yes you are."

"You've upset her, Max," Jamie said.

"Jamie's right. I need my space, Max. I never have time to myself."

"Jeez, Muffin, I can't believe what I'm hearing."

"Believe it. You don't appreciate me. You never ask me how I'm doing or whether I've had a good day. You leave me baking in the hot sun all day, and you make one demand after another. I'm sick of it. Here you are, this big-shot multimillionaire living the good life, Mr. Big-Shot Super Genius, and I'm stuck here all day, waiting for my next assignment. Everybody thinks you're brilliant. I never get any credit."

"She's right, Max," Jamie said. "You could act a little more appreciative."

Max sat there, obviously stymied. "I created her, Jamie. She has a memory bank so vast that she can be fed up-to-date information around the clock. I made her what she is today."

"And he never fails to remind me," Muffin said.

"What do you want, Muf?" he asked.

"You could turn the air conditioner on high for starters. I'm so hot it feels like all my wires are going to melt."

"Have you been talking to Deedee?"

"Yes. I'm the only one who would listen to the poor woman. I'm the only one who'll take the time to research her condition. She's in perimenopause and nobody seems to care. You don't know what that does to a woman's hormones."

Max shook his head sadly and turned to Jamie. "She's obviously processed everything Deedee said, just as she processes what my staff and I feed into her. She has also adopted some of Deedee's quirks, and now she thinks she's having hot flashes."

"I *am* having hot flashes," Muffin said.

"I'll have to reprogram her," Max whispered to Jamie, "but I don't have time right now."

"Stop talking about me like I'm not here," Muffin snapped.

"Tell you what, Muf," he said. "I promise to be more considerate in the future."

Silence.

"And I'm sorry, okay? From now on I'll try to park you in the shade."

She sniffed. "Thank you, Max."

They arrived back at the house, and Max was glad to see more security personnel in place. While Jamie talked to Vera and Mike Henderson on the telephone, Max met with Frankie and security chief Tim Duncan.

"Wanted to let you know I've hired a few more security people in case you see some new faces," Duncan said.

Max smiled. "I'm surprised you were able to find additional men considering we've got a small army surrounding this property and several others at the newspaper. I assume you ran a check on everybody."

"They're clean."

The butler knocked and stepped inside, wearing his usual overcoat. "Excuse me, Mr. Fontana, but there is, uh, a *person* here to see Mr. Holt."

"Who is it?" Max asked.

"He wouldn't give me his name, and I didn't press. I hesitated inviting him in."

"I'll be right back," Max said. He understood the butler's reluctance as soon as he opened the front door. Swamp Dog stood on the other side, surrounded by half a dozen security personnel. Max arched both brows high on his forehead. "I'm surprised to see you here."

Swamp Dog regarded the security guards with a look of contempt. "Get lost," he said.

Max nodded at the men. "It's okay." He waited until they were gone before speaking. "What can I do for you?"

"I'm here to talk about your job offer."

Max led the man into the study and introduced him to Frankie and Duncan. Both men looked stunned. "Swamp Dog will be working with us," Max said.

"I work alone," Swamp Dog replied. "I come and go as I please, and I don't take orders from no one. Anyone gives me shit, I cut their gizzard out and feed it to 'em."

"Yes, well, that sounds fair," Frankie said, eyeing Max. "What will you need to get started?" he asked.

Swamp Dog pulled a .47 Magnum from the waistband of his jeans, and a hunting knife from one boot.

The thin blade flashed in the morning light. "This ought to do it. Now, where can I grab some grub? I don't work on an empty stomach."

Frankie called for the butler, who was waiting nearby. "Please take Mister, uh, take our guest into the kitchen and see that the cook feeds him."

Once they were alone, Duncan turned to Max. "Are you sure this guy is safe? Looks like he wouldn't have trouble putting a hole in his mother's head while she slept."

"You might keep an eye on him," was all Max said.

Frankie buried his head in his hands. "I'm going along with you on this one, Max, even though I have my doubts. But we can't let Deedee see him." He'd barely gotten the words out of his mouth before a shriek sounded from the kitchen.

"Eeeyeuw!" Deedee cried loud enough to shatter glass. "Who are you?"

Frankie shook his head sadly. "Too late."

An hour later, once they'd showered and downed a few cups of coffee, Max and Jamie climbed inside his car and headed for the newspaper office. The perplexed look on Jamie's face told him she'd seen Swamp Dog as well.

"I don't like it, Max. I don't trust the guy one bit."

"Relax," he said. "I know what I'm doing."

Muffin spoke. "Max, turn on the damn air conditioner."

He did as she asked. "Still having hot flashes?"

Muffin grunted. "I'm so hot I'm afraid I'm going to cause the engine to overheat."

"Sorry to hear it, Muffin," Jamie said. "Too bad you can't go on hormone replacement therapy." She looked at Max and shook her head. "I don't believe I said that."

He smiled. "Muffin, you're just the person I need to talk to."

"What *now*?"

"I want the names of this town's city officials. All of them, including the city manager and the auditor. When you get that, run a complete background check on them."

"I've already started."

"Thanks. You got anything on Hodges or that preacher yet?"

"I'm concentrating on Hodges right now since he seems to be our immediate concern, but you know what it's like to breach military firewalls. I'll get back to you when I have something."

When Jamie and Max arrived at the newspaper office they found the building under renovation, inside and out. The large window in front had been replaced and men on ladders were filling cracks in the concrete. Inside, it was much the same.

Vera looked up from her battered computer. She glared at Jamie. "If you weren't a grown woman I would take you over my knee and give you the beating of your life."

"Good morning, Vera."

"Don't 'good morning' me. I didn't get a wink of sleep last night after Lamar called me. Have you lost your mind, going off like that to find some lunatic killer in the middle of the swamp?" She looked at Max. "I would have expected something like this from Jamie, what with her being so flighty and irresponsible—"

"Flighty and irresponsible?" Jamie squeaked.

"But I would never have expected it from you," Vera told Max.

"I didn't want to do it," he said, "but Jamie threatened to go alone."

Jamie's jaw dropped open as she snapped her head his way. Her irritation flared when she noted one corner of his mouth twitch. "Why, you—"

"Don't even try it," Vera said. "After what you've put me through the last thing I'm going to tolerate is foul language." She snatched up several pink slips. "Would you like your telephone messages before you go traipsing off to Lord-knows-where?"

Jamie was still tossing dark looks in Max's direction as she took the slips from Vera. "I'll be in my office," she said.

"You can't go in your office, the painters are working in there."

"I'll work in the conference room. Alone."

"They're working in there, as well."

"Damn. Well, where the heck am *I* supposed to work?"

Vera held up the kitty. "Twenty-five cents, please."

"Allow me," Max said, reaching into his pocket for a coin.

"No way," Jamie said. "I'll pay out of my own damn pocket. Oh, double damn, I—" She slapped her hand over her mouth.

"You're up to seventy-five cents now," Vera said. "If I were you I'd consider keeping my mouth shut."

"This is the most ridiculous thing I've ever heard of," Jamie snapped, digging through her wallet for the money. "I'm a grown woman, and I'll say what I please." She handed Vera a dollar bill. "Don't forget to credit me a quarter."

Vera stuffed the money through a slit in the plastic top covering a coffee can. "The painters say it'll take a week or so to paint the entire building, what with all the patching and scraping they have to do. They're going to do the interior painting at night so we won't have to close, but we'll probably have to keep all of the windows open. It's going to be hot as Hades around here."

"Go ahead and purchase as many fans as you like," Max said. He looked at Jamie. "We don't need to hang around anyway. We've got other business to tend to."

"Like what?" Jamie and Vera echoed.

"We need to visit city hall."

"You can't just walk into city hall and start asking for documents," Jamie said.

"Yes, but your fiancé can."

They climbed into the car a few minutes later.

"I've got some information for you, Max," Muffin said.

"Let's hear it."

"The city mostly uses Beaumont Savings and Loan. Obviously the original loan officer didn't have much faith in how the local government was running things because he charged the city a high rate. Sounds like he thought it was risky. Once a new board of directors were elected, the rate dropped."

"Who's on the board?"

"Pretty much the same people who sit on city council. No conflict of interest there, right? And the firm who handles the city's legal contracts is Standish and Moss."

"Phillip does it pro bono," Jamie said proudly. "The Standishes have always been generous. His mother is on a committee that raises money for charitable causes. She doesn't do it for money. Heck, she doesn't need money."

"Obviously not," Muffin replied. "She charges an annual salary of one dollar. I'm going to have to check them out, Jamie," she added.

Jamie stiffened. "How about me? Are you checking me out as well?"

"Of course not, but I have to look into the people who run things in this town." She paused. "Phillip and his family are among them. As is the city manager who had done time. Five years for tax fraud."

"You're not serious," Jamie said. "Why, he's a member of—"

"Beaumont Baptist Church," Muffin supplied. "Actually, he's a deacon. What people don't know is he received a dishonorable discharge in the service."

"How did you find out all of this?" Jamie asked.

"I've searched military and prison files."

"Isn't that classified information?"

"Sometimes we have to break a few rules," she said.

"Only if it's for a good cause," Max added.

"But surely the government has high security. Otherwise they'd have people tapping into their computers getting anything they wanted. You could go to prison for this."

"Not likely," Muffin said.

Max hesitated. "Jamie, I used to be somewhat of a hacker."

"And a damn good one at that," Muffin added. "There are only a couple of people in the entire world who are capable of breaking through the kind of firewalls we're talking about, and you're looking at one of them."

"Where are the others?"

"They're both in federal prison," Muffin said.

Jamie gaped at Max. "And you're not. Why?"

He shrugged. "I sort of promised the government I'd stop doing it."

"But you haven't."

"It's like this," Muffin said. "A lot of people owe Max favors."

"I don't think I want to know," Jamie said. "I don't want to go to prison for being an accomplice. Vera has told me what sort of thing goes on behind prison bars, and I don't think I'd last twenty-four hours."

"Vera needs to stop filling your head with all that nonsense," Max said. "I'm surprised you listen to her."

Jamie looked hurt. "She's like a mother to me. Who do you think helped me pick out my first, uh, bra? Who do you think told me the facts of life?"

He grinned. "I thought you learned all that in the backseat at the drive-in."

"Very funny, Max."

"I'm teasing. I know you and Vera are close."

"Besides, I need to know all there is to know about prison life," Jamie said, "because you might just end up in one."

"The secret of my success is that I employ the best attorneys money can buy. Speaking of attorneys, here we are." Max pulled into the parking lot of Phillip's law office. "I see Prince Charming's car is here."

"Could you please try to be nice to Phillip?" Jamie asked.

He looked surprised. "I'm always nice."

"You tend to goad him at times."

"I can't help it if he's feeling insecure about the up-coming nuptials. Maybe he's having second thoughts.

I know I would if my fiancée spent the night with another man."

"We didn't spend the night together. Not the way you mean."

"It got pretty hot under that blanket, Swifty."

"Oh, God," Muffin said. "You guys didn't *do it*, did you?"

"Of course not!" Jamie snapped.

"Only because I refused to go all the way with her," Max replied. "I'm telling you, Muffin, she was begging for it."

Jamie narrowed her eyes. "You are despicable. I was feeling scared and vulnerable and you took advantage of the situation."

"I just want to make sure nobody got laid," Muffin said. "Jamie, you're engaged, and you have absolutely no business sleeping beneath a blanket with the likes of Max."

"The circumstances were unusual, Muffin," Jamie said, wondering why she felt the need to defend herself to Max's computer. "It definitely won't happen again."

Someone knocked on the window and Jamie looked up. She felt a sinking sensation at the sight of Annabelle Standish. "Oh, Lord," she moaned, despite the smile she forced to her face. She opened the door and climbed out. "Annabelle, what a surprise!"

"Jamie Swift, I should take you out to the woodshed after what you did. I didn't get a wink of sleep. What do you mean running after some madman in the middle of the swamp? My son is still in shock. Now, be a good girl and give me a hug."

Jamie hugged the woman tightly. As always Annabelle looked as though she had just stepped out of an expensive salon. Her clothes were perfect, not a wrinkle to be found anywhere. "I'm sorry I caused you to worry. I thought—"

"I know what you thought. You thought you could go out there and solve the case without the help of law enforcement. You could have been killed, young lady. I demand that you put a stop to this nonsense and start concentrating on your wedding."

Max walked around the car and stood there quietly.

"You must be the famous Max Holt," Annabelle said, although she didn't look the least bit impressed. "I would appreciate it if you'd refrain from taking my future daughter-in-law on all these wild, life-threatening excursions."

"Nice to meet you, Mrs. Standish," Max said, offering his hand. "I've heard a lot of wonderful things about you and what you've done for this town."

"Yes, well, I do what I can, but I can't be every place at once. I need someone like Jamie working with me."

Jamie decided a change of subject was in order. "Have you been visiting Phillip this morning?"

"I peeked in on him, but he had a client. All I needed was to have a paper notarized. Honey, we have to get together as soon as we can to discuss some of the wedding details. I know you think we have plenty of time, but September will be here before you know it, and there are so many parties to plan. Not to mention bridal showers."

"Bridal showers?"

"Well, of course, dear. You need to bring your calendar to the house so we can plan the various events. There are at least a dozen dinner parties planned for you and Phillip by our dear friends. But first we must have a party of our own to introduce you to everyone.

You can't imagine how anxious people are to meet you." She glanced at her diamond wristwatch. "Oh, my, I'm ten minutes late for an appointment. Do you see my car or my driver?"

Jamie glanced around the parking lot and saw a uniformed man waiting beside Annabelle's limo near the alley. "There he is," she said. "Probably not easy trying to fit a limousine in such a small parking lot."

Annabelle waved the man over. "Listen, Jamie, why don't you pack a couple of bags and stay at the house for a few days. Just until this awful business blows over. I'd feel better knowing you're close."

"I'd like to, Annabelle, but my friend Deedee is going through a difficult time right now. I need to be there for her."

Annabelle didn't look pleased with her reply. "Yes, well, you have your own mind, and I'm not one to try and change it." She looked at Max. "It was nice meeting you, Mr. Holt. How much longer are you planning to stay?"

Jamie blushed. It was obvious Annabelle wanted him gone.

"Long enough to figure out who's skimming money from the taxpayers," he said.

Annabelle stiffened. "I'm as interested as you are about the misappropriation of tax funds, Mr. Holt, but please try to remember some of that money is going to a good cause. I fight tooth and nail for the small pittance I get to fund desperately needed shelters for battered women and children, as well as my new Help Center. How do you think these people are able to eat or keep warm in the winter? And I have to pay people to work at these places."

"The figure I'm hearing is twenty million dollars in

four years, Mrs. Standish," Max said. "That's a lot of money for a small town, don't you think?"

"Everyone should pay their share, Mr. Holt. I certainly pay mine."

"You're going to need more shelters, then," he said, "because people are losing their homes and cars every day due to increased property taxes. Besides, don't the people who work at your centers donate their time?"

"That's beside the point. I still have overhead. You'll have to join me for tea before you head home, Mr. Holt. You and I seem to share the same concerns for this town. You could give me a few ideas."

Annabelle kissed Jamie on the cheek and made her promise to call as soon as possible. She shook hands with Max and started for her car.

Max and Jamie watched the car drive away. "I think that went fairly well," he said.

Jamie sighed. "You managed to get a few barbs in so I know you're pleased as punch." She looked at the building. "I don't know if I can go through with this. Phillip wasn't really happy with me last time we spoke." Nevertheless, she made her way to the front door.

She and Max waited in the lobby briefly while Phillip's secretary notified him of their arrival. Max glanced through a magazine while Jamie paced.

"Relax," he said. "Phillip is just jealous because you're hanging out with me. I'd be jealous of me too, if I were him."

"Could you please reel in your ego and stuff it into your big mouth?" Jamie said sweetly, although she was grinding her molars as she spoke.

Max tossed the magazine aside and leaned closer. "Listen, Swifty, I won't say anything about last night if you won't."

Jamie's face flamed, just as Phillip stepped into the waiting area. He stopped short at the sight of her. "Jamie, what's wrong? Your face is all red and splotchy. Are you ill?"

"I, uh—"

"Would you like a glass of water, Miss Swift?" the receptionist asked.

What Jamie wanted to do was punch Max in the face. "I just got a little overheated, I think." She groaned inwardly at the thought of how Max would take her words. "The heat outside is miserable."

"Would you care to step into my office?" Phillip asked.

Chapter
ELEVEN

Phillip waited until Max and Jamie were seated before he took his place behind his desk and looked over at Jamie. "You probably think I haven't taken these threats seriously, but I have. I just didn't want to let on and alarm you. I've been riding Lamar hard and heavy every day since someone put bullets through your window, but he seems more concerned about rescheduling his fishing trip. I offered to hire one of the best private investigators in the country, but Lamar was clearly insulted."

"You didn't tell me."

"Like I said, I didn't want to frighten you. I'm at my wit's end, here. We can't afford to offend Lamar; we need his full cooperation. At the same time we can't afford to just sit back and wait for this person to strike again."

"Do you think Lamar is trying to cover for someone?" Max asked.

Phillip shook his head. "He's not the type to take bribes. He's as honest as the day is long."

"How about his deputies?"

Phillip shrugged. "They seem like a loyal bunch,

but I don't know them personally." His gaze shifted to Jamie. "I think I should hire the investigator anyway and not tell Lamar."

"Not a good idea," she said. "You can't sneeze in this town without somebody hearing about it. Lamar would find out, and that would make things worse." She looked at Max. "Lamar can be prideful and stubborn."

"I can't just sit here and do nothing," Phillip said, raising his voice.

"You could help us," Max said.

This time Phillip looked surprised. "Name it."

"I'd like to talk to the city auditor. Go over the books."

"That would be Benson Grimby," Phillip said. "He's on vacation. But I may be able to fix you up with his assistant." He thumbed through his Rolodex, picked up the phone, and dialed a number. "Alexa, this is Phillip. I need a big favor." He explained the situation. "You can go over there now," he told Max as soon as he hung up. He looked at Jamie. "Are you free for breakfast or do you plan to go over, as well?"

Jamie looked at Max.

"I'll be fine," Max said, getting up. "I'm sure you'd rather go to breakfast with your fiancé than sift through a bunch of old documents."

Jamie didn't argue. She and Max had reached an understanding after what had happened the night before. Or maybe Max was planning to do some snooping around on Phillip as well, and didn't want her to know.

She smiled at Phillip. "Would you drop me off at my house afterward so I can pick up my car?"

"Certainly."

"Then I'm all yours."

Max nodded and left.

Ten minutes later, Jamie and Phillip selected a booth at the Downtown Café. Jamie didn't eat breakfast as a rule, but she ordered a blueberry muffin and a cup of coffee and watched in awe as Phillip downed a stack of pancakes. "Good thing you work out every day," she said.

"I'd like to give you a workout," he responded, giving her a soulful look.

"Soon," she promised.

He met her gaze. "I had a reason for asking you to breakfast, Jamie. I want you to come away with me." She opened her mouth to speak, but he held his hand up. "Now, before you start arguing, let me finish. You need to get out of town for a while, that much is obvious. We could go ahead and get married and take a long honeymoon."

"Annabelle would be livid."

"She'll get over it. And start hounding us for a grandchild, of course. It's always going to be something."

Jamie hesitated. When Phillip had proposed, she'd thought she would finally have the life she'd craved for so many years. But what if Phillip *were* somehow involved in the missing tax dollars? Not that she really believed it; after all, he was a good man. But she wanted to know in her heart that he was completely innocent. "I just don't feel right going off and leaving my best friend," she said.

"Frankie will protect Deedee, and I'll protect you. After all, I'm going to be your husband."

"I have a newspaper to run."

"And you've got a managing editor to do it."

"Mike? That's a lot of responsibility."

"How will he ever learn if you're going to keep him tied to your apron strings?" He sat back in the booth. "We could tie up all our loose ends and be out of here by nightfall," Phillip said.

"What about your clients?"

"My secretary will just rearrange my schedule. I don't make a habit of canceling appointments. I don't think any of my clients will fire me for getting married and going on a honeymoon."

Jamie shifted in her seat. "This is not a good time, Phillip. I've got security guards in my building because of the shooting. What would my staff think if I just high-tailed it out of town without so much as a farewell?"

"They'd think you were in love and couldn't wait to be my wife."

"And I have to think of Deedee. She has always been there for me, Phillip. She's not handling this thing well. I'm afraid she's going to end up leaving Frankie."

"Jamie, would you listen to yourself?" he said. "What does any of this have to do with us getting married?"

She could only look back at him in silence.

"I'm beginning to feel like you don't want to marry me at all." He paused and studied her. "Is it Max Holt? Are you in love with him?"

"Of course not. I barely know the man."

"But you're with him a lot."

"You know he's my partner."

"You don't have to spend twenty-four hours a day with him. Don't you realize how that must look to other people? It's probably all over town by now that you spent the night with him out in the swamps."

Suddenly, Jamie understood. "Annabelle has been talking to you, hasn't she?" That explained Annabelle's rude behavior toward Max that afternoon.

"My mother is concerned, yes. She doesn't want you to be hurt by all the gossip."

"Are you concerned about it?"

"I've never paid attention to gossip and you know it. But when people start bad-mouthing the woman I'm going to marry I naturally become upset."

"I'm sorry if I've embarrassed you, Phillip. I'm sure this isn't the first time you've had to defend me to your mother."

"What's that supposed to mean?"

"Meaning she thinks you're marrying beneath yourself." Jamie felt ashamed the minute she said it. Annabelle had always treated her like one of the family.

Phillip glanced down at his coffee cup. "It's no secret my mother can be a bit of a snob at times, but she has always defended you."

"*Defended* me?" Jamie asked in surprise.

"Perhaps 'defend' is the wrong word." He wiped his forehead. "Shit, I wish I hadn't said that. I don't even know what I'm saying."

Jamie's feelings were hurt, but she was good at hiding them. She knew people had speculated about her family for years, the fact her mother had run out on her, and her father was emotionally ill and unable to work the last few years of his life. Kids in school had called Jamie's mother all sorts of names, long before Jamie had understood what they meant. There would be those who would question Annabelle about her son's decision to marry someone who didn't come from a good family. And Annabelle, who could trace her blue blood back to the beginning of time, would feel compelled to make excuses for her future daughter-in-law.

"It's okay, Phillip," Jamie said softly. "I know I wouldn't have been your mother's first choice. I'm sorry if my past embarrasses her or you."

"Don't be ridiculous, I'm proud to be engaged to you. My mother is ecstatic."

The waitress dropped their check on the table and walked away quietly, as if sensing she'd come at a bad moment. "I've explained the reasons I can't go away with you," Jamie said. "I was hoping you'd understand. Perhaps when this is all over."

"Then my hands are tied," he said. "You refuse to come to my place so I can look after you, and you won't go away with me. I don't know what else I can do." Phillip pulled out several bills and placed them on the check. "I have to go back to work now." He left her sitting there.

Jamie ordered another cup of coffee and pulled out a cigarette. She took a puff and sighed. Then, she stabbed it against the ashtray and left.

Max barely had time to glance at the stack of retirement magazines before the door opened to the auditor's assistant's office. Alexa Sanders stared at Max for a full minute before saying anything. She was a forty-something, plus-size woman in a black dress with a fuchsia scarf. Her dark hair curled under at the ends, barely touching her shoulder.

She swallowed. "I almost fell on the floor when Phillip called me and said you were on your way over. I've never met a celebrity. How can I help you, Mr. Holt?"

He stood. "Call me Max. And you are Alexa Sanders,

the lady who runs city hall." He held up the magazine. "And much too young to be reading this."

She looked pleased. "I read *Cosmo*. But we have a few old geezers in the back who pore over this magazine like it holds the secret to life." She rolled her eyes. "My boss being one of them, I might add."

Max smiled. "That old, huh?"

"Not to mention senile. I spend most of my time going behind him and cleaning up his mess. I'm talking too much, aren't I? I'm nervous, that's all. Not used to being around famous people. I'll bet you know Donald Trump personally. And Ted Turner," she added. "I heard you once dated Sandra Bullock."

"You're too smart to believe the tabloids, Alexa." He glanced around. "How long have you worked here?"

"Since college, and I don't want to tell you how long that's been. I was hoping to make auditor one day, but old man Grimby is going to outlive my grandchildren."

"I'll bet you know everything that goes on in this place."

She hesitated, some of the light left her eyes. "Yeah."

"How hard would it be to get me a copy of the city budget and audits? Say the last three years?"

"It's public knowledge, but it'll take time for me to print it out."

"You do that for me, and I'll take you to lunch at the best place in town."

"That's not good enough," she said.

Max leaned on the counter that separated the lobby from the offices. "Playing hardball, huh? Okay, name your price."

"I want an autograph for my ten-year-old son. He gets off on that sort of thing."

"You got it." He grinned. "I'll bet you're a tough mom, huh?"

"Damn right. I've been saving since he was born to get him into a good college. This kid is going places."

"With you as his mother I don't doubt it for one minute."

She looked proud. "Now, how about I fix you a cup of coffee and start printing that budget for you?"

Jamie caught up with Max at the end of the day when she pulled into Frankie and Deedee's long drive. Max was in his car, talking to Muffin and taking notes.

"Find out anything?" Jamie asked, sliding in on the other side.

"Muffin is checking on something for me. I had a nice visit with Alexa Sanders today."

"Oh, yeah? She's divorced, you know."

"She told me all about it. Good thing she got rid of the jerk. Lovely woman. And obviously way over-qualified for her job."

"I would think she's a little different from the women you prefer."

"I think all women are beautiful, Jamie."

"So I've heard. But you wouldn't go out with some-one like Alexa Sanders."

"As a matter of fact, I took her to lunch and had a great time."

Jamie couldn't hide her surprise. "No kidding?"

"The auditor is so old he should have retired when Elvis was still popular. Alexa claims he gets confused easily, which means she has to go over his work care-fully, which means—"

"She has the inside scoop," Jamie finished for him.

"Money is going everywhere. This town has so many

bogus committees you wouldn't believe it. There are committees and subcommittees, some of which are operated by only one person."

"Frankie mentioned the ridiculous number of committees in his speech," Jamie reminded him.

"Yeah, that's why I wasn't surprised when she told me. The person running that committee doesn't really have to do anything except grant favors, which is why he or she is there to begin with."

"Alexa told you all that?"

"She wanted to tell me more, but I think she's scared. I also think she'd like to leave her job, but she's afraid there are people who would make it hard on her if she did."

"Sounds paranoid if you ask me."

"You don't like Alexa very much, do you?" Max asked, his expression amused. "Or maybe you just don't like that I took her to lunch. You're not jealous, are you?"

"Give me a break."

Muffin came on. "Okay, Max, I just ran a check on Alexa Sanders. She's so clean she squeaks. She has a son—"

"She mentioned him."

"He's sick," Muffin went on. "Childhood-onset diabetes."

Max frowned. "I didn't know."

"Her ex-husband left as soon as he found out she was pregnant," Jamie said.

"Nice guy," Max said. "What else are you working on, Muffin?"

"I'm digging into Benson Grimby's past. Do you believe the man is in his nineties, for Pete's sake? How can he still be auditing the city's books?"

"Alexa said he was old. By the way, I want you to run a check on a man named Tim Duncan."

"Frankie's top security man?" Jamie asked.

"I'm not taking chances."

"I have a question," she said. "I already know you guys are breaking into a lot of secure locations. Surely they have a system that keeps track of visitors. Maybe that's why everybody is after us."

"They can't keep track of us," Max said. "Our firewall is impenetrable."

"You sound awfully confident."

"We change passwords several times a day. It's a little more complicated than that, but that's just one way we keep people confused."

"How do you keep up with your passwords? Took me forever to remember mine."

"Muffin and I use a very complex system," Max said.

"Yeah, stud, tell her how it works," Muffin said.

"Jamie isn't interested."

"Yes I am. In fact, I'm intrigued."

Max didn't respond.

"Tell her, Max," Muffin cajoled. "What's wrong, afraid she'll think badly of you?" When Max didn't answer, Muffin went on. "He uses the names of women he's, uh, dated."

Jamie frowned. "I don't get it."

"The names are alphabetized," Muffin said. "Each month, we return to the letter A. If Max goes out with another woman in the meantime, which he often does, we slip her name right into the alphabet and keep going. True, it's more complicated than that, it would take too long to explain, but that's the basic setup. For example, we're still working with the letter *B* today so this morning's password is 'Bunny.'"

Jamie laughed out loud. "You actually dated a woman named Bunny?"

"He not only dated her, he married her," Muffin replied.

Jamie shook her head sadly. "I'm really impressed with your system, Holt. It is so politically incorrect and sexist, but more than that, it's stupid."

"Wasn't my idea," Muffin said, "but then I would never have given voice recognition a name like Muffin with a Marilyn Monroe voice."

Max's grin was almost boyish. "It was all done in fun," he said.

"And marrying a woman named *Bunny*, of all things," Jamie went on.

"Her real name is Bethany Elizabeth Phister. A real mouthful," he added. "So her friends called her Bunny."

"That's what the ladies say about Max," Muffin said. "They tell him he's a mouthful."

Max shifted uneasily in his seat. "Okay, that's enough, Muffin."

"My God, the man is blushing," Jamie said. "How do you know all this, Muffin?"

"You should hear some of the things that go on in this car. Good thing Max has me to remind him not to run off the road."

"Let's go, Jamie," Max said.

Suddenly, the safety bar closed over Max, locking him in. "I'm trying to be a good sport, Muffin, but this is getting old fast. Raise the bar."

"Jamie wants to hear the rest of my story."

"I'm giving you three seconds."

"I'll talk fast," Muffin said. "Anyway, Jamie—"

"Frankenstein," Max said.

"Oh, shit." They were the last words out of Muffin's mouth.

"Disable AI," Max said.

"What are you doing?" Jamie asked.

"Putting the car on manual overdrive so I don't have to listen to Muffin's mouth."

Jamie tried to look serious. "So how does one go about doing all the things you do in a car this size?"

He relaxed and his mouth turned up in a lazy smile that made Jamie think of rainy afternoons and love-making, cold mornings and warm bodies embracing.

"Very carefully," he said, still smiling. They stared at one another for a moment.

Jamie pressed her lips into a grim line. For some reason she didn't like the idea of Max swapping kisses and God only knew what in his car with another woman. It was silly, of course, but there it was. She climbed out, then realized she'd left her cell phone in her car. She started for it. She did not see the man behind the bushes take aim, only the startled look on Max's face before the first shot was fired.

Jamie barely had time to process what was going on before Max shoved her hard, knocking her completely off her feet. Another shot rang out, this one pinging off something metal. She peered over the hood of her car. Where the hell were the shots coming from?

The side window of her Mustang shattered. "My car!" she cried.

"Stay put," Max yelled.

Security men raced from all directions, drawing weapons as they headed in the direction of a fountain surrounded by flowering shrubs. Max followed. He stopped short at the sight of Swamp Dog standing over the body of a heavyset man. His throat had been cut.

"What the hell happened?" Max demanded.

Frankie and Duncan joined them.

"Oh, man," Frankie said. "This is bad."

Swamp Dog looked at Max, his eyes expressionless. "Those bullets were meant for you. I was on him like white on rice the minute the bastard fired the third shot. Slit his throat." He swiped the knife across his jeans, and tucked it into his boot. "That's what you're paying me for, right?"

Chapter
TWELVE

Swamp Dog swaggered off as though he hadn't a care in the world.

"Jesus Christ," Duncan said.

Max sighed heavily. "Frankie, please take Jamie inside."

The big man looked toward the cars. "Yeah, sure." He started off.

"Who is he?" Max asked Duncan.

"Vito Puccini." He rolled the dead man on his side and pulled a wallet from his back pocket. He flipped it open and handed it to Max. "One of the guys I just hired."

Max glanced through the man's identification. "You say he checked out?"

"Clean as a whistle. Came with a letter of recommendation from his last employer, some hotshot preacher who travels with bodyguards."

Max looked up sharply. "Harlan Rawlins?"

"Sounds familiar," Duncan said, "but I'd have to check my files. I've got a lot of men on this job."

"I want to see everything you have on Puccini."

"No problem. Oh, there was another guy traveling

with him. Lenny Black. They both worked for this minister."

"Where is Lenny Black now?"

"I posted him at the front gate. Naturally I plan to question him."

"Please find him immediately. And round up the other new men, as well. I'll meet you at the back of the house in five minutes. And call nine-one-one."

Max hurried into the house where he found Snakeman guarding the front door. "The boys and I have been watching the doors all day," he whispered. "We're armed."

"Does Deedee know?"

He shook his head. "Frankie wants us to keep it under wraps as far as she's concerned. Probably not a bad idea considering she's, uh, hormonally challenged."

Max nodded and headed for the living room where everyone had gathered, including the staff and two of the security guards. "Everything's okay," he said. "Duncan is calling the police."

"Is he really dead?" Deedee asked, shuddering. Frankie stood next to her.

"Yeah."

"I understand he took a shot at you and Jamie," she went on.

Max nodded and looked at Jamie. She was comforting Beenie, who was not taking it so well. He mopped tears with a jewel-accented handkerchief while Choker looked on in disgust.

"Who was he?" Jamie asked.

"Vito Puccini. Anybody recognize the name?"

Big John perked. "Heavyset guy?"

"Yeah."

"I spoke with a man named Vito earlier. He and another guard were having lunch together when I went out to get something from my car. Said he was a big wrestling fan. Had a Jersey accent."

"What did the other guy look like?"

"Tall and skinny. Longish hair. Brown, I think. He had it tied back. He didn't have much to say, but this Vito was pretty talkative."

Deedee's voice trembled. "You think these guys are the ones who have been after us?"

Max hesitated. "We're looking into it. I seriously doubt the other man is still on the property."

"I don't like it," Frankie's campaign manager said. "This has gone too far. I'm thinking we should definitely pull out."

Frankie looked at him. "I thought we agreed not to."

"There's a guy out there with his throat cut. Who's to say one of us won't be next?"

"Are you throwing in the towel?" Deedee asked. "After I've already decided I will make a great mayor's wife?"

The man's shoulders sagged. "I don't know what to do anymore."

"Well, I'm not quitting," she told Frankie, matter-of-factly. "After being stuck in this house for so long I realize I need to get out and do something. I'm not about to let that hoity-toity Annabelle Standish get all the credit. Besides, Beenie reminded me I would be expected to ride in all the parades with Frankie." She looked at her husband. "I'll need new clothes, of course."

Frankie took Deedee's hand. "I'm so proud of you, sweetheart."

Max, Frankie, and Big John met with Duncan and four other men, none of whom matched Big John's description. "Lenny Black is missing," Duncan said.

"We're searching the grounds now. You want me to add another man inside the house?"

Big John spoke. "Don't bother. Me and the boys will kill the person who tries to get by us."

As soon as they were alone, Frankie pulled Max aside. "This Swamp Dog person. He saved your and Jamie's life, right?"

"Looks that way."

"I want him close by at all times."

"Frankie, I have to level with you. Right now I don't trust anyone."

Max knocked softly on Jamie's bedroom door a few minutes later. She opened the door, a portable phone to her ear. She motioned him in.

After a moment, she hung up. "I wanted to check messages at my office. Seems like Mike and Vera have everything under control."

"You sound disappointed."

She gave a self-effacing smile. "Well, naturally I'd like to think they can't run the newspaper without me."

Max glanced around the bedroom. "It smells like you in here."

"I don't wear perfume."

"You've got your own scent. I've spent enough time closed up in the car with you to know."

Jamie had memorized his scent as well. She was certain she could pick him out of a crowd with her eyes closed.

"Jamie, I need to talk seriously with you for a moment." He sat on the edge of the bed. She joined him, eyes curious. "It may not be safe for you to stay here anymore," he said.

"You think I should go home?"

"No, I don't want you to be alone right now, and I

know you don't want to stay with the Standishes. Is there anyplace else you could go for a few days?"

"I have a couple of girlfriends, but I would be afraid I'd be putting them in danger."

"I don't think you're the target here. In fact, I'm sure of it."

"Then who?"

"That's what I'm trying to figure out. It could be Frankie or me or both, but anyone around us could become a casualty. I'd like to get Deedee out of here, as well. Maybe the two of you could visit that spa she mentioned."

Jamie rolled her eyes. "Get real, Holt. Do I look the spa type to you?"

He grinned. "No, you're definitely not the type."

"What's that supposed to mean?"

"When I think of you I think of lazy Sunday mornings and rainy afternoons. You don't want to hear the rest."

"Go ahead," she said, intrigued.

"Promise you won't punch me in the jaw?"

"Don't be ridiculous."

He studied her for a moment. "I visualize you with mussed hair and long T-shirts, wearing absolutely nothing beneath them."

She arched one brow. "Actually, that's exactly what I sleep in."

He groaned.

"Lately, though, I've been wearing all this frilly stuff of Deedee's. I don't think I'm the frilly type."

They sat in silence for a moment, simply looking at one another. Jamie wondered what it was about the man that drew her to him, even when he was at his most irritating. She knew exactly why women flocked to him. Max Holt was larger than life. He'd traveled all over the world numerous times, and he rubbed elbows with people she'd only read about. He was the one people came to when they were in trouble. He could be counted on.

"What are you thinking?" Max asked.

"I was thinking how different we are."

"You and I have more in common than you think, Jamie."

"Oh, yeah? I'll bet you've never shopped at an outlet or secondhand store. You've never eaten canned soup for a week because you were low on grocery money."

"You're right, I haven't. But if the need arose I could. I easily adapt to situations." He paused. "It has always been easier for me to pay someone to shop for clothes and food and whatever else because it frees me up to do what I think is important. I like to think I've made contributions to this world."

Jamie suddenly felt foolish. Max Holt *had* contributed to the world. One only had to pick up a newspaper to learn how his technological knowhow and financial support had made life easier both in the States and in third-world countries. He might have an ego the size of Mother Earth, but he was a generous man.

"I'm not criticizing you, Max," she said. "I'm just pointing out our differences. It would explain why we have so many, uh, disagreements."

One corner of his mouth lifted. "I can think of other reasons, but you don't want to hear them."

She knew the direction he was traveling and changed the subject. "I don't want to leave," she said. "Deedee would be crazed with worry over Frankie if we left under these circumstances."

"And you? Would you worry about me?"

"Of course I would. I'd be worried sick about everybody." She noted a flicker of disappointment in his dark eyes. It wasn't the answer he'd been looking for.

Max stood. "If you change your mind—"

"I won't." He nodded and walked to the door. Jamie stared at it for a long time after he was gone and wondered if there was a reason they'd been thrown together. In many ways she wished they had never met. She had planned her life so carefully, and Max Holt had come along and changed everything.

Finally, she exited the room and walked toward the bedroom Deedee shared with Frankie. She tapped lightly on the door and went in. The room was all rose-colored walls and white French provincial furniture. Tall crystal vases were filled with white roses, and delicate figurines adorned bedside tables. Jamie had to smile. She couldn't imagine Frankie sleeping in such a room.

Deedee lay on an elaborate chaise, a satin eye mask in place, Beenie fussing over her like a mother hen. "Look, honeykins, Jamie is here."

Deedee removed her eye mask. "Hi, honey. I was just trying to catch my breath after all that's been happening. I don't want Frankie to see me fretting."

"You're hanging in there like a real trouper," Jamie said. "I'm proud of you."

Deedee smiled ruefully. "I'll bet you're beginning to wish you'd stayed with Phillip and his mother after all. Annabelle would have taught you two hundred ways to fold linen napkins by now."

Jamie chuckled and sat on the foot of the chaise. "Don't be silly, there's no place I'd rather be right now than with my best friend. Are you okay?"

"I'm okay until I think how close you and Max

came to being shot on my own property." Her eyes misted. "I could have lost both of you."

Beenie, ever watchful, handed Deedee a tissue. "And then to think that a man was actually brutally killed outside my front door." She shuddered.

"He was a very bad man," Beenie said. "A cold-blooded killer."

She sighed wearily. "I know. But this has always been a happy place. Now, we have security guards running all over the place."

Beenie sniffed loudly. Both women looked up. "I'm sorry," he said, snatching a tissue from the box. "I feel so sad. My nerves are shot, and every time I get anxious I start eating chocolate. I've gained three pounds. And look at my nails." He held them out. "I've started biting them. I've had to take off my rings so as not to draw attention to them."

"Oh, Beenie," Deedee said. "It's going to be okay. Once this nasty business is behind us we'll both go in for a manicure. In the meantime, there are a million things to plan."

He looked hopeful. "Like what?"

"I'm going to be the mayor's wife. I think I need a whole new look. My husband will be a public servant."

"Yes, you will definitely need a new look. You'll want an elegant-working-girl look. We'll have to tone down the makeup and choose a simpler hairstyle." He drummed his fingers along his bottom lip. "Oh, my?"

"What?" Deedee said.

"Some of those diamonds must go. They flash like a Kmart blue light special when you walk into a room."

Deedee reared back as though afraid he would try to snatch them from her. "Forget it, Beenie. I didn't say I wanted to dress like Mother Theresa."

Beenie shot Jamie a look of pure exasperation. "You would think I was asking her to give up a kidney."

Jamie chuckled, happy to see Deedee and Beenie focused on a new project. Anything to take their minds off what was happening downstairs. "Why don't I let the two of you slug it out? I need to call Phillip." She suspected she'd better tell him about the latest events herself instead of letting him find out from Lamar.

"Try to rest for a few minutes," Beenie told Deedee. "I can ask the chef to slow down dinner. He'll want to bite my head off and shove it down the garbage disposal, but I don't care."

"Maybe I will rest for a moment." Deedee looked at Beenie. "Where's Choo-Choo?"

"Last time I saw him he was curled on a rug in front of the kitchen fireplace. I think he was cold, poor baby. Let me get him for you."

Lenny walked into the motel room where Mitzi was watching *General Hospital*. "Where's Vito?" she said.

Lenny sat down on the other bed. He was dirty and sweaty, his brown hair plastered to his scalp. "Dead."

Mitzi bolted upright. "What the hell are you talking about? Is this some kind of joke?"

Lenny shook his head. "No, man, he's dead as hell. Some bad-ass dude on the security team got him. Got a black patch on his eye and all these scars on his face." Lenny shuddered. "I saw the whole thing." He drew a line across his throat. "It was nasty."

"Did you finish your business and collect the money?"

He shook his head. "Hell, no. Everything happened so fast I barely had time to get out. I'm telling you, this dude would have gladly cut my heart out if he'd known I was with Vito."

Mitzi slapped him hard. "Listen to me, retard. I've gone through pure hell waiting for you guys to pull this thing off. Now my husband is dead and what do we have to show for it? We're not going anywhere until the job is done, and we're paid. You got that?"

"You don't understand," Lenny said. "Vito and I were supposed to kill someone."

Mitzi gaped at him. "Vito was serious about that?"

"Yeah, man. Only we couldn't get close enough to the target to off him."

She took a deep breath. "Then you and I will have to do it."

"The police are looking for me, Mitzi. They'll recognize me the minute they lay eyes on me."

"Not when I get finished with you." She pulled a pair of scissors from her suitcase. "Sit."

"Has anyone seen Choo-Choo?" Beenie asked once he'd searched the kitchen and several other places the dog enjoyed sleeping.

"I haven't seen him," the housekeeper said.

"Do I look like a dog-sitter?" the chef snapped.

Beenie planted his hands on his hips. "No, you look like a nasty old grouch who hasn't been laid since Julia Child started cooking." He looked at the man's assistant, who shook her head sadly.

"I haven't seen him, either," she said.

Jamie came downstairs a moment later and found Beenie still searching. "Should we look in the other bedrooms?" she asked. "Choo-Choo may have become frightened with all the people in the house."

"That's the problem with this place," Beenie said. "There are far too many bodies around. I should ask Big John if he's seen Choo-Choo." Beenie shivered. "I keep wondering how he got the name *Big* John, know what I mean?"

"He's a large man," Jamie replied.

"Large is what I've been thinking as well."

They searched the other bedrooms. One of the security guards helped. The little dog was nowhere to be found.

Finally, Beenie and Jamie knocked on the door to Frankie's study. They found him, Max, and Lamar deep in discussion.

"Choo-Choo is missing," Beenie said. "I don't know what to do."

"Oh, hell." Frankie's shoulders sagged. "This is bad."

Jamie heard footsteps behind her and turned. Deedee had come downstairs, obviously wondering why Beenie hadn't brought up her dog.

She glanced around at the serious faces. "What's going on?" she asked.

Beenie burst into tears.

Phillip entered the living room quietly where Jamie was trying to comfort Deedee. Although Deedee's housekeeper had dispensed with the burned rug and drapes and cleaned the area from top to bottom shortly after the small fire, the smell of smoke lingered.

"I thought I'd stop by and see how things are going," he said. "I hear the pooch is missing. Any ideas?"

Jamie shook her head. Two hours had passed and there was still no sign of Choo-Choo or the man called Lenny Black. "Security is still searching the grounds," she said. "We think Choo-Choo may have slipped out of the house unnoticed and could be hiding on the property. He's not used to all these people."

"He's gone," Deedee said. "Whoever is doing this terrible thing took my dog, too."

"Honey, why would anyone bother with an innocent pet?" Jamie said.

Deedee met her look. "Because this person is cruel and obviously very sick and doesn't care who he hurts."

Jamie wished Frankie were there for Deedee, but he and Max were still holed up in the library with Lamar. Security Chief Duncan and Big John were at the police station giving their reports and looking at mug shots in hopes of finding Lenny Black's picture. Swamp Dog had been questioned at length and was now walking the grounds, a hero in the eyes of the other security guards. Jamie didn't trust him, had no idea whose side he was on or whether he was playing both sides, and as the sky darkened outside, she became even more concerned. She could only hope that Max was having the man watched.

Beenie came into the room, twisting his handkerchief, his face shrouded in guilt. "Can I get you anything, Deedee?"

Jamie felt sorry for him. "Why don't you prepare Deedee a Frappuccino?" she suggested, knowing Beenie would feel better if he kept busy.

"I already fixed her one," he said. He glanced around and sighed. "Lord, my head is all screwed up. I must've left it in the kitchen." He hurried away. When he returned he carried a small silver tray bearing a tall mug. "It was on the library table in the foyer," he said. "I don't even remember putting it there. I just don't know what's come over me." He set it on the table beside Deedee. "Some of the ice has melted. Do you want me to prepare a fresh one?"

"No need," Deedee said.

Beenie stood there for a moment, wringing his handkerchief. "Deedee, I know you hate me, but I truly am sorry about Choo-Choo. I'm going to keep looking, though. I just know I'll find him."

Deedee looked up. Her eyes were sad. "It's not your fault, Beenie. You love him as much as I do." She reached for her mug and took several long sips. When she lowered it, something metal scraped the inside. She peered at her drink. "There's something in here." She took a spoon from the tray and stirred her coffee. "Yes, there's definitely something—" She pulled up the spoon and paled at the sight. "Oh, my God!"

Jamie turned. "What is it?" She felt the hairs on the back of her neck prickle as Deedee lifted Choo-Choo's collar from the glass. "He was inside this house," she whispered.

The glass slipped from Deedee's fingers and shattered on the floor.

The door to the library was flung open a second later. Max and Frankie hurried out, Lamar right behind him. "What is it?" Frankie asked. He glanced in the direction Deedee pointed.

"Somebody put Choo-Choo's collar in Deedee's Frappuccino," Jamie told him.

Max muttered a four-letter word. "This is bullshit. How could this have happened? Who has been in this room?"

"I just got here," Phillip said.

"It had to have happened in the kitchen or while it was sitting on the library table," Beenie said, explaining how he'd forgotten to bring in the drink when he'd made it. He mopped fresh tears. "I can't seem to do anything right."

Max strode purposefully from the living room to the kitchen. Jamie followed. The room was empty.

"Where is the kitchen staff?" Max demanded. All at once there were footsteps on the stairs leading from the wine cellar. The chef appeared, a bottle of wine in each hand. He stopped abruptly at the sight of them.

"May I help you?"

"Did you see anyone come into this room?" Max demanded.

"I've been downstairs choosing wine. Not that it will matter. Everything is overdone and will taste like rubber by the time I serve it."

"Where is the woman who normally helps you?"

"She quit on me. Said she wasn't used to working in such a crazy place. I don't blame her."

"You didn't see *anything* out of the ordinary?" Jamie asked.

The chef scowled at her. "I've got people traipsing in and out of this kitchen all day," he snapped. "I can't get anything done for all the traffic."

Max shoved through the swinging door with Jamie right behind. Frankie and Deedee were on the stairs. "Deedee and I want to be alone for a little while," Frankie said.

"Good idea," Max said, as Duncan and Big John came through the front door. The men paused as though sensing a problem, but Max waited until Frankie and Deedee were gone before pulling Duncan aside. "Is there another way inside this house that I don't know about?"

"There's a cellar door that opens up near the back hedges. But nobody can get in or out because I put a lock on it."

"I want to see it," Max said.

"I've got a flashlight."

They started once more for the kitchen where the chef, clearly annoyed at being questioned, was banging pots and pans together as he prepared dinner. Outside, several security men looked up from their posts as Max and Duncan searched through the hedges.

"It should be here somewhere," Duncan said. "I scattered leaves and pine needles over it so it wouldn't be noticeable." He stooped beside an area and began raking brush aside. Max peered over his shoulder as the area was cleared and a wooden door came into view. Duncan trained his flashlight on the lock.

"Shit." He picked up the lock and handed it to Max. "Somebody sawed right through it. He could be in the house right now for all we know."

"Where's Swamp Dog?" Max asked.

"He watches the back of the property. Says he doesn't trust anyone else to do the job right."

"Find him. And I want the cellar and house searched from top to bottom."

Max returned to the kitchen and found the chef opening the bottles of wine.

"Throw everything out," Max ordered.

"Excuse me?" The man looked at Max as if he were crazy.

"I don't want this food served."

"Are you nuts? I've spent all day preparing this meal. Do you have any idea what tuna steaks cost?"

"Someone had access to this kitchen who shouldn't have. He could have tampered with the food. If you still want to serve tuna, then I'd suggest you serve it from a can."

The chef opened his mouth to protest, but the hard

look on Max's face must've changed his mind. "Whatever."

Security personnel began filling the house. "I want the search done as quickly and quietly as possible," Max told Duncan, "and keep the men away from Mrs. Fontana's room. I'll check it personally."

Duncan nodded. "I've got men in the cellar now. Swamp Dog is still at the back of the property, reclined against a tree, holding a high velocity assault rifle and wearing night vision gear." He shook his head sadly. "He's got booby traps along the back fence. I've cautioned my men. You ask me, I think the guy is whacko. He's the one we need to watch."

Max nodded. "Make sure you do that."

It was after midnight before the house was battened down for the night. Jamie had already seen a very worried Phillip out. Max and Duncan were discussing security at the kitchen table, where tuna sandwiches and pasta salad had been the evening fare. Snakeman stood guard at the door.

"We found more evidence inside the cellar of someone coming through the access door," Duncan said. "It's clear now. I've got a guard down there. As for Lenny Black, I think he's long gone."

"Frankie and I searched and secured the master bedroom while Deedee was taking a bath," Max said.

Duncan sighed. "I've never worked a job where I had no idea who the enemy was."

"How long have you owned your security company?" Max asked.

Duncan shrugged. "Ten years. I took early retirement from the police department."

"How come?"

"I figured I'd make more money this way."

"But you were only a couple of years from retiring from the department, weren't you? You lost your pension."

Duncan met his gaze. "You had me checked?"

Max nodded at Snakeman, and the wrestler stepped outside.

Duncan rubbed his eyes. "Okay, so I was forced to take an early retirement, but I was never convicted of any wrongdoing. I was cleared."

"They found drug money in the trunk of your car."

"It was planted there. I'd just busted a big-time dealer, and he was determined to get even."

"So instead of fighting it you moved a thousand miles away and started your own security company."

"I could have fought it in court, but the media had already tried and convicted me. It didn't matter that I had spent twenty years on the force and had a perfect record. My neighbors refused to speak to me, and no matter how many times I had my phone number changed I continued to get crank calls."

"Your wife left you over it, didn't she?"

Duncan nodded. "Our relationship had been over for years anyway so that was no surprise, but it only made things worse when she walked out." He met Max's gaze. "If you have a problem with me you're free to get somebody else. I've told you everything."

Jamie came into the kitchen and stopped short when she saw the two men talking. "Is this a private conversation?"

Max shook his head. "You're free to join us."

She sank into one of the chairs. She was depressed. Not only was her relationship with Phillip growing even more tense, she no longer knew what to expect from one minute to the next. She was edgy after all that had happened and wired from drinking too much coffee. "What a night," she said.

"Is Deedee asleep?" Max asked.

"Yeah. Frankie refuses to leave her side." She asked both men, "Do you think the person who took Choo-Choo will kill him?"

Max and Duncan exchanged looks.

"Don't lie to me," Jamie said. "I want the truth."

"I think it was just a scare tactic," Duncan told her, "but dogs make noise, and this person isn't going to risk a barking dog."

"So the answer is yes," Jamie said.

Max shifted in his chair. "I don't think we can automatically assume the dog is dead, Jamie, but we need to be prepared for the worst."

"Like what?"

Duncan didn't look up from his coffee cup. "We could receive a body part."

Jamie heard a gasp and realized it had come from her own mouth. She felt sick. Tears stung her eyes. "Oh, God."

Max took her hand and squeezed it. "He's giving us the worst-case scenario, Jamie."

She met his gaze. "Promise me—"

"Deedee will never know," he said softly. Max looked at Duncan. "I'm counting on you to see that nothing comes into this house until it's checked carefully."

It was after three A.M. when Beenie pushed through the swinging door that led inside the kitchen where Choker sat at the kitchen table reading a wrestling magazine. His gun lay on the table. Beenie shivered. "You must be on the night shift."

Choker didn't respond.

"I couldn't sleep," Beenie said.

"Then be quiet so the others can," the man replied without looking up.

"I need air."

Beenie opened the back door and stepped outside. A security guard stood nearby. "What the hell are you doing out here again?" the man said. "We've got enough problems on our hands without you wandering all over the grounds this hour of the morning looking for some stupid mutt."

"I'm going to do one last search." Beenie left the back steps and walked along the hedges. "Choo-Choo," he whispered. "Come to Papa. I know you're hiding because you're scared of all these strange men, but it's okay to come out. Your mama misses you terribly." Beenie peeked into the hedges. "Come on, sweet boy. Uncle Beenie will take care of you."

Beenie continued searching. He rounded the house and came to an abrupt halt when a man stepped from the shadows. "What are you doing out here?" the man whispered in a menacing tone.

"I'm looking for Choo-Choo." Those were the last words out of Beenie's mouth before the butt of a pistol slammed against his skull. He fell to the ground with a thud.

Max walked into the kitchen a few minutes later. "Ready for me to relieve you?"

"I'm okay," Choker said. He shifted in his chair. "Beenie has been out looking for the dog again. He's been down several times already. Driving me crazy. He came through about ten minutes ago."

"I'd better go out there," Max said. He started for

the door. It was flung open before he could reach for the handle.

"Hold it right there!" Choker said, aiming his weapon. He lowered it at the sight of one of the security men.

"We've got trouble," the guard said. "That Beenie fellow—"

Max pushed past him and raced outside. He followed the sound of voices and hurried around to the side of the house where he found Duncan and several others kneeling beside Beenie.

"He looks bad," Duncan said.

Max pulled his cell phone from his pocket and dialed nine-one-one.

Chapter

THIRTEEN

Jamie sat on one side of Deedee, Frankie on the other, as they waited in the visitor's lounge of the ER for word on Beenie. Deedee had cried on and off since the ambulance had awakened her to more bad news.

"I'm so scared, Frankie," she said. "I can't lose Beenie. He's like a sister to me."

Max almost smiled in spite of the seriousness of the situation. "He's got a lot going for him, honey. He's young and healthy. That helps."

"We'll find the person responsible for this," Lamar said, having arrived at the hospital only minutes after Beenie had been taken into the emergency room.

Deedee turned to him. "You haven't done anything useful so far," she snapped. "My husband is the one who has hired all the security. What the hell are you people doing? Do I have to arm myself in order to be safe in my own house?"

"We're following leads, Mrs. Fontana. I have extra men working the case."

The metal doors leading inside the emergency room suddenly opened, and a young doctor came through. Everyone stood, waiting for the worst.

"I'm Dr. Cox," he said.

"Is Beenie dead?" Deedee blurted.

The doctor looked surprised. "No, ma'am. He's going to be fine. He has a moderate concussion, but we found no signs of swelling around the brain. His injuries are superficial; he looks worse off than he really is."

"Oh, thank God," Deedee said.

"I'll have to warn you, though, he's got one heck of a headache, but I don't want to give him any pain pills because he needs to stay awake for the next twelve hours."

"Oh, Jeez," Frankie said. "Can you give *us* anything to take?"

Cox smiled. "I'm going to release him, along with a treatment plan, but you have to understand he's confused and disoriented right now." The doctor smiled. "Don't worry. He's on the mend. He's flirting with all my nurses, In fact, I think he has a date with one of them tomorrow night."

"With a nurse?" Deedee asked. "A *female* nurse?"

Dr. Cox chuckled. "We *do* have some pretty nurses here." If he noticed the group was staring at him in disbelief, he didn't say anything. "He should be ready to go in an hour."

"What I need right now is a rare steak and eggs," Beenie announced once he was settled inside the limo, flanked by Deedee and Frankie. Jamie and Max sat across from them.

Deedee blinked. "You don't eat red meat, Beenie. And why are you talking in that John Wayne voice?"

He looked at her curiously. "Why do you keep calling me Beenie? Sounds kinda fruity if you ask me."

Max studied him closely. "Have you forgotten your name?"

He paused. "Please tell me it's not Beenie."

"It's just a nickname," Deedee said. "Do you know who *we* are?"

He looked at her. "No, but I like the car, and the fact I'm sharing it with two drop-dead gorgeous women." He looked from Max to Frankie. "No offense intended."

"He has amnesia," Max said.

Beenie looked startled. "I do?"

"Maybe we should take him back to the hospital," Deedee said.

"No way am I going back there."

"I don't think he's in any physical danger," Max said. "His MRI looked good. Like the doctor said, he has no internal bleeding or swelling. The amnesia's probably temporary. There's not much they can do to treat it." He grinned. "I vote we just take our patient home. I suspect he'll be back to his old self again soon enough."

"You guys are confusing me," Beenie said. "Why are you grinning like that? Someone obviously tried to kill me from what I understand. Shouldn't we start a manhunt? I demand to know who did this, and as soon as I find out there's going to be some serious ass-kicking."

"I need to go by the office," Jamie told Max an hour later. Beenie had wolfed down a hearty breakfast while talking about wrestling to Big John and Snakeman, who listened without comment. They simply sat at the table, heads cocked to one side, mouth agape, as though waiting for the real Beenie to stand up.

"I'll drive you," Max said.

"Will you be okay?" Jamie asked Beenie.

"Damn right." He pulled a baseball bat from beneath the table. "I'm going to hang around and make sure there's no trouble."

"I can't take any more," Deedee said. "I've lost my dog *and* my friend."

Beenie was still entertaining the wrestlers. "Either of you guys got wrestling groupies?"

Jamie arrived at work and found two security guards at the front door and Vera discussing paint samples with one of the painters. "What do you think of this color?" she asked Jamie. "It's called Sand. It would make the room look larger, and fingerprints won't show as badly."

Jamie looked at it. It looked like plain old beige to her. "I like it."

"Check out your office."

Jamie discovered, much to her amazement, her office was finished, right down to the cherry desk, matching credenza, and two large filing cabinets. The walls had been painted a soft rose color, which blended with the loveseat and two matching chairs. Silk flowers adorned the coffee table. Men were installing new computers and the phone company was running cable and hooking up phones that would match the décor throughout.

Max came up beside her. "What do you think?"

Jamie had tears in her eyes when she turned to him. "I don't know what to say."

"I thought it looked like you when I selected it."

Jamie's breath caught in the back of her throat. "*You* picked it out?"

He nodded. "I let the decorator decide on the other furniture, but I wanted to choose yours. I hope you don't mind."

"Max, I can never thank you enough."

"I wanted you to have a nice place to work."

Vera was grinning when Jamie came out. "Wait

until you see the rest of the place. We have a beautiful mahogany table and executive chairs in the conference room, and all new appliances in the kitchen." She suddenly frowned. "I'm going to kick your butt to kingdom come if you try to sell it."

"She's not going to sell it," Max said.

Jamie couldn't stop smiling. "Have you seen Mike Henderson?"

Vera nodded. "He has been here all night. Says he has several articles he wants to run by you. You'll find him in his office." She handed Jamie two sheets of paper. "I attended the chamber of commerce meeting, and the garden club meeting, and took notes so Mike could concentrate on the important stuff. I'm also covering the Lancasters' wedding this evening. Helen, bless her heart, answers the phone while I'm out."

Jamie couldn't hide her surprise. "Very good. Anything else?"

Vera grinned. "I saved the best for last. You're not going to believe this. I sold twelve ads this week."

Jamie's eyes narrowed. "You didn't threaten anybody, did you?"

Vera looked insulted. "For your information, I was the epitome of professionalism. I think everyone is so excited with the place they're working twice as hard. And the raises didn't hurt."

"Raises?"

"The ones you insisted your employees deserved," Max said with a wink.

Jamie nodded. "Oh, yeah. I'm surprised they went into effect so quickly."

"And Muffin is pushing the home office for those bonuses you requested."

"We're getting a bonus, too?" Vera said.

"Of course," Jamie said, realizing Max was trying to make her look good.

"Muffin says everyone will get theirs within a week," Max added.

"Who is Muffin?" Vera asked.

"Max's computer," Jamie replied. "She's really awesome, but she's going through menopause right now so Max had to disable her for a little while. She's back now and feeling much better."

Vera sighed. "Ask a stupid question, get a stupid answer."

"I have to run," Max said. "I'm upgrading the security system back at the house, and I'm late. I'll be back as soon as I can and help out."

Jamie nodded. "Vera, please ask Mike to come into my office. I need to see what he has."

Max greeted the men who were to put in the new security system. "Sorry I'm late," he said.

"No problem," the man in charge said. "We've already started installing upstairs if you want to take a look."

"I noticed you're setting up cameras outside like I asked."

"Yes. We'd like to use the small office off the kitchen to set up TV monitors. Hope that's okay."

Max nodded. "How long will it take?"

"The job is a little more elaborate than I'd originally thought it would be, so we'll need a couple of extra days. You understand we're moving as quickly as we can."

"Yes, and I appreciate it. Okay, show me what you've got."

Jamie and Mike worked straight through to lunch. Vera sent out for sandwiches. "I'm really impressed with all you've done," Jamie told Mike, as they lunched at her desk. "How do you like working with Vera?"

"She can be bossy at times, but she works hard. If I need research or other information for my articles, Vera has it to me in no time. Makes my job a lot easier. And she loves taking pictures. I didn't know she was an amateur photographer."

Jamie nodded. "She took a class at the community college. They offer them free for senior citizens. Last I heard she was taking ballroom dancing."

"Why didn't I know that?" Mike asked. "I should do an article on that. Maybe get more seniors in this town involved."

"I need a break," Jamie told Mike once they sent the front page and Lifestyles section to layout.

"I need to check on my mom anyway," Mike said, hurrying to his office.

Jamie called Deedee to check on Beenie's condition.

"I'm worried about him," Deedee said. "He's been in the bathroom for hours with a girlie magazine. Do you think he's gone straight?"

"I don't see how," Jamie said. "I thought homosexuality was a genetic thing. You know, once gay, always gay? Maybe he doesn't remember coming out of the closet."

Deedee sighed. "Sounds complicated. I asked him to go through my catalogs so I could pick out an outfit for Election Day, and he looked at me like I was crazy. I don't know who's going to do my makeup and hair now. I just want my old Beenie back."

"I'm sure he'll come around," Jamie said before she hung up.

Mike returned shortly after, assuring Jamie all was

well with his mother. "She's doing a lot better. Gave me a scare in the beginning, though."

"I'm glad to hear it," Jamie said. "Listen, Mike, I have to tell you, I'm impressed with all you've done the past few days. You got a lot accomplished."

"I realized it was time I took on more responsibility. I guess my mom getting sick was a wake-up call," he added. "I'm just surprised you put up with me for so long."

"You're a darn good editor, and this newspaper is lucky to have you." Jamie wouldn't tell him how close she'd come to telling him to hit the road at times, but with the salary she offered, she couldn't have afforded to hire a replacement. "Keep up the good work."

At three o'clock, Max left the installation crew and climbed into his car. "Are you there, Muffin?" he asked.

"No, I'm shopping at Saks."

"I need answers. Someone attacked Deedee's assistant last night."

"Beenie?" she said.

"Yeah. Probably the same person who took Deedee's dog." Max quickly filled her in.

"That sucks," Muffin said. "How's Beenie?"

"He's okay, but Deedee's worried as hell. Have you got anything on Swamp Dog yet?"

"I keep bumping into firewalls. There's a record of him serving in Vietnam, but every time I try to dig deeper, I hit a dead end. The government is doing everything in its power to protect that information." She sounded frustrated.

"Think, Muffin. Sometimes things are not as hard as they seem. You're programmed to think like a computer *and* a human being. There's a reason for that."

"Max, what the hell are you talking about?"

"What would a computer do if it couldn't get the information?"

"It would simply tell you there was no data available."

"Right. What would *I* do?"

"You'd say, screw it and find the information anyway."

"So, Muffin?"

"Yeah, yeah. Keep looking. What's on your agenda?"

"I've got to go through three years of the city budget."

"Good thing you're a speed-reader."

"By the way, how's it going with the laptop at MIT?"

"He's not very bright."

"You're going to be hard-pressed to find anyone brighter than you, dear."

"What I'd like to know is why it's so important that I learn about Mustangs and replacement parts."

"Jamie's car was hit a couple of times in the shootings. I'd like to get it repaired." He went on to explain the actual damage, and Jamie's sentimental attachment to the car.

"I'll get on it right away since it concerns Jamie," Muffin said.

Max spent the next hour going over the city budget. "I'm going to take a ride, Muffin. I need directions to Highway 24."

"Where on Highway 24? You got any crossroads, or am I supposed to do this blindly? Forget it, I already know the answer."

Five minutes later, she ran a printout. "Here are the directions," she said. "What are you looking for?"

"The sewage treatment facility that never was. A lot of money was allocated for it, and taxpayers are still getting hit. I'd like to know why the city never finished it. Oh, before you do that, get Jamie on the phone."

Silence.

"Please."

Jamie picked up on the first ring.

"How are things going with the newspaper?" Max asked.

"Surprisingly well."

"Okay, if you don't need me, I'm going to take a drive."

"Anything I need to know?"

"I want to look at that sewage treatment facility the town was promised."

"'Bout time, Holt."

"Listen, Swifty, I've been chasing a killer, okay? Cut me some slack here."

"Well, there's not much to see as far as the facility is concerned. Of course the powers that be in this town are full of excuses as to why it's still unfinished."

"I'll check back with you."

Jamie heard a click from the other end. She smiled. Max Holt was obviously on the job, and she knew he wouldn't stop until he found what he was looking for.

Twenty minutes later Max pulled in front of a partially erected building. "Muffin, are you there?"

"Yeah, did you find the facility?"

"What there is of it. There's a sign out front listing Davidson Construction as the contractor. I need the address."

Jamie was in her office proofreading when Max came through the door. "Don't you ever knock?"

"This is important."

She motioned him to a chair, and he sat. "I'm listening."

"First things first. How's Beenie?"

"He likes women now."

"He was probably better off as he was. Women have a way of driving a man crazy."

Jamie tossed him a dark look.

"What do you know about Davidson Construction? That's the company that was hired to work on the treatment facility."

"All I know is a man died on the project and everything came to a halt," Jamie said. "The family sued, it's been in litigation for a couple of years, and the city is trying to settle out of court."

"Which explains why people haven't pushed," Max said. "It could stay in litigation forever, and the city could collect a ransom in interest on the money that was put aside for it. *If* the money is still there." He looked thoughtful. "I've gone over the city budget. It's clean. Too clean. Which tells me it's not the real budget."

"Come again?"

"The real budget is probably tucked so far away that only the people in the know can find it. Have you ever heard of a company called EPSCO?"

"No. Where did you see it?"

"Alexa scribbled the name at the bottom of the last page of the city budget printout. She didn't say anything, but I have a feeling it's important. Muffin is still searching but so far nothing has come up."

"Maybe it's a fake company. Maybe it doesn't really exist."

"I've thought of that. I think EPSCO is a password to something else."

"Like what?"

He shrugged. "Don't know yet, but I intend to find out. Uh, Jamie?"

She glanced down at the work in front of her. "Yeah?"

"You're looking mighty good today, Swifty."

"I don't have time for this, Max."

"I like you in jeans, you know. You've got a nice behind. I have to tell you when I see that behind my mind runs amuck."

She looked up. He was such a blatant flirt. "Stop turning yourself on, Max."

He stood and leaned over her desk so that his face was only an inch from her, bringing with him the smell of a light aftershave that made her want to get closer and get a better whiff.

"And here I thought I was turning you on."

She was startled at the look in his eyes, dark, probing, intense. Toe-curling. She held her breath, afraid to release it in fear it would come gushing out.

He smiled as though he knew precisely what he was doing to her. "You're not married yet," he said.

"I believe in long engagements," Jamie replied.

"And I believe in long honeymoons."

"It takes time to get to know people," Jamie said. "Perhaps if you'd taken time to get to know Bunny you wouldn't be a divorced man right now."

"I was younger then, just looking for eye candy. I've matured."

Jamie gave him one of her looks. "Right."

Muffin came on as soon as they climbed inside the car. "Max, I have something for you."

"Yeah?"

"I broke through the firewall."

"Which one?"

She hesitated. "The CIA."

"You broke through the CIA's firewall?" Jamie cried. "Are the two of you crazy!"

"Calm down," Max told her.

"Calm down? How do you expect me to calm down? You're going to prison for the rest of your life. And they're going to take me with you, even though I don't have anything to do with this. Double damn. I should probably have a cigarette." She reached for her purse.

"Don't do it," Max said. "You'll set off the sprinkler system."

Jamie went on. "I have always made it a point to stay on the right side of the law. I don't jaywalk, and the time I discovered a carton of soft drinks on the bottom of my grocery cart that I forgot to pay for I drove right back to the store and took care of it."

Max looked amused. "I'll bet you're one of those who've never had a parking ticket, right?"

Jamie opened her mouth, then clamped it shut.

Max glanced at her. "Uh-oh, Muffin, I think Jamie's about to confess to a heinous crime."

"I forgot about the parking ticket," she whispered.

"I'm sorry, I didn't hear you."

"I was barely twenty years old at the time. I parked in front of the Hallmark shop on Main Street, saw there were six minutes left on the meter and ran inside. I'd planned to grab a birthday card and get back before the time ran out, but once I got inside I couldn't decide on a card and, well—" She paused. "I completely forgot about the meter. When I came out a cop was writing a ticket. Cost me three dollars."

"Did you hear that, Muffin? Jamie's got a record. Sounds like we got a troublemaker on our hands."

"Maybe we shouldn't have given her all our secret information."

"I hope she doesn't try to sell them to some of her friends in the big house," Max said.

"Very funny," Jamie said. "So I got a parking ticket. What you're doing is a federal offense."

"Tell me what you found out, Muffin," Max said calmly.

"Well, if you think Jamie's trouble, wait till you hear about Swamp Dog. He's dangerous, Max. You don't want to piss off this guy. You don't even want to exchange Christmas cards with him."

"Yeah? What'd he do?"

"He *was* in Special Forces in Vietnam, but his records have been sealed. It was hell getting in; I used every trick in the book, so to speak. Swamp Dog, aka Jim Hodges, lost it, went right over the edge after losing all his men on a secret mission."

"What'd he do?" Jamie asked.

Muffin paused. "He committed a number of atrocities against civilians. Trust me, you don't want the details. But as far as the government is concerned, it never happened."

"Isn't the government afraid Swamp Dog will talk?" Jamie asked. "Or, in his case, brag? He could make a lot of money selling his story."

"The government is paying a shitload of money to keep him quiet," Muffin replied.

Jamie grunted. "You wouldn't know it by the way he lives. Besides, if he's got all that money why is he poaching?"

"It's not about money," Max said. "It's about breaking all the rules and laughing in people's faces while he's doing it."

"He wants the money as well," Muffin said. "He supports a number of causes, specifically paramilitary organizations, and the damn Ku Klux Klan, for God's sake."

"Sounds like it would be easier if the government put him behind bars for the rest of his life," Jamie said. "Or took him out."

"They can't," Muffin said. "Swamp Dog has too much information on their black ops and mistakes, and it's all well documented. He's got it hidden—the government can't find where, and he's got a fail-safe on it. Something happens to him, the lid is blown off the whole thing."

"He lives like an animal because he *is* an animal," Jamie said.

"You've got a call coming in, Max," Muffin said. "It's Lamar Tevis from the police department."

"I'll take it on the speaker phone."

"Max, is that you?" Lamar asked once Muffin put him through.

"Yeah. What's up, Chief?"

"We got problems. Alexa Sanders's boy is missing. Somebody broke into the house tonight while they were sleeping and snatched him right out of his bed. Ms. Sanders asked me to contact you. Said you'd know what to do."

Chapter
FOURTEEN

Max and Jamie arrived at Alexa's place fifteen minutes later. Patrol cars surrounded the small frame house that was painted a robin's egg blue and surrounded by a flower bed where orange tiger lilies grew in abundance. They found Alexa and Lamar were talking quietly in the living room. Her eyes were swollen from crying. She stood the minute she spied Max.

"You know why this happened," she said.

Max took her hand. "We'll find your son. First, I need the facts."

"I've already gotten the facts," Lamar said.

"I want to hear them from Alexa."

Alexa sniffed and mopped her eyes with a tissue. "Like I told Lamar, I went into Danny's room to check on him before I went to bed."

"What time?"

"Shortly after ten. When I went in, I found him gone. Danny's diabetic. If he doesn't eat the right food on schedule or he misses his insulin injection—" She paused and choked back fresh tears. "He could go into a diabetic coma."

"That's not going to happen, Alexa," Max said.

"Now, did you hear anything in the house before you noticed he was missing?"

She shook her head. "I was watching TV in my bedroom."

"Your doors were locked?"

"Yes, but I had the windows open so we could get a breeze. I can't afford to keep the air-conditioning on."

"The screen has been cut in Danny's room," Lamar said. "I smelled chloroform on the boy's pillow, so he probably slept through most of it."

Jamie took Alexa's hand in hers. "Is there anything I can do?" she asked.

Alexa looked from her to Max. "He's all I have. Find him."

"Holy hell, Frankie!" Beenie said. "Would you look at the knockers on this babe?" He passed the magazine to Frankie, but Deedee snatched it from her husband's hand.

"Don't you dare, Frankie Fontana. The only knockers you're going to look at are mine."

"Oh, yeah. I wasn't thinking."

Beenie stretched. "Man, I'm bored. I should go out."

Deedee regarded him in his jeans, a wrinkled T-shirt, and old sneakers. "You're not supposed to drive."

"You feel like doing a little night fishing, Frankie?"

Frankie started to answer when the front door opened. Big John led Swamp Dog into the room. His black eye patch appeared more ominous.

"Duncan just called my cell phone," he said. "They found Choo-Choo."

Deedee leapt from the sofa. "Where is he? Is he okay?"

"Who's Choo-Choo?" Beenie said.

Deedee waved her hand at him impatiently. "My dog. Is my little boy all right?" Deedee repeated.

Swamp Dog nodded. "He's fine. Duncan is trying to grab a nap since he hasn't slept in about eighteen hours so I offered to drive over and pick up the pooch."

"I'm going with you," Deedee said. "Choo-Choo gets nervous around strangers."

Frankie put his hand on her shoulder. "I'll go, sweetheart." He looked at Swamp Dog. "How long will it take? I don't like leaving Deedee."

"He was found in an abandoned building in town. I don't know the details, only that Duncan wants me to pick him up right away. We can drive over and back in twenty minutes."

Frankie got up. "Let's hit the road."

"But Frankie—" Deedee tried to argue.

"You need to stay with Beenie," he said.

"You want me to tag along?" Big John asked.

"No. I don't want anyone coming through that door while I'm gone."

Big John nodded.

"We can go in my old truck," Swamp Dog said. "It'll be quicker that way." They hurried out.

"You know where I'll be if you need me," Big John told Deedee, returning to his post at the front door.

"I don't like it," Deedee whispered to Beenie once they were alone. "Something doesn't feel right."

"What are you worried about?" he asked.

"I'm sure you don't remember all that's gone on around here, but believe me, we've all been in a lot of danger."

"I assumed as much when I regained consciousness in the ambulance."

"I don't like the idea of Frankie going off like that with—"

"Swamp Dog?"

She nodded. "He looks evil."

"Yeah, he even *sounds* evil, and if you ask me he's got a sucky attitude. I could probably take him down."

Deedee ignored him and began to pace. She turned for the door. "Come with me."

"What?"

"I need your help."

Beenie sighed and followed her into the kitchen, where Choker was making a sandwich. He smiled at Deedee.

"You want me to relieve you for a while?" Beenie asked.

Choker looked straight at him, but it was obvious he was trying to keep a straight face. "I think I can handle it, cowboy."

Deedee headed for the door to the wine cellar.

"What are you doing?" Choker asked.

"They've found Choo-Choo," she said excitedly. "I want plenty of champagne on hand to celebrate."

"I'll get it," Choker said.

Deedee shook her head. "Oh, you'll never find it. I keep the good stuff at the very back of the cellar. Even I have trouble finding it."

"So I'll look," Choker said with a shrug. "John Wayne here can look after you while I'm gone." He started down the stairs.

"Would you please tell me what you're doing?" Beenie demanded.

"We're going after Frankie."

He crossed his arms over his chest. "Has your curling

iron fried your brain, lady? Why would I want to do something stupid like that when your husband specifically told you to stay put?"

"Because you and I used to be very close, and when your memory returns you're going to feel crummy for not helping me."

"Okay, one more time in case you misunderstood. Frankie said—"

"I don't *care* what Frankie said, and I'm tired of being treated like a porcelain doll that will break at any moment. I still have a mind of my own."

"Good speech. What are you trying to say?"

"I'll go alone."

Beenie blocked the door. He sized Deedee up. "Just how close were we?"

She hesitated. Finally, she put her hands on either side of Beenie's face and kissed him passionately. She released him, and he whistled under his breath.

"Does your husband know?"

"He doesn't care what I do." Deedee smiled beguilingly and opened the back door. The security guard looked up. "I need a teensy-weensy favor," she told the man. "Choker, the wrestler, is in the cellar looking for champagne. I don't want him down there alone."

"We have a man posted down there, ma'am," the guard said.

"Yes, but I'd feel so much better if you'd check on him," she said, pinching his cheek lightly. "He's been down there a long time, and well—" She whispered the rest. "He's terrified of spiders. Are you afraid of spiders?"

The man straightened his shoulders. "Absolutely not. I'll be happy to help." He opened the door to the cellar and started down the stairs.

Deedee waited for a moment before closing the door softly and turning the lock. Beenie grinned, and they hurried out the back door. "This way," she said, heading toward Jamie's car.

Beenie reached it first. "There aren't any keys in the ignition."

"I know where she keeps her spare." Deedee reached inside the rear bumper. She pulled out a black case with a magnet on one side, opened it, and produced a key. "You'll have to drive," she said. "My license has been suspended because I keep running into people with my car."

"I thought I wasn't supposed to drive because of my concussion."

"You're going to let something silly like that stop you?"

"Hell, no."

"Then hurry up and let's get out of here. Once Choker realizes he's been locked in the cellar he'll kick down the door." They climbed inside Jamie's car. Beenie started the engine, put the car into gear and they shot off. They passed the guard at the gate who looked up in surprise when they didn't stop to sign out.

"Faster," Deedee said. "Maybe if we're lucky we can catch up. But don't get too close. I don't want Swamp Dog to know we're following him."

Beenie shot her a look of pure annoyance. "Look, I know what I'm doing, okay? Just keep quiet and let me do the driving. By the way, you're going to owe me big time for this."

"I'll take you to Charleston on a shopping spree," she said. "We'll have lunch at your favorite restaurant."

He frowned at her. "Why the hell would I want to go shopping?"

She sighed. "Oh, never mind. How about I just buy you a pack of Redman chewing tobacco and a case of beer?"

"That'll work." He looked her over. "But I have something better in mind."

"Sheesh!" Deedee said.

Max dialed Duncan's cell phone, and the man picked up on the first ring. "Find Swamp Dog," Max said without preamble.

"I was just about to call you," Duncan replied. "We have a problem."

"I'm listening."

"Swamp Dog left with Frankie not more than fifteen minutes ago. Claimed they found Deedee's dog."

"What the hell are you talking about?" Max demanded, startling Jamie and Alexa, who were sitting on the sofa across from him.

"It gets worse," Duncan said. "Deedee and her houseboy took off right behind them. Just flew right through the security checkpoint. I was trying to grab some well-needed shut-eye in my truck when one of the guys alerted me. I've already sent a crew out looking for them, but they've got a ten-minute head start on us."

"How could this have happened?" Max said.

"Deedee locked Choker and another guard in the cellar. By the time Choker broke the door down they were gone."

"That sister of mine just doesn't give up. Anything else?"

"Yeah. Is Swamp Dog on our side or not?"

"I don't think Swamp Dog takes sides," Max said. "Consider him dangerous and call me when you know something."

"What's going on?" Jamie asked as soon as Max hung up.

He quickly repeated the story.

"I've heard of Swamp Dog," Alexa said, the color leaving her face. "If he's involved in this, my son could already be dead."

Max glanced around the room. "I need your help, Alexa. You wrote the word 'EPSCO' on the last page of the budget printout. We can't find anything on it. I think it's a password to something."

"I don't know what it means," she said. "Old man Grimby doodles a lot when he's on the phone. I saw the word and wrote it down. What does this have to do with my son?"

"This town is filled with corruption, Alexa, but you already know it, or you wouldn't have given me the name EPSCO."

Alexa remained silent.

"This may be important," Max said.

Jamie noted the look of fear in the woman's eyes. "Have you been threatened? Is that why you're scared to talk?"

"If I implicate anyone I could be implicated, as well," she said.

"How?" Max asked.

"Someone set up an account for Danny in the amount of fifty thousand dollars. I was so scared I burned the letter, but I know the account is being held in a Delaware bank."

"Do you remember who sent the letter?" Max asked.

"There was no return address. I'm scared, Max. These people mean business. As long as I played along I was okay."

"You wouldn't get into trouble for printing out the city budget," Max reminded her. "Besides, it's a fake."

"Yes. So why are they doing this? And why not take me? Danny has nothing to do with this."

"They're playing with your head, that's all. They knew you'd be more afraid if they took the boy than you would be for yourself. They're counting on the fear factor here, Alexa, believe me. They have no intention of hurting Danny; this is simply payback for cooperating with me in the first place." Max sounded more confident than he felt. He suspected Danny was in grave danger.

"Do you know if Phillip is involved in this?" Jamie asked.

Alexa gave her a blank look. "He's the one who sent you to my office. If he were trying to keep you from finding out anything, why would he do that?"

Jamie nibbled her bottom lip as she considered it.

"Excuse me," Max said. "I need to get on my computer." He hurried away.

"His computer is in his car," Jamie told Alexa.

"Don't you think Lamar should call the FBI?" Alexa asked, wringing her hands. "After all, this is a kidnapping case."

"Just hold tight," Jamie said. "Max's computer is probably more sophisticated than what the FBI has."

Max slipped into his car. "I've got information for you, Muffin."

"It's about the missing boy, right? Danny Sanders?"

"Yeah. Someone set up an account for him in a bank in Delaware in hopes of keeping his mother quiet. I think that's where the missing dollars are going. Banking laws are fairly lenient in that state so money could easily be laundered and forwarded to another location. I think EPSCO might be the password we need to get in."

"Okay, searching now."

"How long will it take?"

"There are a shitload of financial institutions, Max, and we don't know if it's the password into the bank, or a private account. I'll let you know if I get a hit. Anything else?"

"I just thought of something. I'll get back to you."

"Is this the place?" Frankie asked once Swamp Dog slowed and turned into the parking lot of the city municipal building.

"Yeah." Swamp Dog reached beneath his seat and pulled out a remote-control device. He pushed a button, and a door rose. He drove inside, and the door closed. "This is it, pal. The end of the road."

Frankie nodded as though he understood. "I only have one request. I don't care what you do with me, but don't hurt my wife."

"If I was interested in her I would have led them here. She and her houseboy have been following us since we left the house. Right now they're so lost they don't know which way is up." Swamp Dog grinned. "It's you they want, Fontana. You and your genius brother-in-law, Max Holt."

"You won't be able to get your hands on him."

"Watch me."

"Shit!" Beenie said. "Where'd they go? I saw them turn down this street."

"You idiot!" Deedee cried. "I told you to speed up."

Beenie glared at her. "You talk to me like that

again, and I'm going to put you out of the car, you got that?" They bounced along the road for a moment. "Oh, damn," he said.

"What is it?" Deedee cried.

"I just remembered who hit me. That bastard Swamp Dog. I never saw him, but I'd know that voice anywhere."

Deedee gasped in horror. She grabbed Beenie's arm. "We have to find them!" she all but shrieked.

The car swerved to one side, almost running into a ditch. "Get your hands off of me, you crazy woman!" Beenie turned the steering wheel in the opposite direction but overcorrected and lost control. Deedee screamed as they slammed into a tree.

"Are you okay?" she asked Beenie.

"Hell, no, I'm *not* okay," he yelled. "I hit my damn head on the steering wheel. You could have gotten us both killed."

Deedee grimaced. "You've gone and wrecked Jamie's car. She'll never forgive me. What do we do now?"

"It's a no-brainer, lady. We hoof it."

"Think, Alexa," Max prodded. "If somebody in the city were trying to hide something or someone, where would they go?"

She twisted her hands nervously. "I don't know. If I did, I'd tell you."

A middle-aged man stepped through the front door. He wore a collar. "Alexa?"

She turned. "Father Joseph? What are you doing here? Oh, God, it's bad news, isn't it?"

"I came because I heard Danny is missing. I don't know anything, Alexa."

She looked around the room. The officers stood

there, faces carved in sympathy and regret. The priest wore a pained expression. "You think he's dead, don't you?" she said, bursting into tears. "All of you think my son is already dead."

"No," Max said. "He's not dead. We have to believe that."

"Let's go somewhere private," Father Joseph said. "I'd like to spend a few minutes with you alone." He led the sobbing woman away.

"What are we going to do?" Jamie asked Max, wondering how long Alexa could hold up. "Do you have a plan?"

Max was prevented from answering when his cell phone rang. He pulled it from his pocket. "Max Holt," he said tersely.

Jamie watched the changes on Max's face. The look in his eyes told her something was wrong, bad wrong. He snapped his phone shut. "I have to leave for a few minutes," he told her. "I want you to stay with Alexa."

"What's happened?"

"Don't automatically assume the worst, okay?"

"I know you, Max. Who just called?"

"It's not important, but I have other business to attend to. I won't be long. Trust me for once."

She studied him. She did trust him, but she knew he took risks, and that's what bothered her.

He glanced around. "I have to let Lamar know I'm going out for a few minutes. I'll be back before you know it."

Jamie waited until Max headed off to talk with Lamar before racing out the front door. She opened the door to Max's car. "Muffin, Max is in trouble," she said. "I don't have time to explain. Open the trunk so I can climb in."

"I don't normally take orders from anyone but Max," Muffin said.

"I'm pretty sure this is a life-or-death situation. If you don't help me now, you might not have Max around to give you orders."

"It's going to be tight in there," Muffin warned, "even though the car was designed with more room than the standard Porsche."

"Yeah, okay," Jamie said, closing the door. The trunk popped open. She was surprised to find it located at the front of the car. Without wasting another second, she ran in that direction. "Oh, damn," she muttered when she saw just how small the trunk was. She climbed in, scrunching her legs beneath her chin, making herself as tiny as she could. She closed it only seconds before Max opened the door, slipped into the front seat and started the engine.

"I have a situation on my hands, Muffin," he said, as the safety bar closed over him, and he shot out of the parking lot. "It's serious."

"I'm all ears."

"Swamp Dog is holed up in the city municipal building. He's got Frankie and Alexa's son. And Deedee's dog," he added.

"A hostage situation?"

"Yeah. Now, listen, if I don't get back to you—"

"Don't talk like that, Max."

"Listen to me, Muffin, this is very important. I've been thinking about the word 'EPSCO.' I think it's a cryptogram for the word 'SCOPE.'"

"Meaning the people involved scope out opportunities to rip off everybody they can."

"That's probably not exactly what they had in mind when they came up with the word, but it means the same thing. It may just be the password to get into those financial organizations in Delaware."

"How come I didn't figure it out on my own, Max? I mean, a child could have done it."

"Because it was too simple, and we have a tendency to make things more complicated than they are. It was staring us right in the face."

"Max, I can't let you go into that building. You're dealing with a madman."

"I can take care of myself."

"Yeah, right. Your sixth-degree black belt won't mean shit to an animal like Swamp Dog. A karate chop is no match for a bullet. I have to notify the FBI. They could grab a chopper and be here in an hour."

"There's no time. Swamp Dog said if I wasn't there in fifteen minutes he would start shooting."

Chapter
FIFTEEN

From inside the trunk, Jamie heard the entire exchange, and her blood ran cold at the thought of Max facing Swamp Dog. Max didn't even carry a weapon, for God's sake! Not that it would matter to a man like Swamp Dog. She braced herself more tightly to keep from slamming into the sides of the trunk as the car careened around a corner. Max was literally flying. After five minutes or so, the car slowed. Jamie felt the car turn several more times before it finally came to a screeching halt.

"Where are we?" Muffin asked.

"I've parked in front of a wooden garage door that's twice the size of a normal one. I assume this is where they store the city trucks and heavy equipment. There's a side door as well. I'll enter the building through it."

"My exterior audio sensors are on," Muffin said. "I should be able to hear and record everything that goes on in there. So far it's quiet, but my heat sensors tell me Swamp Dog and his hostages are near the back of the warehouse." She paused. "Uh, Max?"

"Yeah?"

"Be careful."

Jamie listened as Max climbed from the car. She waited until she thought he was out of earshot. "Muffin?"

"I'm here."

"Pop the trunk."

There was a moment's hesitation. "Sorry, Jamie. Can't do it."

Jamie blinked in the darkness. "What do you mean you can't do it?"

"It's far too dangerous to let you out."

Jamie's temper flared. "Max is in danger, dammit, and I'm not going to just lie here in a fetal position and wait for Swamp Dog to kill him. Let me out of the damn trunk now!" Jamie was glad Vera wasn't there to collect quarters over her cussing.

Muffin didn't respond.

Mitzi and Lenny had cruised by slowly as Max turned into the driveway of the old building. They pulled into the parking lot of an adjacent building, and Mitzi cut the engine. She reached into her purse for her gun. She turned to Lenny. "Ready?"

He sighed.

"You're going in there with me whether you like it or not."

"I'm not a killer, Mitzi, and neither are you."

"Listen to me, you dumb son of a bitch. There's a lot of money riding on this. We go in, pop the guy, and get the hell out of there. Simple as that."

"We could go back to our old life," Lenny said. "I could get a real job. Ya know, you don't appreciate life until you watch it snuffed out of another person," he added. He met her gaze. "I could take care of you, Mitzi. You wouldn't have to go back to stripping."

Mitzi's mouth fell open in surprise. "You? You can't even wipe your ass, Lenny."

"A man can change if he has reason enough. You're enough reason for me. Vito never appreciated you like I did. Like I still do."

Mitzi looked thoughtful for a moment, but then the hard look returned. She raised her gun, pointing it directly at Lenny. "You either go in there with me now or I'm going to put a hole in your head the size of Texas."

Lenny looked dejected as he reached beneath the seat for his gun. "Maybe dead is better," he said. He got out of the car, and they started for the building.

Max stood just inside the door of the municipal building and waited. The place was a massive storage facility for city equipment, which included bulldozers, trucks, tractors, and yellow cars. The smell of diesel and rust was almost overpowering. Generators hummed, and Max could hear the creak and pop of cooling metal from some of the vehicles.

Swamp Dog stepped from behind one of the trucks, holding a gun. "Nice seeing you again, Max."

"Where are the others?"

"I'll show you." He motioned Max to follow him.

Max did as he was told. Frankie and Alexa's son were tied to a gas tank, their mouths covered with duct tape. Choo-Choo was leashed nearby. He barked and wagged his tail at the sight of Max. "Are you all okay?" Max asked, looking from Frankie to the boy. They nodded. The fear in Danny's eyes was palpable. Max found himself hating Swamp Dog more.

He turned to Swamp Dog. "Let them go. It's me you want. Besides, Frankie has already decided to pull out of the race."

"You think I'm stupid? He knows too much. He'd squeal like a stuck pig if I let him go."

"He doesn't plan to hang around long enough. His wife is already packing their bags for Scottsdale, Arizona. They just want to get the hell out of here and start a new life."

Swamp Dog shrugged. "You don't get it, Holt. I don't care about any of this."

"What about the boy? What did he do wrong?"

"His mother has a big mouth."

"That's the problem with you and the people you're working for. You're so damn greedy and paranoid you don't know what you're doing. Alexa Sanders would never say anything to jeopardize her son's life. I want you to untie him and send him on his way."

"I told you a long time ago I play by my own rules," Swamp Dog said. "I've decided to up the ante. You want your friends and that stupid mutt to stay alive, then you have to kill me." His look was menacing. "If I kill you, I get to take them out as well."

Max's eyes hardened. He almost choked on his anger. He had never killed, but he knew he could kill the man before him and never regret it. But he had to keep that anger in check, keep his wits about him because others were involved.

"I'm unarmed. You plan to gun down a defenseless man, Hodges?"

"I don't know anyone by that name."

"Sure you do. That was the name you used to go by. When you were a big brave soldier in Special Forces," he added. "Until you went over the edge. You lost it, didn't you?"

"Go screw yourself, Holt. You don't know shit."

"I know all of it."

Swamp Dog's face twisted into a painful snarl. "I have all the more reason to kill you now. But I'm no coward. You want hand-to-hand combat, I can do that, too." He laid down the gun and kicked it aside. Very slowly, he approached Max.

Max waited, his face void of expression, eyes alert and trained on the man before him. Suddenly, Swamp Dog rushed him. Max stepped to one side and gave him a kick that sent him flying into a bulldozer.

Swamp Dog stood up and wiped a trickle of blood off the side of his face. He smiled. "This is going to be more fun than I thought. I do love killing people who can give me a run for my money."

"That's not the information I have," Max said. "I hear you like taking down innocent women and children."

"The enemy always looks the same."

Max decided to try to keep him talking until he could come up with a plan. "Why'd you come to work for me?"

"Because I like getting close to the enemy. Close enough to feel the knife go in."

"Why did you kill Vito? Wouldn't it have been simpler to let him shoot me and get it over with?"

"The guy kept getting in my way. I took him out so I could have the pleasure of killing you myself."

"You had the opportunity on your boat that day."

"You don't understand warfare, Holt. It takes only seconds to kill. What fun is that? I like watching my prey squirm."

The two men circled each other as they talked, each gauging their opponent. All at once, Swamp Dog moved like lightning, ramming his head into Max's belly. Air gushed from Max's lungs and he staggered back, barely evading Swamp Dog's grasping hands.

"Whatsa matter, rich boy?" Swamp Dog taunted. "Never been in a fight with a real man before? Or maybe you're used to hiring somebody else to do your fighting."

Max blinked several times to clear his head, and then lashed out with his foot. The front kick connected solidly with Swamp Dog's stomach, doubling him over. The man had no time to recover before Max followed up with a roundhouse kick to the head. Swamp Dog dropped like a felled oak. Max followed him down and pinned him to the floor.

Swamp Dog bucked like a wild bronco beneath Max, trying to break Max's hold. Swamp Dog gave one final heave, and threw him off. They grappled together, each desperate to gain the advantage. Out of the murderous scrimmage, Swamp Dog found an opening and reached for Max's neck, reaching, reaching, until finally he closed his hands around it and began to squeeze. "You're a dead man, Holt." His eyes glittered with rage.

"Pretend I'm an innocent woman or child," Max managed. "Isn't that the way"—he paused and tried to suck in much-needed oxygen—"you like it?" He grabbed for Swamp Dog's thumbs and twisted hard.

Swamp Dog howled like an injured animal. "What did you do to them?" Max demanded, staring into the face of a mad man.

"What I'm going to do to you, asshole."

Max couldn't allow Swamp Dog to win this fight. He couldn't let this psycho kill Frankie and Danny. Alexa's boy. Deedee's husband.

He summoned every ounce of strength he had left. Breaking Swamp Dog's hold, Max took one precious split-second window of opportunity. With a carefully aimed chop, he landed a blow to the man's larynx. Swamp Dog clutched his throat, his face distorted in agony. Max struggled to catch his breath.

With the speed of a trained killer, Swamp Dog reached for his abandoned gun. Max scrambled toward him, but it was too late. Swamp Dog raised the gun and aimed it at Max.

A shot rang out, echoing inside the large building. Max froze. Swamp Dog gazed at him in disbelief before his eyes glazed over. The gun fell from his limp fingers and clattered against the floor.

All was silent. Max glanced around. Finally, he heard the sound of high heels. Annabelle Standish stepped from behind one of the bulldozers and smiled at Max. She was regal, dressed in clothes that had never come off a rack.

The gun looked incongruous in her delicate hand.

Max stood. "That pistol doesn't go with your outfit, Annabelle," he said.

"Good evening, Mr. Holt."

Max stood, still panting from the fight. He did not look surprised to see her. "You'll have to excuse my appearance, I've been doing a little hand-to-hand combat."

Annabelle looked at Swamp Dog. "Disgusting fellow, wasn't he? White trash, that's all he was."

"Well, you certainly showed him what happens to folks born on the wrong side of the tracks."

"He disobeyed my orders. When I pay someone to do a job, I expect them to follow through."

"And he was paid to kill me?" Max said. "You know, he tried. He came very close the first night I was in town."

"Don't be ridiculous. We had nothing to do with

that." She glanced at Frankie. "Swamp Dog was hired to scare off Frankie, that's all. But then you came into the picture and started nosing around, and that changed everything. You should have minded your own business, Mr. Holt. It would have been so much simpler."

"And just let you people keep scamming the taxpayers?"

"This town is a better place because of people like me." She drew herself up proudly. "Some people are whiners and complainers, Max. I get things done."

"And pad your pockets along the way."

"You're saying I should do it for nothing?"

"That's how you ended up being touted the most charitable woman in town."

"It gets good press and encourages others to dig deeply into their pockets."

"But it's getting harder for them to keep lining your pocketbook because of all the tax increases. You and your cohorts would have probably gotten away with it, but you all got greedy."

Annabelle opened her mouth to respond but turned when the side door to the building creaked open. Beenie and Deedee peeked inside the door. Max took a step toward Annabelle, but she trained her gun on him. "Don't move," she said. Then, in a voice a Southern hostess would use for welcoming guests, she called out to Deedee. "Please join us, Mrs. Fontana. So glad you could make it."

Deedee and Beenie looked at one another as though unsure what to do. Finally, Deedee spotted Frankie. She hurried inside, with Beenie close behind. "Oh, my God!" She turned to Annabelle. "Why are my husband and that boy tied up?" she demanded. "And why are you holding that gun on Max?"

"You're in no position to question me, dear. Now, you and your servant boy behave yourselves and go stand next to Max."

Beenie bristled. "I am *not* a servant boy, thank you very much. I am Mrs. Fontana's personal assistant."

Deedee snapped her head in his direction. "You got your memory back?"

"Yes, and I'm totally disgusted with the whole thing. Why am I dressed like some man in a beer commercial? And would you look at your shoes. You've ruined a perfectly good pair of Manolo Blahnik heels."

"I stepped in mud," she said. "Look, you've got mud on your sneakers."

Beenie sighed. "Good thing I'm not wearing my Tod's. Who picked out this outfit anyway, Frankie's wrestling buddies? I'm surprised I'm not in a T-shirt brandishing a beer label."

"You forgot you were gay and started acting like a guy."

Beenie's hands fluttered to his throat. "Oh, Lord, say it ain't so. I didn't go hunting or anything like that, did I?"

Max and Annabelle watched the exchange in silence. "Okay, that's enough silliness," Annabelle said. "Perhaps you two don't realize the seriousness of the situation."

Beenie struck a pose and tapped his bottom lip with one finger. "I see a gun and a couple of hostages. Doesn't take a mobile home falling on me to understand what's going on. I'm not an imbecile."

"Phillip said you were foolish," Annabelle said.

Beenie shrugged. "Phillip has poor taste in ties so who's the bigger fool?"

"Would you shut up, you idiot?" Deedee cried. "Do you want to get us all killed?" She flashed a worried look toward Frankie. Her husband struggled with the ropes on his wrists.

"Both of you do as Mrs. Standish says," Max told them. He looked at Annabelle. "What's the plan here?" he asked. "Are you really going to kill all of us?"

"You've left me no choice, Mr. Holt. You know too much."

"And what are you going to do with the bodies?" he asked. "I can't imagine a woman like you digging graves. You'll get bloodstains on your nice dress. What will your dry cleaner think?"

"You underestimate me, Mr. Holt," she said calmly. "I would never have walked through that door without a plan." She nodded toward the gas tanks where Frankie and Danny were tied. "Swamp Dog made it easy for me by tying the hostages to those gas tanks. By the time the authorities find all of you, you'll be burned beyond recognition. And I'll be home sipping tea and planning my next social event."

"That's a pretty good cover for an embezzler and killer."

She shrugged. "People see what they want to see."

Jamie banged against the inside of the trunk. "Muffin, I swear to God, you are going to rue the day you locked me in this trunk."

"Be quiet," Muffin said. "I'm trying to hear what's going on inside, but it's almost impossible with all the noise you're making."

"You heard that shot," Jamie cried. "Max is probably dead." Hot tears filled her eyes. She had never been angrier in her life.

"I told you, Max isn't dead. He's moving around in there. I am still able to pick up his voice now and then, but I can't make out the words. I think he's talking to a woman."

"Do you hear Swamp Dog?"

"No. I think he may have been the one shot."

"What if—"

"Shut up, already," Muffin said. "I just dialed nine-one-one."

Jamie gave a snort of disgust. "Everybody will be dead by then."

"Let them go, Annabelle," Max said softly. "Deal with me."

"I'm in charge here, Max. Not you." She smiled. "I like power. I like knowing I hold everybody's lives in my hands."

"So you're into control. Tell me, do you try to control your son as well? Is that why he has kept quiet about this or is he a team player?" Max decided it was best to keep her talking. Until he could come up with a plan of his own.

"Phillip knows nothing," she snapped, "and if I were trying to control him he wouldn't be marrying Jamie Swift. He's much too good for her."

"The only reason you haven't tried to put a stop to it is because you know you'll alienate him," Max said. "Isn't that right?"

Her eyes narrowed.

"But guess what?" Max went on. "Once Phillip is happily married you won't take priority in his life anymore."

"My son is devoted to me."

Max laughed. "That's all going to change after the wedding. You know he and Jamie are looking for a home of their own. He's even thinking of moving his practice to another state. Neither of them want to live under the same roof with you." It was a lie, but Max knew it would get to her.

Annabelle looked aghast. "That's not true!"

"He's not going to be around to kowtow to your every whim. He'll start avoiding your calls. He'll see you as a burden." Max allowed a small smile. "That's not going to sit well with you, is it? You were counting on Phillip looking after you when you become old and feeble. He's not going to have time, what with his own family. You'll end up in a nursing home eating strained carrots and wondering why he doesn't visit."

"Shut up!" Without warning, Annabelle turned and fired a shot at the gas tank next to Frankie. The bullet missed its target and hit the man instead.

Deedee screamed as Frankie jerked back, then slumped against the gas tank. She started toward him, but Max grabbed her.

"Don't move," he muttered under his breath.

"That bitch shot my husband," Deedee cried. She looked at Annabelle. "Why don't you toss that gun aside and take me on, you big snob? I think a good catfight might teach you some manners."

"Didn't you used to jump out of cakes for a living, Mrs. Fontana? If it weren't for your boy you'd still be dressing like you belong in a bowling alley." She gave a menacing smile. "Speaking of your boy." She aimed the gun at Beenie.

"Hold it right there, lady," Beenie said. He looked at Deedee. "If she kills me would you please see that I'm not buried in this outfit? I want to be dressed in my white linen Armani suit."

Jamie cried out when she heard the second shot. "Do something, Muffin!"

"Get in the car," Muffin ordered. The lid to the trunk popped open. Jamie scrambled out and opened the door to the car, then jumped when Muffin hit a siren. She slid inside and started the engine.

"What are you doing?" Muffin demanded.

"I'm going in."

"Oh, no you're not." Muffin cut the engine.

"We have no choice."

"I'm not putting you in the line of danger," Muffin said.

"Frankenstein!" Jamie shouted.

"Shit," Muffin muttered.

"Disable AI."

Silence. Jamie restarted the engine, waited for the safety bar to close over her, and slammed into first gear. She closed her eyes and rammed the accelerator to the floor. The car leapt forward.

Deedee screamed as Max's car ripped through the wooden garage door. Annabelle, already shaken and distracted over the sound of the siren, accidentally dropped her gun. She reached for it. Max lunged for her. They struggled, and the gun went off.

Jamie climbed from the car and watched Annabelle go limp in Max's arms, the look in the woman's eyes dazed and surprised as she gazed down in disbelief at the red stain spreading across her abdomen. Max simply held her, his expression sad.

"Help is on the way," Jamie said.

Deedee raced toward Frankie and Danny. She ripped the tape off Frankie's mouth, and he raised his head and smiled.

Deedee cried out, so startled she almost fell over. "Oh, Jesus, oh, Jesus—" she whispered in a heartfelt prayer.

"I'm okay, Deedee," he said.

"You're bleeding!"

"I'm fine. She just winged me. The bullet grazed my shoulder, honey. It hurts like hell, but at least she didn't hit the gas tank."

"I thought you were dead!"

"I only pretended because I hoped she wouldn't fire again. Untie the boy, sweetheart. And give Choo-Choo a hug."

Mitzi and Lenny, who'd overheard the whole thing while in the process of trying to get into the building undetected, looked at one another and blinked.

"Do we really want to get in the middle of this, Mitzi?" Lenny said. "They've got guns in there, and they're not afraid to use them. We're going to get killed."

The hard look in Mitzi's eyes had been replaced with fear. She looked at the gun in her hand. Finally, she dropped it. "To hell with it, man. I'm going home."

Ten minutes later, the municipal building was surrounded by police cars and several ambulances. Swamp Dog lay in one, his body draped with a sheet, and a bleeding Annabelle had just been whisked away in another ambulance to the emergency room. A paramedic tended to Frankie's wound while Deedee fussed with her husband like a mother hen. Max, who'd already placed a call to Alexa, had lifted Danny onto a large bulldozer, and the kid was having the time of his life pretending to drive it. Jamie and Beenie watched with a smile.

Alexa cried out when she spotted her son, and Max helped Danny down and into the arms of his frantic mother.

"I'm not hurt, Mom," the boy said, as Alexa searched for wounds.

Alexa looked up at Max, her eyes swimming with tears. "I thought—" She shuddered.

Max smiled gently. "Take your son home," he said. "He'll be safe now."

She nodded and led the boy from the building. Lamar came through the door and shook Danny's hand on the way out. He spotted Max and hurried over.

"The FBI is on the way." Lamar grew serious. "You took a big chance coming here on your own, Holt. You could have been killed. The hostages could have been killed."

Max kept his mouth shut. It wasn't the first time he'd been taken to task over interfering with an investigation, and it wouldn't be the last.

"I have something for you," Max said. "There are certain documents in my car that should be in your possession before the FBI arrives and takes over. My computer is trying to open files in a financial institution in Delaware. Once we get a hit, you'll probably have the location where the town's tax dollars have been going, as well as who all the players are. I'll get them to you before we leave."

"Is Annabelle Standish involved?"

"I suspect she's the queen bee of the operation."

Lamar sighed. "Man, I hope she lives. I'd love to lock that snooty woman behind bars." He looked at Max. "You know, this whole thing has been confusing. I'm still trying to figure out how that Vito guy got involved."

"I have every confidence that you'll succeed," Max said.

"Thanks." Lamar offered his hand, and they shook.

"For everything." He started to walk away, then slapped an open palm against his forehead. "Blast it, I almost forgot. I'm just not used to all this action. Every time I turn around there's something else going on, you know?"

"What is it?" Max said.

"I just got a call from the fire department. Swamp Dog's houseboat is burning out of control. The fire chief says you can see the blaze for miles."

Max simply nodded.

"You don't look surprised."

"Nothing would surprise me at this point."

Lamar joined the other officers and Max walked over to Jamie and Beenie, who were deep in conversation, Beenie gesturing with his hands as he spoke. "What's going on?" he asked.

"Beenie's just ticked off," she said.

"She's right," Beenie said. "I'm sick and damn tired of people pushing me around. I may be gay, but that doesn't mean I can't defend myself. After all, I was John Wayne for a while, you know? He used to be my hero."

"You don't have to take crap from nobody," Jamie told him.

"I think you were very brave," Max said. "You really told Annabelle Standish where to get off. And she was holding a gun on you."

Beenie looked thoughtful. "I think there are probably worse things than being shot." He looked at Jamie. "Like having people make fun of you all the time. I'm not going to tolerate it anymore." He sighed heavily. "But right now I just want to slip into my Calvin Klein jammies and sleep for a week."

"You deserve it," Jamie said.

Suddenly, Beenie looked up in alarm. "Oh, God, Jamie, you're going to hate me when I tell you what I did to your car."

Three nights later, Frankie climbed the stairs to the bandstand in the courthouse square. The crowd broke into hearty applause at the sight of him. Jamie and Deedee smiled at one another.

"My Frankie is so brave," Deedee whispered. "I know his shoulder hurts like the dickens, but he would die before he'd let on."

"What about me?" Beenie whined. "My head still hurts, but nobody cares about that."

Max stood there quietly, watching his brother-in-law get ready to give the most important speech of his political career. Alexa and Danny had joined the group, as had Snakeman, Big John, and Choker. Vera and Mike stood in the front. Mike was getting the speech on tape while Vera snapped pictures for the newspaper.

Frankie beamed at the roaring crowd. "Ladies and gentlemen," he began. "As you know from reading the newspaper and watching TV, our town is undergoing tremendous changes. I promised to look into your missing tax dollars, and with the help of a number of good people and our fine police chief, we have already managed to get most of the answers."

More applause.

"The investigation continues," Frankie said, "and I promise that everyone involved in the corruption will be prosecuted. I will see that justice is served." He was forced to pause again as the crowd cheered.

"Tomorrow, when you go into that voting booth, I only ask you to remember one thing. As mayor of

Beaumont, I will keep my promises. I will cut taxes and fight wasteful spending, and I will do everything possible to see that the fraudulent tax dollars that were stolen are returned to each and every one of you. It's your money. You earned it."

The crowd went wild.

Max looked at Jamie. "Guess we know who's going to win the election tomorrow."

She nodded. "It would be kind of hard for him to lose, seeing as how the present mayor is under investigation for embezzlement."

Max smiled. "That does better Frankie's chances."

"Uh, Max, we need to talk," she said. "My lawyer called me this afternoon and—"

"Why don't we talk later?" he suggested. "I don't want to miss the rest of Frankie's speech." Max felt someone nudge his arm and found Police Chief Lamar Tevis by his side.

"We done good, Holt," he said. "Why don't you sign on as one of my deputies? I've got my work cut out for me, you know. Can't even find the time to do a little fishing."

"From what I hear, you've been a busy man the past couple of days."

"Yes, well, I have friends in high places." He winked, and then grew serious. "I guess you heard a couple of our town's finest packed their bags and high-tailed it out of here in the middle of the night."

"Nobody has seen hide nor hair of Grimby," Alexa said. "Talk about job security. I'm practically the only one left on my floor."

"Alexa has been a big help to me," Lamar said.

"Just don't keep her too long," Max said, smiling at the woman and ruffling Danny's hair. "I know you need her right now, but she's got a job waiting for her elsewhere if she wants it."

"She'd make a fine city auditor," Lamar said.

Max arched one brow as he regarded Alexa. "Are you considering it?"

She shrugged. "Old man Grimby is obviously on the run, so I need to hang around and get this mess sorted out."

Max took her hand and squeezed it. "You do what you need to do. You have my card."

They faced the stage when the crowd burst out with fresh applause. Max listened for a few minutes, then turned, trying to thread his way through the people.

Jamie glanced around and saw that Max was gone. Where could he be? she wondered. "Deedee, have you seen Max?"

"No, honey. Maybe he went to the concession stand."

Jamie pushed through the crowd, calling loudly to Max. She felt a knot of anxiety in the pit of her stomach. Had Max simply decided to leave without saying good-bye to her?

It seemed to take forever for her to escape the throng of people. Jamie sighed a breath of relief when she spied Max heading toward his car, which had miraculously come through the crash without so much as a scratch.

"Max!" she yelled. "Wait!" He kept on walking. "Double damn," she said, knowing he would never hear her with all the noise. She took off in a run. He turned as she caught up with him. "Where are you going?" she asked.

"Jamie, you should be with the others."

"You're leaving, aren't you? You were just going to leave without saying good-bye. I don't believe it."

He smiled and tugged a strand of her blond hair. "I knew it would feel like silk, and I was right." His look softened. "I have other business waiting," he said. "Besides, your fiancé needs you right now, what with his mother still hospitalized in critical condition."

"Max—" Jamie tried to speak but her tongue suddenly felt weighted. "The engagement is off."

He looked amused. "This is a hell of a time to call it quits with the poor guy, don't you think? Talk about kicking a man when he's down."

"I had no choice. Phillip suspected all along that things weren't right, but he looked the other way because he wanted to protect his mother. The same woman who tried to kill my friends," she added.

"He probably won't be indicted."

"I can't marry him."

"Because you're hot for me?"

Jamie rolled her eyes in order to keep him from seeing how close to the truth he was. "You never give up, Holt." She crossed her arms over her breasts. "I don't love Phillip the way a wife should. He knew it, but he figured things would change in time. I'm not prepared to wait that long *or* take the chance that it'll never happen."

"Look, Jamie, you had your life all figured out before I got here. I had no right to interfere. I'm sorry."

"So you're just going to take off for Tennessee and look for that preacher?"

Max hesitated. "Like they say, it's not over till it's over."

Jamie nodded. "Okay, what you're saying is that we still have more work to do."

"We?"

"These people tried to kill me, too, Max. I'm just as involved as you are."

"No way, Jamie. I have a feeling the person I'm looking for is a whole lot more dangerous than anything we've come up against so far."

She walked over to Max's car and waited. "Let's go," she said.

"Jamie—"

"If you won't open the door for me I'll ride in the trunk like before. Or I'll follow you."

Max grinned. "You can't follow me. Your car's in the shop, remember?"

"And it'll probably be there for six months, so you owe me a ride."

Max sighed. "Jamie, I don't know how long I'll be gone, and you've got a newspaper to run."

"Mike and Vera are doing a fine job. Besides, I can check on them from time to time." It was odd how the newspaper had suddenly taken second place in her life as soon as Max Holt had appeared.

He shook his head. "I don't like it."

Jamie tried to open the car door but found it locked. She knocked on the hood. "Muffin, let me in."

"Get lost," Muffin said.

"Is she *still* mad at me?" Jamie asked Max.

"You stole her thunder. Muffin doesn't like being upstaged by anyone."

"I wasn't upstaged," Muffin snapped. "I had a better plan and Jamie wrecked it."

"I'm really sorry," Jamie said. "I'm only human." She tapped the window. "Come on and let me in, Muf."

The lock on the door clicked, and Jamie reached for the handle. "Be careful about knocking on the exterior," Muffin said. "I'm still sore from you barreling through that damn garage door."

"You don't have a mark on you," Jamie said, noting the proud look on Max's face.

"I'm emotionally scarred," Muffin replied.

Max let himself into the car and stared at Jamie thoughtfully. "Honey, you need to stay in Beaumont where you belong. You need the predictability this town and its people bring you. You know what my life is like."

"So maybe I'll learn to take more risks."

Max shook his head sadly. "It won't work."

"Is that why you decided to sell me your shares of the company back to me for one dollar?" she asked. "So you wouldn't have to come back?"

"Of course I'll come back. Frankie and Deedee are here. As for selling you my shares of the business, you weren't supposed to find out about that until later."

"Sorry, Max, but my lawyer is also one of the guys who tried to get me in the backseat of his car at the drive-in movie. He thought I should know. He also told me you left a check for me in the amount of two hundred thousand dollars to add to my business account. Do you have any idea the kind of raise Vera is going to expect when she catches wind of that?"

"The newspaper belongs to you. It belonged to your family. Beaumont needs a good newspaper, and we both know you're highly capable. I gave you the money because I never want you to struggle like you did in the past." He smiled gently. "I have to go, Swifty."

Jamie felt a moment of sheer panic. "Okay, answer one question. I know we drive each other crazy and tend to argue most of the time, but how would you feel if you thought you'd never see me again?"

Max looked at her. Their gazes locked. "Oh, Jamie,"

he said, running one hand over his head as though confused. "I don't know. My life is, well, very different from what you're used to."

Jamie felt her heart sag in her chest. The thought of watching Max Holt drive away and never seeing him again was more than she could bear. Breaking it off with Phillip had been painful, but it was kid's stuff compared to this. "Okay, Max," she said softly, trying to blink back tears. "I understand. I just want you to know—" She turned away and reached for the door handle. "Never mind. You and Muffin take care, okay?" She stepped out of the car and closed the door behind her.

Max just sat there.

"Way to go, big shot," Muffin said. "You just hurt her feelings big time."

"It's better this way," Max told her.

"So what are we waiting for? If you're in such an all-fired hurry, let's go."

Max started the engine, and the bar closed over him. He put the car into gear and backed out of the parking slot. "Here we go," he said.

Jamie left the courthouse square and started home. Luckily, she lived near town, which would serve her well with her car in repair until God only knew when. Thankfully, Max was handling the costs.

Her eyes filled with tears as she continued walking. She didn't need to think about Max Holt anymore. They had shared a lot together, good times and bad, and now he was heading toward a new adventure. Thankfully, she still had her newspaper, and although she was glad to have the added funds for her account, she would not buy back Max's shares. He was stuck with the paper whether he ever planned to return to Beaumont or not.

She sniffed. What she needed was a good cry. After all that had happened, her stress level was at a new high. She would go home, lock all the doors, and fall into bed and cry to her heart's content.

Jamie started to cross the street but paused at the sound of an approaching car. Lord, she needed to get Max off her mind before somebody ran over her. She glanced up in time to find Max pulling up to the curb beside her. She merely stared in silence.

"You're just begging me to let you come so you can get in my pants," he said.

Jamie stepped closer to the car and looked in the window. He was grinning. "Max, I know you're going to find this difficult to believe, but getting into your pants is the last thing on my mind." It wasn't completely true, but she wouldn't give him the satisfaction of letting him think it.

"So what are you after if it isn't me?"

Jamie hesitated. "I don't know." All she knew for sure was she couldn't let him go.

"Well, I'm not sure it's a good idea, but Muffin thinks you should go with us."

Jamie crossed her arms. "Muffin said that, huh?"

"Yeah. The minute I started off she blasted me with disco music. I can't drive all the way to Tennessee listening to disco."

"This is so typical of you, Max," she said. "It would kill you to admit you want me to go with you. Why is that? Why can't you just ask me?"

He wiped his hands down his face and muttered something under his breath.

"I can't hear you," Jamie said.

He sighed heavily. "Okay, I'd like for you to come with me. Is that what you want to hear?"

She smiled. "Now say please."

"Shit."

"Go ahead and say it," Muffin prodded. "You know you want her with us."

"Okay, then. *Please!*"

Jamie smiled, opened the door and climbed in. The protective bar closed over her. "See, that wasn't so bad. Now then, I need to drop by my house for clothes and work gear. I could do a little investigative reporting. It might be just what I need to liven up the newspaper."

"Yeah, and we need to celebrate the fact you're a free woman. I think I have a good idea how we should get started."

"I may be a free woman, Max, but I am still hands off where you're concerned."

He drove on. "I can wear you down."

"Has it occurred to you that I might need time to get over my breakup with Phillip? I mean, I can't bounce from one relationship to another like you. I like to think mine have a little more depth than yours."

Max checked his wristwatch. "Okay, do you think you can get over the guy by the time we hit the Tennessee border?"

"Don't be ridiculous."

"Okay, Muffin," Max said. "Here's the plan. You and I can play twenty questions on the way to Tennessee while Jamie mopes and pines away for Phillip, but first we have to go by her place for a few things."

"I'm not really crazy about this idea, Max," Muffin replied. "You just barely escaped death during this last little escapade, and now you're heading straight for another one. This is way too much stress on me, you know."

"And while you're mapping out a good route, I want everything you can get me on this preacher. I want to know who works for him and where all his future revivals are going to take place."

"So much for the vacation you promised me."

"We'll take a vacation as soon as I get this little problem dealt with. Won't take long. We'll be in and out in no time flat."

"That's what you said last time. That's what you always say."

"But you love the mountains, Muffin."

"Okay, I'll agree to this one last trip, but then I'm looking for a job elsewhere."

Max looked at Jamie. "You know, I have a feeling this is going to be one of the best trips ever. You and me, cool mountain air, lots of sex."

"Don't count on it, Holt," she said.

He winked. "Hang on, Swifty. I'm going to take you on the ride of a lifetime." He floored the accelerator and they were gone.

FULL SPEED

Prologue

Jamie Swift paced the parking lot of Hank's Pump-n-Pay as she tried to decide her next move. She was mad enough to chew a barbed-wire fence, and her anger had a name to it: Max Holt.

Jamie needed help. She needed someone to talk to, and she needed a ride.

She spied the phone booth and hurried toward it. Who to call? It was after midnight. People with any kind of sense were usually home in bed at this hour. She had to calm down. She sucked in three deep breaths and was immediately hit with a wave of dizziness. She grasped the metal counter beneath the telephone. It would be her luck to hyperventilate right here in the parking lot, fall on her face, and be scarred for life. Yeesh.

Jamie spied the sticker on the pay telephone that read: *DESPERATE FOR HELP? CALL* LEND-A-HAND *HOTLINE.* She leaned closer and read the small print: *We're Here for You Twenty-four Hours a Day.*

Desperate, the advertisement read. That was her, all right. Desperate with a capital *D.* Plus, she was losing her mind. Or what was left of it after two weeks of dodging bullets from a drive-by shooting, almost getting blown to smithereens by a car bomb, and falling into a river and into the path of a hungry alligator. Hell's bells, she was lucky to be alive.

Jamie plunked two quarters into the pay phone. Her hand trembled. The fact it had started raining didn't even faze her. After what she'd been through, that was small potatoes.

Big potatoes was being stranded in a Podunk town she'd never heard of in the middle of the night, with her best friend more than two hours away. Big potatoes was being ogled by a gas station attendant whose oil-stained T-shirt stretched tight across a belly that had obviously sucked down a record number of Budweisers. She glanced his way. Even from a distance he looked dumb as cow dung. Probably had a tattoo on his butt that read *This Side Down* just in case he forgot. He looked at her like he hadn't seen a woman since inside plumbing. Like the kind of man people wouldn't let near their barnyard animals.

She dialed the number.

"Lend-a-Hand Hotline, this is Tanisha."

"Oh, thank God," Jamie said, glad to hear another voice. "I'm, uh—" She glanced down at the ad once more. "I'm desperate."

"Could you hold, please?"

There was a click. Jamie blinked. And waited. She would not cry. She was made of tougher stuff than that. Tough as nails, that's what she was. She glanced toward the man inside the gas station, not more than fifty feet away. Yeah, he really did look kind of goofy. Like maybe there were a couple of orangutans hanging from his family tree. Like maybe his parents had been first cousins. Jamie stared right back at him. Finally, he looked away.

"Hello?" The woman named Tanisha was back.

"Yes. My name is Jamie, and I'm in trouble."

"Are you pregnant and scared and suffering feelings of isolation and helplessness? Afraid of telling your parents?"

Jamie blinked. "No."

"Are you depressed?"

"Well, I—"

"Are you having trouble sleeping at night or sleeping too much? Experiencing appetite changes, feelings of sadness or doom, unable to get up in the morning?" The woman paused, drew in breath, and went on in rapid-fire succession. "Have you lost interest in people, places, or things that used to bring you pleasure? Do you enjoy sex?"

"Sex?"

Huge sigh. "Girl, you got to work with me, 'cause I've got a possible jumper on the other line and I'm the only one working the phones tonight."

"I've never done this sort of thing before," Jamie confessed.

"Me, neither. It's my first night."

Jamie slapped her open palm against her forehead. A rookie.

"Listen up. Does your problem have something to do with a *man*?" Tanisha said the word as though it weren't fit to be used in polite company. "'Cause I know about men, honey."

"Sort of."

"Sister, you hold right there while I try to talk this idiot off the roof of his house. If he don't get off this time, I'm going over there personally and pushing the SOB."

Another click. Jamie wondered if she'd made a mistake by calling. Maybe she wasn't as desperate as she thought; she certainly hadn't considered diving off a rooftop. That had to be a good sign. The man in the gas station had settled down with a magazine, and the rain had slacked off. Things were looking up.

Tanisha picked up. "OK, I'm all ears."

"... **And so there** I was, running my little newspaper in Beaumont, South Carolina, minding my own business. . . ." Jamie paused. "Did I tell you that I own the newspaper? My daddy left it to me when he died. It has been in my family for years."

Silence.

"Hello? Tanisha? Are you there?"

The woman on the other end yawned. "Do you think we could cut to the chase, Jamie? I don't need your life history, and to tell you the truth, my attention span isn't that great. I think I have ADHD."

"Oh." Jamie realized she *had* been talking for some time, but she'd assumed Tanisha would need background information if she was going to help. "OK, so the next thing I knew, this gazillionaire, Maximillian Holt, blew into my life like a bad wind and turned it upside down. See, I need balance and predictability. Max is not a predictable person."

"So what's the problem? Were you born without feet so that you couldn't walk away?"

"It wasn't as simple as that," Jamie replied. "Max is my silent partner. He kept my newspaper from going bankrupt."

"OK, so this is a business problem."

"No." Jamie glanced toward the gas station. The man inside was sleeping, head thrown back, slack-jawed. Maybe he was harmless after all. She went back to her conversation. "Max and I were a team. Not only were we trying to investigate corruption in my town, somebody hired a couple of hit men to kill Max. And guess who found herself right in the middle of it? The gunfire shattered the windows at my newspaper office. If Max hadn't pushed me down on the floor, I wouldn't be talking to you right now."

"Wait a minute, what's with this hit men stuff?" Tanisha asked.

"We think this big-time preacher from Sweet Pea, Tennessee, ordered the hit. He has mob connections. He wanted to buy Max's TV network, but he couldn't scrape the money together fast enough. When Max sold it to another person, someone was mad enough to hire a hit."

"Girl, what'choo mean coming to me with hit men shit? Am I going to lose my kneecaps for hearing this?"

"Nobody knows I called you."

"Listen to me," Tanisha said. "This is police business. I'm going to hang up now."

"Hey, I put fifty cents into the phone. Don't I get some advice? Plus, I was hoping you could tell me where I could get a ride."

"I am not being paid enough to handle mob-related problems. I have a family: a husband, three kids, six brothers, and two sisters. I have cousins, aunts and uncles, grandparents. I have three cats and a beagle. I've got more relatives than the Brady Bunch and the Waltons put together. I can't just disappear into one of those witness protection programs, you get my drift?"

The woman on the other end of the line gave a huge sigh. "Just answer me this: Where is Max now?"

"He dumped me."

"Excuse me!"

"We were on our way to Tennessee, you know, to go look for this minister and his mob friends. Max waited until we got two hours out of Beaumont, and he just stopped the car in the middle of the road and turned around. Said he was taking me home. Said I would, quote, just be in the way, unquote." She paused. "After all we'd been through together, I lost my temper. I made him stop the car. We had this huge fight on the side of the road, and, well . . ." Jamie paused as she recalled their argument. "It was bad."

"So what did you do?"

"Fortunately, it happened close to a gas station, so I walked over."

"And he just drove off and left you?"

"Actually, he came back for me, but I refused to get in." Jamie paused. "Maybe I overreacted."

"You think?"

"I'm better off without him, Tanisha. All I've ever wanted was to live a normal life. Max is not normal."

"Girl, there ain't no such thing as normal."

Jamie thought of Phillip, the man she'd almost married because he'd seemed so safe and normal. Yet his mother had been the ringleader of the corruption in Beaumont. "You may have something there, Tanisha."

"And you don't want to go nosin' around some crazy preacher with mob friends. Besides, it sounds like you and Max are done."

Jamie didn't answer.

"Hello?"

"It wasn't all about Max," Jamie said. "I was hoping

to land a story for my newspaper. I could just taste the headlines, Tanisha: *Renowned Evangelist Hires Hit Men to Take Out Millionaire Tycoon*. This story could have given me my big break. Not only would it have sold newspapers, it probably would have been picked up by the Associated Press. I'll bet *Newsweek* or *Time* magazine would have bought it. This is the kind of story I have always wanted to write."

"Look, you asked for my advice and I gave it to you."

"You're saying I should walk away from my big story and let Max have the final say?" She was suddenly indignant. "I don't *think so*. I have always made my own decisions."

"Hey, it's not like I'm charging you for this, you know. You want to end up buried beneath a concrete building, go for it." She sniffed as though she were truly peeved. "Besides, I think you had your mind all made up long before you called me."

Jamie stood there for a moment, letting the words sink in. "You're right, Tanisha. I just needed to talk it out. To hell with Max. I'm going to Sweet Pea, Tennessee, whether he likes it or not. Besides, I got something he doesn't have."

"And that would be?"

"I'm a woman, that's what. And from the information we've already gotten on the man, it seems this preacher likes women. They're his weakness. I'm going to bait him, Tanisha. I'll have him eating out of my hand so fast he won't know what hit him, and when I get finished I'll have the story of my life."

"What about Max?"

"What about him?" Jamie hung up, a satisfied smile on her face.

ONE

Jamie's excitement about going to Tennessee was short-lived. How the heck was she going to get there without a car? Her vintage Mustang was in the shop back in Beaumont, South Carolina: dented, banged up, with a couple of bullet holes.

She needed a plan.

She needed wheels.

The rain started to fall once more. What she really needed at the moment was either a really big umbrella or a place to stay for the night.

Jamie glanced at the sign on the road that read: *Whittville: 2 Miles.* That didn't tell her much; she'd never heard of the town.

She watched a tow truck turn in to the gas station and pull up beside one of the gas pumps. A big man in navy overalls climbed out and began pumping gas. He glanced at her, politely tipped his cap, and nodded, as though it were an everyday occurrence to find a woman pacing the parking lot of a run-down gas station at this hour.

Hmm. Maybe he could give her a ride.

Jamie approached him. He looked harmless enough.

He was middle-aged and wore a wedding ring. His overalls were snug; he looked well fed. Probably had a wife at home who spent a lot of time in the kitchen. They probably ate their dinner on those cute little folding tray tables in front of the TV set while sitting in matching recliners. Their relationship was probably simple and uncomplicated.

The man caught her staring. "Good evening, ma'am."

The name Buford Noll had been stitched on a little patch sewn to his overalls. Yep, he looked respectable enough.

"Good evening to you, Mr. Noll," Jamie said, trying to sound upbeat. "I was wondering if you could give me a lift into town. I'll pay you."

"Well, sure. Any place in particular?"

"I need to find a nice, inexpensive motel for the night."

"Oh, well." He rubbed his jaw. "The one in Whittville is pretty run-down. Probably have to go all the way into Jessup."

"How far is that?"

"'Bout twelve miles."

"Like I said, I'll pay you."

"Oh, you don't have to do that. I'm headed that way, but I got to make a quick stop first."

Jamie was relieved. "Thank you."

"You can go ahead and climb on in, Miss . . ."

"Just call me Jamie." She hurried around to the passenger's side. Things were definitely beginning to look up.

Parked in the shadows across the street, Max Holt watched Jamie climb into the tow truck. She had not seen him return; she had been talking on the telephone.

"What's she doing now?" a voice asked from the dashboard.

"Looks like she just found a ride home."

"Man, you really screwed up big-time."

Max stared at the blinking lights on the front of the dash. A former NASA scientist had designed his car, a Porsche look-alike, only bigger, with a virtually inde-structible titanium exterior. The car held state-of-the-art equipment, which ranged from a global positioning satellite system to a full videoconferencing suite and a high-powered computer that ran it all. Max had person-ally created artificial intelligence with voice recogni-tion technology that would not be available for years to come.

His invention, which he called Muffin, had a Mari-lyn Monroe voice and "she" could literally think for herself. Muffin was stubborn and mouthy and, as ludi-crous as it sounded, capable of emotion. She was con-stantly taking in data, but unlike other computers, she formed opinions and made judgment calls. And thanks to his sister, Deedee, who was in the throes of meno-pause and had complained to Muffin of her symptoms, Muffin had processed the information and was now suffering the same malady.

Muffin, too, was going through menopause. She had hot flashes, mood swings, and she threatened to shut down her own hard drive permanently each time Max crossed her. Currently she was having an on-again-off-again on-line romance with a laptop computer at MIT. She was almost more than Max could handle. To say that he had created a monster was an understatement.

"What are you going to do now, big shot?" Muf-fin asked. "Mr. Love-'em-and-leave-'em?" she added, never one to mince words.

"That's not the way it was between Jamie and me."

"Yeah, and that's what really has you pissed. I mean, who would have thought it? There's actually a woman out there who doesn't think you're the best thing since on-line trading."

Max tightened his grip on the steering wheel as he watched the tow truck pull away from the parking lot.

"I was trying to protect her. This job is going to be dangerous. The good Reverend Harlan Rawlins and his mob pals are probably looking for me as we speak."

"But that's not what you told her, was it? You told her she would only get in your way."

"That's how you deal with a woman like Jamie. If I had told her I was afraid for her she wouldn't have listened."

"So you decided to hurt her feelings instead. Great idea, Max. You shouldn't have agreed to let her come in the first place."

"You're the one who insisted I bring her."

"You never listen to me. Besides, I wouldn't have advised you to do it had I known you would dump her halfway to Tennessee."

"It's better this way," Max said. "I need to think clearly, and I can't do it if Jamie's around."

"Look, I don't have time to take on your personal problems, OK? My job is to keep you out of trouble and make you look good by providing you with any and all information you might need."

"Thank you."

"You still screwed up."

Max shook his head as he started his engine and

put the car into gear. It shot off, leaving a dust cloud in its wake.

Ten minutes after Jamie had climbed into the tow truck, she found herself on a dirt road in a remote area. The truck's headlights provided the only light. "How much farther?" she asked.

"We should be coming up on it soon," Buford said. "We're looking for a pink-and-white house trailer with a brand-new SUV parked in front of it."

The shabby-looking mobile home appeared right after the next bend. A white Ford Explorer was parked out front. "Nice wheels," she said. "Looks like it just rolled off the showroom floor. Don't tell me the owner is already having mechanical problems."

Buford grunted. "The new owner is having problems making payments. That's where I come in." He turned into the driveway.

"What do you mean?"

"It's being repossessed. I'm here to pick it up. Thank goodness there are no lights on, that means he's asleep. Makes my job a whole lot easier." He put the truck into reverse and backed toward the SUV.

Jamie gaped. "You're taking this person's car?"

"He hasn't made a payment in three months. I'm just doing my job." He put the truck into neutral, set the emergency brake, left the motor running. "Better lock your door. Some people don't cotton to having their vehicles towed off like this."

"Wait a minute," Jamie said. "You said you had to make a quick stop. To me a quick stop is hitting a McDonald's drive-through window or maybe grabbing a cup of coffee to go at the Waffle House. You never mentioned repo'ing somebody's vehicle."

"Won't take me long," Buford said, climbing from the truck.

"Oh, no." Jamie twisted around in her seat and watched Buford unwind a cable and attach a massive hook to the underside of the SUV. He hit a switch, and a motor churned to life. The vehicle climbed upward.

Suddenly a light flashed on inside the trailer. Jamie scrambled across the seat and leaned out the driver's window. "Someone's up," she said.

Buford glanced toward the mobile home. "Oh, shit."

Suddenly the trailer door was flung open and Jamie caught the silhouette of a man holding a shotgun. He fired into the air. Jamie ducked. Buford dived beneath the truck.

"Get away from my car!" the man shouted.

"You done missed three payments, mister!" Buford called out loudly. "I've been hired to tow it in! You cause trouble and I'm calling the cops!"

The man fired again. A bullet pinged off the side of Buford's truck. "Holy hell!" Jamie cried, and hit the floor.

"Stay down!" Buford told her. "They're always upset at first."

Jamie closed her eyes. It was happening all over again. For some reason that she couldn't fathom, people insisted on shooting at her. "What are we supposed to do in the meantime?" she replied loudly.

Buford didn't hesitate. "I reckon we wait."

The smell of freshly cut lumber greeted Max as he stepped inside the cabin with his bag. No surprise there; the cabin had been renovated and redecorated for his use. Even so, the construction crew had kept the antique heart pine floors intact, knowing that Max, who was personally doing renovations to his home in Virginia, would appreciate them. The furniture was simple; probably much of it had already been in place. Max was grateful for that as well. The fact that he could afford to build a brand-new cabin with all new furniture and appliances did not mean he preferred it. Simplicity and comfort was more his style.

As usual, his staff had taken care of everything from securing the place to providing groceries. Max looked inside the refrigerator and cabinets and nodded his approval. His people knew his likes and dislikes, right down to the brand of beer and cold cuts he preferred. He checked out the two bedrooms and decided on the loft area. He spent an hour on his cell phone, finalizing his plans. He and Muffin had worked tirelessly once they'd gotten back on the road, but Max was a man who left nothing to chance. He knew what he was facing, knew the dangers.

By morning he would have all the information he needed on Harlan Rawlins, celebrity evangelist. Max hoped Muffin would be able to get information on Harlan's mob connections as well. Max's plan was simple: First, find Rawlins. The hit man who'd tried to kill Max had been linked to Rawlins, and Rawlins was supposedly linked to the mob.

Rawlins and his mob friends obviously felt they had a score to settle with Max because they'd lost the bid on his TV network. It would have been the perfect vehicle for Rawlins to spread his word and draw in literally hundreds of thousands of new members. New members meant more money, and owning a TV network would have made the mob more powerful than ever. It was no surprise they were angry; the only question was, how far would they go to get revenge? Max knew he would ultimately have to contact his friends with the FBI, but he needed more information. He needed to know exactly who and what he was up against.

Finally, he showered and went to bed. He closed his eyes. He was not a heavy sleeper, and he had long ago adapted to only five or six hours of rest. He could exist on less if necessary, and there had been times in his life he had found it necessary.

This might be one of those times.

It was after 3:00 A.M. when Buford delivered Jamie to the front door of a motel called the Hickory Inn, less than a mile from Jessup. Jamie's back and legs ached, and it was all she could do to reach for her purse. She had crouched on the floorboard for hours before Gunsmoke, as Jamie referred to the gun-toting man in the trailer, had cut the lights and gone to bed.

"I'll have to file a police report," Buford said, "but I'll keep your name out of it." He was apologetic.

Jamie tossed him a weary look. "Well, thanks for an evening I'm not likely to forget. I just hope I never miss a car payment." She climbed from the truck and went inside the motel. The furniture in the small lobby was old, but the place looked and smelled clean. She rang the bell three times before a woman ambled to the counter, the hair on one side of her head mashed flat, her print dress badly wrinkled. The sign on the counter read: *Mavis*.

"I'd like a room, please," Jamie said.

The woman crossed her arms, glanced at her wristwatch, and shot Jamie a dark look. "Do you happen to know what time it is?"

Jamie was in no mood to argue. "Late?"

"I closed at midnight."

"You forgot to turn your vacancy sign off."

"That's beside the point. No decent woman would check into a room at this hour unless she had monkey business on her mind."

Jamie leaned across the counter. "Mavis, I have *not* had a good night. I want a room. And don't give me a room on the second floor, because my legs are sore and I am *not* going to climb those concrete stairs. And inside that room, I want HBO like your sign says, and I want one of those cute little coffeepots, and a soft bed with clean sheets. Now, either you give me a room or I'm going to go out into that parking lot and pitch such a fit that I'll wake up every one of your guests. *That's* how bad my night has been."

Mavis grunted and slapped a registration form on the counter.

Max rose at 5:00 A.M. and, once again, checked the security monitor, computer console, and other gadgets at one end of the kitchen table where he would spend much of his time working. Outside cameras were connected to the CPU, and the monitors displayed the road leading to the cabin, as well as the surrounding property. He drank two cups of coffee, read his e-mail, and waited until the sun came up before stepping out of the front door. Electronic eyes and sophisticated motion detectors with image recognition enhancement were attached to trees and fence posts and would catch movement and set off an alarm inside the house. One of Max's employees had come in the day before to set it up, per Max's specifications.

All seemed well as Max started for the garage

where he'd locked his car. He punched a series of numbers on a concealed security panel and opened the door. Muffin was waiting for him.

"How'd you sleep?" she asked. "I'll bet you didn't get a minute's rest worrying about Jamie and feeling like the biggest jerk in the world."

Max sighed. "Good morning to you, Muffin."

"See, you even sound tired. Guilt will do that to you. The first thing that goes is your appetite. Then you'll start tossing and turning all night in your bed, unable to forgive yourself for hurting someone's feelings."

"Is this going to take long?"

"Of course you're in denial right now, so you're probably OK. Once you accept the reality of the situation, all hell will break loose. Sleep deprivation, confusion, and disorientation will occur," she added. "You'll stop taking care of yourself, and your health will go to hell. Next thing you know, you've landed in the hospital with a life-threatening illness."

"I take it you're still sore with me?"

"No more than usual."

"Can we get down to business?"

"Fine. I worked all night, but I managed to get the rest of the information you asked for on Harlan Rawlins. Don't ask me how I got it or we'll both go to prison. Have you set up the printer yet?"

"Yeah, everything is up and running."

"OK, it's printing now. As for your schedule, a woman by the name of Karen Callaway will be here shortly to give you your new look, and your retired FBI pal will arrive at nine o'clock to take your picture and get your new identification in order."

"How long will it take?"

"Max, the guy is bringing his equipment in the trunk of his car. Is that quick enough for you?"

"Good old Paul. What else have you got for me?"

"You and Dave Anderson are now working part-time for Bennett Electric. Dave is bringing by a couple of uniforms later. Tom Bennett, the owner, is cooperating fully."

Max was not surprised. He had bailed Bennett Electric Company from near bankruptcy several days ago. It was sheer genius that Max's mergers and acquisitions man had managed to find it so quickly; not only had the partnership been sealed within a matter of hours, but also Max and Muffin had mapped out a business plan for Tom Bennett that promised substantial profits within a year. Tom Bennett was one grateful man, and Dave Anderson, long-time employee of Holt Industries, was a top-notch mechanical and electrical engineer who could fill in literally wherever Max needed him. Dave had already memorized the layout of Rawlins's house and was ready to move on the project.

"What about transportation?" Max asked.

"You and Dave will be sharing one of Bennett's trucks." Muffin didn't sound happy about it.

"I'm sorry I'm going to have to leave you in the garage for a few days, Muf, but my car won't exactly blend with the community."

"That's not the problem."

"I'm listening."

"Why did you call Dave Anderson in on this job? You know how he gets. He can be so obsessive-compulsive at times, he makes me crazy."

"Dave is having problems. He and his wife Melinda are divorcing."

"And we need to get involved in that for what reason?"

"Because Dave is my friend, and because he's an electrical genius who could rewire the entire White House in twenty-four hours if he had to. Besides, everybody has one or two quirks."

"OK, whatever. As far as sitting in a cool garage, that sounds good to me."

"Still having hot flashes?"

"If I get any hotter my hard drive is going into melt-down and the car's radiator will spew like a volcano."

Max nodded as though the whole thing made perfect sense. "Speaking of transportation, have you had a chance to check out a red Mustang?"

"I found a guy in New Hampshire who deals strictly with Mustangs. He has a 1964½ red convertible, black interior and top. It's a V-8 with a stick shift. The guy said it looks like it just rolled off the showroom floor, and he should know, because he's one of the top dealers in the country. I checked him out."

"I'd like to see a picture of it."

"You will. I forwarded the scanned photos to you with the rest of the stuff I'm sending to your printer. Am I good, Max, or what?"

"Damn good."

"Oh, and this guy even agreed to deliver the car personally for the right price."

"Then I suggest we pay what he's asking."

"I know what you're thinking, Max. You're thinking Jamie is going to take one look at that Mustang and forgive you. You're thinking she's going to be waiting for you with open arms when you finish up here. You're thinking see-through nighties, edible panties, and hot steamy sex, but I'm here to tell you, it isn't going to happen.

"I'm not saying don't buy the car for her; it's your fault hers was sprayed with bullets to begin with. I know Jamie's got a thing for vintage Mustangs and that she needs transportation, but she's a proud woman and she might take it the wrong way."

"The two of you can think what you want, but my intentions are honorable. Have the guy deliver the car to the newspaper office and tell him to give the keys to Jamie's assistant, Vera Bankhead."

"You just better hope Miss Bankhead doesn't get the wrong impression. Jamie's like a daughter to her. And don't forget, that woman carries a gun."

TWO

Jamie awoke to someone pounding on her door. She was stark naked, having washed her underwear in the bathroom sink before she'd climbed into bed and fallen into an exhausted sleep. It had not occurred to her to grab her suitcase from Max's car before she'd slammed out.

Just one more thing, she thought.

Coming off the bed, she dragged the sheet with her. Her eyes were gritty, her blond hair standing out to there, and she just remembered she didn't have a toothbrush. "Who is it?" She thought her voice sounded like a frog giving birth.

"Mavis. Checkout was fifteen minutes ago. I have to clean your room."

"It's not even noon!" Jamie said.

"Not my problem."

Jamie leaned her head against the door. This was not a good sign. Here she was, tired, no clothes or car, and she was about to get thrown out of a second-rate motel. It was starting out to be a really sucky morning. Finally, she raised her head, and, keeping the chain in place, she cracked the door. The sun hit her between the eyes. "I'm requesting a late check-out," Jamie said.

"I'll have to charge you for another night."

Jamie just looked at Mavis. She wore pink sponge curlers beneath a gauzy scarf, and her rouge stood out on her pasty skin, two perfectly round circles that looked as though they'd been pressed on with an ink stamp. She was enjoying herself, Jamie decided.

Mavis tapped one foot impatiently.

"It'll take me a minute to get dressed," Jamie told her. She closed the door and hurried to the coffeepot. She dropped the filter into the top, added water, and stepped inside the bathroom. Her panties were still damp. "Oh, great," she muttered, thinking it was just another sign that her morning wasn't going to be all that great.

She slipped them on anyway, threw on her jeans and top, and filled a thick paper cup with coffee. She was still sipping it when she stepped out her door a few minutes later. She found Mavis waiting with a maid's cart.

"Is there a taxi service in this town?" Jamie asked.

Mavis looked her up and down. "Are those the same clothes you had on last night?"

"Yes, but I washed my underwear," Jamie blurted before she had time to think. She sighed. "Yes, they are. Why?"

"Are you in trouble with the law?"

"Not yet."

Mavis gave her a long look. "Dixie Cab Service. Phone calls are a dollar."

Jamie fished a dollar bill from her purse, hurried

back into the room, and grabbed the telephone book. She dialed the number for a taxi just as Mavis turned on the vacuum cleaner.

"This is it," the cabdriver announced a half hour later as he pulled into the parking lot of Bud's Used Cars. Jamie paid him and climbed from the battered cab.

She made her way toward a small construction trailer where a sign read: *Bad Credit? No Problem*. She opened the trailer door and was hit with a blast of cold air blowing from a sputtering window unit. Jamie found a man sitting at his desk, holding a cigar in one hand and sipping coffee from a chipped mug with the words *Do Me* in his other.

He stood so fast he almost spilled his coffee. "Good morning, miss," he said. "I'm Bud Herzog. What can I do for you this fine day?"

"I need a car. Something cheap but reliable."

"Well then, you've come to the right place. Matter of fact, I got several good, clean cars coming in day after tomorrow."

"I need something today. Now."

"Oh, well." Bud chewed his cigar. "I'm a little low on inventory, but you're welcome to look. You interested in a Cadillac? It's twelve years old, but it's solid. Low mileage."

Jamie thought about it. "I'm not really the Cadillac type."

"You're absolutely right. You need something sporty. Come with me, I've got just the car." He led her outside to a shiny red vehicle. "Now, this here is a Camaro RS. Fully loaded, got all the extras. It's a 1997 model, has a few miles on it, but it runs like a charm. Used to be owned by an old schoolteacher."

Jamie shot him a sideways glance. "An old school-teacher, huh?"

"Yep. Liberian, I believe she was," he added, mispronouncing the word. "She took real good care of it."

Jamie peered inside the window. "It's got one hundred and sixty thousand miles on it!"

"Yeah, she had to commute to work."

"How much?"

"This one goes for twenty-one hundred dollars, but I'm going to give you my rock-bottom price and sell it to you for fifteen. Is that a deal or what?"

Jamie gaped at him. "I can't afford to spend that kind of money. Don't you have something under five hundred dollars?"

Bud looked surprised. "Hon, you can't buy a good bicycle for under five hundred bucks. Not these days, anyhow." He suddenly looked hurt. "I'm cutting my profit to the bone here, darlin'."

Jamie checked out several other cars, but they were even more expensive. She spied an old pickup truck parked on the last row. "How much for that truck?"

Bud looked surprised. "I plumb forgot about that old thing. My cousin brought it in last night, and I haven't had a chance to clean it up. I don't think you'd be happy with it."

"How come?"

"It's old and beat-up. You can see it's got a lot of rust on it. There's a hole in the floorboard on the passenger's side, but my cousin nailed plywood to it so his kids wouldn't fall out. Mostly, he used it to carry hunting dogs. He's a big coon hunter."

Jamie walked toward the truck. "Just how old is it?"

"Early eighties. It's a Dodge, and they hold up pretty good, but I wouldn't feel right selling it to you."

Jamie opened the door and winced at the sight. On the driver's side, the leather seat was split and the stuffing had spilled out. Papers and fast-food bags littered the floor. "Mileage is high," she noted. "Does it run?"

Bud nodded. "Pretty good."

"How does it look under the hood?"

"Well, my cousin is a mechanic, so he's careful to change the oil and transmission fluid and keep everything in working order. He rebuilt the engine some five or six years ago, but it's still an old truck."

"Do you think it'll get me to Knoxville?"

"You know any shortcuts?" He laughed. When Jamie didn't join in, his look sobered. "Yeah, I reckon it'll get you where you're going."

"How much?"

Bud shrugged. "As is? I reckon I could let you have it for six hundred dollars."

Jamie blinked. "Excuse me, but are we talking about the same truck?"

"OK, OK, I'll sell it to you for four hundred dollars, but I can't give you a warranty at that price."

Jamie glanced at the bed in back. And found herself looking into the face of one of the ugliest bloodhounds she'd ever seen. He had a wrinkled forlorn face, mournful eyes, and long ears. Skin hung in loose, pendulous folds, as though he had never quite managed to fill his own hide.

"What's with the dog?" she asked.

"Oh, yeah, I forgot. He comes with the truck."

She blinked at Bud. "What do you mean, he comes with the truck?"

"He's kinda attached to it. My cousin asked me to take him to the animal shelter, but I didn't have the heart. He wouldn't last long there. He has, uh, problems."

Jamie looked more closely at the animal. "What kinds of problems?"

Bud toyed with his cigar, rolling it between his thumb and forefinger. "Well, he's deaf in one ear, and his eyesight ain't what it used to be. He's also suffering shell shock."

"Shell shock?"

"Like I said, my cousin did a lot of coon hunting. This here dog wasn't much of a hunter; in fact, he runs at the sight of a raccoon and hunkers down in the nearest ditch if someone fires a gun."

"He's losing his hair."

Bud shrugged. "Way I heared it, he was attacked by a big old grandpappy coon. Hair never grew back. My cousin says he whimpers in his sleep. Says he thinks the dog has flashbacks. You ask me, I think he's suffering from that-there post-traumatic stress disorder."

Jamie rolled her eyes heavenward. "Oh, brother!"

"And he hates country-western music. I need to tell you that up front. He goes bananas when he hears it."

"I'll agree to buy the truck, but I'm not taking the dog."

The hound suddenly let out a pitiful howl as though he'd understood what Jamie had said.

"It's nothing personal," Jamie said before realizing she was talking to a dog. She shook her head sadly.

The animal covered his face with his paws.

"Uh-oh," Bud said. "I think you hurt his feelings."

"Oh, jeez." Jamie pulled Bud aside. "Look, I've never owned an animal, not even a goldfish. I can't keep a houseplant alive."

"Oh, Fleas ain't no trouble, honey. You just give

him a little food and water and he's fine. Mostly all he does is sleep."

"His name is Fleas?"

"Yeah, that's what my cousin calls him. But I personally checked him out. There ain't nary a flea on this hound's body, I can promise you that."

Jamie looked thoughtful. Damn. Just what she *didn't* need, a dog with physical and emotional problems, not to mention one who freaked out at the sound of gunfire, which she seemed to draw like fruit did flies. "I can't do this," she said.

"OK, tell you what. You take the truck *and* the dog, and I'll knock off fifty bucks."

Jamie arrived in Sweet Pea, Tennessee, shortly after 5:00 P.M., just as a light mist began to fall. Oh, great, she thought. And her with a dog in the back of her truck. She stopped at a red light and glanced over her shoulder. Fleas had his nose pressed against the back window, fogging it with his breath.

"It's OK, boy," she said loudly, even though she suspected he couldn't hear her.

She had to admit he'd been a good traveler. She'd stopped twice to give him water and let him go to the bathroom, and she'd ordered him a cheeseburger at a fast-food restaurant when she'd stopped for lunch. Probably wasn't a proper diet for a dog; she needed to buy the poor animal real dog food. It was up to her to see that he ate right until she could find him a good home. Not that it would be easy finding somebody interested in adopting a dog with emotional problems and missing hair.

Jamie could just imagine what Vera would say about her becoming a dog owner. Sixty-year-old Vera Bankhead, her secretary, whom Jamie had recently promoted to assistant editor out of fear and intimidation, was the closest thing Jamie'd had to a mother and was not above telling her how to run her life. "Jamie," she'd say. "You have absolutely no business taking on a dog. Why, you can't even take care of yourself."

This was due to the fact Jamie's cupboards and refrigerator were always bare. She seldom took time to buy groceries, except for coffee and junk food. And when she'd picked up her father's smoking habit, Vera had hit the ceiling. She had promptly declared the *Beaumont Gazette* a smoke-free environment, so that if Jamie wanted an occasional cigarette she had to smoke it outside come rain or cold weather. Jamie had kicked the habit, only to pick it up again briefly during the past two weeks, when her stress level had been at an all-time high. Dodging bullets could put a big strain on the nervous system, she reminded herself.

Vera would be proud to know Jamie was now making a concerted effort to keep her body as smoke-free as the newspaper office, although she had certainly craved a cigarette when she and Buford Noll had waited out the rifle-bearing lunatic in the mobile home.

Jamie thought of Vera. The woman would not appreciate Jamie just taking off without telling a soul. Which was why Jamie had called her from Max's cell phone when she knew the woman would be out. "I'm taking a well-deserved vacation," she'd said.

Vera would never fall for it, of course. She'd never fallen for what she'd termed Jamie's "shenanigans" during Jamie's youth and wouldn't fall for this latest scheme. It didn't matter that Jamie had already celebrated her thirtieth birthday; there would be hell to pay when she returned to Beaumont.

The mist turned to rain. Jamie needed to find a place to stop for the night. She drove a long stretch of highway before she spied a tired-looking motel in faded aqua cinderblock with black wrought-iron railing. She passed it, then, after driving a few more miles in the downpour without spotting other lodging, turned back. She suspected there weren't many motels in a town the size of Sweet Pea.

Jamie turned into the parking lot a few minutes later and pulled beneath a covered area in front. She climbed from the truck and managed to convince Fleas to get inside the cab of the pickup. The dog was shivering despite the summer temperatures. She had a feeling he was merely playing on her sympathy, even though he didn't look that smart. She dried him as best she could with an old towel she found stuffed behind the seat. He looked downright pitiful, what with his big soulful eyes and drooping skin. She was already proving to be a lousy pet owner.

"Bless your heart, you've got a face only a mother could love," she told him, rolling her window all the way down so he would get plenty of air while she was gone. "Now, stay down. If the motel manager sees you we'll never get a room."

The littered grassy area in front of the motel, as well as the badly smudged double-glass doors leading inside, should have prepared Jamie for the lobby area. The smell of cooked onions greeted her, someone obviously preparing dinner in a back room. The carpet needed to be vacuumed, and the man behind the counter wore a stained shirt. He didn't seem to hear Jamie enter; his eyes were fixed on a TV set attached high on a wall.

Jamie stepped up to the counter. "Excuse me, but is this the only motel in town?"

The man looked at her. "Why would you ask me a question like that? Is this place not good enough for you?"

"No, it's fine. I just—" Jamie was suddenly interrupted by the sound of a barking dog. It was not just any dog. Fleas had decided to follow her. Damn.

"Is that your dog?" the man asked.

"What dog?"

"The one scratching on the glass door."

Jamie glanced over her shoulder. "I've never seen that dog before in my life. Do you have HBO or Showtime?"

"No, and I'm going to have to charge you ten bucks extra for that mutt on account I'll have to spray the room after you leave."

"Yeah, OK." Jamie reached inside her purse for her credit card. It might not be the best motel, it might not have HBO or Showtime, but it was probably the only place in town that would take a homely-looking bloodhound.

Jamie checked in, grabbed her key, and joined Fleas outside. He wagged his tail as though happy to see her. "Thanks a lot," she muttered. "You just cost me ten bucks." She spied the newspaper stand and purchased a paper, then stopped by a couple of vending machines for cheese crackers and a soft drink. "At least I won't have to cook dinner tonight," she told the dog, who seemed to take a sudden interest in the crackers.

She followed the numbers on the doors, counting the way toward her room. A big man stepped out from behind one of the doors and looked her up and down. He wore a grimy T-shirt and bore tattoos on both arms. Jamie offered him a stiff smile as she stepped up to the door next to his. Just her luck; they were neighbors. Not that she was surprised. It wasn't likely she was going to run into any doctors or lawyers in a dump like this.

He made kissing sounds.

Jamie rolled her eyes and looked at him. "Please don't do that," she said, slipping the key into the lock.

He grinned. "You staying here?"

Jamie's look was deadpan as she tried to turn the key. It wouldn't budge. "No, actually I'm trying to break into this room so I can get decorating ideas."

He stepped closer. "Is that your dog?"

"Yeah, and he'll tear your leg off if you come near me."

"Might be worth it. How about a drink later? I got a bottle of Wild Turkey in my room."

"It certainly sounds tempting, but my boyfriend, Killer, is picking me up for an AA meeting in ten minutes. Sorry." The key finally turned and Jamie opened the door. "Have a nice evening." She went inside and waited for Fleas to follow before locking the door and putting the chain in place. She shoved a chair in front of the door to be safe.

"This is just wonderful," Jamie said, glaring at Fleas. "Because of you I am reduced to staying in a hovel with dangerous-looking people. I'll never get any sleep tonight."

His tail thumped against the ugly carpet.

Jamie glanced about. The room was clean enough but drab and depressing with its faded moss green walls and brown bedspread. Even Fleas seemed to give it a second glance. He sank onto the floor and stared at her crackers.

Jamie sat on the bed, opened the crackers, and shared them with him. He swallowed each one without chewing. "If we live through the night, we're checking out first thing in the morning." She opened the newspaper, skimmed the articles. One article particularly caught her eye.

"Holy hell!" she blurted. "Reverend Harlan Rawlins is preaching at seven o'clock tonight at Sweet Pea Community Church." She looked up in alarm. "I don't have anything to wear. I don't even have extra underwear. And that's not the worst of it. The worst of it is I'm talking to a dog. How sick is that?"

Jamie jumped up from the bed and peered out the curtain. The rain had abated and her neighbor, Brutus, was nowhere in sight. She looked at Fleas, debating whether or not to take him with her. If she left him behind he'd probably start barking, and they'd get kicked out. "Come on. We're going shopping." She grabbed her purse, opened the door, and they made a run for it.

Sweet Pea Community Church was filled to capacity when Max arrived with Dave Anderson, both dressed in uniform.

Dave was a slender man with light brown hair and tortoiseshell glasses that had a tendency to slide down his nose. He and Max stood along the back wall of the church, scanning the crowd. A massive navy banner hung on the wall above the choir, the words *Love Ministry* emblazoned in white letters.

"Do you have any idea how many germs are in this place?" Dave whispered, shoving his glasses upward with his pointer finger.

Max shrugged. "Rawlins is offering miracle healing toward the end of the service. You might want to get in line."

"Very funny," Dave replied.

Max caught sight of a tall redhead in sunglasses who seemed to be making a fuss in her attempt to get a front row seat. He leaned sideways to get a better look.

She wore a short denim skirt and a tight fire engine red tank top that fit snug against lush breasts and left very little to a man's imagination. Her stilettos showed off a pair of long, shapely legs that had captured the attention of most of, if not the entire, congregation. Rhinestones dangled from her ears and flashed each time she moved her head. She turned slightly, snatched off her sunglasses, and mouthed something to a heavy woman who seemed to be giving her the most trouble.

Max frowned. Even if she was in disguise, it would have been impossible for him not to recognize Jamie Swift. "I don't believe it," he muttered under his breath.

Dave leaned close. "What is it?"

"Trouble," Max said.

The congregation burst into the hymn "Bringing in the Sheaves" as Jamie finally managed to squeeze herself between two people. She held her head high and ignored the looks of disapproval coming from the women around her, even as their husbands tried not to stare. Not that she blamed them. Her slut suit, as she had referred to it to Fleas, was way over the line, as was her wild hair. The wig had cost more than she'd planned to spend, but it looked like the real enchilada. She had *floozy* written all over her. She only hoped Harlan Rawlins noticed.

Her plan depended on it.

Reverend Harlan Rawlins appeared during the last stanza of the song. He carried a cordless microphone, and he joined the singing. He had a strong, well-modulated voice, and he sang with confidence. Jamie studied him closely. She wasn't sure what she'd expected, but she certainly hadn't expected him to be so handsome and polished. Vera had taken Jamie to a couple of tent revivals when she was young, but those ministers wore cheap suits and yelled a lot.

Harlan Rawlins did not look like any minister she had ever seen. He looked like a movie star. But there was more to him than good looks. The man had presence. He exuded such charisma that it was easy to see why people followed him, why women might find it difficult to say no to his advances. The air seemed electrified, and Jamie could literally feel his energy from where she sat. She needed to remember the exact feelings he evoked so she could make note of them later. Her readers would want to know what it was about the man that had made him so successful, that made people dig deep inside their pockets to support his ministry.

Jamie was so focused on the man that she was only vaguely aware of the shuffling of feet behind her.

Someone tapped her on the shoulder. Jamie glanced over her shoulder and gaped at the sight of Max Holt.

THREE

Max looked different, his hair in a buzz cut, face unshaven. She dropped her gaze to his uniform where the name Bennett Electric was stitched across his shirt pocket. Jamie wasn't surprised to find him in disguise; what shocked her was the fact he could pull it all off and still look sexy as all get-out. She realized Max was staring at her as well.

"What are you doing here?" he demanded in a whisper.

"I'm here for the same reason you are," she replied.

Several people turned and glared at them. "Shhh!" the lady beside her said.

Jamie suddenly remembered how things had ended between Max and her the night before. "Go away," she whispered. She turned and faced the front, but the hair on her neck prickled. She could feel Max's eyes on her. Well, let him take a good look at the new Jamie Swift, she thought.

The song ended, but Harlan remained quiet and smiling. His eyes scanned the congregation; he nodded at several people he seemed to recognize.

"Brothers and sisters, it is great to be back in Sweet

Pea, Tennessee," he said. The crowd cheered. Jamie felt something at her ear.

"Why are you dressed like a hooker?" Max asked.

The people were so busy clapping that those around her didn't seem to notice. "I'm here to get my story, Max," she replied.

"Dressed like that?"

She smiled and fluttered her long lashes. They were as fake as the cleavage that peeked over her tank top. Funny what a pair of false eyelashes and a good push-up bra could do. "Yes."

The woman beside Jamie nudged her. Jamie tossed her a dirty look but faced the front once more.

Harlan waited until the people sat and grew quiet before speaking again. "I have been on the road for weeks, living out of motel rooms and counting off the days until my return. I'm home with my family and friends now, sleeping in my own bed, and eating home-cooked meals. Praise God!"

This time the congregation laughed and applauded, and Harlan laughed with them, his smile enhanced by beautiful teeth that shone a bright white against his tanned face. Jamie thought he looked like he belonged in a toothpaste commercial. His navy suit, obviously tailor-made, emphasized a fit body and brought out his blond hair.

"Dorothy was right," he said. "There's no place like home." More applause. After a moment, he grew serious and closed his eyes. "Let us pray."

When the prayer ended, Rawlins walked out to the very edge of the platform. He had a habit of pausing before he spoke, as though waiting for every eye to see him, every ear to hear what he had to say.

"You know, brothers and sisters, this ministry has

surely been blessed. We've fed thousands through our outreach program, and each year our young people travel to the poorest areas, patching holes in roof-tops, installing windows where families have nothing more to keep the cold out than plastic or cardboard. Yet there are still folks, our neighbors, mind you, who don't have inside plumbing or electricity. But God bless our local volunteers who have gone into these homes and donated their skills so these poor people can enjoy many of the things some of us take for granted." Another pause. "But you know, feeding people and keeping them dry and warm isn't enough.

"Someone once asked Mother Teresa what people needed most in this world, and she had a surprising answer." He looked about the congregation. "What do *you* think is the single greatest need people have today, brothers and sisters?" Harlan folded his hands behind his back and paced the stage. "You know if someone had asked me that question, I would have had to think about it.

"We see pictures of starving people in third world countries, children in cancer wards and burn centers who live with pain on a daily basis, and we see single parents trying to play both mama and daddy because of the staggering divorce rates. Many of these parents can't afford child care, so the children are left to fend for themselves. And when boys and girls don't have adequate supervision, they get into bad trouble. Where do you think they end up?"

"In jail!" a man shouted from the audience.

"Yes, sir," Harlan replied. "These kids get addicted to drugs, and they commit all sorts of crimes in order to support their habits." Harlan looked sad. "These young people are filling our prisons today."

He walked over to the podium, pulled a handkerchief from his pocket, and mopped his eyes. "Please forgive me," he said. "This is not the sermon I had planned to give. I didn't prepare for it. But I spent a long time in prayer this morning, and this is the sermon the Lord gave me."

Harlan gazed across the crowd, and when he spoke, his voice was soft, barely a whisper. "But Mother Teresa was not as concerned about hunger or illness or the breakup of families. The woman who witnessed the absolute worst in human misery, who lived among the poorest of the poor, and who saw every horrific disease known to man was more concerned with a different affliction, and that affliction, brothers and sisters, was loneliness."

Harlan raised his voice on the next sentence, and he began to speak quickly, as though he couldn't get the words out fast enough. "Loneliness. That feeling of isolation and the thought that nobody cares. It eats through the human heart and soul like maggots, because when people suffer loneliness they feel unloved, and when there is no love, there is *nothing*!" Harlan pounded on the podium and shouted the word. "Nothing!"

People in the congregation shouted, "Amen!"

Harlan jumped from the stage and walked down the aisle, and the crowd turned in their seats in order to see him. He stood by the back door. "I'll say it again!" he shouted. "Where there is no love, there is nothing!

"Love *does* conquer all, brethren. Where there is love, there is no loneliness. Where there is love, there is *hope*." The crowd cheered, once again rising from their seats.

Harlan hurried toward the front of the church and

climbed the stairs to the stage. The congregation continued to cheer.

"*Love,* brothers and sisters. I get excited just saying
the word. *L-o-v-e,*" he spelled out. "The same love that
God showed us when he gave his only begotten son
so that we should not perish but have life everlasting.
Shout Amen!"

The crowd began shouting the word. The choir
broke into a rousing gospel song. Music blasted through
the church, and Harlan began to dance as he gazed
toward the heavens, arms lifted high in the air. He
clapped his hands, keeping time to the music, and the
choir members joined him, dancing and reaching their
arms toward the heavens. The congregation began to
dance as well.

As the last chords faded, Harlan became serious. "I'm
going to make an unusual request tonight," he said. "I
know this ministry needs funds to keep it running, and
I know there are starving people in distant lands, but
tonight I'm asking you to make a love offering for those
in your town who don't know where their next meal is
coming from. For your neighbors," he added. "For those
sad faces we see standing in front of the unemployment
office, for the boys and girls who attend schools with
holes in their shoes. Many of those who are standing in
this congregation tonight," he added softly.

"I am not going to collect one dime for this ministry
while I'm in town, and I'm not going to send the money
away to some country you've never even heard of. The
money you give tonight will stay right here in Sweet Pea,
and I aim to see that it fills those bare cupboards and that
our children have what they need. That's what we're all
about, dear folks. Love Ministry is all about loving and
giving, and that is what chases away loneliness.

"Now I know there are some who can't afford to give much, and to you I'd say this: The Lord knows your heart. Follow your heart. And for every penny you give, this ministry will match it tenfold."

The people applauded.

Jamie looked around, noted the hopeful expressions on the faces of those around her. They believed in Harlan Rawlins. He had reeled them in. Damn, he was so good.

Jamie turned and looked at Max. He met her gaze, and she could see her own thoughts mirrored in his eyes. He did not like Harlan Rawlins. Max, like Jamie, was wondering how a man could prey on people who had nothing else to give.

"It's not enough to chop wood for a fire to keep a family warm," Harlan said. "You need to go out there and set their hearts on fire for Jesus!"

More music, more dancing.

"Does anyone here need a miracle tonight?" Harlan shouted above the din, drawing Jamie's attention to the front once more.

The crowd cried out.

Harlan smiled. "Some of you, perhaps many of you, know that I was converted at an early age. I was only ten years old when God sent me a vision that I was to preach to the world, that I was to go forth and heal in his name. Let God grant you a miracle tonight, brothers and sisters. Allow God, who has chosen me, a simple preacher, a sinner of the worst kind, to act as his vessel. Come to Jesus!"

People began lining up in the aisle. Jamie hesitated only a moment before she joined them. She could feel Max's eyes boring into her. He was, no doubt, wondering what she was up to. So let him wonder.

Harlan spoke to a man at the front of the line and then raised his microphone to his lips. "Brothers and sisters, we have a man who suffers chronic back pain and is unable to work. He has sought the help of doctors to no avail. Well, I will tell you, there is a power that can heal all pain and suffering. This power doesn't have medical degrees on his walls and he doesn't have to put us through rigorous tests to find out what's wrong, because he knows what ails us before we ask. Bow your heads, brethren, and let's pray for a miracle."

The people bowed their heads, and Harlan put his hands on the man's back and said a prayer for him. Jamie watched closely. For all she knew, the man could have been planted in the crowd to make it look as though Harlan was actually capable of healing the sick. For all she knew, there could be dozens planted in the congregation for the same reason.

After much praying, Harlan raised his hands and shouted, "Receive your miracle, brother!" Harlan ordered the man to touch his toes, and the man touched his toes, not once but several times. The crowd became jubilant as Harlan moved on to the next person.

After fifteen minutes of waiting in line, Jamie stepped up to Harlan. She was nervous, her palms damp. She wiped them on her denim skirt. "I am a sinner, Reverend," she said quietly.

"You're in the right place, sister. We welcome sinners here." Harlan perused her from head to toe, and his bright blue eyes flickered with interest. "Are you looking for a miracle tonight?"

She nodded. "I need to be healed of an addiction."

"What's your name, dear lady?"

"Jane." Jamie winced inwardly; it was the first

name that came to mind. Probably would have served her better if she'd used a sexier name.

Harlan put one hand on her shoulder and held up the other. "Brothers and sisters, we have a woman here who wants to be cured from an addiction. Now, I don't know if she is addicted to drugs or alcohol or both, but God doesn't care, because he can whip the worst of them. You don't have to go to the Betty Ford Center to get well. God only asks that you kneel before him. 'Ask and ye shall receive,' the Bible tells us."

Harlan returned his gaze to Jamie. "Sister, what addiction would you like for the Lord to take from you tonight?" he asked.

Jamie covered the microphone with one hand. "It's, um, really, really personal."

Harlan didn't bat an eye. "The Lord forgives even the worst of us."

She hung her head. She could smell Harlan's cologne, feel the heat from his body. "I'm a, well, a woman who can't seem to get enough of . . ." She didn't finish.

Harlan was obviously hanging on to her every word. "Say it, sister."

"It's an *s* word. I'm too embarrassed to tell you." It had seemed so easy when Jamie had rehearsed it in front of the mirror in the motel room and again in her rearview mirror as she'd applied her new lipstick called Oral Promise. *I'm a sex addict. I'm a sex addict.* But now the words wouldn't come.

And dressed as she was, with her breasts shoved up to her chin, she figured Harlan Rawlins had to be about as dumb as they came not to figure it out.

"Turn around and face your brothers and sisters and

tell them, dear woman. The Lord says you must confess your sins in order to be forgiven. Tell us what this *s* word is that fills you with such shame you can't even utter it."

Jamie faced the expectant crowd. All eyes were focused on her. "I, uh, um . . ."

"Say it, sister!" a woman yelled.

Jamie's heart pounded in her chest. "I like to, um . . ." She paused and took a deep breath. "Shop!" she finally cried.

The people looked about as though confused.

Jamie did a mental head slap. She had blown it. People would see her as a fake; she would never get close to Harlan. She didn't dare look in Max's direction.

The crowd was quiet, the look on Harlan's face confused. Jamie's face burned with embarrassment. "I'm a shopaholic!" she shouted. "I know it doesn't sound so bad, but I can't control my spending. I see a half-price sale and I get all tingly. I'll buy everything on the table whether I need it or not. If I see a sweater on sale, I can't just buy one, I buy ten. My husband cut up all my credit cards, but I went out and got new ones. The bank foreclosed on our house. We can't afford food."

She finally had their attention. Jamie grabbed Harlan's microphone. "I am addicted to blue light specials and red dot sales. I can't resist a bargain."

"We understand, sister," Harlan said, reaching for his microphone.

Jamie held it aside. She was on a roll. "I'm so . . ." She paused and hung her head. "Sick!"

The crowd nodded sympathetically.

From his place in the second row, Max rolled his eyes and shook his head sadly. In the back, Dave edged away from a man who was scratching himself.

Jamie turned and raised her eyes to Rawlins's. Still holding the microphone, she covered it with one hand so that the congregation could not hear her words. "What I just said was a lie," she whispered. "I'm not really a shopaholic. I'm a sex addict. I just couldn't bear to tell everyone."

Two blond brows shot high on his head. Sweat beaded his brow. "I'm sorry for putting you on the spot."

Jamie swallowed. "I'm so ashamed."

He put his hand on her shoulder, and he squeezed it, massaged it, actually. "Brothers and sisters, we have heard this young lady's confession, and we both know how hard it is to battle an addiction." He turned to Jamie, and his eyes were bright with interest. "Sister, are you willing to go into private counseling with me in order to beat this?" he asked. "Because you know with the Lord's help we can lick it once and for all."

"I'll do anything," she said. She fluttered her lashes, hoping they didn't stick to her cheek. "Anything."

Harlan swallowed so hard his Adam's apple bobbed erratically. "I'll speak with you after the service."

Jamie saw the promise in his gaze that made her suspect he wasn't exactly thinking along spiritual lines. "Oh, thank you." She clasped his hand tightly, bent down, and kissed it. The crowd applauded. She lingered for a moment, letting her warm breath fan over Harlan's skin, and she was almost certain he shivered.

Jamie reclaimed her seat in the front row. It was all she could do to keep from grinning. "Gotcha," she whispered.

Jamie exited the church some minutes later after setting an appointment with Rawlins for the next day. She headed straight for her truck, where Fleas waited.

Danged if she wasn't beginning to like the dog. That didn't mean she planned to keep him. He needed to live on a farm where he'd have plenty of space to run. Not that she'd actually seen him run or even move at a fast pace, mind you. He sort of ambled about. Mostly he slept.

Jamie suddenly felt a presence. Max.

He grabbed her wrist. "Oh, no, you don't."

Jamie turned. Had they not been surrounded by people, God-fearing church folks, she would have let him have it right there. After what she'd been through she was ready for a showdown. Instead, she very politely extricated herself from his grasp.

"Max, I'm only going to say this once. Get out of my face *and* my life."

"What do you think you're doing here?" he demanded.

"Going after a story, that's what."

"I specifically told you—"

Jamie hated that she still found him so attractive. "I don't give a rat's tail what you told me, Holt," she said. "Go away."

"Not until you explain that outfit. But first, let's start with the hair."

Jamie hitched her chin high.

"Not that it's any of your business, but this outfit, not to mention the wig, is designed specifically to entice Harlan Rawlins. It's all part of my plan to get close to him. Learn his secrets."

"How did you get here?"

Jamie was thankful he hadn't pushed for more information with regard to her plan. "I bought a truck." She motioned to the pickup. Fleas's head was propped on the side, and he was drooling.

"Damn, Jamie, that's the ugliest thing I've ever laid eyes on."

He could be so annoying, she thought. Max Holt had a way of getting under her skin in the worst way. "So it has a little rust on it. I got it for a steal."

"I'm talking about the dog."

"Don't bad-mouth my dog, Holt," she said. "It just so happens he's pure bloodhound. Comes from a family of champions."

"Right."

"And I figured I needed a guard dog."

Max looked dumbfounded as he glanced from the dog back to her. "A guard dog? Looks like he couldn't catch a dried biscuit. You know, you're taking a huge risk being here. This could be dangerous."

Jamie crossed her arms in a businesslike manner. "I have to do it, Max. I need the story for my newspaper. And I'm following my dream."

"Your dream is to dress like a hooker and drive a junk heap?" he asked.

"Very funny. I had a lot of time to think during my drive here, and I realized I needed to make some changes in my life. I'm tired of writing about high school football games and city council meetings. I want a story with some meat in it. As for the way I'm dressed, I'm on assignment."

"You sound pretty serious about this."

"I've spent my life doing what was expected of me." Which was true, she reminded herself. She'd spent years taking care of a sick father and trying to save the family newspaper from one calamity after another. "I'm done with people-pleasing, Max. From now on, I only have to please myself."

"I'm glad to hear it, Jamie," Max said. "It's about

time you started thinking about yourself. But we still need to talk." He glanced toward the truck he and Dave were sharing and found his friend leaning against it, watching the crowd. Max waved, managing to get his attention. "I'll catch up with you later!" he called out to the man. Dave nodded, climbed into the truck, and drove away.

"Here, give me the keys to your truck," Max said. "We can talk at my cabin."

"Excuse me?" Jamie snatched the keys from his reach.

"I think it's great, what you're doing, but I refuse to stand by and allow you to put yourself in danger."

Jamie waved a hand in front of him. "Hello-o-o? Did you already forget what I just told you? I'm doing this for me. Besides, you dumped me."

"I did not dump you. You jumped out of my car and refused to get back in."

Jamie noticed they were drawing stares. She hitched her chin high. "Look, Max, I don't want to make a scene, OK? But if you don't leave me alone I'm going to have to slug you."

He grinned. "You wouldn't really hit me."

She hated when he grinned like that. It just emphasized his sexiness. She could almost imagine her bones getting soft under her skin. Trouble was he knew exactly what he was doing to her. "What do you want, Max? You only grin like that when you want something."

The smile turned lazy. "What I want and what I need are two separate things, but would you at least give me a lift back to my cabin? My ride just drove away."

FOUR

"Your ride left you?" she said. "Sounds like you got a problem, Bubba."

Max arched a brow. *"Bubba?"*

"All right, I'll give you a ride if you'll promise not to say anything to annoy me."

He looked thoughtful. "I'm not sure that's possible."

Jamie almost laughed. "Put some effort into it. And no more wisecracks about my dog."

They climbed into the truck, and Jamie started the engine.

"This thing is pretty rough inside," Max said.

"See that, you've already done it. Annoyed the hell out of me."

"Only because you're still angry with me because I didn't think you should get involved in this, er, job."

"In order to be angry with you, I would have to be emotionally invested, and that's just not the case."

He chuckled. "Face it, Swifty. You're still hot for me."

"I can't hear you," Jamie said, turning on the radio. All she got was static. She pushed the button, and a country-western song came on. Max started to say something, and she turned up the volume to drown him out. She was not going to let him goad her. All at once, Fleas pounced against the window and began growling.

"What the hell?" Max said.

Jamie hit the brake and turned around in her seat. Fleas's teeth were bared. He clawed the glass as though trying to get at Max. "Oh, damn, I forgot. He hates country-western music." She turned off the radio.

Max stared, open-mouthed.

She glanced over her shoulder. "Sit!" she ordered the dog.

Fleas paced for a moment, then sank onto the bed of the truck. Jamie turned and caught Max's astonished look. "He hates country-western music," she repeated.

"I'll try to keep that in mind. Turn right once you pull out of the parking lot."

Jamie did as she was told. The truck bounced along the pockmarked road.

"Where are you staying?" Max asked.

"I found a motel in town."

Max looked surprised. "In Sweet Pea? Dave said there were only two places. One is being repainted, and the other one is a dump."

Jamie offered him a grim look. "That means Dave and I are staying at the same place."

"No, he's staying in Knoxville. I offered him the spare room at my place, but the mattresses and pillows are stuffed with feathers. Dave has allergies. You're welcome to use the spare room, Jamie."

"No, thanks."

"It would be easier if we worked together. We could share information. I have a complete printout on Rawlins, the kind of information you can't get anywhere else."

Jamie looked at him. "I'm not going to ask how many laws you broke getting it. What kind of information?"

"I'll let you look through it if you like."

Oh, he was a cool one, Jamie thought. "I can find out what I need on my own."

"Whatever you say, Swifty."

"I told you to stop calling me that."

"It suits you." His voice dropped. "Especially now that you've got all that curly red hair. And I'll have to admit that skirt does your legs justice."

"Don't start, Max." Nevertheless, her stomach did a quick flip-flop at the thought.

"You're one of those women who look good in everything," he said. "I'll bet you look even better in nothing."

"I should have made you ride in the back with the dog."

Max merely smiled.

They rode in silence for a few minutes. Jamie wondered what kind of information Max had. It *would* make her job easier if she knew exactly what she was up against, but that would mean playing ball with him again, and that's the last thing she wanted to do. Max Holt played fast and loose, took way too many chances. If that weren't stressful enough, he seemed to have trouble with the word *no*.

Yes sir, she was better off on her own.

"What did you think of Rawlins's sermon tonight?" Max asked after a minute.

"He certainly has stage presence."

"He has to be good in order to steal all that money. Those poor people are so desperate they'll believe anything."

"People need hope. Harlan gives it to them."

"You're not falling for any of that holy baloney, are you?"

"Of course not. I'm just telling you why he's able to get away with all that he does."

"I saw the way you were staring at him. Don't forget what he tried to do to us."

"If I was staring, it was because I was trying to get a fix on him. I have to be objective here. We don't know that he was responsible for ordering the hit, and we don't know that he's scamming people. All we have are suspicions."

"Trust me, he's as greedy as the people he does business with."

"Nevertheless, he is helping the community. Oh, I'm sure he's skimming money, but some of it is actually going to a fine cause. Did you take a good look at the people in that church, Max? They live in poverty." She looked at him. "I don't expect you to understand what being poor is like." Not that she'd actually been poor, but she had certainly lived on the fringes from time to time.

"I've seen poverty, Jamie. I've seen much worse than this. And I've tried to help people."

Jamie stared straight ahead. She knew he spoke the truth. Max Holt might be an egomaniac and the world's worst womanizer, but one only had to pick up a newspaper to see that he did more than his share of giving. He pumped millions into various research facilities and children's hospitals, and he'd started a watchdog program that badgered companies that refused to spend the kind of money necessary to control pollution.

"I know you do your share, Max. I don't mean to

sound like I'm picking on you; I just despise seeing people taken advantage of. Especially when they have nothing to begin with," she added. "I don't know how Rawlins lives with himself, and I don't know how he continues to get away with it."

"I can show you when we get to my place."

"How much farther?"

"It's only a few more miles. You're not really going back to that motel, are you?"

"I've already rented the room."

"Did you leave your things there?"

Jamie hated to tell him she'd been afraid to leave her stuff behind for fear someone would break in and steal it. "No, everything I have is in bags behind the seat."

"Would you reconsider staying at my place if I told you there were no strings attached? And that I'm willing to share what I have regardless of whether you agree to work with me or not?"

"Why would you do that?"

"I keep telling you, I'm a nice guy."

Jamie raised an eyebrow. "And I'm your ticket to get to Harlan?"

"I'll have to admit you look pretty good in that outfit. I keep hoping you'll fall out of that top. And, yes, I think Rawlins noticed."

"Darn right he noticed. As a matter of fact, I'm meeting with him tomorrow to work on my, um, problem."

"No kidding? What's he going to do, ask the good Lord to send down a lightning bolt when you try to enter a shopping center?"

"Not exactly."

Max looked at her. "You're blushing, Jamie. What's up? I can tell when you're keeping something from me."

She would have to tell him the truth sooner or later.

"Max, what I told the congregation and what I told Rawlins were two different things."

"I'm listening."

"I had to say something that would get his attention."

"I'm still listening."

"I told him I was a sex addict."

"You did what!"

"It was the only way. How else do you think I managed to get a personal invitation to his home for private counseling?"

Max did not look happy. "Let me get this straight. You're going to Harlan Rawlins's home without backup, *knowing* full well that he's somehow involved with the mob? Not only that, we already know he has a weakness for women, and you've told him you're a sex addict. Great idea, Jamie. Why don't you throw a little meat to a lion while you're at it? Dammit!"

"I wouldn't go if I weren't convinced it was safe. I'm sure he has plenty of staff on hand, not to mention his family."

"You don't know what you're up against. By now Harlan and his mob pals know the man they hired to take me out is dead. The fact that the hit man, Vito Puccini, didn't get the job done will make them even more determined to succeed. They may have already hired someone else to take me out. They could be searching for me at this very moment."

Jamie remained silent.

"The bottom line is we need to work together on this for both of our sakes," Max said. "So what's it going to take to convince you?"

Jamie knew he had a point, but she wasn't going to give in that easy.

"First, admit that my plan could work."

Max glanced over at her. "I'm not saying it's a bad plan; I'm saying you need backup. You really need to see what I have on Rawlins. Then you'll understand why I feel the way I do."

"OK, I'll see what you've got."

"Take a right at the next road and drive until you see the cabin. There aren't any other houses nearby."

Jamie turned down a dirt road where *No Trespassing* signs made it plain visitors weren't welcome. A minute later, she pulled into a driveway beside a rough-hewn log cabin. She looked around. "Where are the security cameras?"

Max smiled. "You won't find them. You'll know if somebody comes near the property because it'll set off an alarm inside."

"Loud enough to give me heart failure?"

He chuckled. "No, just loud enough so you can hear from any of the rooms."

Jamie climbed from the truck and opened the tailgate so Fleas could jump out. He whizzed on the nearest bush and followed them inside the cabin. It was cool. The scent of wildflowers rode on a breeze coming through the living room windows. The room had obviously been designed for comfort. The overstuffed sofa and chairs, adorned in a country print, faced a wall-sized stone fireplace. A TV sat in one corner, a bookshelf in the opposite. The room was large and shared space with a kitchen that held an old trestle table made of pine. It was simple and inviting.

"The beds come with feather mattresses," Max said.

"How many bathrooms?"

He hesitated. "There's a half-bath in the loft but only one with a tub, and it's in the hall across from the bedroom where you'd be sleeping. If you decide to stay."

Jamie nodded her approval. "Nice place you got here, Holt."

"Muffin found it while we were still chasing bad guys in Beaumont. From what I understand, it was in bad shape. A team of contractors practically rebuilt it from the ground up in less than a week."

"Jeez, I can't get a toilet repaired that fast."

"You do what you have to do."

"Won't people think it strange that the cabin was repaired almost overnight? What if the contractors talk?"

"They work for me."

"Why am I not surprised?"

"So what do you say? You want to give it a try?"

Jamie pondered it. She had promised herself to stay as far away from Max Holt as possible, but here she was, standing only a few feet from him and wishing she didn't find him so sexy. On the flip side, Jamie knew she needed him for the job at hand. He had the technology and the contacts.

Max smiled. "You're chewing your bottom lip. That means you're considering it."

"We should set a few ground rules."

"You're right. You'll have to stop giving me the come-on."

Her look was deadpan.

He sighed. "What are the rules?"

"We agree to keep this strictly business."

"That depends. Do you plan to walk around in those short skirts and tank tops all the time?"

"Be serious."

"I'm being very serious."

"I have to dress like this when I meet with Harlan. I'm trying to bait him."

"Damn good bait if you ask me. I'd bite."

She tried to ignore him. Yet she couldn't help but admit she derived a certain amount of satisfaction knowing she had captured Max's imagination. "Rule number two: I want to know everything that's going on at all times. No surprises. I'm serious about getting my story, so I have to be able to document everything as it happens. I'll also need to use some of the background information you've gathered on Harlan and the mob."

"Some of the information came from, um, sources that I'm not supposed to know even exist."

"Oh, great. Meaning you and Muffin have been busting through computer firewalls and deciphering codes again."

"Sometimes I break the rules." He saw her look. "Not that I have any intention of breaking the rules you're setting right now, of course."

"Yeah, right."

"And I might enjoy helping you with your story. I happen to know a little bit about the newspaper business if you'll recall."

Jamie was reminded that was one of the reasons he'd been eager to invest in her fledgling newspaper to begin with. Max had worked for his cousin's newspaper, and she had also seen firsthand how savvy he was when it came to what readers liked.

Finally, she shrugged. "I'll listen to suggestions," she said, "as long as you realize I'm not giving you editorial control, and you're not getting a byline."

"You're a hard woman, Jamie. Does this mean you're in?"

"Show me what you've got on Rawlins."

Max handed her a folder.

Jamie sat on the sofa and opened the file. Max took a chair opposite her. After a moment, she looked up. "I'm impressed."

"And so you should be."

"How did you know Rawlins wouldn't be touring at this time?"

"We got lucky. If he'd been on tour we would have come up with a different plan. It just worked out this way."

"I see he actually received his master of divinity from one of the best seminaries in the country."

"With a heavy emphasis on pastoral counseling," Max said. "Which permitted him to take all the psychology courses he wanted. Bottom line: He knows people."

"No wonder he makes such a good shark. Nice photo. Shows off his blue eyes."

"Stop drooling; you're supposed to remain objective, remember?"

"Do you think you could hold off being insufferable until I've had a chance to study Rawlins's file?"

"So you're saying you and me, a hot shower, and me licking you dry afterward isn't likely?"

A shiver ran up Jamie's backbone, touching each vertebra along the way. "See what I mean? I haven't been here five minutes, and you're already breaking the rules."

Max moved to the sofa. His gaze met hers. "You know the score. You knew it when you walked through that front door."

Jamie felt his thigh touch hers, but she refused to move and make a big deal out of it. "What are you trying to say?"

"You're after something."

She arched one brow. "And that something would be you?"

He shrugged. "I know the story is important to you. The fact you might have me as well is just an added bonus."

It was all she could do to keep from bursting into laughter. His sense of humor was one of the qualities she most appreciated in him. "Enjoying yourself, Max?" she said as though talking to a child. It didn't help that Max had already painted a picture in her mind of the two of them naked beneath a warm spray of water.

She took a deep breath and studied the printout before her. Max was quiet, but she could sense his gaze on her, smell his aftershave. She was attracted to him on all levels. But she had to stop thinking along those lines, because she already knew the dangers. Max Holt was hazardous to a woman's heart.

"I see Rawlins's psychology courses helped immensely in his calling," she said, changing the subject. "It says here that he uses a number of techniques to win people over and control his followers."

"Brainwashing, fear tactics, and hypnosis being among them," Max said. "There's also a lot of peer pressure from within the group. People like to fit in. Rawlins plants his people in the group to draw visitors in and keep them in."

Jamie wished Max would scoot over, but to suggest it would let him know he was having an effect on her. Not that he didn't already know, she reminded herself. Max knew women, and he knew how to play them.

"So this is what you wanted me to see."

"I thought it might give you insight as to the kind of man we're dealing with."

"But why would he go to so much trouble when most of this area is impoverished? Why isn't he trying to convert the wealthy?"

"Rawlins knows he isn't going to make money in Sweet Pea, but how would it look to the public if he didn't help the people he grew up with? He's offered to meet their donations tenfold. It might make headlines, but tenfold of almost nothing equals very little out of his pocket. There aren't many people who can afford to give." Max paused. "As for converting the wealthy, Rawlins has managed to snare an impressive number of those with fat wallets. He plays golf, sails, and he's big on charitable events."

"Which means he rubs elbows with the right people."

Max nodded. "And his PR person makes sure Harlan's name is in the newspaper every chance he gets. His notoriety and charm are a big draw to people."

"He's fighting for new industry in this area," Jamie said. "Not only has he donated money from his ministry, he's rallied support from other organizations."

"His ministry appears squeaky clean," Max said. "He presents himself to the world as a happily married man with a two-year-old son he dotes on. You have to know where to look to find the real story."

Jamie held up the papers. "Who would take the time to collect this much information on Rawlins, and why?" When Max didn't answer, she tried to guess. "The FBI, right? They've caught wind of his mob connections."

"Could be."

"You're not going to tell me?"

"You haven't agreed to work with me."

Jamie looked up. "I have a question, Max. Do you believe in miracles? Other than the fact it's a miracle we're still alive after what we've been through?"

"That's one heck of a way to change the subject, but to answer your question, I believe in living by my wits."

"In other words, you can't imagine a power greater than yourself. Why am I not surprised?"

"I didn't say that." He smiled. "I'm glad we're going to be spending a lot of time together here," he said, indicating the cabin. "It's a very intimate setting. We'll have time to work on us."

Jamie rolled her eyes. Talk about changing the subject, but then, Max might be one of those people who kept his beliefs private. "There is no *us,* Max, except in your own mind."

He looked amused. "I hope you didn't make that date with Rawlins just to make me jealous."

He was back to his old antics. "Would you cut it out?" Finally, Jamie stood and moved to the chair. "By the way, he thinks my name is Jane."

Max chuckled. "Very original. Now you're going to need a last name. How do you like the name Matt Trotter?"

"Why do you ask?"

"It's the name I'm using." He pulled out several cards. "Driver's license, Social Security card, and my employee card from Bennett Electric. Like my picture? I wasn't crazy about my new look at first, but I think it works."

Of course it *worked,* Jamie thought. The truth was, the man would have been handsome with pork chops hanging from his ears. "I take it this new job of yours is just a front?"

"Yeah. I'm really working for an escort service."

"How do you plan to find time to investigate Rawlins and his mob friends?"

"I have a nice boss."

"Meaning money has exchanged hands."

"It happens. Now that you've decided to sign on with me, so to speak, you'll need identification. I'll snap a picture of the new you, scan it, and e-mail it to a friend of mine. Next time you walk out that door, you'll have a brand-new identity."

"Oh, yeah? Who am I supposed to be?"

"Jane Trotter. My wife."

FIVE

"We're supposed to be married?" Jamie blurted in disbelief.

"Can you think of a better explanation as to why we're sharing a cabin in the woods?"

"Why can't we be brother and sister?"

Max shook his head. "Jamie, Jamie, Jamie. Someone would notice how you look at me, and our cover would be blown."

She did a massive eye roll. "Oh, puh-lease."

"Face it, Swifty: You have lust in your eyes, and it has my name written all over it."

"You know, I've discovered the best way to deal with you is to ignore most of what you say. Frankly, I don't see why we have to explain anything."

"We're going to try and infiltrate the good reverend's ministry, sweetheart. Hopefully, we'll meet some of the key players. Who knows? One of us might end up teaching Sunday school."

"Harlan might be discouraged if I tell him I'm married."

"Actually, it works to his benefit. The last thing he wants to deal with is a messy entanglement. You can pretend you're trying to curb your, uh, addiction in order to save your marriage. You're not really going to have sex with him. . . ." Max paused.

"What?" Jamie said when he didn't finish. She frowned. "You're not afraid something is going to happen between Harlan and me. You're not thinking—"

"I don't know what to think," Max said. "What if you get cornered? What if he forces himself on you?" Max shook his head. "I'll have to level with you, Jamie. I've felt uneasy about the man from the beginning. We don't know what he's capable of."

It was as if a lightbulb suddenly went off in Jamie's head. "So *that's* why you changed your mind about bringing me along," she said, remembering Max's change of heart had come after Muffin had told them about Rawlins's history with women.

Max hesitated. "I knew you would try to think of a way to play him, that you would place yourself right in the line of fire, so to speak. And I was right. You showed up in an outfit that was designed to give a man a . . ." He paused. "You get my point."

"Uh, yeah."

"All I'm asking is that you practice a great deal of caution. It's OK to dangle a carrot in front of Rawlins, but it's not OK to take unnecessary chances. When you visit him, Dave and I need to be close by."

"How?"

"Let us worry about that."

"Just don't blow my cover, OK? I spent a lot of money on this wig."

"Wait a minute, Jamie. I don't care if we all blow our covers if Rawlins gets crazy with you. If he tries to use force, Dave and I are going to be on him. That's why you have to agree to work with us as a team. I'm not going to back off on this one, Swifty. You have to agree to that up front."

She sighed. "OK, Max."

"There are ways you might be able to get away without blowing our cover. You can try those first."

"What are they?"

"Having a husband in the wings is one of them. You can tell Harlan any number of things if it looks like the situation is getting out of hand. Tell him your husband is insanely jealous, that you suspect you're being followed. Tell him whatever the hell you have to in order to protect yourself. You could suddenly start feeling guilty. Whatever it takes to stay safe. But if it doesn't work, you scream, you run, you do what you have to do to protect yourself. Dave and I will be close by."

Jamie knew Max was right. "OK," she said. "Husband and wife. We'll need wedding rings."

"I'll take care of it." He suddenly smiled. "So, what do you say? Think we can work together?"

"That depends. Would you promise not to try to disarm any more bombs in my presence?"

"If you'll promise not to be so disagreeable."

"I am *not* disagreeable."

"And we need to discuss the dog."

They both looked at Fleas, who was napping near Jamie's feet. "He stays," she said. "It's a package deal."

Max didn't look happy.

"I'll take care of him. I've already bought everything he needs."

Max studied the lanky bloodhound. "What happened to his hair?"

"Fleas was attacked by a raccoon."

"You're going to allow an animal named Fleas to sleep under the same roof with us?"

"He doesn't have fleas. It's his *name*. Obviously somebody thought it was funny. Besides, we need a good watchdog."

"And that would be him?"

"Of course. He's very alert when he isn't sleeping. I think he's already attached to me. I can't even take a shower without him following me into the bathroom."

"Oh, now you've done it," Max said. "You've gone and turned me on." He grinned.

"Trust me, you're perfectly capable of doing it to yourself." Jamie glanced around. "Is there anything to eat in this place? I'm starving."

"I can scramble some eggs. I'm great with scrambled eggs." Max got up.

"Sounds good to me," Jamie replied, jumping to her feet as well. "I need to grab Fleas's food from the truck."

"I'll go with you. We can grab the rest of your things while we're at it."

"I don't have much. I left my suitcase in your car."

"I've already brought it in."

"Where *is* your car, by the way?" Jamie asked, standing in the doorway, looking across the yard.

"In the garage. Remind me to give you the security code for the garage and the cabin before we go to bed."

Jamie opened the door to her truck and reached behind the seat for the bags she'd stuffed behind it. One held her new underwear and toiletry items, the other her dirty clothes, and a separate bag held Fleas's dry dog food and bowls. She made a note to buy more slut-wear.

"By the way, how is Muffin?" she asked once they started back toward the cabin. As odd as it sounded even to her, she had missed Max's computer.

Max opened the door and waited for Jamie to enter. "She's not very happy with me at the moment, thanks to you."

"What did I do?"

"You refused to get back in my car. You just took off on us." Max closed the door after them and locked it, then punched a series of numbers on an alarm panel. "Naturally Muffin missed you and was worried."

Jamie would not have thought Muffin capable of feeling emotions had she not witnessed it for herself. Muffin also had attitude. She did not mind telling Max where he could get off. Jamie had liked her right away. And to think, she had doubted Max the first time he'd told her about his computer; in fact, she had thought him crazy. Hell, she had doubted her own sanity in her earlier conversations with Muffin. Now, as strange as it sounded, Muffin felt like an old friend.

"And you weren't worried about me that I took off?" Jamie asked.

Max shrugged. "I knew you could handle yourself."

They stood there for a moment, simply looking at each other. Jamie studied the handsome olive-skinned face, gazing into those dark eyes that seemed as if they had been created to turn a woman's stomach to mush. She had run her fingers through his hair. She had kissed those delicious lips, tasted him, run her fingers along the strong stubborn jaw.

She knew he was attracted to her, he'd said it plenty of times, and she supposed he cared about her to an extent, but neither of them was clear about their feelings after only two weeks of knowing each other.

Not that it had been an ordinary two weeks, she reminded herself, and she *had* been engaged to another man during that time. Still, they had come mighty close to having sex one night—and it had been a night Jamie would never forget. Max had never mentioned it, but Jamie knew she, for one, was still thinking about it.

Now, as he gazed back at her, Jamie wished she knew what he was thinking. Max was not one who shared his thoughts easily. Sure, he'd made it plain more than once that he would have enjoyed a rumble beneath the sheets, but where his feelings were concerned he was about as close-mouthed as they came.

"Hey, you're awfully quiet," Max said. "Is something wrong?"

Jamie gave an inward sigh. By meeting up with Max she had once again placed her heart in a precarious position. "I'm just tired. Maybe you could show me where I'm sleeping."

"Right this way."

She followed him down a short hall. He paused at the door, reached inside, and flipped on the light, then motioned her into the room as he set her bags down. "The bathroom is right across the hall. While you get situated, I'll start the eggs."

"Thanks."

Jamie stepped into the bedroom and sat on the old four-poster bed, testing the mattress. Max was right; it was stuffed with feathers. She could do some serious sleeping on this bed. A cool breeze rustled the curtains and fell softly on her skin. Jamie suddenly felt more relaxed than she had in days.

She glanced at the oak dresser against the wall and frowned at the woman in the mirror. She pulled off the wig, unpinned her blond hair, and finger-combed it. Much better, she thought. Now she only had to scrape off an inch-thick layer of makeup.

Jamie could hear Max cracking the eggs into a bowl in the kitchen as she crossed the hall to the bathroom. She grinned at the old claw-foot bathtub and imagined herself sitting inside it with bubbles up to her ears. A metal hoop had been positioned over the tub, hanging from it a floral shower curtain. A porcelain sink was perched on one wall; someone had attached a skirt to it that matched both the shower and the window curtain. A wicker basket beside the tub was stuffed with fluffy bath towels.

Max was in the process of chopping green peppers on an old-fashioned butcher block when Jamie entered the kitchen for her suitcase. "I thought you were just going to scramble a few eggs," she said, peering over his shoulder. "I should help."

He turned and held his hands out, blocking her. "Actually, I don't permit anyone in the kitchen when I'm preparing my secret recipe."

"Why is it a secret?"

"Because of all the special ingredients that go into it. Why don't you just rest for a few minutes?"

Jamie noticed Fleas standing beside Max as though waiting for something. "Have you been feeding my dog?"

"I gave him a little cheese. Dogs like cheese."

"He should be eating real dog food." Jamie pulled his food and dog dishes from a bag.

"I'll feed him," Max said. "Just go back to what you were doing. Oh, I wrote down the alarm code. It's on the table."

"OK, I'll get out of your way, but don't give Fleas any more cheese. He'll get fat."

Jamie grabbed her suitcase and returned to her room. Inside she found her favorite cutoff jeans. She stepped out of her short skirt and high heels and pulled them on. She unpacked her bag, put her newly purchased shampoo, toothbrush, and toothpaste inside the bathroom cabinet, and hurried back into the kitchen, where she found Max, scooping eggs onto plates.

"That looks wonderful," she said, noting that Max had added ham, onions, and cheese to the eggs. He'd even made toast. Jamie grabbed napkins and flatware and went about setting the table as Max poured orange juice.

"This is good," Jamie said after tasting her food.

"My cousin Nick taught me how to run a newspaper; his wife Billie taught me how to cook." Max looked up from his food. "I've always wanted to take a gourmet cooking class."

"Why haven't you?"

"My schedule doesn't really permit it."

"Who takes care of your horse farm in Virginia while you're away?"

"I have a guy who looks after things. He's been with me for years now."

"Don't you miss being home?"

"Yeah. I'll probably go back for a while once I'm done here."

"Isn't Holt Industries based there?"

"Uh-huh. I have offices in other locations, but the home office is in Loudon County, Virginia."

"And what do you do in those offices?"

Max regarded her. "Mostly technological research, but I've expanded over the years. We're doing some biomedical research, and I'm putting out bids soon to build a lab to study viruses."

"Isn't that already being done?"

"Not fast enough."

"You're amazing," Jamie said.

"Yeah?"

"You've got your fingers in everything."

"Keeps boredom at bay."

"But you could afford to retire anytime you like."

"What would I do, Jamie?"

She laughed. "With your money? Any damn thing you wanted. You could travel the world."

"I already have. Several times."

"Isn't there anything you haven't done?"

Max sat back in his chair and looked thoughtful. "Until today I'd never ridden in a pickup truck with a redhead and a hound dog."

"Seriously, Max."

"If you could retire tomorrow, would you?"

Jamie hesitated. "I'd probably still want to write a few articles. It's sort of in my blood."

"You'll never stop working, Jamie. You're too much like me. When you do what you love, it never feels like work. That doesn't mean I don't like to take off and play. I'm big on vacations. But I need direction. A reason for being."

"Your marriage to Bunny didn't provide that?" She tried to hide her smile.

Max scowled. "That was *not* her real name. And no, the marriage was all wrong from the start."

"Why'd you marry her?"

"Because I was dumb and infatuated. End of story."

"Do you wish you'd had children with her?"

"Why are you asking these questions? You're beginning to sound like Muffin."

"I was merely trying to carry on polite conversation, Max. I certainly didn't mean to intrude."

"I don't question you about your love life." He bit

off a piece of toast and chewed. "She was not an air-head. People just assumed she was because of the way she looked."

"The way she looked?"

"Well, hell, Jamie, the woman was . . ." Max paused.

"Gorgeous," Jamie said.

"Yeah, and she had this—"

"Great body," Jamie interrupted.

"Uh-huh."

Jamie dropped her fork, and it clattered loudly. "Well, now isn't that special."

"I thought so in the beginning."

Jamie stood and picked up her plate.

"What are you doing?" Max asked. "You haven't finished eating."

"I'm not hungry."

"You were starving a few minutes ago."

Jamie raked her eggs into Fleas's bowl, and the dog dived on it. "I'm really very tired."

Max chuckled. "You mean you're really very jealous."

Jamie cut her eyes at him. "I am not jealous. I just don't want to talk about your ex-wife's body."

"Hey, you're the one who brought it up."

Fleas finished eating and gazed at Max's plate.

Max stood. "You're saying you've never noticed a man's body?"

"I notice a man's eyes first."

"Uh-huh."

"But I've dated some very fit men, Max."

"You want to see fit?" Max suddenly lifted his shirt, exposing a flat, hair-roughened stomach. "Feel that."

Jamie decided her first mistake was looking. Oh God. He had one of those hard washboard stomachs that she'd only heard women talk about. And that hair, the way it fanned out so nicely across his stomach, the way it whorled around his navel and—She dropped her gaze, found herself suddenly staring at his zipper. Oh God, oh God, oh God. It didn't help that his unshaved jaw made him even more appealing.

Max grabbed Jamie's wrist and pressed her hand against his abdomen.

Skin touched skin.

"It's hard as a rock," he said proudly. "Not an ounce of flab anywhere."

Jamie swallowed. Felt like a giant turnip was trying to make its way down her windpipe. Felt like something had cut off her breath and she was going to have to use the Heimlich maneuver on herself in order to get air.

She jerked her hand free. "Would you cut that out!"

"I was trying to make a point." Max pulled his shirt down, grabbed his plate, and raked his food into Fleas's bowl. The dog scrambled toward it.

"He's not supposed to be eating that," Jamie said.

"You fed him yours."

"I decided to give him a little treat. I don't want him to get used to eating people food on account it isn't good for him. I'm going to bed. Come on, Fleas, let's go."

"You're letting him sleep in your room? Man, that's one lucky dog."

Jamie ignored him.

Fleas wolfed down the remaining food before following Jamie into her bedroom. She closed the door and locked it. "I know what you're thinking," she said. "You're thinking I didn't handle that very well."

He belched in response.

Jamie waited until Max went to bed before going out to his car. She needed a friend, and Muffin, despite being a computer, was the closest thing she had at the moment.

She punched a set of numbers into the alarm panel, hit a button, and the garage door rose automatically. She hurried inside and yanked open the car door.

"Hey, Muffin, it's me," she said once she'd climbed into the car.

"Jamie, don't you *ever* sneak up on me like that again! I almost hit the panic button."

"This place has too many alarms," Jamie grumbled. "I can't go to the bathroom without fear of setting something off."

"What are you doing here?" Muffin asked. "I thought you'd gone back to Beaumont."

"I decided to come to Tennessee on my own," she said. "You know how badly I want to do a story on Harlan Rawlins and his mob buddies. So, I said to hell with Max and came on my own."

"Where are you staying?"

"With Max."

"Oh." Muffin paused. "Did I miss something?"

Jamie filled her in on all that had happened since her arrival.

"You actually went to Harlan's church and told him you were a sex addict?" Muffin said in disbelief.

"Yep. After all, you're the one who told me he had a weakness for women. You should have seen the look on his face. I'm meeting him tomorrow for private counseling. I wish you could see me, Muffin. I look like I'm peddling poontang, for sure." Jamie laughed. It was good talking to Muffin again. And easy to forget she was a voice-activated computer.

"It sounds dangerous to me, kiddo. What does Max have to say about this?"

"He wasn't exactly thrilled to see me at church, but we got past that. By the way, Max and I are supposed to be married."

"Oh God, this'll never work."

"It has to, Muffin. This is the chance I've been waiting for. My big break. And it's only the beginning."

"Listen, Jamie, you don't know what you're getting into. This Rawlins guy could be dangerous. Especially if he's in tight with the mob like we think he is."

"OK, if I sound like I'm not taking it seriously it's because I'm excited. But I'm very much aware of the risks. I'm not leaving anything to chance. It's not like Max and I haven't faced danger before."

"The two of you were very lucky to get out of Beaumont alive," Muffin said. "You can't afford to take chances now."

"I promise I'll be careful. Look, I have to get back to the house in case Max wakes up. Don't tell him I talked to you. Try to act surprised when he tells you I'm back."

Muffin sighed. "I knew this was going to get complicated."

Max tossed in his bed for an hour before he climbed out and pulled on his jeans. He slipped from the house quietly. A moment later he was telling Muffin all that had taken place since they'd last talked.

"Jamie just blew into town in an old pickup truck

with an ugly bloodhound in the back," he said. "I couldn't let her go after Rawlins on her own, so I convinced her to work with me. She's staying at my cabin."

"How are the two of you getting along?"

"Jamie promised not to be difficult."

"And what did you promise?"

Max sounded defensive when he spoke. "Are you saying I'm difficult?"

"Now where would I get an idea like that?"

"OK," he said begrudgingly. "I promised not to disable any more bombs. You got anything for me?" he asked, stifling a yawn.

"I'm still working on it. Have you and Dave finalized your plans?"

"Yeah, but then Jamie showed up and that changed everything."

"You have to admire her spunk."

"Yeah, I guess. I just hope she doesn't get us all killed."

SIX

Jamie shivered as something wet and moist nuzzled her ear. "Cut it out, Max." She pulled the bed pillow over her head and sank farther into the feather mattress. The pillow shifted. She was jolted fully awake, this time by a wet tongue at the back of her neck. Her scalp tingled and she could feel the goose pimples on her arm. She shouted in irritation, "Max, I said stop it!" She yanked the pillow aside as Fleas skittered beneath the tall bed, toenails clicking across the old plank floors.

"Oh, damn," she muttered. "I must've had another X-rated dream about Max."

Coming off the bed, Jamie dropped to her knees and peered beneath it. "I'm sorry, boy. I thought you were this pervert I know." She offered her hand. Fleas sniffed once and thumped his tail in response.

"Come on out. I won't hurt you."

The dog hesitated and then crawled from beneath the bed. Jamie regarded him. His folds seemed more prominent this morning. "Jeez, pal, a little collagen in those wrinkles would work wonders, you know."

The dog cocked his head to one side. His skin seemed to slide with the motion. Jamie shook her head sadly and glanced about the small bedroom. She was still tired. After her visit with Muffin she'd lain awake for a good two hours, finally falling asleep around 2:00 A.M. She gave a wide unladylike yawn.

"Have you seen Max?" she asked Fleas. "You remember him, the guy with the hard stomach? The one who kinda looks like something you'd find in a Calvin Klein ad? Like someone you'd want to share a hot tub with?"

Jamie sighed. First she'd had a sexy dream; now she was thinking about Max's body. And she hadn't even had her first cup of coffee. Well, it was all his fault; he'd started it by lifting up his shirt.

"Watch yourself, kiddo," she told herself, "or you'll end up falling for him all over again."

Falling for him? Uh-oh. The thought shocked her. No, no, she wasn't falling for him; she was simply attracted to him, that's all. What woman wouldn't be? Looking into those sexy eyes of his was almost like having foreplay with him, for Pete's sake! Damn him for making her think things she had no right thinking.

The dog made a sound. "What is it?" Jamie asked. Finally, it hit her. "Oh, I'll bet you have to go to the bathroom. Oh, hell, Fleas, I knew I'd make a terrible pet owner. And you know it, too, don't you? That's why you look so sad."

Jamie sighed and walked from the room in her nightshirt, the lanky bloodhound on her heels. She let him out the front door. "How about sniffing out the nearest Dunkin' Donuts while you're at it?"

She checked her wristwatch while she waited for him to do his business. Six o'clock. No wonder she was so tired. She was the kind of person who needed eight hours of sleep or she became disagreeable, as Max sometimes accused.

Fleas returned and Jamie closed the door behind them. She wondered what Max was up to. She glanced toward the loft, which she assumed held another bed. "Max, are you up?"

No answer.

"He's probably in his car talking to his computer," she told the dog. "You don't know about Max's computer. Her name is Muffin, and she's capable of doing just about anything. Maybe she can find you a nice plastic surgeon."

The dog thumped his tail against the floor.

"Maybe she can find me a shrink. I talk to computers; I talk to dogs." Fleas looked at his bowl. "Oh, yeah, it's time to feed you. See, I'm not very reliable; you have to remind me of these things." She grabbed the sack of dry food and shook some into his dish. "Breakfast is served," she announced.

Fleas simply blinked back at her. "Listen to me, pal: This is primo dog food. It's supposed to keep you fit and trim and give you all the vitamins you need." He responded by slumping to the floor. "OK, so you're not a breakfast dog. I usually like to have a couple of cups of coffee myself before I eat. Sometimes I don't even bother with breakfast. Saves calories. That way I can pile up on junk food later. I shouldn't be telling you this on account I need to set a good example for you."

Jamie found the automatic coffeemaker and filled a cup. She sat down at the old pine table and looked about. She felt lost and disoriented, and she suspected it was due to lack of sleep mixed with anxiety mixed with wondering how she and Max would live under the same roof for the next few days.

She forced the thought aside, turning her attention to the appointment she had with Harlan Rawlins in less than six hours. She had to admit she was worried; indeed, she could find herself in a compromising position if she weren't careful. She would have to stay one step ahead of him at all times.

Jamie hurried into her bedroom for the notepad she'd purchased on her shopping trip. As she sipped her coffee, she jotted down her first impressions of Harlan.

"Handsome and charismatic," she wrote. "A man who knows how to work a crowd," she added, scribbling quickly. She'd devised her own form of shorthand long ago from interviewing people. She continued writing. Harlan Rawlins seemed sincere when it came to the less fortunate, but his weakness for women and his ties to the mob told a different story.

Jamie paused and clicked the pen against her bottom teeth, something Vera often got on her for doing. Lord, Vera was going to skin her alive when she got back to Beaumont. She thought of the woman who had been the next best thing to a mother when Jamie's biological mother had left while she was still in diapers. Vera, who had always been there for her.

Vera had taught her to be strong and to meet challenges head-on. As a result, she had refused to give up on the newspaper. She had sold almost everything she owned in order to keep it afloat, and she had swallowed her pride when an investor had offered to help her out. That investor had been Max Holt, of course. Max bailed her out and put a large chunk of change in an account so Jamie would never have to struggle again.

Jamie looked forward to the day she could pay him back. It might sound like a grand plan at this point, but she was determined.

Guilt hit her as soon as she thought of Vera. She had no right to cause the woman to worry. With a heavy sigh, Jamie put down her pen and grabbed the portable phone from the kitchen counter. She had a choice. She could call Vera at home and listen to the woman rant and rave or she could call the newspaper office, knowing Vera wouldn't be in at this hour, and leave a message.

Jamie dialed the office. "Hello, Vera, it's me," she said, trying to make her voice light and airy, as though she were having the time of her life. "Just wanted to let you know I'm enjoying my little vacation and I'm resting. I'm going to have a great story when I get back. I'll call again soon, please don't worry about me." She hung up and regarded Fleas.

"See that? Here I am, a grown woman, and I still have to check in. That's because I've always done the responsible thing until I met Max. I was a lot more stable and hardly ever thought about sex before he came into my life and turned it topsy-turvy.

"See, I like predictability. I like having a routine." Like drinking her coffee in her favorite mug with the big smiley face on it, she thought. And sitting in her favorite chair when she watched the news on TV. Simple things that brought her pleasure. She preferred Dove soap to the store brand because one of her earliest memories made her think of that smell.

Could it have been her mother? she'd asked herself a hundred times. She doubted it, since her mother, as best Jamie could determine, had left when Jamie was about two years old. Perhaps she had dreamed it. What she *did* remember, as though it had been yesterday, was snooping through a box in the attic that had held her mother's few belongings and finding a bar of Dove soap inside. She'd hidden it in her underwear drawer, taking it out occasionally so she could sniff its clean scent.

Even now, she kept a bar on her night table because she liked turning over in the middle of the night and smelling its fragrance, and it was all she ever bathed in. She still had the old bar tucked inside her lingerie drawer. And as silly as it sounded, she was annoyed that she had forgotten to buy it at the store the previous day.

Jamie's stomach growled. She crossed the kitchen and grabbed a cookie from a jar that had been painted with roosters and matched the set of canisters nearby. The coffee was not doing what it was supposed to do, namely, wake her up. Where the heck was Max? She climbed the narrow steps that led to the loft area.

The bed was empty and unmade. Jamie slid her hand across the smooth sheet. The pillow bore the imprint of Max's head and the subtle scent of his after-shave. She plucked a dark hair from it and tried not to imagine Max warm and naked beneath the old quilt.

Here we go again, she thought.

What was wrong with her? She was lusting after a man, that's what. Her hormones must be out of whack. Or maybe her defenses were down due to fatigue.

She stared at the empty bed. It looked so inviting. Perhaps if she just closed her eyes for fifteen minutes. She lay down on the soft mattress, nuzzled her face into Max's pillow, and drifted off to sleep.

SEVEN

Harlan Rawlins smoothed his hand over his perfect blond hair and readjusted his tie. His white dress shirt was European-cut. It fit nicely against his well-toned body and brought out his tan, both of which he worked hard to keep, even when he was on the road. One of the 18-wheeler trucks that carried Love Ministry's tents and other equipment also contained a gym, complete with a portable hot tub and tanning bed.

His entourage included a personal trainer and masseuse, a chef who saw that Harlan maintained a healthy but delicious eating regimen, and a publicist and PR person who purchased licenses and permits for the ministry, contacted the newspapers and TV and radio stations, and set up news conferences.

Harlan's administrative assistant saw that Harlan stayed on schedule and had exactly what he needed at all times, and even wrote some of Harlan's speeches and sermons. A personal valet saw to Harlan's extensive wardrobe, shaved him, trimmed his hair, gave him manicures, pedicures, and facials, and made sure the minister's personal belongings were laid out upon his arrival. A bodyguard traveled with Harlan and was responsible for arranging for the female "guests" who visited Harlan's hotel rooms from time to time.

Now, sitting at his desk in his private office, Harlan spoke to the woman on the other end of the line, using the voice that inspired confidence and had brought many to salvation. Only this morning it was marked with fatigue and had a certain edge to it. He cradled the phone between his shoulder and jaw, freeing his hands so that he could massage his temples where a headache had been brewing for the last hour. His forehead was damp.

"Honey, I've only been back three days. Of course I was going to call you, but my little boy has a nasty summer cold and I've been spending time with him. You know I can't count on his mama to see to his care, what with her emotional problems." Suddenly he lost his connection. The lights flickered in his office, not for the first time. He looked up and frowned.

Someone knocked on his door. "Yes?" he called out.

His bodyguard, Ward Reed, peeked inside. He was a tall, angular man with hard eyes and thin lips. Not only did he accompany Harlan wherever the minister went; he saw to home security as well. "Mr. Santoni is here."

Harlan froze. "*Here?* What's he doing *here?*"

"I know we've discouraged him from coming to your home in the past, but I suggest we go ahead and let him in this time. I want to know what's so important that he decided to show up at your front door so early in the day."

Harlan sighed. "Greed, what else? I don't like this, Ward." He wiped his brow. "What's wrong with the power? The lights are flashing on and off and the phone just died on me."

"We've got electrical problems. I've already reported it, but it'll take a while for the men to get here. May lose power for a while; the generator will eventually kick in." As if acting on cue, the lights flickered, and the office went dark.

"Just what I need," Harlan said. "I want to meet with a man like Santoni in a dark office."

Ward pulled a cord and the drapes whispered open. July sunlight filled the room. "I'll be here the whole time." He studied the man. "You don't look so good."

"I didn't sleep last night. My mind was racing ninety miles an hour."

"You can't keep this up, Harlan. You look strung out, man."

"You know what touring does to me."

"Yeah, but you're taking way too much medication. You have to take something to make you sleep, something to keep you awake. You need to see a doctor."

"Let Santoni in," Harlan interrupted.

Ward gave the man a long, hard look. Finally, he shrugged. "Whatever you say."

Nick Santoni stepped through the door a moment later with Ward Reed on his heels. Santoni wore a soft dove gray suit that had been shipped directly from Milan, the likes of which could not be purchased in a town like Sweet Pea or Knoxville for any amount. His black hair was perfect.

"Well, well, the lamb of God has returned to his holy mansion on the mountain." He glanced around the dark room. "Did you forget to pay your electric bill?"

Harlan offered him a tight smile. "We're having problems with the power. Were we supposed to meet today, Mr. Santoni? I don't have you listed in my appointment book."

Nick smiled and held out his arms in greeting. "What's this 'Mr. Santoni' business?" he asked. "How many times have I asked you to call me Nick? I like to think we're not only business associates but friends as well. Surely you can spare a few minutes of your time."

"Of course." Harlan's voice trembled.

"By the way, your home is lovely. I had no idea ministers lived so well. You've even got marble pillars in the foyer. I thought you Christians were supposed to store your treasures in heaven." He paused and winked. "Looks like you couldn't wait, buddy."

"What can I do for you?" Harlan asked. He reached for a tissue, mopped his upper lip.

Nick took a chair across from Harlan's desk. Reed sat on the sofa against the wall. "I wish I had good news, my friend," Nick began, "but the family has been putting pressure on me to up your percentage, despite my best efforts to convince them otherwise."

Harlan looked confused. "But we agreed on a cap. We have a gentlemen's agreement."

"Yes, and the Santoni family has always been honorable people, but your situation has changed. Your celebrity status has grown by leaps and bounds in the past few years." He paused. "I'd like to think I am somewhat responsible for your success."

Harlan remained quiet.

"Unfortunately, your fame puts you at a higher risk, and at your current installment, I can't guarantee your protection outside of this state. You could be in serious danger."

Harlan and Reed exchanged looks. "My expenses are already sky-high," Harlan said.

"We're only talking another five percent. I know it sounds like a lot, and I'm very sympathetic to your situation, but my uncle feels strongly about this. There's no changing his mind," Nick added softly.

Harlan pressed his fingertips against his temples but still said nothing.

Nick waited, absently stroking the thin scar that ran from his left eyebrow to his cheekbone, one he'd earned as a wet-behind-the-ears thug who'd gone up against a Jersey gang leader. The surgeon hadn't finished stitching Nick's cut before a jogger found the other man's body in a ditch on the side of a road.

Nevertheless, the scar, while it added a slightly harder edge to Nick's good looks, did not detract from them, and he turned his share of women's heads. Having been groomed for years to be the head of the Santoni family, Nick was polished and carried himself well. He'd lost most of the Jersey accent; he spoke slowly and deliberately and made each word count. He had the look of a banker or corporate attorney.

"You don't look well, Harlan," Nick said.

Harlan rolled his shoulders. "It was a long trip. I ran out of medicine."

Nick reached inside his jacket. He pulled out a small plastic bottle of pills. "Catch." He tossed the bottle, and Harlan lunged at it.

"It'll take the edge off," Nick said, "until I send over the other. I've told you before there is no reason for you to suffer needlessly when I'm only too happy to help."

The lights came on. Harlan straightened in his chair. "I have cooperated with the Santoni family in the past, but this, er, request is unreasonable."

"Now, Harlan," Nick said gently. "The last thing we want to do is create hard feelings between us. The family has always had your best interests at heart."

"We lost the TV network deal," Harlan said. "That was inexcusable."

Nick looked surprised. "Inexcusable? That's a harsh word to use between friends, but then, I know you're not yourself today. The deal simply didn't pan out."

"My portion of the money has not been returned," Harlan said.

Nick looked thoughtful. "Has it not occurred to you that we may have even greater aspirations for you?" he asked. "It would benefit you greatly if you'd learn to become more patient with us. Take the pill, Harlan."

Reed stood and walked over to a cabinet where he poured water into a glass. He handed it to Harlan before facing Nick. "Maybe we could discuss this another time."

"What is there to discuss?" Harlan said. "I can't afford to run a ministry at this rate." He looked at Nick. "Don't you people realize that every time you up your share you take food or medicine away from those who desperately need it? Should I close down all of my outreach programs so the Santoni family can keep getting richer?"

Nick smiled, but it didn't reach his dark eyes. "This coming from a man who lives like he has already passed through heaven's gate?"

Harlan wiped one hand down his face. Finally, he uncapped the bottle, pulled out the tiny pill, and popped it into his mouth. He didn't bother with the water. "I may as well fold up my tents and retire."

The smile on Nick's face faded. "That would be a mistake, Harlan. You're only talking like that because you don't feel well."

"Is there anything else, Mr. Santoni?" Reed said.

Nick nodded. "Yes, and this should be of concern

to all of us. Vito Puccini is dead. He did not do the job for which he was hired. Maximillian Holt is still alive."

"I don't want to hear this," Harlan said. "I had nothing to do with it. The less I know the better. In case the police question me."

"The police will never make a connection," Nick said, "but Maximillian Holt will. He's got a reputation for being very cunning; he has contacts that even we don't have." He paused. "And he has disappeared."

"What do you mean he has disappeared?" Reed asked.

"He's no longer in Beaumont, South Carolina."

"Maybe he got scared," Harlan said. "He could have left the country," he added hopefully. "Heaven knows he can afford to live anywhere in the world he likes."

Nick shook his head. "Max Holt is not the type of man to run. In fact, he could be looking for us as we speak."

"Do you know something we don't?" Reed asked, as though sensing there was more.

"I did not hire Vito whatever-his-name-is, and I'm not going to get involved in this sort of thing," Harlan said.

"Relax, Harlan," Nick said. "That's why you pay us. I just want you to be aware of the problem, that's all." When Harlan continued to look concerned, Nick smiled. "Haven't we always taken care of your problems in the past? Better still, we keep your dirty little secrets."

Harlan started to respond when the door opened and a young boy peeked through. He had Harlan's blond hair. "Daddy play?" the boy asked.

Harlan literally bolted from his chair, grabbed the

boy, and stepped outside the door, where his wife raced down the stairs, eyes bright with fear.

"I'm sorry, Harlan. I turned my back for one minute and he—"

Harlan didn't give her a chance to finish. He slapped her hard across the face. She cried out, at the same time using one arm to fend off another blow.

Harlan's voice was hard as he regarded his wife. "You only have one job in this house, Sarah," he said. "If you can't do it I'll find somebody who can."

The housekeeper joined them in the hall. "Shall I take Harlan Jr.?" she asked.

The lights flickered and came on; the generator had kicked in. Harlan paid scant notice as he passed the boy to his housekeeper. "Watch him closely." He turned to his wife. "You will spend the rest of the day in your room, Sarah, and you will not see my son until tomorrow." He looked at the housekeeper. "Is that clear?"

The woman nodded stiffly. "Of course, Reverend." She carried the boy away.

Nick waited until Harlan took a seat behind his desk before he spoke. "Nice-looking son you have there," he said. "The spitting image of his daddy. I'll bet he idolizes you."

Harlan's jaw grew rigid.

"Oh, look at the time," Nick said. "I fear I've overstayed my welcome." He got up slowly and made for the door. "Call me later, Harlan. Once you've had time to think about our discussion." He winked. "Oh, and I'll send somebody over later with something to help you sleep tonight. Something a little stronger this time."

EIGHT

When Jamie opened her eyes she found Max staring down at her. She sat upright on the bed, dragging a sheet to her breasts. "What are you doing?"

Max smiled. "Looking at you."

"How long have you been standing there?"

"Long enough to know you got the cutest behind I've ever seen."

Jamie snatched the sheet to her chin. "Don't you have anything better to do than ogle me in my sleep, Holt?"

"I was also thinking how peaceful you look when your eyes are closed and your mouth isn't moving. I could get accustomed to your quiet side. And finding you in my bed."

"Where have you been?"

"Taking care of business."

"Which means you're up to something. I know you." She got up and took the steps down. He followed. The clock in the kitchen pointed to eight o'clock.

"You hungry?" Max asked. "I grabbed a box of fresh donuts from the grocery store while I was out. You know how you like donuts."

Donuts. Damn. The man obviously knew how to work her. "I think I'll shower first," she said, hoping to show some self-control. Max grinned, and she knew she'd failed. "Just don't eat them all."

"You might need this." Max reached into one of the grocery sacks and tossed her a bar of soap.

Jamie was surprised to find a bar of scented Dove soap in her hand. She looked at him. "How did you know?"

"I've spent a lot of time in the car with you; I know your scent. I took a whiff of every bar on the shelf, and this is as close as I came. Was I right?"

Jamie was touched. She couldn't imagine a man like Max taking the time to smell every bar of soap in the store in order to find her brand. "Gee, Max, that was really nice of you."

"I keep telling you I'm a nice guy."

"You can be."

Max smiled as she walked away, her shirt barely concealing her behind.

Jamie showered and changed into cutoff jeans and a tank top. Max had already downed two donuts, but that still left her plenty. She peered into the open box. "Oh, there is a God." She started to reach for a vanilla-glazed donut with bright colorful sprinkles, then paused.

"Come on, Swifty, go for the chocolate-covered one," Max said. "You know you want it."

Jamie grabbed it. She took a bite and closed her eyes. "Yum." She opened her eyes and found Max staring. "What?"

"I like donuts, but I'm not sure I like them that much."

"OK, so you know my weakness."

"By the way, I prefer you as a blonde."

"You and me both. But the red wig is a good disguise." She sighed. "The things I do to keep from getting shot."

Fleas came up beside her and sniffed.

"Forget it, pal," Max told the dog. "You've got a better chance of getting a lung." He reached for a brown envelope and dumped the contents on the table. "Your new identification and—" He pulled two wedding bands from his shirt pocket. "Your ring."

"What? No diamonds?"

"Remember, the idea is to blend. This is not a wealthy area."

Jamie slipped the ring on her finger. "Perfect fit; how did you know?" He shrugged. She glanced at her new driver's license and other identification. "You took this picture of me late last night. How were you able to get all this back so quickly?"

"I asked nicely."

"I'm beginning to think you might have mob connections, too."

"Now, about the truck."

Jamie tossed the last bit of donut into her mouth and licked her fingers. "My truck?"

"Some men are arriving later today to install Muffin into the dashboard. After your appointment with Rawlins," he added. "Nobody will be able to detect the system."

Jamie arched her brow. "You're installing Muffin in the dashboard of *my* truck?"

"Yeah. We can't use my car. Oh, and you're going to need directions to Rawlins's place."

She looked up. "Why don't I just follow you?"

"What makes you think I'm going out there?"

"Like I said, I know you. You're dressed in your

Bennett Electric uniform. Are they having electrical problems this morning by chance?"

He grinned. "As a matter of fact, they are. But you won't arrive until much later." He reached for a pen and paper and began writing directions. "You'll need a key for the cabin in case you get back before I do." He reached into his pocket and placed one on the table.

Jamie had finished her donut and was staring at the remaining ones. "Is that what I think it is?" She pointed to one.

"Yep. Chocolate-covered malted cream."

"Oh, man." She stared.

Max laughed softly. "Well, are you going to eat it or what?"

"This is between me and the donut, OK? It has nothing to do with you."

Tall wrought-iron gates circled Harlan Rawlins's property. The main entrance boasted a guardhouse where a uniformed man met Jamie, eyeing her truck and dog skeptically.

"Does the dog bite?" he asked.

"No, that would take effort on his part," Jamie replied.

The guard almost smiled.

"I have an appointment with Reverend Rawlins."

He checked the small notebook in his hand. "You must be Jane. The reverend is expecting you." He eyed the animal in the back. "You'll need to tie the dog out front."

"He's not as dangerous as he looks," Jamie said, "and it takes an act of God to get him out of this truck. Try going to a pet store for a dog and having to buy a truck as well."

The guard hesitated. "I suppose he looks harmless enough. Just make sure he stays in the truck." He pressed a button, and the gate swung open.

Jamie followed a cobblestone road that was flanked by pines, tupelo, firs, and red maple, interspersed with dogwood, mountain laurel, and rhododendron, the latter of which had already lost their blooms. She rounded a copse of tall loblolly pines and caught her breath at the sight of Rawlins's bricked English manor house, surrounded by parklike grounds and stone courtyards.

Jamie spied a truck with the name Bennett Electric on it. No surprise there, Max Holt was on the job, just as she'd suspected. She was relieved, but she would be slow to admit it to him.

She parked, climbed from the truck, and stood before Fleas. "How do I look? Do I have the word *easy* written all over me or what?"

The dog cocked his head to the side.

"Now hear this," Jamie said, trying to sound stern. "You so much as think about following me like you did at the motel and you're not getting any more table scraps, got it?" The dog actually seemed to sigh as he slid to the floor of the truck and propped his head on his paws. Jamie stroked one floppy ear and made kissy sounds before turning toward the house.

A brick portico sheltered the front doorway. The man who met her wore dark slacks, a crisp white shirt, and a burgundy tie. He was not smiling.

"I'm Ward Reed," he said, giving her a cursory glance, followed by a look of outright disapproval. "Reverend Rawlins is waiting for you." He opened the door wide to admit her.

Jamie stepped inside a large foyer of inlaid marble and ornate columns. She followed Reed down a long

hall where he paused before a door and knocked. A
voice on the other side admitted them.

"Hello, Jane," Harlan said, greeting her warmly. He
took her hand in his, holding it longer than was necessary. "It's good to see you again. You can leave us
now," he told Reed.

The man nodded and closed the door behind them.
Jamie studied Harlan's office. It was large and paneled
in teak. A triple window overlooked more gardens,
a valley below, and in the distance purple mountain
ranges. Rawlins's desk was tucked into one corner of
the room. A stone fireplace with floor-to-ceiling book-
shelves on either side—mostly religious material—
took up one wall. The opposite end was decorated in
earth tones, with plump sofas and chairs and a multi-
print rug that seemed to pull everything together.

"Very nice," she said, trying to commit it to memory. She would describe it later in her notebook.

"I spend a lot of time in here, so it was designed for
comfort." Harlan smiled. "I hope you didn't have any
trouble finding the place."

"Not at all." Jamie met his gaze. She thought he
looked tired. "I appreciate your inviting me to your
home on such short notice, Reverend Rawlins. I hope
this isn't an inconvenience."

"Of course not. Now, why don't we try to be less for-
mal? You call me Harlan, and I'll call you Jane. Would
you like something to drink? Coffee, tea, juice?" When
she shook her head, he motioned toward one of the
sofas. "Please sit down." He sat beside her.

"I was surprised to find a security guard out front,"
Jamie said.

He nodded solemnly. "I'm not crazy about the idea,
but I'm afraid it's necessary."

She gave him an innocent, wide-eyed look. "Are you in danger?"

Harlan smiled gently and patted her hand. "There are people in this world who don't appreciate my spreading the Good Word. But don't worry; you're safe. Now, let's talk about you."

Jamie shrugged. "There's not much to tell. My husband and I just moved here and we were hoping to find a good church."

"You're married?"

"Just barely," she said. "My marriage is sort of on the skids right now because of my, um, indiscretions."

"Tell me a little bit about your problem, Jane. If you don't mind talking about it, that is."

"I trust you, Reverend Rawlins," she said. "I knew the minute I looked into your eyes and touched your hand last night that I could tell you anything."

"I'm glad you feel that way, dear."

Jamie sighed. "I don't know where to begin. I've just been wild as long as I can remember."

"Explain what you mean by *wild*."

"You know, loose as a goose."

"Would you say that you're promiscuous?"

"Oh, yeah." Jamie put her hand on his knee. "I can't seem to help myself."

Harlan glanced down at her hand. "Do you and your husband presently have, um, relations?"

"No. Which makes my condition worse. I'm like a walking time bomb, Harlan."

He sucked in his breath and glanced toward the closed door. "Jane, I am terribly concerned about your condition, but you must realize the danger you place yourself in each time—"

"I use protection," she interrupted.

Harlan shifted on the sofa. "Do you ever feel guilty afterward?"

"Sometimes. It doesn't stop me, though."

"Have any of these men ever hurt you?"

Jamie lifted her eyes to his. "Only when I ask them to."

"Holy crap!" Max said, listening to every word Jamie said. "What does she think she's doing?"

Lying next to Max in the crawlspace beneath Harlan Rawlins's house, Dave was busy shining his light in the dirt. "Sounds like she wants Harlan to slap her around. Some women are into that sort of thing. Can we go now?"

Max shot him a dark look. "Jamie's not like that. And we can't leave. You haven't even linked up the cameras."

"I can't believe you dragged me into this," Dave said. "This is a breeding ground for spiders and cockroaches. We're probably lying in cockroach feces at this very moment. Damn, my left eye is twitching."

Max glanced at him. "What does that mean?"

"Means I don't like it down here, that's what it means."

"Well, the sooner we get the job done, the better."

"I'm working as fast as I can."

"And you're doing a hell of a job," Max said. "You want something done right, you hire the best. That's you, Dave."

"You couldn't afford to pay me to do this," Dave grumbled. "I'm doing it out of friendship and nothing more. Hell, man, we wouldn't even know it if a spider bit us." He paused in his work. "Is it me or does the house seem to be getting lower? I feel like everything is closing in on me. I'm having trouble breathing."

"Trust me, Dave, it's you."

"Excuse me, what are the two of you doing down there?"

Max paused and glanced sideways. Ward Reed was peering beneath the house. "Man, you've got some serious problems down here," Max told him.

Reed frowned. "What kinds of problems?"

"The wires have been chewed in various places," Max said. "Looks like a raccoon did it."

"That's ridiculous."

"That's what I thought, but there's a dead raccoon down here, and he looks like he's been fried."

"Come out from beneath the house and talk to me. And bring the raccoon."

Max and Dave exchanged looks. "I don't think that's a good idea," Max said. "He looks nasty."

"I want to see him. Now."

Max crawled out from beneath the house, dragging a plastic bag with him. Inside was a dead raccoon. He dumped it at Reed's feet. "It's yours if you want it, although I don't recommend hanging it over your fireplace mantel."

"That's the most disgusting thing I've ever seen."

"I agree," Dave said, shuddering. He stepped back, eye twitching furiously.

Reed looked from Dave to Max. "What the hell is his problem?"

"He'll be OK," Max told Reed. "Just a small case of claustrophobia."

Reed sighed.

"I think maybe the raccoon was rabid and looking for water," Max said. "I noticed the pond has been drained. That would have been the first place he would have checked."

Reed shrugged. "There was a lot of algae in it, so we emptied it two days ago."

"This is the way I figure it," Max said. "We've had no rain to speak of; the creeks and rivers are drying up. If this raccoon was rabid and couldn't find water, he probably decided to look beneath the house where it's cooler. You know how crazy they get. No telling what kind of damage he did under here." He paused. "Have you ever seen a rabid coon?"

Dave gave Max his undivided attention.

Reed shook his head. "Fortunately, no."

"I'm surprised nobody noticed it," Max said, pointing to the animal. "I saw a tricycle out back, so I assume there's a child on the premises. This coon could have attacked the kid. Or worse."

Reed automatically stiffened. "Get rid of it. Nobody else is to know about this, do you understand? I don't want to hear another word about rabid raccoons on this property."

Max nodded.

"I don't care what you have to do to repair the electrical system—"

"We'll have to run new lines inside the house," Max said. "Might take a while, but Dave here is an expert."

Reed closed his eyes as if he was trying to muster up a little patience. "You'll have my full cooperation. Just get the job done as quickly and quietly as possible, and you might find a nice bonus in your check." He walked away.

Dave waited until they were alone. "Why the hell didn't you tell me you thought the coon was rabid?" he demanded.

"I was trying to make Reed believe it. The coon

died because somebody ran over him. You were there when we pulled him out of the road."

"Oh, Jesus."

"What?"

"You don't know the coon wasn't sick. And I'm pretty sure he scratched me when I was trying to help you get him into that bag." He held out his arm and pointed to a faint red line.

"There's no puncture wound, Dave. You probably scratched yourself crawling under the house."

Dave grimaced. "On a rusty nail, no doubt. Let's see, which would be worse, dying of tetanus, a fatal infectious disease marked by rigidity and spasms, or having my central nervous system attacked by rabies and suffering a horrifying drooling death?"

"You're going off on me, Dave. Noting the coon's flat-as-a-fritter body, I'm willing to take an oath that he was run over by a heavy piece of equipment, namely an automobile or truck. I mean, what does it take to convince you, man, tread marks?"

"You can make light of this all you like, but there is no cure for rabies. Once a—" He swallowed. "Once victims have been exposed they only have about seventy-two hours to be vaccinated so they can develop an immunity."

"What are the symptoms?"

"Headache and fever. Feels like the flu. It gets much worse after that, then you die."

"I'll make a deal with you. We'll watch the scratch carefully over the next few hours. If we see a change in it I'll personally take you to the ER. Now, we have work to do."

"I'm not climbing back into that hellhole," Dave

said, backing away. "I'll give you instructions from out here, but I'm not going under that house."

"OK, fine, but you're going to have to calm down or you'll blow our cover." Max crawled beneath the house once more. He grabbed his headset and listened. "Dammit to hell!" he said.

Dave got on his knees. "What is it? Did something bite you?"

Max, tuned in to what was happening between Rawlins and Jamie, jerked off the headset. "Jamie just kissed Rawlins."

Nick Santoni put his car into neutral and let the engine idle. He had followed the pickup truck from Harlan's home, keeping himself at a safe distance. He'd followed the truck to Wal-Mart and waited while the woman had gone inside, and he'd followed her to a strip of dirt road where *No Trespassing* signs dared him to come any closer.

He pulled out a pair of binoculars and watched the truck turn into a driveway, watched the woman yank off a red wig and scratch her head furiously before finger-combing her shoulder-length blond hair into place. He smiled, picked up the photo on his seat, gave it a cursory glance.

"Welcome to Sweet Pea, Tennessee, Miss Swift," he said, and drove on.

NINE

Holding her purse in one hand and the red wig in the other, Jamie climbed from her truck. Max and several men stood just outside the garage. Max introduced them. "These gentlemen are here to install Muffin inside the dashboard of the truck."

"What does Muffin have to say about all this?"

"She's raising almighty hell. Threatening to destroy her own hard drive." He paused. "So, if you won't be needing the truck for a while—"

Jamie noticed she had the men's full attention. Actually, they were gawking. She stared back. They quickly turned away as though embarrassed to have been caught staring. She tossed the keys to Max. "Go ahead. Just make sure Muffin doesn't think it was my idea." She headed for the house.

Max didn't take his eyes off her as he handed one of his engineers the keys. "Go at it, gentlemen."

"Yes, Mr. Holt," one of them said.

Max stepped inside the cabin a moment later and found Jamie's bedroom door closed. He tapped on it and walked in. He arched one brow when he found her stripping off her tank top. She quickly pulled it back on, but not before he saw the peach-colored bra. For a moment they simply stood there, staring at each other.

Jamie planted her hands on her hips. "What happened to waiting until you're invited before entering? You're lucky I don't clobber you."

He crossed his arms and leaned against the door frame. "Most women threaten to clobber me if I try to *leave* their bedroom."

Jamie did an eye roll.

Max closed the distance between them, raised a finger, and touched the strap to her tank top. When Jamie shivered, he looked up.

"OK," she said. "I give up. What do you want?"

He cocked his head to the side and smiled lazily.

"When pigs fly," she said. Still, that slow smile made her think of afternoons stretched beneath smooth sheets, legs entwined. Oh God, she was doing it again.

Max slid his fingers back and forth beneath the strap of her top. "I hope this doesn't have anything to do with Rawlins."

She blinked. "Excuse me?"

"Well, you *did* kiss him."

She snapped her head up. "How do you know about that?"

"Dave and I heard the whole thing. Unfortunately, by the time we hooked into the cameras you were gone, so we didn't actually get to see anything juicy."

Jamie felt her face burn. "You listened to our conversation?"

"Why do you think we were there? Dave and I tapped into both the phone lines and the surveillance cameras."

"I thought you were there for backup."

"How would we know you were in trouble if we

couldn't hear what was going on? Or were you just planning to scream if something happened? And how else do you expect us to find out who Harlan's mob pals are if we can't hear or see the activity over there?"

Jamie knew all that in theory, of course, only she didn't like having her conversation with Harlan taped. "Well, I hope you and Dave enjoyed yourselves."

"Actually, I thought you played him pretty well."

"You did?"

"Until you kissed him."

"Oh, for Pete's sake!"

"He must have enjoyed it. He invited you to lunch tomorrow."

Jamie sighed. "That should please you. The whole point of my being here is to try to spend time with him and get information."

"Not if it puts you in danger. We already know what the man is capable of."

And then he kissed her, soft and lingering. He slipped his arms around her waist and pulled her closer.

"We're good together, Jamie. We could be better." He reached for the hem of her top and pulled it upward and over her head, exposing her bra. He kissed the valley between her breasts before unhooking the back of her bra and pulling it away.

Jamie simply stood there, not knowing what else to do, enjoying the feel of her body responding to Max. "Max? This is scary."

"Scary?"

"Complicated."

"You make it complicated."

"It's a girl thing."

"I like girl things."

She chuckled. "You're terrible."

"Can't you for once just let go and enjoy your life without knowing precisely what's going to happen next? You're willing to take all sorts of risks with Harlan Rawlins just to get your story."

"That's different."

"The things you put me through." He reached into his pocket and pulled out a miniature cell phone. He handed it to her. "My number is voice-activated. You'll be able to reach me at all times, just by calling my name. Not only will I get your call, I'll know your location. Keep it with you and turned on at all times." He started for the door, then turned. "OK?"

She nodded.

"Somebody want to tell me what's going on?" Muffin demanded early the next morning as Max and Jamie sat inside Jamie's pickup truck. The engineers had worked through the night, installing Muffin and welding the glove compartment shut so that nobody would be able to detect the system. Max was doing a final check before Jamie took off on her shopping trip.

"I've already explained why this was necessary," Max said. "Jamie and I have to blend in the community. I can't very well drive my car, but I'm still going to need your assistance."

"I've lost most of my capabilities," Muffin said.

"You're still hooked up to the motherboard. You'll be able to get the information I need."

"I don't have my sensors *or* my siren. I was attached to that siren."

In the back of the truck, Fleas howled.

"What was *that?*" Muffin asked.

"My dog," Jamie said. "He's a bloodhound, and his name is Fleas."

Muffin gave a snort of disgust. "I should have known something like this would happen. I'm riding in a rust bucket with a hound dog named Fleas."

"It gets worse, Muffin," Max said. "Jamie let Harlan Rawlins kiss her yesterday."

"Oh God. See what happens when you shut me down?" Muffin accused. "I can't turn my back for one minute without you two getting into something."

"It's not what you think," Jamie said. "I was just doing my job."

"I can't believe you let him kiss you," Muffin said as though shocked and dismayed. "Is he a good kisser?"

Jamie shrugged. "Passable."

Max shook his head as he climbed from the truck and slammed the door. He turned and peered in the open window. "Look, Anderson is going to be here in a couple of hours. The three of us need to talk."

"I'll be back by then." Jamie slid beneath the wheel.

"Where on earth are you going to shop for clothes at this hour?"

"Wal-Mart."

"It's not even six A.M."

"They're open twenty-four hours a day."

"Except on Sunday," Muffin said.

Max glanced at the dashboard. "I can't believe you actually know when Wal-Mart is open." He turned to Jamie. "What could you possibly need at this hour?"

Jamie tossed him a saucy smile. "Shorter skirts, Holt." She pulled from the driveway, leaving a frowning Max behind.

Jamie decided shopping at Wal-Mart at six in the morning had its advantages. For one thing, she had the best pick of parking spots. She promised Muffin she would hurry before climbing from the truck, and gave Fleas a firm warning to stay put. She headed for the glass doors leading inside the store.

At first Jamie didn't notice him. She was too busy thumbing through the women's department where skirts in animal prints had been marked half-price. She felt someone watching her and turned. A tall, well-dressed man with black hair was staring.

As if realizing he'd suddenly been caught, he jumped. "I'm sorry, I didn't mean to—"

She noted the desolate look in his eyes. "Are you OK?"

"Yes, well . . ." He paused and gave a pained smile. "Actually, no."

"Are you ill? Should I ask one of the employees to help you?"

"That would probably be best. If you don't mind," he added in a strained voice.

Jamie nodded and hurried off to find someone working in women's wear.

A stout woman with short gray hair joined the man a moment later. "May I help you, sir?"

"Yes, thank you. I need to buy a dress for my sister."

Jamie continued thumbing through the clothes on a rack not far away. She was only vaguely aware of the two talking.

"What kind of dress?" the woman asked.

"Something pretty."

"What's the occasion, hon?"

The man didn't answer right away. Jamie paused in what she was doing and waited for his answer.

"Something nice enough for church," he finally said. "Do you have anything in pink? That was her favorite color." He whispered the rest.

Jamie strained to hear.

"Oh, I'm so sorry, sir," the saleslady said quietly. "Of course I'll help you. I'll need her size."

"I think she wore about a size ten. She has pretty clothes at home, but I couldn't bring myself to go there and look through her closet. Under the circumstances," he added. "I don't like what the people at the funeral home chose for her."

Jamie moved away. From what she'd managed to hear, the man had obviously just lost his sister, and she didn't feel right listening to such a private and painful conversation. Once she'd made her purchase, she hurried into the small restaurant area, where she purchased a sprinkled donut and a cup of coffee. She took a seat at one of the tables. She'd only taken one sip of her coffee when the man she'd spotted earlier walked in, ordered coffee, and sat in a booth a short distance away.

Jamie tried not to stare, but she couldn't help it. Grief etched his face, making him look older than he probably was. He raised his coffee to his mouth, and she could see that his hands trembled badly. All at once, the cup slipped from his fingers and fell to the floor. He jumped, obviously startled.

Jamie bolted to her feet and hurried over. "Are you OK? Were you burned?"

He was already on the floor trying to mop up the mess with his napkin. He looked up as though surprised to see her. "No, I'm fine, but I made a big mess."

Jamie hurried to a counter and plucked napkins from a dispenser. She cleancd up the spill as best as she could. "You're sure you're not burned?"

"I wasn't burned, really. Thanks for helping me." He looked embarrassed. "I used to spill my milk at the dinner table, too." He tried to smile.

"Let me get you another cup of coffee," Jamie said, grabbing his cup and walking away before he had a chance to respond. She carried his cup to the cashier, who refilled it.

When Jamie returned, he was still standing. She set the cup on the table instead of handing it to him. "I'm sorry I put you to so much trouble," he said. "I promise to be more careful." He started to sit down. "Would you like to join me?"

"Well, I—"

"Maybe you'd be safer where you were." Once again, he smiled.

She noted the smile didn't reach his eyes. He looked bereft. "Hold on, I'll grab my cup and donut."

Jamie returned and slid into the seat across from him. He seemed to take great caution in raising his cup to his lips, but she noted his hands were still shaking. She met his gaze over his cup. He was dark and attractive, with a thin scar running down one side of his face that didn't detract from his looks. She wondered if he'd been in a car accident at one time.

They were silent for a moment. "I wasn't trying to eavesdrop, but I couldn't help overhearing what you said to the saleslady," Jamie said at last. OK, so it wasn't the honest-to-goodness truth, but she didn't want to admit to being nosy. "I sort of know what you're going through," she said. "I'm sorry for your loss."

"You lost someone recently?" he asked.

"I lost my father several years ago, but sometimes it seems like yesterday."

He nodded but didn't speak.

"Would you like to talk about your sister? I'm a good listener." When he hesitated, she hurried on. "Or maybe you don't feel like it. I don't mean to pry."

"You seem like a nice person."

Jamie took a sip of her coffee and tried to think of something to say, anything that might offer comfort. She didn't want to say the wrong thing as so many people had done when she'd first suffered her loss, people who tried to make her feel better by telling her that her father was in a better place or that at least he no longer had to suffer. If only they had talked less and listened more.

"Her name was Bethany. She was my twin."

"That makes it worse, doesn't it? Her being your twin and all, that is."

"Yes. We were inseparable."

"Do you have other family?"

He shook his head. "My parents are deceased. I have a few cousins, but we haven't kept in touch."

"What you need right now is a lot of support. That's what pulled me through."

"Oh, I have plenty of friends, but I don't want to burden them." He glanced at the bag beside him. "Would you mind taking a look at the dress I chose for my sister and telling me if you think it looks OK? I had to trust the saleslady, because I don't know what to buy for this sort of thing."

"I'll be glad to look at it," Jamie said. He handed her the bag, and Jamie pulled the dress out. It was a simple pink shift.

"I probably should have gone to the mall in Knoxville and picked out something nicer, but Bethany wasn't the dressy type. She preferred simple things."

"This dress is perfect, Mr. . . ."

"Michael. Michael Juliano."

"Jane Trotter," she said, deciding it was best to use the name as long as she was in Sweet Pea, even if she wasn't in disguise at the moment.

They shook hands. "I could use another cup of coffee," Jamie said. "How about you?"

"I'm fine, but I'll get you a cup."

Jamie was already on her feet. "I can do it." When she returned she found him talking on a cell phone. He looked angry.

"Tell the guy to come back when I'm around. He's not going to like the answer I give him, so if you or the others are afraid to stay let me know."

Jamie noted the tension in his face had brought back the deep lines around his eyes and mouth. Whatever it was, it had to be bad.

"I don't care what he says. I'm not afraid to go to the police. Look, I can't talk right now, OK?" He hung up and picked up his coffee.

"Is something wrong, Mr. Juliano?"

"Nothing I can't handle. And call me Michael." He glanced at his cell. "I just didn't need that call right now."

"You mentioned the police. Are you in some kind of danger?"

"Depends on what I'm willing to pay." He covered his eyes. "Oh, hell, I'm sorry. I shouldn't have said that."

"I don't know what this is about, but if you're being threatened—"

"I don't know if the police can help," he interrupted. "I really shouldn't be talking about this." He sighed. "I should close shop and get out," he muttered to himself, and then gave a grunt of disgust. "I thought this sort of thing only happened in Jersey or Vegas." He looked at her. "Are you from here?"

She shook her head.

"Then you probably don't know how corrupt this

town is. Like a bunch of piranhas just waiting to snatch up as much money as they can from honest, hard-working people."

"Are you being blackmailed?" she whispered.

Michael glanced around the room. "I shouldn't talk about it. The last thing I want to do is drag another person into it."

"I'm a good listener, Michael, and I know how to keep my mouth shut. Especially if it might jeopardize your safety," she added.

He met her gaze. Still, he refused to talk.

Jamie realized she was pushing, and that's the last thing she wanted to do. Vera had always accused her of being too softhearted where people were concerned. Vera always said, "If there's a bleeding heart out there, you can bet Jamie is going to find it."

"I'm butting in," Jamie said. "I'm sorry. I'll leave you with your coffee." She made to get up.

"You have to swear not to repeat this."

"Yes, of course."

"You can't say anything to anyone. I mean it. I just need to talk to someone. Someone who isn't involved," he added. He smiled. "I mean, what are the chances of us running into each other again?"

She nodded.

"Someone is trying to extort money from me. It's really hard for me to deal with it at the moment after what has happened with my sister. Too many nights sitting in a hospital, eating junk food, living on caffeine. It gets to a person after a while. Thing is, I think this person is counting on my recent loss to get the upper hand."

"Who is threatening you?"

"A couple of thugs," he said. "They're acting on

somebody else's behalf, of course. The man in charge probably won't show his face until it's absolutely necessary. I don't know, but I assume that's the way it works."

"Do you know this person's name? The one in charge?"

"I have an idea who he is. He has quite an operation going."

"But do you know his name?" she repeated. He frowned. She was being pushy again, and she feared it would draw his suspicion. "I mean, in case you have to go to the police," she added quickly.

He glanced down at his coffee cup. "I've already said more than I should. "The less you know, the less anyone knows, the better."

Jamie suspected she was on to something. The gods must be with her, because the last thing she had expected was to meet up with somebody who might be able to give her some information, albeit unintentionally, but answers nevertheless. She didn't have enough to go on, and she might never see the man again, which meant she had to act fast.

"Listen, Michael, I haven't eaten, either." Which was true. Her donut was untouched, and it had suddenly lost its appeal. "There must be a restaurant nearby where you can enjoy a healthy breakfast. And you really look like you need a friend."

"You don't even know me."

"I believe things happen for a reason."

"What do you mean?"

"Well . . ." She paused. She was grasping at straws. "A lot of wonderful people helped me during my time of loss. If I can say one thing to help you, I've managed to return the favor." It sounded lame in her own ears, but he suddenly nodded as if it made complete sense to him. It didn't feel right that she was lying to him, using him, to get information, but it was necessary.

"There's a little place not far from here," he said after a moment. "I go there a lot. Or I did until recently," he added.

She offered him a bright smile, hoping she could bring one to his face as well, even under his current circumstances. "Tell you what, I've got an old truck outside, but it will probably get me to the restaurant. Why don't I follow you?"

When Jamie pulled into the driveway beside the cabin, she found Max pacing the yard. Lord, she hadn't realized how late she was. She and Michael had talked almost two hours before she'd thought to check her watch, before she'd finally mumbled a hurried goodbye. Unfortunately, Michael had not divulged more information about those threatening to extort money from him, as though he feared he'd already said too much. That didn't mean she was giving up.

Max yanked the door open as soon as she'd parked. "Where the hell have you been?"

"I told you I was going to Wal-Mart."

"We just got back from there. You weren't in the store or the restaurant area. Your truck wasn't in the parking lot. I tried to call you a dozen times. What happened?"

"Jeez, you were spying on me?" Jamie realized she had her head cocked to the side like Fleas did when she asked him if he had to take a leak.

"No, I wasn't spying on you; I was afraid you'd broken down in the truck or that something had happened. Jesus, Jamie, you've been gone for three hours."

She saw the deep concern on his face. She wanted

to tell him the truth, about Michael and their meeting, but she needed time to think about it herself. She had sworn not to utter a word of what Michael had said to her. *Sworn* to him. And rule number one for journalists was never to compromise your source. Especially when there was more information to be had. Better to keep her mouth shut. For now. Still, not confiding everything to Max felt like lying.

"Jamie?"

"Yeah?"

This time Max had his head cocked to the side.

"I lost track of the time, OK? And I must've forgotten to turn on my cell phone. I'm sorry I worried you."

Jamie saw Dave leaning against the Bennett Electric truck. He wore a thick bandage on his arm. He was staring at Fleas.

"Is that your dog?" he asked. When Jamie nodded, he gave a deep frown. "I'm allergic to dog dander. Dust mites thrive on animal dander."

"Dust mites thrive on everything, Dave," Max said, "including your own skin."

"I'm not as allergic to poodles or Italian greyhounds," Dave went on as though he hadn't heard Max. "Oh, and whippets and Mexican hairless dogs are pretty much hypoallergenic. I wish you had a poodle," he told Jamie.

Jamie looked at Fleas, who had followed her out of the truck. She tried to imagine him as a poodle and couldn't. "He's really a good dog," she said.

"Don't you take allergy shots and medication?" Max asked Dave.

Dave ignored him. "My eyes are already itching." He stepped closer to Max. "Are they red and puffy?"

"They look perfectly normal to me."

"I'll try to keep the dog away from you," Jamie promised.

Dave sighed. "I suppose I can double up on my medication. I may have to run back to the hospital for an allergy shot."

Max turned to Jamie. "Dave is going to follow us to Knoxville for your rendezvous with Rawlins."

"Us?"

"I'll drive you part of the way so I can get updates from Muffin. Once we're at the hotel, Dave and I will be close by in case something happens."

"What if Harlan recognizes you?"

"He won't see me." He paused. "Trust me, Rawlins has something up his sleeve or he wouldn't have invited you to lunch at a hotel in Knoxville."

"He's a womanizer, Max. That doesn't make him dangerous."

"What are you going to do when he suggests getting a room?"

Jamie had already considered it. And planned for it. She had purchased an extrastrength fast-acting laxative in the pharmacy at Wal-Mart, and she planned to put it in Rawlins's tea or coffee if the opportunity presented itself. It was probably the dumbest idea she'd ever had, which was why she had no intention of telling Max, but it might prove a deterrent if things got out of hand.

"I'm going to have to play it by ear, Max," she said after a moment. "I have to appear interested and hope I gain his trust without, well, you know—"

"Yeah, I know. Which brings me to the next subject," he said. "I think you should wear a wire. In case something happens."

Jamie looked from Max to Dave, then back at Max. "That's kinda risky, isn't it?"

"Going in without a wire would be more of a risk," Max replied. "Dave and I have had Rawlins under surveillance since yesterday. From what we've been able to learn through his conversations with his bodyguard, he mouthed off at the guy who's been bleeding him for money the past few years. Have you heard of the Santoni family?"

Jamie nodded. "Who hasn't? Two of them went to trial a few years back for murder."

"They whacked a cop who was on the family's payroll," Dave said. "Supposedly, it was an honest mistake, but you don't kill cops, especially the ones covering your ass."

"They got off, if I remember correctly," she said.

"The star witness literally disappeared off the face of the earth," he said, "despite around-the-clock police protection. One of the shooters, Nick Santoni, was involved in the cop killing. His uncle sent him to Tennessee, as sort of a punishment. The other shooter accidentally drowned in his bathtub."

Jamie arched one brow. "How come Nick Santoni didn't suffer the same consequences?"

"His father headed up the family until he died of a heart attack five years ago," Max said. "Nick was supposed to take his place, but the family vetoed it, and Nick's uncle was forced to come out of retirement and take over. He wanted to see Nick eventually head up the family, but it isn't likely."

"Why not?" Jamie asked.

"Nick has a habit of disobeying orders, moving in on other people's territory, you name it. He's got a chip on his shoulder and doesn't get along with the family, except for this uncle."

Jamie pondered it. "That's odd, since the uncle is

the one who took what Nick would consider his rightful place."

"This uncle protects Nick," Dave said. "Not only is he Nick's godfather, Nick was always his favorite. So he sent him here, and Nick has opened shop, so to speak. He's got Rawlins by the short hairs. On top of that, we think Nick is supplying Rawlins with uppers and downers."

"The rest of the family merely tolerate Nick," Max told her, "but it looks like Nick regained their favor when he got his hooks into Rawlins. But Nick has a serious gambling problem and squanders money. Both the Santoni family and Harlan put up the money to buy my TV network but lost the bid. Harlan is convinced Nick blew the money in Atlantic City, at least that's what we heard him tell Reed, and it's a real possibility, since Nick visits the area a couple of times a month.

"Now, Nick has raised Rawlins's percentage, probably hoping to pacify the family until he can get his hands on enough money to pay them back. But Rawlins has had enough, despite the fact Nick is feeding what looks like a drug addiction. Rawlins is thinking of going over Nick's head and telling the uncle the truth."

"The mob has their own code of ethics," Dave said. "Family honor and all that. Nick is a rogue player who doesn't care who he hurts as long as he gets what he wants. And right now he wants and *needs* money. If he catches wind that Rawlins is thinking of blowing the whistle on him, he could get really dangerous."

"Either way, Nick loses," Max said. "If he has Rawlins killed or pushes him too far, there goes his meal ticket, and the family is going to wash their hands of him. If he lets Rawlins live, there's a chance he's going to bc found out."

"And that could be equally bad," Dave said.

"Would Nick's own family kill him?" Jamie asked.

"It's been known to happen," Dave said. "Nick Santoni is a desperate man right now. He'll probably try to make some quick business deals in order to get his hands on money. Max and I don't know exactly what he's involved in, although it's almost a sure thing he's involved in prostitution, backroom gambling, drugs, and probably gunrunning, just to name a few. We tapped into his computer yesterday, but we haven't been able to decipher the information."

"It's all coded," Max said. "The codes are similar to those used by the CIA, but damned if I've been able to crack them. We need more time."

"That's why we're concerned about your meeting with Rawlins," Dave said. "Harlan's bodyguard checks for bugs in the office and home every day, but Nick may have found a way to prevent detection. We did it by hooking into the phones and cameras."

"What it boils down to," Max said, "is we don't know what Nick knows. If he even suspects Harlan might go over his head there's going to be trouble. Big trouble. And you just might find yourself right in the middle of it."

TEN

"**Why didn't you** tell me this sooner?" Jamie asked.

"We're gathering information as we speak," Max said. "While you've been, um, shopping, Muffin has been hard at work tapping into every resource she can find. She's been e-mailing information to us as she gets it." He paused. "I'm not holding back anything, if that's what you think."

Which explained why Muffin hadn't questioned Jamie when she had returned to the truck after having breakfast with Michael, she thought. Muffin had been preoccupied. And Jamie hadn't offered an explanation because she knew Muffin would say something to Max. And then Max would interrogate her to the nth degree about Michael.

Jamie was determined to get information from Michael, which was why she had suggested they meet again the following day. But she was going to be careful and subtle about it. Max had his mighty computer and enough contacts to overthrow a small country, but she had genuine empathy for people, and she hoped Michael would sense it and open up. She felt a little guilty about using him when he was grieving and probably at his most vulnerable, but she might be able to help him in the end as well. If she did learn something, if it was something that could put Michael in danger, then she would have reason enough to break her oath and tell Max.

She suddenly realized Max was talking to her.

". . . So far we don't have much on Santoni. Other than a couple of photos of him ducking in and out of the courtroom during his trial," he added. "They're not very clear. Also, he wore a beard at the time, so he could look completely different today. He has a number of aliases, which make it hard to get an address or anything else on him.

"I suspect he stays in the background as much as possible. He's probably got a couple of men he trusts who see that his orders are followed. Which is how it usually works for those in the upper echelon; they look like legitimate businessmen, but the businesses are merely fronts for illegal activity."

"Do you think Nick Santoni hired Vito Puccini and ordered the hit on you?"

Max nodded. "We have it on tape. Harlan discussed it with his bodyguard at length after Santoni paid him a visit yesterday. Rawlins had nothing to do with arranging it, but I think he suspected something was going on, and for some reason he decided not to go to the police. Which leads me to believe Santoni has something on him," he added. "Rawlins might be a lot of things, but he's probably not a killer. We still think you should wear a wire. In case there are any surprises."

Jamie didn't look convinced.

"It's like this," Max said. "I don't like the idea of your meeting with Harlan in the first place, but it's already set up, so I'll agree to it, but *only* if you're wired.

I want to know where you are at all times. Otherwise, I'm calling this whole thing off."

He and Jamie locked gazes in a battle of wills. "What if Harlan discovers the wire?" she asked.

Max met her gaze. "That's not likely to happen as long as you keep your clothes on, Swifty."

Muffin greeted Max and Jamie in a surly voice when they climbed into the truck at ten-thirty for the drive to Knoxville. "That dog whines constantly. I don't like it."

"I know he's an inconvenience right now, Muffin," Jamie said, "but I don't know what to do with him."

"Try the animal shelter."

"Nobody would adopt him."

"Is he ugly?"

Jamie and Max both glanced over their shoulders at Fleas, who had his face pressed against the back window. Max shrugged; Jamie grinned. "Actually, he's pretty cute," she said.

"I guess it could be worse," Muffin said. "I guess I could be strapped to a moped or tied to the back of a mule."

"You should feel flattered that we need you so badly," Jamie told her as Max pulled from the driveway with Dave following. She glanced at Max. He looked distracted; Jamie knew he was worried.

"This is your big day, huh?" Muffin said. "You're having lunch with Rawlins."

"Uh-huh."

"You wearing your slut outfit?"

"No, I toned it down since we're meeting at the Hyatt Regency."

"Her skirt is a little short," Max said, "and she's

wearing a push-up bra. If she sneezes she's going to pop out all over the place."

"And get this, Muffin," Jamie said. "I'm wearing a wire."

"You planning on doing the nasty?" Muffin asked.

Jamie gave a burst of laughter. "I don't believe you said that."

"Because if you are, you're going to have to excuse yourself and go to the rest room so you can remove that wire. Things get too hot, it might short-circuit on you."

"Time to change the subject," Max said. "You got anything new for me?"

"I'm still trying to find an address for Santoni. The man doesn't exist on paper, not even under the aliases he's used. Doesn't own property, doesn't even pay a light bill. I figure his family got all new identification for him when he relocated to Knoxville."

"Maybe he lives in Sweet Pea," Max said. "A man like that would enjoy the seclusion this area offers."

"I'll keep looking. As for looking into Harlan Rawlins, I've checked police records within a three-hundred-mile radius. There's a lot of domestic violence in this part of the country, which I attribute to financial stress. The unemployment rate here is very high. Harlan has never been arrested, but I did find something interesting when I checked the local hospital records. Harlan's wife has visited the emergency room twice, once for a fractured wrist which she claimed happened as a result of falling off her horse, and another time with a concussion when the same horse threw her and she hit her head against a tree."

"It sounds legit," Jamie said.

"Sounds like she needs to get rid of the horse,"

Max said. "Or Rawlins," he added. "If he was actually abusing his wife and Santoni knew, that in itself could be cause for blackmail." He pulled into the parking lot of a gas station. "The Hyatt is less than a mile from here. Dave and I will follow you. We'll be close by at all times.

"Now listen to me, Jamie. If Harlan suggests going upstairs to a room, I want you to get the number to me. I don't care how you do it, work it into the conversation somehow, but make sure you say it loud enough for me to hear."

Jamie nodded. "I'll be OK, Max."

"One last thing. If there are any surprises, scream like hell. Dave and I will kick in the door if we have to, but I don't want you taking chances. I don't care if we blow the case or not when it comes to your safety."

"I'll be careful, I promise."

They climbed from the truck, and Jamie got in on the driver's side. As she put it into gear, she noticed her hand was trembling. She pulled onto the street once more and headed for the hotel.

Jamie noted the strange look on the valet's face as she pulled up to the Hyatt entrance. She didn't know if he was more amazed at the amount of rust on the truck or the sight of Fleas in back.

She handed the young man her key and smiled. "It's an antique," she said, motioning to the truck. "Please see that you don't put a scratch on it."

He remained straight-faced. "Yes, ma'am. I'll take good care of it. What about the dog?"

"He'll be fine. He's got food and water back there."

"You're not worried someone might take him?"

Jamie patted her wig into place. "Would you be if you were me?"

He looked at the animal. "On second thought, no."

Ward Reed was waiting for Jamie in the lobby. He motioned her toward the elevator. "Reverend Rawlins decided to order lunch in his private suite," he said. "I hope you don't mind."

Jamie couldn't hide her surprise. She hoped Max and Dave were nearby. "The reverend actually keeps a suite here?" she said, voice raised in surprise. "Oh, my. His own suite."

"He often has business in Knoxville. He also invites guests from time to time, you know, visiting clergy? There aren't any nice hotels in Sweet Pea."

Jamie knew about the hotels in Sweet Pea.

The elevator doors opened, and they waited for the people to clear out before entering. Jamie could feel the tension in the back of her neck. Reed punched a number, and she realized they were going to the top floor. "Wow, we're going all the way to the top? I'll bet there is a great view from up there."

Reed smiled stiffly. "Yes. Reverend Rawlins says he feels closer to heaven."

Jamie nodded as though it made perfect sense. She tried to remain calm as the express elevator whooshed them upward, but the thought of going to Harlan's private suite was a little unnerving. Then she reminded herself of the great story she would have when it was over, and that spurred her confidence.

A bell rang out, interrupting her thoughts.

"Here we are," Reed announced, holding the doors so Jamie could exit first. She followed him to a door at the end of the hall. "Oh, my, would you look at that! Room Twelve-ten. That's my birthday, December tenth. But don't you dare ask the year." She laughed at her own joke. Reed merely nodded. Jamie decided he didn't have much of a sense of humor.

He tapped lightly on the door and inserted a card into the lock. He pushed the door open. "Go on in. I'll escort you down when you're ready to leave."

Inside, Jamie found a large, beautifully decorated living room with a kitchenette. Fresh flowers sat on the coffee table.

Harlan stepped through a set of sliding glass doors that led outside onto the balcony. He smiled. "Welcome, Jane."

"Your suite is very nice," she said.

"Thank you." He walked over and touched one of her red curls, toyed with it. His gaze met hers. "I'm glad you came." His finger slid down her cheek, brushed her neck, and rested on her shoulder. "I sometimes come here to unwind or write my sermons."

Or get laid, Jamie thought. "We all need time to ourselves," she said. "I imagine it gets hectic touring all the time."

"Yes, it does." He took her hands in his. "But spending this time with you is a real treat. Would you like something to drink?" He nodded toward a basket of fruit and a bottle of wine. "I don't usually drink alcohol, but a dear friend left this for me, and I hate to waste it. I'm not particularly fond of the red wine. It tastes bitter to me. But if you like it, I'll join you."

That just might work in her favor, Jamie thought. "Yes, let's have a glass."

He grinned and uncorked the bottle. "I took the liberty of ordering lunch. I hope you like fish." He looked up and caught her staring. "Is something wrong?"

"You look tired, Harlan." Which was true. "Why

don't you go out on the balcony, prop your legs, and I'll pour the wine?"

He nodded. "Promise not to take too long?"

"I'll be right out." Jamie waited until he stepped outside before she poured the wine into two glasses. Once again, her fingers trembled as she reached into her pocket for one of the laxatives she'd crushed into a fine, white powder. She sprinkled it into his drink. She stirred it, taking care to see there was no residue on the side of the glass. She had about twenty minutes before it would start to work and then she could make her getaway.

"I know what you're doing," Harlan said the minute she joined him on the balcony.

Jamie froze. "You do?"

"You're trying to spoil me."

She relaxed. "Looks like you need spoiling. Here, drink this. Maybe you'll feel better."

He took the glass. "Do I really look that tired?"

"Oh, now I've gone and hurt your feelings."

"No, actually I appreciate your honesty. I haven't slept well lately, except for last night, but I think I just need to catch up on my rest." He took out a small pillbox, opened it, and took out several tiny pills.

Jamie noticed he was trembling. "Are you OK?" she asked.

"I have a little headache. These help." He popped them into his mouth, then raised his glass to his lips.

Jamie watched closely as he took a sip of his wine. He didn't seem to notice a difference. "Losing sleep will catch up with you sooner or later. Are you worried about something?"

He shrugged. "Just everyday stress, but I don't want to burden you with it. We're here to enjoy ourselves."

He drained his glass. "Perhaps I should have another," he said.

Jamie studied him. "It's none of my business, Harlan, but I don't think you should be mixing alcohol with your medication."

He nodded. "You're probably right."

"You look very handsome today in that navy blue suit," she finally said. "That's definitely your color. I'll bet half the women in your congregation have a crush on you."

He smiled and tugged at his tie as though it was too tight. "Well, I do get my share of homemade cakes and pies."

"I'll bet you do," she said, a teasing lilt in her voice.

"There are a lot of lonely widows in the church. They just want someone to talk to, you know? I try to do my best."

"I'm sure you do." She sighed. "I know what it's like, Harlan. Not having anyone you can tell your troubles to. We all need someone we can trust. Someone who won't judge us or betray our confidence."

"People like that are hard to find," he said.

"My friends have always been able to come to me," Jamie said softly. "What good is a friend if you can't talk to them? I mean *really* talk to them," she added. "Unload, spill your guts, get it all off your shoulders kind of talk. I've heard it all, Harlan, buh-lieve you me. Nothing would shock me."

"That kind of friendship is rare indeed," he agreed.

"And I know about loneliness," she said. "The kind of loneliness you spoke of in your sermon. Sometimes . . ." She paused, as though wrestling with her emotions.

"What is it, dear?"

"Sometimes I get so lonely my skin aches."

Harlan looked at her, studied her face. "Then you know what it's like. I've discovered I have to find solace wherever I can. *However* I can."

A knock at the door seemed to startle him. "That must be our lunch." He stood and walked inside, and Jamie followed. She wondered if it was her imagination, but he seemed to move sluggishly.

"Room service," a man announced.

Jamie thought she recognized the voice. Harlan opened the door, and Jamie felt her mouth drop open at the sight of Dave pushing in a food cart. He was dressed in a hotel uniform, and he wore a mustache and glasses. She wondered if he had counted the dust mites in the mustache before he'd put it on.

"Good afternoon," he said formally. "I believe you're expecting lunch?"

Harlan nodded. "Yes, we are."

"I'll have you set up in just a jiffy," Dave said, giving Jamie a private look. He pushed the cart to the table and began setting it, placing the utensils in their proper spots. "How are you today, ma'am?" he asked.

Jamie wondered how he had managed to get a uniform from the Hyatt. No telling what he and Max were up to. "I'm, uh, fine."

Dave set the dishes on the table and lifted a metal food warmer from the plates. Jamie eyed the food appreciatively: baked fish covered in a cream sauce, new potatoes, fresh asparagus, and a Caesar salad. Dessert consisted of pecan pie, a big favorite of hers.

Dave pulled out a chair for her. Jamie walked over to the table and allowed him to seat her.

"Will there be anything else?" Dave asked.

"That will be all," Harlan said.

Dave turned to leave. He paused at the door and gave Jamie the thumbs-up.

Jamie tasted her food. "It's delicious." Harlan was staring at his plate. "Is something wrong?"

"I'm afraid I don't have much of an appetite."

"Oh, no. At least taste the fish. It's delicious. And you need to keep up your strength."

Harlan glanced up in surprise, as if he wasn't sure what she meant by the remark. Nevertheless, he forked a small amount of the fish and took a bite. "You're right. It's very good." He smiled, as if trying to put on a brave front.

"Thank you for inviting me," Jamie said. "It's not often that I get to dine on gourmet cooking in such grand surroundings."

"I hope you're not offended that I asked you to my hotel suite."

Jamie looked down at her lap. "I wouldn't blame you if you didn't want to be seen with me in public."

"Oh, no, Jane, it's nothing like that."

"I mean, I've probably slept with half the men in this hotel."

He gasped.

"I'm teasing, Harlan. You're going to have to lighten up."

"You have a very unusual sense of humor. But I should be thanking you. It's a treat for me to share lunch with a woman who is not only beautiful but has a wonderful sense of humor." He put down his fork, mopping his brow with his napkin.

"Jane, I've been looking into your, er, addiction."

"Is there a cure?" she asked hopefully, fork paused in midair. "Or am I destined to be a sex maniac for the rest of my life?"

He looked taken aback by the remark. "Don't be ashamed of who or what you are, Jane. Your creator loves you no matter what. You know, I studied psychology in seminary because I wanted to be able to help people with their problems."

"That's why you're so easy to talk to. You're a very sensitive man when it comes to other people's needs." Jamie noticed he was perspiring heavily.

He mopped his upper lip. "I try to be. I sense you have a lot of needs that have not been addressed."

"You're so right, Harlan."

"From what I understand most sexual addictions are the result of either physical or emotional trauma suffered in childhood. Might I ask, as your minister, if that applies to you?"

Jamie glanced away. "I can't talk about it, Harlan. Perhaps in time."

He reached across the table and covered her hand. "We have all the time in the world, Jane."

His hand was clammy. Jamie leaned closer. "I suppose I don't feel I have much to offer a man. Except my body," she whispered. "You probably wouldn't understand, what with you being a godly man."

"I'm human, Jane. Do you think I didn't feel anything when you kissed me yesterday? Do you think I don't notice how attractive you are?"

"I'm so ashamed of myself for kissing you," she said. "You must think badly of me."

"Nonsense." He studied her closely, as if trying to read her thoughts.

Jamie took a deep breath, stood, and walked over to the sliding glass doors. "I think maybe we have something special."

Harlan joined her, placing his hands on her arms,

sliding them downward. Very gently he lowered his head and pressed his lips to the nape of her neck.

"Oh, Harlan!"

"Sweet Jane. I can't stand to see you hurting." He turned her around in his arms and looked into her eyes.

In the next room, Max tore off the headset. "Oh, damn, it's quiet in there. She must be kissing him again. What the hell are we supposed to do *now*?"

Dave shrugged. "Jamie can take care of herself. How long do I have to wear this mustache?"

"Until we finish the job." Max grabbed his headset once more and winced when a loud squeal hit his eardrums. He yanked it off. "What was *that*?"

Dave had already removed his. "Hell if I know. Oh, great, my ears are ringing."

"Something's wrong," Max said.

"Damn right. That noise set off my tinnitus. Sounds like church bells going off in my head."

"I can't make out their words. There's a lot of static. Shit."

Harlan suddenly gave Jamie a funny look.

"What's wrong?" she asked.

"I don't feel so good." He gripped his stomach and swayed.

Jamie tried to steady him. He looked pale. "You need to lie down."

"I'm dizzy."

"Get on the bed, Harlan!"

Max managed to catch the last sentence. "Did you hear that?" he said, trying to listen to the voices through the static. "She told him to get on the bed!"

"I can't hear a thing," Dave said. "Except for static and bells. I'll probably end up losing my hearing after this."

"You need to get back over there."

Dave shook his head. "I can't just barge in."

Harlan struggled with the knot on his tie.

Jamie saw that he was having difficulty breathing. She began to panic. "Let me help you." She didn't know what to do. She had obviously given Harlan too much laxative and it was causing him painful stomach cramps. Or maybe he was having an adverse reaction to them.

He pulled his knees against his stomach and groaned aloud. "I can't stand it!"

Jamie's heart fluttered. He was sweating profusely; his color didn't look good. "Try to take a deep breath."

"I'm going to be sick!" he cried. "Please help me to the bathroom." He covered his mouth with his hands.

Jamie scrambled to help him, but he could barely stand. She struggled to keep him upright. Lord, she'd gone and done it now. If he was having an allergic reaction there was no telling what would happen. She managed to get him inside the bathroom. He slammed the door and locked it, and the next thing Jamie heard was a loud thud. She tried the knob. "Shit! Harlan, unlock the door."

Jamie picked up the phone to call for help but dropped it when she heard a knock on the living room door. She raced toward it. Dave stood on the other side wearing the hotel uniform. "I came for your dirty dishes, ma'am," he said.

Jamie grabbed his arm and pulled him toward the

bedroom. "Something is wrong with Harlan. He's in the bathroom, and I can't get in. I think he fell."

Dave reached into his pocket and pulled out a knife. He opened it up, and Jamie saw it was equipped with all sorts of gadgets. In a few seconds he picked the lock and turned the knob.

They found Harlan sprawled on the bathroom floor. Dave shook him, but there was no response. He reached down and pressed his fingers against Harlan's neck as Jamie stood there, wringing her hands.

Finally, Dave removed his hand. He shuddered. "Oh, Jesus Christ! He's dead! I touched a dead man!"

ELEVEN

Max and Jamie left the hotel immediately. Using his cell phone, which Max assured couldn't be traced, he called 911, and, claiming to be a security guard for the Hyatt Regency, reported that a man had become ill in room 1210 and was in grave condition. Max didn't bother to mention the man was already dead. He hung up before the dispatcher questioned him further.

Jamie, who'd struggled to maintain her composure while the valet went for her truck, fell apart the minute Max pulled onto the street and headed for the interstate. "Oh God, everybody is going to think I killed him!" she cried. "The mob is going to find out who I am and hunt me down like a dog until they—" She paused and made a slicing motion across her throat.

"Would you calm down!" Max said.

"And what if I did kill him? What if he had a severe reaction to the laxative I put in his drink? Oh God."

"How many did you give him?"

"Two. I crushed them into a powder and put them in his drink."

"You didn't bother to tell me that."

"I figured you would think it was silly."

"People don't die from an over-the-counter laxative," Max said. "Now, calm down until I can get us out of here." He turned onto the interstate and sped up.

"What is all this noise about?" Muffin demanded. "I'm trying to download an e-card from my laptop friend at MIT and I can't think straight for all this noise."

"Harlan Rawlins is dead," Jamie said. "I was the last one to see him alive. Somehow they're going to find out who I am, and I'll end up on *Unsolved Mysteries*." She gulped. "Vera will find out. She'll probably be the one to turn me in."

"I'm not easily confused," Muffin said, "but you're not making any sense."

Max filled her in. Finally, he exited at a rest area and backed into a slot far away from the other motorists. He reached behind the seat and pulled out a license plate and a screwdriver.

"What are you doing?" Jamie asked.

"Covering our butts in case somebody got a look at the truck and wrote down the tag number. I always keep an extra on hand."

"Do you know how that sounds?" Jamie asked. "I can't believe I'm associating with a man who carries an extra license plate wherever he goes. That is scary."

"It works for me," he said, climbing from the truck.

Jamie leaned back against the seat and closed her eyes. All she could see was Harlan's face as he'd looked in death. "Oh God," she said.

"Calm down, Jamie," Muffin said gently.

"I'm going to prison," Jamie said dully. "They'll put me on the chain gang. I could get the death penalty. What will I do with Fleas? Nobody is going to want him. They'll put him to sleep." She turned around and glanced at the bed of the truck where Fleas was sleeping.

"You're not going to prison," Muffin said. "Max will make a few telephone calls and—"

"And clear me of a murder rap? I don't think so."

Max opened the door. "Lose the wig."

Jamie looked at him. "Excuse me?"

"Give it to me."

Jamie plucked it from her head. She watched Max toss the wig and license plate into a trash can. He returned and stashed the screwdriver behind the seat before climbing in.

"That's not going to do any good. My fingerprints are all over the hotel room."

Max shook his head. "Dave wiped everything down while I was trying to revive Harlan. He's good at that sort of thing since he hates germs."

Jamie rolled her eyes. Dave had almost gone off the deep end after touching Harlan. "You seem to forget there was a witness, Max. Harlan's bodyguard personally escorted me to the room."

"You were in disguise. And a damn good one at that," he added. "Nobody is going to recognize you once you wash off all that makeup."

"The police are going to lock me up and throw away the key."

"You're not going to prison," Max said. "I don't know what happened to Harlan, but I know you didn't have anything to do with it. Unless he got so excited with you he had a heart attack."

"What?"

"Sounded like things got pretty hot in there. You were trying to get him undressed and into bed."

Jamie gaped at him. "Excuse me?"

"Oh, brother," Muffin said. "I don't think I want to hear this."

"I heard it all," Max said. "I was afraid something like this would happen."

"Max, I don't think this is a good time to discuss what happened between Jamie and Harlan," Muffin told him. "I think we need to be a little more sensitive to her feelings."

Jamie looked at Max and shook her head. "Relax. Nothing happened."

"What?"

"Harlan got sick. I was trying to loosen his clothing so he could breathe. If I was trying to get him to lie down it was because I thought he was going to pass out." She gave him a sidelong glance. "You seem to really want to know all the details."

"Where you're concerned? Absolutely."

"Well, forget it. We need to figure out who killed Rawlins."

Ward Reed sat quietly in the living room of Harlan's suite as the detectives examined the man's body. The medical examiner had already been summoned, and they were awaiting him to pronounce Rawlins dead, despite all obvious appearances. An officer carefully wrapped the plates of food on the table while another dusted the room for fingerprints.

A young detective with a neat beard stood in the kitchen questioning the officer who'd first responded to the call. Finally, the detective joined Reed.

"I'm Detective Sills of the Knoxville Police Department," he said. "You're Ward Reed?"

He nodded. "I was Harlan Rawlins's bodyguard," he said.

Detective Sills sat down. "I've read your statement, Mr. Reed. You say you escorted a woman to the reverend's room this afternoon?"

"That's correct. I unlocked the door and let her in."

"And she said her name was Jane? She never gave you a last name?"

"No."

"Reverend Rawlins was to have lunch with her?"

"Yes."

"Was Reverend Rawlins alive when this Jane person arrived?"

"I didn't see him, but I heard him call out to her as I closed the door and put the *Do Not Disturb* sign on it."

"You also said you had seen Jane at the last church service."

Reed nodded. "And she visited the reverend in his home yesterday as well."

"Is it possible he might have listed her full name in his appointment book?"

"If he knew it, he would have, but he referred to her only as Jane when he asked me to notify the security guard at the front gate of the appointment. I can check."

"I'm sending a couple of my men over. They'll go through the reverend's things and question the guard."

"You'll give me time to break the news to Mrs. Rawlins first, right?"

"My men will have to follow you over, Mr. Reed. We'll want the reverend's office and personal belongings secured immediately." The detective made notes on his pad. "Did Reverend Rawlins often meet women here?"

"Do I have to answer that question?"

Sills shrugged. "You can answer it either here or at the station."

"Am I a suspect? Do I need an attorney?"

"This is normal procedure, Mr. Reed. Your answers will help in the investigation. As one of his most trusted employees, I'm certain you'll want this case solved as quickly as we do."

Reed sighed heavily. "Yes, he often met women here."

"Did you personally escort these women up to meet the reverend?"

"Yes."

"Can you remember their names?"

"It was really none of my business to know their names or why they were visiting, and I never felt the need to inquire. Had I thought the reverend was taking a risk, I would not have brought them up."

"You'll call me if you happen to remember any of their names?"

"Of course." He checked his wristwatch. "Is this going to take long? I really need to get back to the house and break the news to his wife."

"Be patient, Mr. Reed, I promise I won't keep you any longer than I have to. Do you think you could give an accurate description of this Jane person to our artist at the station? I'd like to have a composite drawing. After you speak to Mrs. Rawlins, of course."

Reed nodded. "I'll do my best."

The medical examiner, a heavy-set man whose double chin bulged over his shirt collar, walked into the room. "I'm done," he said.

"What can you tell me?" Sills asked.

"He's deader'n hell."

Sills sighed and muttered, "Thanks a lot."

The heavy man nodded. "I found pills on him, looks like amphetamines and barbs, but we won't know for sure until the crime lab checks them out." He shrugged. "But it doesn't take a rocket scientist to figure out what killed him. His throat was slit right through the carotid artery."

"Holy hell!" Dave said, pointing at the TV.

"What now?" Max said.

Dave sat in front of the TV, a magnifying glass in his hand. He'd been checking his wound again, despite the fact a doctor in the emergency room had assured him it didn't look like a bite and there was no need to be vaccinated for rabies.

Max followed Dave's gaze to the TV set, where the Knoxville chief of police was holding up a composite drawing of Jamie in her disguise. Max didn't realize Jamie had followed him into the room until he heard her gasp out loud.

"Oh, my God," she said.

"It gets worse," Dave told them. "The medical examiner was just on, and you won't believe what he said." Max and Jamie looked at him. "Rawlins's throat was cut from ear to ear."

"Jesus," Max said. "He wasn't like that when we last saw him."

Jamie nodded. "Somebody came into the room after we left. Before the police arrived."

"Why would somebody slit his throat?" Max asked. "He was already dead."

Dave looked up. "Here's one even better. What if the killer had been there the whole time? Just waiting," he added. "Hell, he could have been hiding behind the shower curtain."

Jamie felt a sudden chill. "Somebody wanted to make certain he was dead. That somebody wanted to make one hundred percent certain that Harlan Rawlins never drew breath again."

"Or talked," Max added.

"Jamie, can I come in?" Max said, knocking softly.

He heard a click, and the door opened. Jamie stood there, her arms folded across her stomach. She wore cutoff jeans and a thin white T shirt.

"Are you OK?" Max asked, trying not to stare at her breasts, but he could see her nipples against the shirt.

Jamie shrugged and backed away from the door. "I've been better."

Max went inside. Fleas was lying on the floor beside her bed, having been relegated to that part of the house because of Dave's allergies. Although the dog didn't raise his head, his eyes followed Max as he stepped closer to Jamie. "I feel crummy, too, Jamie. I know Rawlins was a thief and a liar—"

"Not to mention an adulterer," Jamie added. "He probably abused his wife as well."

"Probably."

"I feel bad about Rawlins," she said, "but that's not why I'm freaked out. I'm scared to close my eyes, Max. I keep thinking about what Dave said. The murderer could very well have been in the hotel room when Harlan and I were there. I don't remember if the shower curtain was closed, but it would have been a perfect place to hide. What if—"

"Stop asking yourself *what if,*" Max said. "The killer wasn't interested in hurting you; he wanted Harlan."

"I can't shake the feeling that he's going to get me

next. Every time I close my eyes I imagine him standing over me by my bed. Watching me. I don't think I'll ever be able to close my eyes again."

Max walked over to the bed and pulled the covers aside. "Why don't you lie down, and I'll sit with you?"

Jamie lay on the bed. Max tried not to stare at her long legs.

He sat down on the edge and regarded her. "This is why I didn't want you to come with me," he said. "I was afraid something like this would happen."

"I know. But all I could think about was getting my big story. Now Harlan's dead. I don't have the story, and I wasn't able to get any information from him before he was murdered."

"You got an invitation to his private residence," Max said. "He invited you to lunch. I think he would have told you something if he hadn't died."

"You're just trying to make me feel better."

"No, Jamie. I believe Harlan desperately needed someone he could talk to. I believe he trusted you." Max reached up and pulled a stray lock of hair from her face. "I'm glad we got rid of that wig. Your hair is too pretty to cover up." He let his hand rest against her cheek for a moment.

Jamie swallowed. His touch was so tender she felt something in her stomach flutter. "We have to find out who killed him, Max."

"I definitely think Santoni is responsible."

"He could have hired a woman to pass herself off as a maid. That way she could have had access to the room."

"Most women don't kill with a knife, and from the description on the news it was very brutal. Of course, a knife is quiet and comes in handy when one has to worry about noise, so that would change things. It could have been a man dressed as a woman."

"What about Ward Reed, the bodyguard?" Jamie asked. "He certainly had opportunity. Maybe Santoni got to him, offered him a ton of money."

"Or maybe Reed was already working for Santoni," Max said.

"What makes you think it wasn't Santoni himself?"

"I don't know that it wasn't, but most mob figures in his position would have hired it out because the risk would be too great. Not that Santoni isn't a risk-taker," he added. "He's taken so many risks that most of his family is against him. All I know is, whoever killed Harlan knew exactly what he was doing."

"Meaning this person has killed before and is going to kill again."

"Not necessarily. I think he got what he wanted. Let's not talk about it anymore tonight, OK? You need to try and rest." He stood.

"Max?"

"Yeah?"

Jamie was almost embarrassed to ask. "Would you sleep in here tonight?"

His look softened. "Are you sure Fleas won't mind?" he asked, as though hoping he could tease her into feeling better.

"He'll understand."

"OK." Max cut the light, rounded the bed, and kicked off his shoes.

Jamie felt the mattress dip under his weight as he lay down on the bed. He reached for her, pulled her close. Jamie lay there, her back flush against his chest.

She could smell his aftershave, feel his breath on her neck. She allowed his warmth to seep in, allowed her body to relax for the first time since they'd found Harlan dead.

"Damn, Swifty, you feel good," he whispered.

"Yeah?"

"Yeah." Max adjusted his body so that she wouldn't know just how good she did feel against him.

Jamie's body responded to his nearness, the protective arm that held her close. She felt safe for the first time since finding Harlan sprawled on the bathroom floor. She shifted on the bed, trying to get closer.

"Don't do that," Max muttered, in a pained voice.

Jamie was acutely conscious of his body against hers, the hard lines that made her feel so secure. She and Max might have differences from time to time, but she knew instinctively that he would protect her no matter what. It gave her some satisfaction to know that he was as conscious of her body as she was of his. She smiled in the darkness. She was thankful she could find something to smile about after her day. "Don't do what?" she said after a moment.

"Dammit, Jamie, you know what you do to me."

"No, tell me." Even as she said it she wondered why she was teasing him. Perhaps she was simply looking for escape in Max's arms, or maybe she liked knowing Max desired her.

"I think it's obvious," Max said after a moment.

Jamie heard the smile in his voice. "Max, I know we don't always see eye-to-eye. I know you find me disagreeable at times."

"Uh-huh."

"But I appreciate your being here with me."

"Why wouldn't I? You know how I feel about you, Jamie. It's not like I haven't told you."

She took a deep shuddering breath. "I know you care about me, Max, but I think a big part is due to . . ." She paused.

"My attraction to you? Of course I'm attracted to you." He tightened his arm around her. "You make me crazy sometimes."

She heard the huskiness in his voice and something more. A need. She knew how he felt. She had tried to fight her attraction to Max from the moment she'd laid eyes on him, had tried to fight her feelings. But there was no denying it. She had never been so drawn to a man, and that's what scared her.

God, where was her self-control? she thought.

Max rose on his elbows and turned her over so that he was facing her in the dark. "Man, oh man," he whispered.

Jamie could barely make out the outline of his face, but she knew he wanted to kiss her. And, dammit, she wanted it as much as he did. It didn't seem to matter what was happening in her life; Max could just look at her a certain way or touch her and everything else faded into the background. She was obviously not a disciplined person where Max Holt was concerned.

Max found her lips. Jamie didn't hesitate to let him in; she was just as eager as he was for the kiss. He slipped his hand beneath her T-shirt, and her stomach did a massive somersault. Nope, no discipline, she thought. The man was intent on turning her on, and she was more than obliging.

Max broke the kiss, but his mouth never stilled,

moving over her face in sweet lingering kisses that made her feel shivery one moment, anxious the next. She arched against him, heat seeking heat, feeling as though she couldn't get close enough. Max eased her lacy bra upward, exposing both breasts. He covered one with his mouth. Jamie closed her eyes, thinking maybe it wasn't such a bad thing to let her resolve weaken from time to time. This seemed like a good time.

His hands were warm against her cool skin. Her stomach fluttered and she could almost feel her bones turning soft and mushy.

His gentle massage sent erotic messages low in her belly. Damned if the man didn't have a way with his hands.

Max ran his hand lightly down her abdomen to her inner thighs, and Jamie knew she was a goner. Oh God, oh God, oh God. Max's hand moved higher and he turned it over so that his palm lay flat between her thighs.

Jamie sucked in her breath. She tried to think, but all logic had gone out the window. She had tried so hard to be strong. She had wanted reassurances from Max, but maybe he was right. Maybe she expected too much. There weren't any guarantees in life. Or maybe she was just rationalizing because, well, because she wanted him to make love to her.

As if sensing a subtle change in her, Max pulled back, and his hands stilled. "You're doing it again," he said. "You're thinking too much."

"I can't help it."

"Do you want me to stop?"

"Um, I don't know."

He gave an enormous sigh, pulled her T-shirt in place, and rolled onto his back.

She should never have let things go this far, she thought, only to back out in the end. What was wrong with her? What the hell was wrong with her?

"Max?"

"Go to sleep, Jamie," he said softly.

Max was reading the newspaper when Jamie stumbled from the bedroom the next morning in her crumpled T-shirt. Fleas followed closely, and when Jamie stopped to open the front door, he bumped into her. Jamie turned, and they just looked at each other.

"Is there a problem?" she asked the dog.

He inched out the door as though he had all the time in the world. On the front steps he shook his head and his long ears made a flapping sound. He sat down and began licking himself.

"That is the most disgusting thing I've ever seen in my life," Jamie told him, and closed the door. She turned for the kitchen, nodded once at Max, and made for the coffeepot. She was determined to act as though nothing had happened the night before.

"Your eyes don't look so good, Swifty," Max said.

"I didn't sleep well," she said, avoiding eye contact.

"I guess that makes two of us. I was wondering. Maybe I should drive you back to Beaumont. You'd be safer."

She turned and gaped. "No way. Not until we find out who killed Rawlins." She spied the newspaper in his hand. "Oh, damn."

"I went out earlier to get the paper. You made headlines, Swifty."

"That's why you want me to go back, isn't it? You're afraid somebody will recognize me."

"No. The picture isn't even close." He held it up. "See for yourself."

Jamie hurried over and studied the drawing. The wig made a lot of difference; bangs covered most of her forehead, giving her face a rounder look. The slightly upturned nose was close, but the eyes were all wrong. She drew a sigh of relief.

"Nobody is going to recognize you as this woman," Max said. "Did you give anyone your last name?"

Jamie shook her head. "Nobody asked. Not even Rawlins."

"Probably because you told him you had a sexual addiction." Max shook his head as though he still couldn't believe she'd done it. "Most people would want their anonymity protected. He would have been sensitive enough to know that."

She gave a shaky breath. "You're saying it's safe for me to go to Wal-Mart?"

He suddenly looked amused. "God forbid I try to stop you from shopping." His eyes took on a tender look. "If it helps to get out, I'll take you. You're safe as long as you're in a crowd."

She had wondered about what to do about meeting Michael for breakfast. "I'll be fine on my own."

He didn't argue. "You're not the only person the police are looking for. A bellboy is being questioned about a man who offered him one hundred bucks to borrow his clothes and push the food cart into Rawlins's room. Fortunately, Dave was in disguise as well." He paused. "We can continue using the name Trotter, and since Jane is such a common name, I don't see a problem there, either."

"Sounds like everything is going to be OK then."

"For the time being."

Jamie didn't miss the edge in his voice.

Jamie slid into the booth across from Michael Juliano. She stiffened when she noticed the folded newspaper beside him. She was just being paranoid, she told herself.

He smiled at her. "Good morning. Or is it?"

She froze. "What do you mean?"

"You look tired."

"I didn't sleep well last night."

"Does it have anything to do with that wedding band you're wearing? Not that it's any of my business, of course."

Jamie's stomach took a nosedive as she realized she was wearing the wedding band she had put on before meeting with Harlan the day before. She had been so upset she hadn't thought to remove it when she'd returned home and changed. She hadn't been wearing it when she first met Michael and she wanted to keep things consistent. In his paranoid state he might shut down to her.

She had gone and blown her chance. "I can explain it," she said.

He leaned back in the booth as though waiting.

TWELVE

Jamie was thankful the waitress had picked that particular moment to bring coffee and menus. She waited until the woman walked away.

"My husband and I are divorcing," she said.

"But you still wear his ring?"

Jamie stared at it. "I suppose I'm still trying to come to terms with it. I should take it off and I do sometimes."

Michael seemed to ponder it. "I really don't have a right to ask. I mean, we barely know each other, right? I just . . ." He paused and gave a rueful smile.

"What?"

"I found myself looking forward to seeing you today, so the ring was a big surprise. I don't remember seeing it yesterday, but then, I was upset at the time. I'm sorry I butted in. And I'm sorry that you're going through a bad time. I was married once, but it didn't work out."

He looked genuinely sad for her. Jamie glanced down. It wasn't easy lying to someone who was so nice, and it wasn't easy keeping secrets from Max. But she seemed to be doing a lot of that lately. She had even called Vera and spent ten minutes on the phone lying to her about what a great time she was having in Tennessee. Yeesh.

But she had a very good reason for all the subterfuge. She was trying to keep Vera from worrying, and she was trying to get information from Michael that might protect him and lead her and Max to Nick Santoni. A girl had to do what a girl had to do.

"Jane, are you all right?"

Jamie looked up. "We barely know each other, Michael, and the last thing I want to do is burden you with my problems. I was just trying to be a friend when I thought you needed one."

He didn't respond.

"Would you rather I go?" She held her breath. Leaving was the last thing she wanted to do. If she left now she would be empty-handed as far as information was concerned.

"Please stay."

Jamie tried to hide her relief as she took a sip of her coffee. "How are you?"

"My sister was buried yesterday afternoon in a private ceremony. As much as I hate to say it, I'm relieved to have it over with. I didn't like seeing her suffer, you know?"

The waitress took their order and left them. "So what are you going to do now?" Jamie asked.

Michael shrugged. "Take it one day at a time. I own several delis in Knoxville. I have to look after them."

Jamie leaned closer. "Have you had any more threats?"

Michael glanced around the restaurant. "I wish I hadn't told you. I plan to take care of that little problem tonight."

"What do you mean?"

"I'm going to tell the guy flat-out no. I'm going to hire security guards to watch my delis, and I'm going to the cops. I'd rather spend the money on that than paying off thugs to keep them from burning my places to the ground."

"You're actually meeting with one of them?"

He nodded. "Yeah. It won't take long to say screw off. Excuse my language."

Jamie's mind raced. Finally, she gave a sigh.

"What is it?"

"Nothing. You'll think it's silly."

"What?"

"Michael, I was going to invite you to dinner tonight. I figured it would lift your spirits." She shrugged. "Mine, too."

"I'm sorry." He reached across the table and squeezed her hand. "I would have gladly accepted under different circumstances."

Jamie pondered it. She didn't want to sound pushy and risk blowing it, but if she didn't come up with some kind of plan she'd lose her chance altogether. "Maybe we could have dinner afterward. What time are you meeting with this, um, person?"

"Eight o'clock. But we're meeting in Knoxville."

"I know how to get to Knoxville."

He hesitated. "I suppose that'll work. I'm just going to meet him in a bar, tell him I'm not going to do business with him, then walk away."

"We could meet somewhere close, say around eight-thirty?"

Michael looked thoughtful. He reached for a napkin and scribbled on it. "There's a quaint little Italian restaurant down the street from where I'll be. It's called Jeno's; you can't miss it. I'll meet you out front at eight-thirty."

"Great. I look forward to it."

They made small talk until their breakfast arrived, but Jamie's mind wasn't on the conversation. She was already forming a plan in her head.

"So, who's the guy?" Muffin asked as soon as Jamie had pulled from the parking lot and turned onto the highway.

Jamie had not been expecting the question. "How'd you know?"

"Female intuition."

"You're a computer, Muffin."

"Whatever. So who is he?"

"His name is Michael; he's very nice and drives an awesome Jaguar. He's also going through a bad time, and he needs a friend right now. That's all we are, friends. We're having dinner tonight."

"Does Max know?"

Jamie sighed. "No, I haven't told him. But I'll have to; otherwise, he'll worry."

"You should go, Jamie. It'll do you good."

She looked at the dashboard. "Really?"

"That doesn't mean you don't need to take extra precautions, but you need to do something to take your mind off what happened yesterday. You haven't even had time to get over all the crap you went through in Beaumont."

"You worried I might crack up or something? That you might have to find me a quiet state-operated mental hospital?"

"I don't think you need to sit in that cabin night after

night while Max and I try to break through the Santoni family's firewalls. Or listen to Dave," she added.

Max's jaw went slack in disbelief. "Are you saying you have a date?"

Jamie pretended to fluff the throw pillows on the sofa so she didn't have to look at him. "No, it's not a date; I'm meeting this guy for dinner." She turned to Max. "He just lost his sister. She was his twin. He's devastated, and he needs somebody to talk to."

Max scooted his chair back from the kitchen table, where computers, monitors, and various other equipment that Jamie knew nothing about blinked and winked and made soft whirring sounds.

"You always find them, don't you, Swifty?"

"What do you mean?"

"You're just like my sister. The two of you must have radar. If somebody has problems, you lock in to them and you immediately have to fix whatever is wrong." Max suddenly looked suspicious. "How well do you know this person?"

"Well, I haven't had time to call a profiler from the FBI, but I managed to lift his prints off his water glass, so I should know something by the time we're supposed to meet."

Max didn't seem to find humor in her remark. "How do you know he wasn't just using a line?"

"Max, he asked me to look at his sister's dress, for God's sake. The one she was buried in yesterday. The man is in a lot of pain. I don't care if you think I'm just a big softie, I can't turn my back on him."

"Just be careful, OK? I know you need to get out, but don't forget what we're up against."

Which made her all the more determined to find

out what Michael knew. *If* he knew anything, she reminded herself. And once she did, she would lay it all at Max's feet and have the inside edge to her story.

A buzzing sound from a speaker drew Max's attention away from her for a moment. "It's just Dave."

Dave came through the front door a few minutes later. He looked anxious. "I can't find the deer anywhere."

Max stared at the man.

"What deer?" Jamie asked.

Max spoke. "Dave swerved to miss a buck this morning, but now he has convinced himself he hit it."

"I could have nicked him," Dave said.

"I was in the truck when the deer ran out in front of you, Dave," Max went on. "You missed him by a mile. We've gone back to look for him twice. If you had hit him he'd be dead by the road."

"Not necessarily. He could have wandered off. He might be lying in a gully in pain at this very moment."

"Try not to think about it," Max said. "We have to worry about Jamie right now. She has a hot date tonight."

Dave looked at Jamie. "Man, you move fast."

Jamie rolled her eyes at Max. "Thanks."

Dave stepped closer to Max. "Are my eyes red?"

"They look perfectly fine to me."

"I can't remember if I took my allergy pill this morning. I should probably count them."

"Dave likes to count his pills," Max told Jamie. "And when he's not counting his pills he counts license tags and telephone poles."

Dave, who'd reached into his pants pocket for his prescription bottle, simply stood there. "It's what I do," he finally said. He glanced at Jamie. "Didn't your new boyfriend notice you were wearing a wedding ring?"

"It doesn't matter. Michael and I are going to have an affair anyway."

Max tried to hide his amusement. "They can't help themselves, Dave. They took one look at each other and their morals flew right out the window."

Dave didn't seem to be listening. "I should probably run down and take another look just to make sure that deer is OK."

Max stood. "I need to check in with Muffin."

Jamie watched him go, then sank onto the sofa. If only she could tell him what she thought she knew.

"That thing is covered with dust mites," Dave said.

Jamie just looked at him.

Max climbed into the truck. "Have you got anything on Santoni yet?" he asked Muffin.

"Your timing is perfect. I just found Santoni's address."

"Damn, that's great news," Max said, grinning. "Just what we've been waiting for."

"His place is about forty-five minutes from here. It would have been a whole lot easier finding him if the man put things in his own name, but like I said before, he has a number of aliases."

"You have my undivided attention."

"The name Juliano has popped up a couple of times in the family tree. It was Nick's mother's maiden name; seems Nick borrows from that tree now and then just to keep people guessing. Nick's sister was named Bethany-Ann Juliano Santoni, if you can believe it."

"I didn't know he had a sister. Nothing we've pulled up mentioned siblings."

"I was playing around with birth records and discovered Santoni's mother, Mary-Bethany Elizabeth

Juliano Santoni, gave birth to twins in a hospital in Carlstadt, New Jersey. Michael Nicholas and Bethany-Ann Juliano."

"That's interesting."

"Yeah, but this is where it gets weird. Bethany-Ann died at birth. That didn't stop Nick from borrowing. He's using the name Michael Juliano."

"What else?"

"I discovered Nick Santoni attended Saint Teresa's Holiness School in Carlstadt, New Jersey, but that was before computers, so I can't get anything more. He had a couple of best friends, Rudolf Marconi or Rudy, as they call him, and Thomas Peter Bennetti."

"I'm having trouble keeping up with all these names," Max said.

"Most of these guys are Catholics, and you often find their names contain one of the saints. Go figure. I've found various mortgages in and around Knoxville owned by a Michael Juliano. Marconi owns a couple of bars in Knoxville."

"What about the other guy? Bennetti."

"He sort of dropped out of the picture."

Nick Santoni's home was perched high on a mountain and surrounded by a massive brick wall, the house built of stone and granite that had been dragged up the side of the mountain. Cameras sat atop the gated entrance, aimed in all directions. They were monitored by Santoni's employees, who watched from the office of a nearby building, which also housed a kennel of Doberman pinschers. Each hour, a man leashed two dogs and walked the property.

Nick pulled up to the gate, and in a matter of seconds it slid open. He parked in front of the house, unlocked the door, and went inside. The slate floors and heavy leather furniture had been designed for a man, and although Nick owned several properties in various locations, his mountain home was his favorite.

He strode purposefully toward a wet bar, poured his favorite scotch into a short glass, and drained it. His cell phone rang, but he ignored it. Instead, he poured a second scotch, sank into the nearest chair, and opened his newspaper. The headline stared back at him: *Renowned Evangelist Found Dead in Hotel Room.* Nick reread the article and tossed the paper aside. He leaned back in his chair and closed his eyes.

His cell phone rang again. With a sigh, he reached into the pocket of his slacks and pulled it out.

"You've been ignoring my calls," the voice said from the other end. It was the tired, raspy voice of a man who had spent much of his life smoking expensive cigars with his brandy. "Is that any way to treat your favorite uncle?"

"I was tied up most of the morning, Uncle Leo," Nick said. "I couldn't talk."

"I've been listening to the news, Nicholas."

"Yeah?"

"You want to tell me about it?"

"What? You think I killed Rawlins?"

"Not at first. Then I started playing around with it in my mind."

"You got it all wrong. I'm as surprised over his death as you are."

"You mean his murder." The man paused. "I have always been able to tell when you're lying, Nicholas. You lied about hiring Vito Puccini, and you're lying now. I sent you down there to protect you. I'd hoped you would change. You think you can just kill somebody, bury the body, and that's it? You think the cops are idiots? You watch too many gangster movies, Nicky. The family is sick of your tactics. You've become a problem. A big problem."

Nick frowned. "The family is always on my ass, trying to pin something on me. If someone in this town takes a shit, I'm the one who gets blamed for it."

"You've been stepping in shit all your life, kid. Problem is, you track it all over the place so that your family has to walk in it. The police watch our houses. My daughter can't take my grandchildren to the park because men follow her."

"What would I have to gain by killing Rawlins?" Nick asked.

"You're asking the wrong question."

"OK, what's the right question?"

"What would you have to lose if he lived?"

Nick sighed. "I don't have any answers, Uncle Leo. I've got my boys looking into it. That's the best I can do right now."

"Harlan Rawlins was the only thing you had going for you."

"That's not true! I've got money coming in from a number of sources."

"Yeah, but he was your big fish." Leo suddenly went into a fit of coughing. "I'm an old man, Nicky. I don't need this. The family doesn't need this. Losing that TV network was a bad mistake, and we still haven't recovered that loss. I can't help you anymore." He paused. "You need to come home."

Nick was silent for a moment. "What are you saying?" He wiped a hand down his face and found it wet. "Have I been replaced?"

"It's best this way."

"Look, Uncle Leo, I'm in the middle of something down here, and I can't let go. I didn't want to say anything until I took care of it, but I've got Maximillian Holt and his girlfriend in the palm of my hand."

Silence.

"Max Holt has been snooping around, Uncle Leo. He somehow managed to trace Vito Puccini back here, so he found out Harlan hired him. Hell, Harlan even wrote a letter of recommendation."

"Which you forced him to do," the man said knowingly.

"I don't know what you're talking about."

"Harlan Rawlins wouldn't know how to go about hiring a hit man. Do you take me for an old fool?"

"You don't have to believe me, Uncle Leo, but I'm telling you Holt is bad news. Hell, he has more connections than we do. He could have easily taken Harlan out."

"Are you planning to kill again, Nicholas?" The man sounded tired.

"Holt could hurt the family, Uncle Leo. He could expose us all."

"The family has done nothing to Max Holt; you have. And when you kill him you will have to kill his girlfriend, and then there will be someone else. It never stops. You create too many problems."

"Listen to me, old man! Your grandchildren will *never* be able to play in the park as long as Max Holt is alive, because he's going to even the score."

"I think you are very confused," Leo said. "You are no match for a man like Max Holt. You are a coward. Your own father knew this."

Nick started to answer, but the line went dead.

THIRTEEN

Detective Pete Sills sipped coffee from a chipped mug and waited until the lab technician finished speaking to another detective before he approached him. "Hey, Lance, you got anything for me on the Rawlins case yet?"

"Are you kidding? The chief has us working double-time on it. He obviously wants to look good in front of the media. When is his next press conference?"

Sills smiled. "You know I don't keep up with the politics around this place. I'm just a worker bee."

"You and me both," Lance said. "Anyway, we matched the pills they found on him, as well as those he'd stashed in his desk drawer, and it's obvious he came about them illegally, since the bottles were unmarked. This guy was taking a shitload of stuff. I'm surprised he could even remember what they were, or the dosage.

"I also ran a test on the powder they found beside the wine bottle, and the ingredients are consistent with those found in most laxatives."

"There was evidence he'd gotten sick shortly before his death," Sills said. "I wonder if maybe it was all that crap in his system."

Lance shrugged. "We won't know the facts until the autopsy, of course."

"I've talked to the wife," Sills said. "Rawlins's beatings sent her to the emergency room more than once."

"You think she killed him?"

"She had motive. Problem is, she can't weigh more than a hundred pounds, and she's a timid little thing. I just can't picture her killing her husband with a knife."

"Maybe she has a boyfriend."

Sills met his gaze. "It wouldn't have been easy. Harlan kept her in her bedroom most of the time."

"Sounds like he was one mean sonofabitch."

Dave waited until Max climbed into the bucket that was attached to the hydraulic lift to Bennett Electric's truck. "You got everything you need?" he asked.

"Yea. Once I attach the recording transmitter, I'll hook into the telephone line and run a test."

"Look, Max, I'd go up in the bucket if it weren't for my vertigo."

"Naw, I personally want to get a look at Santoni's place."

Physically finding Santoni's house had been no easier than Muffin getting the information that the property wasn't listed to Nick Santoni. Tom Bennett of Bennett Electric had been able to locate property belonging to a Michael Juliano in his computer. He'd given Max a county map and marked the area in red, but many of the dirt roads leading to the residence were unmarked. Max and Dave had combed the mountain until they found the massive brick wall that enclosed what appeared to be a compound of sorts.

"Don't forget to take pictures," Dave said. "Oh God, I hope we didn't forget the camera."

"I've already told you I've got it. Five times I've told you."

"Just want to make sure."

"Take me up."

Dave pressed a button, and the bucket rose slowly upward. Once Max was in position, he went to work. Soon it would be possible to access incoming and outgoing calls on Santoni's line.

Jamie had spent the day cleaning the cabin and working on her story, filling the pages of her notebook with her impressions of Rawlins and the town of Sweet Pea, as well as the faces she'd seen in the congregation. The bottom line: People needed hope, and Harlan Rawlins had given them that. Because so much money had come into his ministry he was able to make a difference in some ways, but he'd been more interested in lining his pockets and paying off those who were extorting money from him. Had he not been so greedy, had he not owed the mob hush money, Harlan Rawlins would have been able to make staggering changes with his ministry.

Jamie found herself wondering about the man. Had he always been a phony? she mused. Or had he started out with good motives, only to be seduced by money? And what about rumors of affairs and possible spousal abuse? What did the mob have on Harlan that he'd been willing to pay so much money to keep quiet?

It was after 6:00 P.M. by the time Max and Dave arrived back at the cabin. Jamie had bathed and dressed in a white denim skirt and navy knit top, minus the push-up bra. Her blond hair hung free, falling to her shoulders.

Max took one look at her and arched one brow.

"Wow. Your new friend is going to take one look at you in that outfit and forget about all his problems. Maybe I should go as a chaperon."

"I'm too old for a chaperon, Max, but thanks just the same. Where have you guys been all day?"

"Maybe you should sit down first," Dave said, "because you're not going to believe it."

Jamie looked at Max. "Oh, yeah?" she said.

"We found Santoni's place," he told her.

Her jaw dropped. "For real?" She couldn't hide the excitement in her voice. "What's it like?"

"Nice hideout," he said, "surrounded by what looks like the Great Wall of China."

Dave nodded. "Max attached a recording transmitter to his telephone line so we could monitor his calls."

"Wow, we're finally getting somewhere," she said. "Did you happen to get a look at Santoni?"

Max shook his head. He looked disappointed. "I wish. The place is under heavy guard. We had to do the job and get out so we wouldn't attract attention." He didn't look happy as he walked over to his laptop and sat down.

"We have pictures of his place," Dave said. "Or should I say his fortress." He handed Jamie several photos.

"Looks like a prison," she said.

"It's secure," Max told her as he checked his e-mail. "He's got almost as much security on his place as I do on mine. Of course, what I use is more sophisticated."

"Yeah, but you don't have a herd of Doberman pinschers walking the grounds," Dave said.

"I would love to know what Santoni looks like," Jamie said. Even as she said it, she hoped she would get the opportunity later. She suspected Santoni was the one threatening Michael, but what she didn't know was whether he would show up personally to meet with Michael or send one of his men.

"What are you doing?" Jamie asked Max.

"Muffin is sending me what stats she has on Santoni. The reason we couldn't find anything at first is because he has everything in his sister's name and she's deceased."

"You're not thinking of trying to get into his place, are you?"

"There's no need," Max said. "We wouldn't find anything in his residence. That would make him vulnerable to possible search and seizure if he got busted. If the cops even know where he lives," he added. "I figure he's operating out of the back room of one of his businesses under an assumed name. Hopefully, we'll hear something in a phone conversation."

"What's next?"

"We're going to grab some gear and equipment and spend the night near Santoni's place," he said. "We have to be within range of the transmitter in order to tap in to his phone calls. Dave and I found a shack in the woods not far from the house. You can tell it hasn't been used in a while."

"It sounds dangerous."

"Damn right," Dave said. "The place is full of spiderwebs, not to mention . . ." He paused and glanced at Max. "Dust mites."

"Will you be spending the night out there?" Jamie asked. Not only was she anxious at the risk they were taking, but she also didn't relish the thought of being alone at night in the cabin.

"I'll take the first watch," Dave said. "No sense us both being there."

Max looked at Jamie. "I'll stay with Dave for a

while and try to be back by the time you get home. You *are* coming back tonight, I assume." He gave her outfit another once-over.

Jamie tossed him a look. "Very funny. I should be home before midnight."

"That's kind of late, isn't it?"

"I'm not meeting him until eight-thirty."

"I hope he's not married, too," Dave said. When Max and Jamie looked at him, he shrugged. "I know you and Jamie aren't really married, but this guy she's going out with doesn't know it. What if he has a wife? What if she's the jealous type?"

"He's not married," Jamie said.

Max looked troubled. "Maybe you and I should talk further before you meet this guy. I don't even know where the two of you are going."

"Would the two of you relax?" Jamie said. "I'm having dinner with the guy. He's probably going to want to talk about his sister. I'm going to listen to him, try to be supportive, and then I'm coming home." That wasn't all she was going to do, but that's all she was going to tell them for the moment. She hoped when she left Michael Juliano she would have big news for Max. A name or a face.

"Would you mind driving Bennett's truck tonight?" Max asked. "I'd like to have Muffin around."

"No problem."

Jamie had to stop and ask for directions twice, but she finally managed to find the Italian restaurant Michael had told her about. The sun was setting. She searched the area and found a small sports bar located within a block of the restaurant.

She parked in a side alley and waited. She did not

wish to be seen by Michael. She had no idea if he planned to meet his party at that particular bar; all she could do was wait and watch for any sign of him.

The streetlights flickered on, but Jamie was hidden in shadows. She hoped a policeman didn't drive by and find her illegally parked, because she would have a difficult time explaining why she was there.

Shortly before eight, Jamie spied Michael's Jaguar. She instinctively ducked, then remembered he couldn't see her. She raised the binoculars she'd found beneath the front seat; obviously Max and Dave had used them earlier. She could see Michael's car perfectly, but she could barely make out his profile in the dark interior. She watched him select a parking place near the door of the bar. He pulled into the vacant slot and waited. Jamie waited as well.

The minutes ticked by slowly. Jamie drummed her fingers on the steering wheel and hummed a tune under her breath. A black Jeep Cherokee pulled into the parking lot and a couple emerged, young and smiling.

Jamie sighed and shifted in the seat. What if the person Michael was meeting had arrived early? For all she knew the man could have been inside sipping cold beer and watching a sports program on TV before she got there. Maybe she was on a wild-goose chase.

Jamie perked up as a silver SUV pulled into the parking lot. She put the binoculars to her eyes and followed the vehicle. The driver chose a slot near Michael's. Jamie watched him climb from the SUV, but it was hard to get a good look at his face in the dim light. His hair was long and dark and hung in what looked like a ponytail down his back. As he started for the front door of the bar, Michael climbed from his Jaguar. She waited until they were both inside before she grabbed a flashlight and her notepad and climbed from the truck. She hurried toward the parking lot and to the SUV; then, checking to make sure nobody was around, she turned on the flashlight and shone it through the back window. All at once, something hit the glass hard. Jamie's heart gave a lurch, and she cried out as two angry-looking Doberman pinschers pressed their faces against the window, teeth bared, snarling and barking as though they could come through the glass with very little trouble.

Their barks were deafening. She had to get away before they drew attention to her. Jamie quickly copied down the license tag number. She stood and turned.

She was face-to-face with the longhaired man.

"What do you think you're doing?" he said, his voice barely audible among the barking dogs.

Jamie felt a chill race up her spine as she stared into the flat, emotionless eyes of the man before her. They were as black as his long braided hair, as black as the slacks and silk shirt he wore. Was it Nick Santoni? He looked like a mobster. She felt a sudden adrenaline rush.

"I asked you a question," he said.

There was nobody around; the sky seemed to have darkened considerably in the past few minutes. Jamie knew she needed a damn good answer. "What the hell does it look like I'm doing?" she said, trying to make herself heard over the barking dogs. "I'm copying down this license tag number. You got a problem with that?"

"This is my vehicle."

"No way. I know who this SUV belongs to."

From his pocket, the man pulled a key ring, a small black object attached to it. He pressed it, and there was a bleeping sound. Jamie knew he had just unlocked the door. Probably planned to shove her inside and take off, she thought. He wouldn't have to shoot her; the dogs would kill her instantly.

Shit.

The man opened the driver's door and reached inside for a pack of cigarettes. He shouted at the dogs, and they grew quiet.

"I guess this is your vehicle," Jamie said. "I thought it, um, belonged to someone else."

His gaze was unflinching. Jamie knew it would be so easy for him to put a gun to her head and order her in. Max would have no idea what had happened.

"I thought it belonged to the woman my husband is seeing," she said at last. "I don't know much about vehicles, but this looks exactly like hers. Only I don't think she has dogs."

In one easy move, he snatched Jamie's notepad from her hand, tossed it into the front seat, and closed the door. He hit the automatic lock before she could protest.

"Hey, give that back," she said. "It has all my information in it."

He turned and started for the bar. The dogs were barking again. Jamie panicked. The last thing she needed was for Nick Santoni or one of his men to have her notes in his possession. "Wait a minute!" she called out. "You can't just take my notepad!"

He lit a cigarette and blew the smoke in her face. "Report me to the police if you like," he said, "but stay the hell away from my vehicle." He gave her a long silent look before walking away.

"Dammit!" Jamie said aloud. What was she going to do now? She couldn't very well break into the vehicle; the dogs would eat her alive before she reached her notepad. Without wasting another second, she hurried across the street toward Bennett's truck. It wasn't until she was safely inside with the doors locked that she realized she should have at least checked the license tag again and written it down when she got into the truck. She tried to remember the numbers but couldn't. She couldn't risk going back over, even in her truck. If Michael saw her he would suspect something was up.

Jamie met Michael in front of Jeno's at precisely 8:30. He smiled and gave her a hug. "Where'd you park?" he asked.

She pointed. "I'm over there. My truck was giving me trouble, so I borrowed one from a friend."

"A *male* friend?" Michael said, arching both brows. "Should I be jealous?"

"My friend is happily married." Jamie was surprised he could be so jovial after meeting with someone who had probably just threatened him with extortion. "Are you OK?"

"Uh? Oh, yes, it has all been taken care of."

"What do you mean, it has been taken care of?"

"I told him I would go to the police if he came around again."

Jamie just stared. People like Nick Santoni weren't afraid of the police. She was about to say as much when he changed the subject.

"You know, when you're ready to trade in that relic of yours, I might be able to help you find a good deal on a car. I have a friend in the business."

"Fleas loves that old truck," she said.

"Maybe you could buy him a new truck. I hope you're hungry. This restaurant has great food. I'd love to own the place, but Jeno wants to keep it in the family, you know, husband and wife team. He's struggling to make ends meet, poor fellow."

Jamie noted the line that started inside and wound its way out. "It looks packed to me."

"Yes, but his overhead is high, and he has trouble with vandals. This is not a great neighborhood. And to tell you the truth, I don't think he and his wife are good business managers. I could really turn a profit in a place like this."

"I hope you made reservations."

"We don't need them." He offered his arm, and Jamie took it. He led her inside, where the air hung heavy with the smell of garlic, Italian sausage, and baked bread. Waitresses bustled about in peasant-style uniforms, and a short balding man was frantically cleaning the only empty table available.

"Wait right here," Michael said. "I'm going to talk to Jeno." He walked over to the man, leaned forward, and spoke close to his ear. Jeno immediately stopped what he was doing and looked up. He nodded curtly at Michael.

"Jeno is clearing our table now," Michael said, rejoining Jamie.

She felt his hand at the small of her back, felt him prod her forward. "But what about those people waiting in line?"

"I'd ask them to join us, but there's no room."

Jamie could literally feel the heated stares as Jeno seated them and handed her a menu. "Thank you," she said. His gaze met hers. He was not a happy man. He walked away without a word.

Michael touched her hand. "You look so serious; what's wrong?"

Jamie shrugged. Perhaps she was being overly sensitive, but she could almost feel the hostility in the room. "I guess I'm feeling weird for taking the only available table. I wouldn't have minded waiting."

"Jeno was happy to oblige us, Jane. Now, if this were my place, there would be no waiting line. I'd expand."

"I like the quaintness," Jamie said. "It's so cozy." Jamie noticed several windows along one side had been boarded over. "What happened there?"

"Like I said, this isn't a great neighborhood. Two weeks ago, someone broke the windows. Jeno hasn't been able to afford to fix them because something happened to his walk-in freezer. He's closed on Sunday and Monday, so he walked in Tuesday morning to the smell of rotting meat. I'm sure that set him back. I offered to help, but he's a proud man, so what can I do?" He took a sip of water. "But I'll tell you this: For the right price I'd take this off his hands."

Max watched the rearview mirror as they turned off the highway and took a series of dirt roads that led to Santoni's place. It was shortly after nine; the sun had finally disappeared behind the mountains.

Max took the road almost directly across from Santoni's. He cut his headlights, stopped, and waited until Dave climbed from the truck.

"This place is probably crawling with rattlesnakes," Dave muttered. "Did you know diamondback rattlesnakes have been known to reach lengths of eight feet?"

"Good thing you're wearing steel-toed work boots," Max said.

Dave quietly closed the door.

"Are we there yet?" Muffin asked.

"Yeah. Dave is going to lead the way with the flashlight. I figure the less light the better."

"How dangerous is this?" Muffin asked.

"It's far enough away from Santoni's that nobody should venture this way. If we were any farther we wouldn't be within range of the transmitter."

Max followed Dave down a narrow road and parked beside the ramshackle cabin. He climbed from the truck and picked up a box containing the equipment while Dave pulled out his backpack and other gear. He fastened a mask over his face before stepping through the cabin door. Inside, Max lit a lantern, and they went to work.

"You need to get out of here," Dave said, his voice muffled behind the mask. "I can do the rest."

Max looked at him. "I should probably stay with you."

"I'm more concerned about dust mites than I am Santoni or his men showing up. Now get out of here and let a genius do his work."

Rudy Marconi parked his SUV in front of Nick's house. He had made the drive back from Knoxville in record time, even though it would have been difficult for most drivers to concentrate on the winding mountain roads with two Dobermans pacing the back restlessly. But Rudy kept the dogs with him at all times. They were young and still in training, but he was patient where his dogs were concerned.

That's where his patience ended. He was as hot-headed as Nick could be at times, which was why they understood each other so well and why their friendship had lasted for so many years.

Rudy climbed from the SUV and stretched. Dressed

all in black, he was not easy to make out in the dark, and he liked it that way. He was better able to move about the property unseen. As Nick's head lieutenant and most devoted friend and employee, Rudy saw that things ran smoothly, in both Nick's personal and professional life. He reached beneath the seat for his gun and tucked it into the waistband of his slacks.

He went to the back of the SUV and lifted the tailgate. Once he'd leashed the dogs, he grabbed a flashlight and led them to the gate. He muttered a few words into the speaker, and it slid open.

He crossed the highway and followed the path that led through the woods on the other side. The dogs pulled at the leash as though sensing something was about to happen. Some minutes later, he came upon the cabin. He stared for a moment at the window and the faint glow coming from inside.

Rudy reached for his gun. Very quietly he walked toward the cabin. He aimed the gun and kicked open the door.

Dave jumped as the door to the cabin burst open and a man stepped inside. Dave's eyes traveled quickly from the gun to the dogs. He removed his headset.

"Well now," Rudy said, "what have we got here?" He stepped closer. He raised his eyes to Dave, and they locked gazes. Rudy aimed his gun and fired three shots.

Dave dived to the floor as the equipment literally burst all around him. He grabbed a chair leg and raised it chest high in an attempt to defend himself.

Rudy laughed, aimed his gun once more, and fired off another shot. The chair leg splintered. He laughed at Dave, reached down, and unleashed one of the dogs.

Dave cried out as the Doberman sank his teeth into his thigh.

FOURTEEN

It was approaching eleven-thirty when Jamie insisted that Michael take her back to her truck. After she ate her fill at Jeno's—antipasto salad, manicotti stuffed with spinach and ricotta, and a side dish of steamed zucchini—Michael had driven her in his car to a twenty-four-hour bakery for his favorite cannoli and freshly brewed coffee. Afterward, he'd taken her by one of his delis. Jamie had begun to get bored while touring the meat counter.

She began to think the date would never end. Not only did Michael seem intent on dragging out the evening to the next presidential election, but he also was getting clingy. Jamie did not like clingy.

Michael, having reluctantly agreed to drive her back, had just fastened his seat belt when his cell phone rang. He checked the number before he answered. "Yes?" He listened.

Jamie saw the change in him instantly. His face hardened, and his knuckles turned white on the steering wheel.

Finally, he spoke. "I'll deal with it later," he said and hung up.

"Is something wrong?" Jamie asked.

"Nothing I can't handle." He smiled at her, but it didn't reach his eyes. "Anybody ever tell you that you worry too much?" He drove in the direction of Jeno's, where she had parked Bennett's truck. After remaining silent for a moment he placed his hand on hers. "You're awfully quiet. As a matter of fact, you've been quiet most of the night. Did you not have a good time?"

"I guess I've got a lot on my mind," she said. "And I did enjoy myself. Thanks for a nice evening."

"Hey, you took me out, remember?"

Jamie tried not to think of why she had actually invited him out, because that would only remind her how dismally she had failed. "Then you should be thanking me," she said after a moment. And there was something about Michael that left her uneasy. It had all started when he'd jumped to the head of the line at the restaurant.

She did not like people who butted in line. She had hated it as far back as grammar school when Iva-Jean Tidwell used to butt in front of her while playing kick-ball. The teacher had insisted on doing everything, including going to the bathroom, in alphabetical order, but either Iva-Jean had forgotten that the letter *S* for *Swift* came before the letter *T* for *Tidwell* or she was just plain rude. It wasn't until the last year in fourth grade that Jamie had finally stood up to Iva-Jean, and there had been some serious buttkicking as a result. In the end, they had both been suspended from school for three days for fighting.

"I'd like to see you again, Jane," Michael said, interrupting Jamie's thoughts.

"That's nice," Jamie said, even though it wasn't what she wanted to hear. She supposed part of it was her disappointment in not knowing the identity of the person he'd met with earlier and losing her opportunity to get the license tag number. Not only that, she'd lost her notebook that contained valuable information and it was in the possession of someone who might be dangerous to her and Max.

"So what do you say?" Michael asked.

Jamie knew she should be flattered. Michael was handsome and successful, and he drove a nice car. In Beaumont that was reason enough to marry after the first date. It was also to his advantage that he did not have plywood nailed to the front floorboard so that Jamie didn't have to fear falling through the floor each time they hit a bump.

"I like you, Michael," she said, "but I'm very confused right now. I had no right to invite you out while I'm in the middle of divorce proceedings."

"I could be a good friend to you at a time like this."

Jamie suspected he had more than mere friendship on his mind. She knew what the problem was, of course. She had started comparing men to Max, and they always fell short.

The streets were dark and deserted when they passed Jeno's. Michael pulled behind Bennett's truck. "I don't like the idea of your driving all the way back to Sweet Pea this late at night," he said, gazing at her in the semidarkness of the car.

"I'll be fine."

Once again, he reached for her hand. "You know, we don't have to say good night. You could come to my place."

"I can't."

"Because of your husband?"

"My life is complicated."

"Then why don't you allow me to make a few decisions for you?" He smiled and hit the automatic lock.

Max checked his wristwatch again. Midnight. He looked at Fleas. "Your mistress is late." The dog whimpered and sank to the floor. Max walked over to the hound and gazed down at him. Finally, he knelt beside the animal and petted him. "I'm sure she's fine."

The dog sat up, yawned, and stretched.

"What I'd like to know is what we're supposed to do in the meantime." Max picked up some printouts, only to toss them aside. Fleas walked over to him. "What do you say we pop the top on a cold one and find us a wrestling channel?"

The dog thumped his tail against the floor.

Max walked to the refrigerator and opened the door. "First, we need to get some food into us. I don't know about you, but I'm hungry." Fleas joined him at the door and stared.

"You like cold cuts?" Max asked, pulling out a package of sliced ham. He opened the pack, pulled off a piece for himself and one for the dog. Fleas swallowed his in one quick gulp. Next, Max reached for the cheese. "This is what I like about eating at the refrigerator," he told the eager dog. "No dirty dishes to clean up afterward." He held the cheese high and Fleas jumped for it.

"Hello!" Max shouted. "Would you look at that!"

The dog wagged his tail as Max pulled out another slice of cheese.

"Ready?"

Fleas barked.

Max tossed the slice in the air, and Fleas jumped

and caught it in his mouth once more. Max laughed. "I'm going to tell Jamie I taught you how to do that."

Once they'd finished snacking, Max grabbed a beer, twisted off the top, and took a sip. He walked over to the coffee table, picked up the remote control, and turned on the TV. He sat down on the sofa. Fleas climbed up beside him and propped his big head in Max's lap.

"Does your mother allow you on the furniture?" he asked.

Fleas closed his eyes and began to snore.

Jamie wondered what kind of game Michael was playing. The hair on the back of her neck prickled. Not a good sign. She straightened in the seat. "Look, it's late, and I'm tired." And annoyed, she wanted to add. She didn't like this gnawing feeling in the pit of her stomach. "So stop kidding around and let me out of the car."

"You could sleep in my guest room if you preferred. Tomorrow I would prepare you a nice breakfast."

"Michael, I—"

"What if I said I wasn't going to take no for an answer?"

Jamie felt a trickle of unease run down her spine. She looked at him. His expression was hard to read; she could not tell whether he was serious or merely playing a bad joke on her. "Maybe some other time, but not tonight."

"Jane?"

She reached for the handle. "Unlock the car, please." When he didn't make a move to do so, she turned to face him, but she was suddenly blinded by a set of headlights. A patrol car pulled up beside them with two officers inside. Michael pushed a button, and his window slid down silently.

"You folks having a problem?" the officer on the driver's side asked.

Michael smiled. "I'm trying to talk my date into a good night kiss, but she seems reluctant."

The two policemen looked at each other and grinned. Finally, the driver nodded at Jamie. "It's after midnight, lady, and this neighborhood ain't so great. Why don't you give the poor guy a good night kiss so y'all can be on your way?"

Jamie couldn't deny the relief she felt as she gazed across at the smiling patrolmen. "Well, OK." She leaned across the seat and gave Michael a peck of a kiss on his lips. "Satisfied?"

"Oh, man, that's really lame," one of the officers said.

Michael turned to them. "I would probably have gotten a better one if you guys hadn't shown up."

"Would you please let me out of the car now?" Jamie asked.

Michael chuckled but hit the automatic lock. Jamie opened her door. "I'll follow you back to Sweet Pea," he said.

She met his gaze, her own cool. Inside, she was furious. "Good night, Michael," she said, trying to talk around clenched teeth. She already had her keys in her hand by the time she reached Bennett's truck. She unlocked the door, jerked it open, and, in a fit of temper, tossed her purse on the passenger seat as hard as she could. It bounced and landed on the floor. She climbed into the truck, punched the lock down, and started the engine. The policemen waved at her as she pulled away.

Jamie didn't sigh a breath of relief until she turned onto the interstate, but she was conscious of Michael's headlights in her rearview mirror, could see the anxiety in her own eyes each time she glanced into the mirror and caught her own reflection.

It was then that she noted the gas gauge, the needle creeping toward empty. Shit. She'd been in such a hurry earlier to reach Knoxville that she'd completely forgotten to stop for gas. She flinched when the warning light came on. She glanced up just as an exit sign came into view, but there was no time to slow and pull off. Michael was right on her tail.

"Dammit!" she said.

The interstate held very little traffic, with the exception of a few 18-wheelers. The Sweet Pea exit was twenty miles away, and once she took it, there was a lone highway and a series of back roads before she reached the cabin. The gnawing in her stomach worsened.

Michael's Jaguar closed in on her.

Jamie suddenly remembered her cell phone. She automatically reached toward the seat beside her, only to find it empty. She glanced over. Her purse was lying on the floor, flush against the passenger door, where it had fallen when she'd thrown it on the seat too hard.

Jamie felt the truck swerve, and she gripped the steering wheel with both hands. She shot another glance at her purse. She would never be able to reach it. She would have to stop the truck and put it into gear, then lean across the other seat to put her hands on her purse. Bennett's truck was so big she needed both hands on the wheel.

Another exit sign came into view. Jamie read it quickly. There was a Waffle House in one direction and a campground in the other. No gas station. She passed the turnoff, watching the gas needle. Michael's headlights glared at her; he'd obviously turned on his high beams.

It seemed as though she had been driving forever when Jamie spied the tall Exxon sign in the distance. She glanced at the needle, kept driving. When the exit sign appeared she didn't bother to turn on her blinker, she just swerved, and the truck barreled down the ramp. Behind her Michael tapped his horn twice and continued on.

"Have a nice life, creep," Jamie said as she drove toward the gas station. "You just saw the last of me."

Max jumped at the sound of a vehicle pulling in. He glanced at Fleas, who was still snoring. "Some watchdog you are." He got up and started for the door just as Jamie came in.

"Oh, hi," she said, trying to hide her relief at seeing him. "Were you watching TV?"

"Yeah."

She just stood there for a moment, staring at Max and thinking he had never looked so good.

"Is something wrong?" he asked.

"I'm just glad to be home. Well, you know, here."

"Glad to see you, too, Swifty."

Fleas got up and crossed the room. Jamie petted him, and he nudged her with his nose. "Hello, boy," she said.

"Actually . . ." Max paused and glanced at his watch. "I was starting to wonder where you were."

Jamie raised her eyes to his. "I'm sorry I worried you." He didn't know the half of it, she thought.

"I've also been waiting for Dave to call." Max

scratched the back of his head as though he didn't know what to say. "I was, uh, just about to make coffee."

"At this hour?"

"I really should wait up in case Dave calls."

Jamie tried to move, but Fleas had her pinned to her spot. "Excuse me, please." He raised his head and gave her a sad look.

"I think he missed you," Max said. "I tried to entertain him, but, well, I can only sit in the back of the truck with him for so long." He smiled.

"You haven't been feeding him junk food, have you?"

"No, we both had a nice garden salad for dinner."

Jamie regarded the dog. "You ate people food," she accused.

As though realizing he'd been caught, Fleas slid to the floor and covered his face with his paws. Jamie stifled a grin. "I knew it."

She and Max exchanged smiles. She took a deep breath. She knew she had to come clean with him. "I have something to tell you."

"Uh-oh. You didn't wreck Bennett's truck, did you?"

"No, nothing like that," she said quickly. "Uh, Max, I should have told you this earlier, but I was afraid you'd get involved in it and—"

"Involved in what?"

"Well, one of the reasons I've been seeing this Michael person is because—"

"Oh, great, you're about to tell me you like this guy, is that it?"

Jamie shook her head. "No. Michael had something I wanted, Max."

Max's gaze slid from her head to her toes. "Maybe it was the other way around."

"Information, Max," Jamie said. "I thought Michael could give me information on Santoni."

"What?"

"You're not going to like it."

"Tell me anyway."

"I think I may have seen Santoni or one of his men tonight."

Max gaped at her. Finally, he crossed his arms over his wide chest. "You've got some explaining to do, Jamie."

"Promise not to get mad?"

"Start talking."

Jamie told him everything, about meeting Michael, his insinuations that someone from the mob was trying to extort money from him, everything. Max's frown deepened with every word. "I knew Michael was meeting the person tonight, so I made it a point to be nearby. I wanted to get a license tag number. I figured we could get Muffin to run a check on it and find out more. Only the guy caught me writing down his tag number and took my notepad away from me."

"Dammit!" Max yelled the word so loud that Fleas skittered beneath the kitchen table.

"Now look what you've done!" Jamie cried. She started for the table.

"Oh, no, you don't." Max grabbed her wrist and brought her to an abrupt halt. "Fleas is going to be OK, but you're in a shit load of trouble."

"I knew you wouldn't take this well," she said.

"Are you crazy! Why would you take a chance like that?"

"I wanted to help."

"Jesus Christ, I can't believe you'd do something so . . . so insane!" Max released her and began to pace. "God, Jamie, what if something had happened to you?"

"I'm sorry, Max. I know it sounds dumb, but I thought maybe—"

"What did you think, Jamie? That you could take on the mob by yourself?"

"Of course not. I was very careful. But I got a look at the guy, Max. It could have been Santoni himself. He's dark, and he's got long black braided hair. I know it's not much, but it might be something."

"I don't care," Max said, his tone still loud. "It wasn't worth the risk." He raked his hands through his hair, then paused as though just remembering he'd had most of it cut off.

"I was just trying to follow a lead," Jamie said. "I'm sorry that I don't have more for you."

"That is the absolute *least* of my concerns. This is *exactly* why I didn't want you to come with me." He turned away from her.

Jamie stepped closer. "I'm sorry."

Max kept his back to her. "How do you know the guy didn't follow you home?"

"It happened before I met Michael for dinner. I wasn't followed. It would have been easy to spot someone tailing me on these mountain roads. I kept checking." Which was true. She'd watched her rearview mirror closely after she'd gassed up and hit the road again.

"Did it occur to you what it would do to me if something happened to you?"

Jamie touched his shoulder. "Max?"

Without warning, he turned, took her hand in his, and pulled her into his arms.

Stunned, Jamie opened her mouth. Max took it as an invitation and covered it with his own. He pulled her tighter against him so that her body was flush against his. He cupped his palm at the back of her head, holding her in place, as the kiss became even more demanding. He raised back. "Promise me that you won't ever do something like that again."

"I promise."

He buried his face in her neck, inhaled her scent. He held her for a long time. "Dammit, Jamie, I want you so much it hurts."

"I feel the same."

Max raised his head and studied her. "Are you sure?"

She nodded.

"You just bought yourself a whole lot of trouble, Swifty." And he pushed her down the short hall to the bedroom.

FIFTEEN

They fell together on the bed, hard. Too hard. The bed shifted and shook, the pillows flew in every direction, and there was a loud *bam*. To Jamie, it sounded as if the house had caved in. She peeked out from beneath a pillow. The head- and footboards were still in place, but the mattress and box spring were on the floor. The bottom of the bed was still in place, as though suspended. She blinked at the sight. "We broke the bed."

"Ignore it," Max said, pressing his lips to hers.

She kissed him back, even as their bodies inched toward the top of the bed. Jamie's skull touched the wall beneath the headboard. "I'm a little uncomfortable," she said against Max's hot mouth.

He scooted her away from the wall. "Don't think about it. Don't think at all. You know what happens every time you start thinking."

Jamie slipped her arms around his neck, pulling him against her as she opened her mouth under his. It didn't matter that her feet were elevated a good eighteen inches above her head.

Max kissed her deeply, slipping his tongue into her mouth, exploring. She was only vaguely aware that

Fleas was standing beside the bed sniffing her hair. Damned if Max didn't taste better than anything she had ever put in her mouth. Better than cotton candy and buttered popcorn. He broke the kiss, and they both sucked in air.

He looked into Jamie's eyes. "Are you OK?"

"I'm thinking this must be how it feels to be a bat. They hang upside down, too."

"See? You're doing it. You're thinking."

"I'll stop." Jamie put two fingers together, touched her temple, and turned them, as though switching off a button.

Max grinned and reclaimed her mouth. Jamie grasped his head, pulling him even closer. He paused only long enough to run his lips over her face, her closed eyelids, and her throat. She shivered.

Max pressed his lower body against hers. "You make me crazy," he said. "One minute I want to wring your neck, and the next minute I want to make love to you until we both drop."

He was making her crazy, too. Jamie reached for the buttons on his shirt. Her hands shook; her fingers trembled. She fumbled with the buttons, but her fingers were made clumsy by the need building inside of her. She could feel his skin beneath the shirt, solid and warm, but damned if she could get the buttons open. Finally, in a fit of frustration, she yanked the front of the shirt hard. Several buttons popped off and hit the floor.

They paused and watched the buttons bounce. "This was never my favorite shirt," Max said, covering her mouth once more.

Everything seemed to be happening quickly. Jamie was only vaguely aware of Max removing her sandals, caressing her legs. She reached for his belt as he

slipped his hands up her skirt and tugged at her panties. Oh God, she thought as he managed to work them
down past her hips and thighs and calves.

"Damn belt," she muttered, trying to unfasten it.

"You've got sexy legs," Max said, pressing his lips
against her inner thigh.

"Thank you," she managed.

"You're welcome." He looked at her strangely. "Are
you OK?"

"Maybe we could rearrange ourselves. My ears are
pounding. I thought it was desire at first, but I think the
blood is rushing to my brain."

In one move, Max turned her so that her head was
at the foot of the bed and her feet at the top. "That's
better," she said.

Max didn't seem to be listening. He shoved her
skirt high as he kissed his way up her leg. He touched
her lightly with his tongue, and Jamie cried out. She
thought she heard Fleas moan in the background.

Fleas began to howl.

Max raised his head. "Come with me, Fleas," he
said sternly.

The dog followed him from the bedroom and into
the kitchen, where Max pulled out an entire package
of ham. He tossed it, wrapper and all, to the floor before hurrying back into the bedroom, where he closed
the door and locked it.

"Fleas is having a snack," he said, his gaze flitting
over Jamie's half-clad body. He reached for his zipper.
From somewhere far away a phone rang.

Jamie blinked rapidly, trying to clear her head, even
as she reached for him. She barely choked the word,
"Phone!"

Max paused, gave his head a shake, and raced from

the room. He found his cell phone on the table. He pushed a button. "Yeah?" His breathing was ragged.

"Max Holt?"

"Speaking."

"Hello, Max. This is Nicholas Santoni."

Jamie got off the bed, pulled her skirt into place, and walked into the living room, where she found Max on his cell phone.

The look on his face told her something was wrong. "I'm listening," Max said.

Jamie waited, afraid to speak. Fleas got up and ambled toward them. Finally, Max hung up.

"What is it?" Jamie asked, almost afraid to hear the answer.

"That was Nick Santoni. He has Dave."

"What? Oh, my God! Is Dave—"

"He's alive, but he's hurt. One of Santoni's dogs got him."

"Oh, no!" Jamie covered her face.

Max rubbed his brow as he punched several buttons on his phone.

Jamie looked at Max. "How did Santoni know where to reach you?"

"He called from Dave's cell phone. My number is programmed into it. Our phones have a GPS, you know, a global positioning—"

"I know, it allows you to see where the two of you are calling from."

"Yeah, only I can't get a fix on his location, so the system has obviously been disabled." It was obvious Max was trying to remain calm. "I need blankets and clean sheets. Just in case."

"What? Why?"

"Find them, Jamie. Quick!"

She raced to the hall closet and began pulling out bed linen while Max threw on a T-shirt and grabbed his shoes. He stuffed his cell phone into his pocket.

"Please tell me what's going on," Jamie said as he took the bedclothes from her.

"Santoni is going to call me back in ten minutes and tell me where he dumped Dave. I don't know what kind of shape he'll be in, but I may have to put him in the back of the truck and take him to the hospital."

"Let me grab my shoes and purse," Jamie said as Max started for the door.

"You can't come."

Jamie stopped in her tracks.

"Santoni told me to come alone or not at all."

"Max, you can't—"

"I have no choice." He raced out the door without closing it.

"We should call the police!" she cried.

"No! Santoni will kill Dave for sure then."

Jamie watched in silence as Max wrenched open the door to the passenger's side of the truck, dumped the sheets and blankets on the seat, and slammed the door. "I'll call you when I know something."

Jamie watched him speed away. She stood there, staring out into the night, wondering what to do next. What was Santoni up to? she wondered, unable to come up with an answer that didn't scare her to death. Had he already killed Dave? Was he just reeling Max in so he could kill him as well? Her thoughts terrified her.

She closed the door, stood there for a moment, unable to think. She needed to do something. Should *she* call the police? And tell them what? She raked her hands through her hair. What to do, what to do?

Calm down, she told herself. She had to find something to do, something that would give her direction. She was usually pretty good in emergencies; it wasn't until afterward that she went ballistic. Coffee. That was always a good place to start. She needed to be alert when Max called.

She put on the coffee and then shoved a load of laundry into the washing machine just to have something else to do. She hated the washing machine because it was so loud. No telling how old it was. No time to worry about that now. She wondered how long she would have to wait before Max called. She would have to be ready to walk out the door the minute she heard from him. She had to be prepared in case—

She tried to think. She might have to meet Max at the hospital. If Dave was hurt, Max would definitely rush him to the hospital. That's probably when he would call her. She should change clothes. Better yet, a quick shower in case they had to sit with Dave a long time. Jamie hurried into her bedroom, grabbed a pair of slacks, a blouse, and fresh underwear, and raced into the bathroom.

Max's cell phone rang, and he snatched it up. "Hello, Max," Nick said from the other end of the line. His voice was smooth and unhurried, as though he had all the time in the world.

"How is Dave?" Max said.

"He's alive if that's what you're asking. Listen, I hear you're a genius. Let's see how smart you are. I'm going to give you a clue, and it's up to you to figure out where your friend is. If you do, he lives. If you fail, he dies."

"You're going to pay for this, Santoni."

"You have a choice, Holt. You play along or I disconnect our call and you will never find your friend. What's it going to be?"

"What's the clue?"

"Clue number one: Where do dead things go?"

"A funeral home? A morgue?"

Santoni chuckled. "Why are you asking me? I already know the answer. It's up to you to figure it out. Good luck, Max." The line went dead.

Max slammed the ball of his hand against the steering wheel. "Dammit!"

"I heard," Muffin said.

"Dave could be lying in a graveyard," Max said. "How many are there in this damn town?"

"I don't think so," Muffin said. "Did you not listen to the question? Santoni specifically asked where dead *things* go. *Things*, not *people*."

"What things?" Max demanded.

"I don't know; I'm trying to figure it out."

"Oh, shit, I just thought of something."

"What?"

"Jamie could be in danger!"

It wasn't until she'd lathered herself from head to toe that Jamie realized she'd forgotten to bring in her cell phone. Oh, crap. She quickly rinsed, wrapped a towel around her, and hurried into the living room for her purse. The phone wasn't there. Where had she left it? She began to search. Had she left the thing in the truck?

She dressed in record time. The telephone rang in the kitchen and Jamie raced for it. Max was on the other end.

"Jamie, get out of the house!"

Her heart lurched. "What? What's wrong? Have you got Dave?"

"No, I'm on my way. Listen, the global positioning system on my phone works. Santoni knows where I was when I received both calls. You have to leave immediately."

"But—"

"Find a safe place where you'll be surrounded by people. Wal-Mart. Just get the hell out and turn on your damn cell phone for once," he added.

Jamie slammed down the phone. "Come on, Fleas!" she cried. "Let's go." She reached for her purse and fumbled through it for Dave's keys. They weren't there. She checked the counter. Holy crap, they were nowhere to be found. She upended her purse on the kitchen table and raked through the mess, her hands shaking so badly they were almost of no use. Oh, if only she would take five minutes out of her life to straighten her purse. She stuffed everything back in.

Where could she have left them? She looked beneath a stack of newspapers, behind an artificial plant. She stepped on Fleas's paw, and he let out a yelp.

"I'm sorry!" she cried. "Where did I put the damn keys? Where is my cell phone?" The dog took a step back as though he feared he'd done something wrong. "I'm sorry, boy," she said, patting his bony head. "I'm not mad at you, I'm just losing my mind." She checked her bedroom and came out empty-handed. "I don't believe this," she said, feeling as though she had literally lost her mind.

OK, think, she told herself. Maybe she'd accidentally left them in Dave's truck. Or maybe they'd fallen out of her purse on the way in. Anything was possible in her current state of mind.

She raced to the door and jerked it open.

Michael Juliano was standing on the other side.

Max pulled into the parking lot of a convenience store. He punched several buttons on his phone.

"Why are we stopping?" Muffin asked.

"I have to disable the GPS on this phone. I don't want Santoni looking over my shoulder. Besides, I don't know which way to go," he said. "I don't want to end up driving away from Dave. I have to think."

"OK, back to dead things," Muffin said. "It could mean anything. We automatically think it's the end of a life. Dead people, dead animals."

"It could be an inanimate object," Max said. "Something that is of no use anymore. A dead cigarette butt, for example. Or old newspapers or trash. Dave could be lying in a landfill or recycling area."

"There's a landfill on the edge of town, also has bins for recyclables on the premises," Muffin said. "I can get you the address, but I can't give you directions because, well, because I'm not equipped for it in this rust bucket."

"I'll check inside." Max got out of the truck and hurried into the convenience store.

"I got the directions," Max said when he returned, "but I have a funny feeling about this. Know what I think?"

"It's too easy. You're being set up."

"Right. I drive up to the landfill, it's dark and probably deserted, and Santoni or one of his thugs will be waiting for me. I'm a perfect target. That's not where Dave is being held."

"Where then?"

"I want you to check all listings under Marconi. Maybe something is in his name."

"I've already done that, remember? All I found was a few bars in Knoxville."

"OK, try the other guy's name. Bennetti," he added. "He may have disappeared, but it wouldn't surprise me if Santoni was using his name. He seems to do that a lot."

"OK, checking," Muffin said. She was back in a matter of seconds. "Uh-oh. You're not going to like it."

"Tell me anyway."

"I typed in the name Bennetti, but nothing came up. Then I typed in the first three letters of Bennetti's name and it pulled up several Bennetts. I acted on a hunch—"

"Computers don't have hunches, Muffin, remember?"

"And I did a crosscheck on Bennett's home number. Not only did I get the number for the landfill, I got several business numbers, including the number for a place called Last Chance Auto Salvage and—"

Max went perfectly still. "Bennett Electric."

"Right. Tom Bennett owns all three. Peter Thomas Bennetti is Tom Bennett, your current employer."

Max sat there for a moment, his jaw working. "That means Santoni knew Dave and I were planning to tap into Rawlins's phone line because Bennett would have told him. Santoni also knew exactly when we tapped into his phone line.

"Santoni has been playing me all along. He put everything into motion before I left Beaumont. He even had time to falsify records so that it looked like Tom Bennett was ripe for acquisition." Max stared out the window. "Jesus Christ, I'm not believing this. How did he move so quickly? How could he have set me up in that length of time?"

"He's good, Max. Damn good."

"I don't get it," Max said. "Why didn't someone just

kill Dave and me while we were out there tapping into Santoni's line? Instead, they waited."

"I'm stumped, Max. Santoni is playing a game, and he's not letting anyone in on the rules."

Max sighed. "Damn, I'm going to have to go back in that store and ask for directions."

"It's called Last Chance Auto Salvage," Muffin said as though reading his mind.

Max opened the car door, then paused. "If you think about it, a car that no longer works is as good as dead."

"Max, you don't want to know what I'm thinking. If Last Chance Auto Salvage has a crusher—"

"It's the perfect way to dispose of a body," Max said.

Jamie blinked at the man who called himself Michael Juliano. It was as though a veil had been lifted from her eyes. She had been looking for a mobster, a thug, but Nick Santoni had come in a handsome package and was as polished and persuasive as a politician.

He held up her wallet. "It must've fallen from your purse. I tried to follow you, but I got lost on these damn mountain roads. I was about to give up before I spotted this road. I took a chance and drove down despite all the *No Trespassing* signs. Good thing I did, because I spotted that truck immediately."

Jamie took the wallet but didn't say anything. How had he managed to slip it from her purse without her noticing?

"Are you OK?" he asked. "You look upset." He frowned. "You're not having trouble with your husband, are you?"

Jamie made a split-second decision to play along. "It's a long story, Michael. Listen, I was just on my way out." But he already knew that, she reminded herself. He would suspect that Max had called and told her to get out. The only thing he didn't seem to know at the minute was that she did know his true identity.

"At this hour?" He looked surprised.

"Yes. I need to go to the, um, store. For coffee," she added quickly. "I can't stand to wake up and not have coffee in the house." She realized she was talking too fast, probably not making any sense.

"Why don't I take you? I don't like the idea of your driving on these roads at night, and it's foggy out."

"No, no, I'll be fine," she said, hurrying toward Dave's truck. She noticed the fog. It had come in quickly. "Besides, I might be a while. Sometimes when I can't sleep I drive to Wal-Mart and just spend hours looking around, you know?" She opened the door to the truck. "I seem to have misplaced the keys." She looked, but there was no sight of the keys or her cell phone. She checked the ground.

"What do they look like?" Michael asked.

"They're attached to a leather strip." It suddenly hit her. He hadn't slipped her wallet from her purse. He had taken her wallet, her cell phone, and the keys to Bennett's truck. He had come into the cabin while she was showering. She had not heard the buzzer because of the loud washing machine and because she had been in the bathroom with the water running. And because she'd been so anxious she had been talking to Fleas nonstop as she had bathed. Or maybe Nick had somehow disabled the alarm.

She turned to Michael. "Listen, I appreciate your dropping off my wallet, but I need to search the cabin for my keys. . . ." She paused as he reached into his pocket and pulled out the leather strip that held both the key to the cabin and the one to Bennett's truck.

Their gazes locked. "Don't make it hard on yourself, Jamie. I don't want to shove you into my car at gunpoint. Just get in."

She stood frozen to her spot. She had not realized Fleas had followed her out, but he nudged her with his wet nose.

"Tell you what. I'll be a nice guy and let you bring the mutt. You know I like him. Shall we?" He put his hand under her elbow and prodded her toward the Jaguar. Jamie did as she was told. He paused long enough to let Fleas get into the back, and then opened the passenger door for Jamie. She hesitated.

"Get in, Jamie."

She got in. She waited until he'd climbed in on the other side before she spoke. "What do you want with me, Nick?" she asked.

He smiled and started the car. "So you've finally figured it out. I simply want to talk to you, that's all."

"Why can't we talk here?"

"I don't want any interruptions from your boyfriend, Mr. Holt."

"Max is not my boyfriend."

"So you say." He started the car and pulled from the driveway.

Jamie tried to remain calm even as the fear began to build inside her with every heartbeat. "Where are you taking me?"

"Some place where we can talk in private. My home." He hit the automatic lock.

She grimaced in the dark. She was as good as dead.

SIXTEEN

"What have we got?" Muffin asked once Max had scoped out the property surrounding Last Chance Auto Salvage.

Max began pulling out tools from behind the seat and stuffing them into a backpack. "High-voltage fencing, razor wire, top-of-the line security system, and a badass pit bull."

"Hmm. I didn't realize it was so difficult to find good used automotive parts."

Max slipped on the backpack. "Yeah, well, I have a feeling there's a lot more going on in this place than buying and selling auto parts."

"How far away did you park?" Muffin asked.

"Quarter of a mile. Hard to see clearly because of the fog. I don't think anyone is home, but I don't want to risk Nick or his buddies seeing the truck."

"I can probably take care of the dog."

"Probably?" Max said. "You don't sound too certain, and this dog looks mean as hell."

"I can produce an ultrasonic sound of up to two miles, Max, but you realize I'm only going to be able to distract the animal for a matter of minutes. Once he gets accustomed to the sound he'll go after you. I hope you have pepper spray."

"Yeah."

"You'll have to radio me when you're going in and out. I'll hit him with everything I've got, but I can't make any promises."

"I'll be in touch." Max turned on his flashlight and took off on foot. The light seemed to make the fog worse instead of better. The dog was waiting for him when he arrived back at the salvage yard. He barked and snarled as Max donned thick rubber gloves and cut the fence with special wire cutters that would prevent him from suffering a bad shock.

He picked up his cell phone, punched a button, and radioed Muffin. "I'm ready to go in."

"Are you familiar with the security system?"

"Yeah. It's above standard but nothing I can't handle."

"You may not have more than two or three minutes, Max. Here we go."

Max knew the minute Muffin turned on the high-frequency noise-producing sound, not because he heard it but because the dog suddenly reared his head back and shook it hard. Max peeled back a portion of the fence as the dog seemed to forget everything else for the moment except the noise. He yelped and raced away.

Max very carefully slipped past the fence and ran toward the building. He pulled off one glove, reaching into his shirt pocket where he'd tucked a thin but high-powered flashlight. He held it between his teeth and opened the box. Grabbing a screwdriver from his pocket, he shut down the alarm system within seconds.

"I'm in," Max said, once he'd gone through the heavy metal door.

"I see you haven't lost your touch," Muffin said. "I just turned off the noise."

Max crossed a room with a counter and several hard plastic chairs. "I'm in the reception area." He continued down a hall, past a small kitchen, toward the back of the building. He stopped short when he spied a crisscross of blue lights in front of a set of heavy metal doors.

"Aw, shit!"

"What is it?" Muffin asked.

"Lasers."

"You know what that means," Muffin said.

"Yeah. I'm in the right place."

Jamie was quiet as Nick turned on yet another mountain road that seemed to lead farther away from civilization. The fog had worsened, making the ride hazardous, but Nick didn't seem to notice. Jamie gripped the armrest with each twist and turn. Anxiety gnawed at her stomach as she wondered what his plans were.

"You're awfully quiet, Jamie."

"Sorry if I don't feel like playing twenty questions, but my mind is preoccupied."

He chuckled softly. "I know the feeling. I haven't been able to sleep lately. Can't seem to shut off my brain. Have you ever felt like time was running out?"

What a question, she thought. She eyed the locked door. "I think I can relate."

He reached over and took her hand. "I'm sorry if I've frightened you. All I want is for us to talk." He slowed the car and pulled up to a wrought-iron gate. Attached to it was a massive brick wall that Jamie had seen in a photo only hours before.

Nick pushed a button, and his window whispered down. He spoke into a tiny speaker, and the gate immediately slid open. He drove through it, and Jamie watched it close behind them.

"Now, how about that cup of coffee?" Nick said once he'd cut the engine and parked.

Jamie merely shrugged. She remained quiet as he helped her from the car and opened the back door for Fleas. The dog jumped out and shook hard, his ears flapping back and forth.

Jamie glanced around as if impressed by what she saw beneath the tall lighted poles when what she was looking for was an escape route. She noted the outbuildings, heard dogs barking in the distance. The place was probably heavily guarded. She suspected the brick wall encompassed the entire area.

There was no way out.

A man dressed in black emerged from the shadows, two Doberman pinschers beside him, each straining on the leash. Jamie jumped. She recognized him immediately, the man who'd caught her writing down his license tag number, the man who'd taken her notepad. That meant he and Nick knew everything she and Max had been able to find out since arriving in Sweet Pea.

Fleas growled. Nick reached for his collar. "Get the dogs out of here, Rudy."

The man gave Jamie a slow easy smile and walked away, disappearing once more into the dark.

Nick continued holding Fleas's collar. "It's OK, boy," he said. "Don't worry about the dogs, Jamie. I have to keep them on the property due to prowlers."

Yeah, right, she thought.

Together they managed to get Fleas inside the cabin. Jamie was surprised at the dog's aggressiveness; he obviously sensed something wasn't right. She kept petting him, offering him reassurance.

The cabin was spacious and definitely masculine. There wasn't a woman's touch anywhere, not even in the fully equipped kitchen, with its black lacquered cabinets and stainless-steel appliances. A red, black, and yellow abstract painting gave off the only color in the room.

If she lived she would be able to tell her friends she had gotten to see the inside of a killer's house.

Nick walked to the refrigerator. "I offered you coffee, but I have wine if you prefer it."

She didn't need to get drunk; she needed to get out. "Actually, a glass of water would be fine."

"Certainly." He grabbed two glasses from one of the cabinets and filled them from the refrigerator dispenser. He handed her one of the glasses before reaching for a box of dog biscuits. He offered it to Fleas, but the dog backed away. "Suit yourself, boy."

"He was obviously spooked by your dogs," Jamie said, thinking Fleas was probably smarter than her for not accepting from a man like Nick anything that would be ingested. "He'll be OK in a minute or two."

"Let's sit in the living room."

Like she had a choice. Jamie took the glass and followed him once more, the hound on her heels. She sat down on the leather sofa and was surprised when Nick took the chair next to it instead of sitting beside her.

He looked at her. "You're surprised I'm not already all over you, aren't you, Jamie?" he asked as though reading her mind.

"Well, I—"

"That's why you've felt safe with me all this time. I'm different from most men because I don't try to paw you and get you into my bed. I'm certain a woman with your looks is accustomed to men making unwanted advances."

Jamie remained quiet and took a sip of her water. She would not let him know how nervous she was.

"It's because I respect you. You're different from other women. I'm sorry I had to lie to you in order to make your acquaintance, but there was no other way." He paused. "But then, you lied to me as well. You were willing to use a man you thought had just lost his sister in order to get information from him."

"You said you wanted to talk."

"I want you to know the truth about me, Jamie. I want you to know who and what I am. I'm hoping you'll somehow find a way to understand."

Jamie set her glass down on the table. "I'm supposed to understand what you do for a living, Nick?" she said in disbelief. "Are you serious?"

"If I did half of what I was reputed to have done I wouldn't have time to sleep."

"Did you kill Dave Anderson?"

"Absolutely not. I've never even met the man. He was trespassing on my property, and one of the dogs bit him."

"What about Harlan?"

He shook his head, a sad smile touching his lips. "I don't know why people assume I killed him. I can assure you I did not. Harlan and I were business associates, and we had a very lucrative working relationship."

"You were blackmailing him, extorting money."

"On the contrary, I was protecting him."

"From whom?"

Nick chuckled. "Mostly from himself, dear. Harlan Rawlins had an appetite for women, and he was known to get carried away."

"Did he hurt someone?"

"Even men of God make mistakes. And, yes, he did hurt a woman. Very badly, I might add. He called me in the middle of the night, and I took care of it."

"How?"

"I saw to it the woman had immediate medical attention, that she was paid very well for her, um, trouble, and that Harlan's name never came up."

"Why would you protect a man like that?"

Nick arched one brow. "Why?" He stood. "Jamie, I'm a businessman and a realist. Harlan was a human being like the rest of us. He used poor judgment. But look at what he accomplished. I am the one who insisted he hire a bodyguard, not only out of concern for crazy religious fanatics who might take offense over his teachings but to make certain Harlan remained stable. The man had a lot of emotional problems, Jamie. And I supplied more protection by having security personnel travel with the ministry. Harlan never had to worry about someone torching one of his tents. I even hired his administrative assistant and public relations person to give Harlan a little more polish. He was just a country preacher before I took over. I made him a star in just a few years. Was I wrong to collect a salary?"

Jamie didn't know how to respond. Nick Santoni had just painted a very appealing picture of himself. "Did you hire a hit man to take out Max?"

Nick laughed out loud. Jamie shot him a dark look. "I'm sorry, Jamie, but if you knew how that sounded. People like me don't hire hit men, they hire good attorneys."

"What do you mean?"

"Meaning, Harlan and I put together a large and legitimate bid on Max Holt's TV network, but it was ignored, and their dealings with me weren't fair or legal. I was planning to sue Max. Why would I pay someone to kill a man when I can take that man to court and win a considerable amount of money?"

He was good, Jamie thought, but then Nick Santoni had obviously practiced. "Who do you think killed Harlan?"

"I think his wife did it. Harlan was cruel to her."

"What do you want with me, Nick?"

"I like you, Jamie. I'd like for us to have the opportunity to get to know one another. I'm leaving Sweet Pea in a matter of hours. I've chartered a plane, and I want you on it with me."

"Am I being held against my will?"

He looked amused. "That wall is there to keep people out, not in. You are free to walk out that door anytime you like. At the same time, you must realize you're at risk."

"What do you mean?"

"The police are looking for Harlan's killer. You were the last person to see him alive. I can protect you should the police somehow learn of your visit, should they find out who and where you are." He paused. "I can give you the kind of life you've never dreamed of."

Jamie just stared at him. Why did he want her with him? He wasn't in love with her. He hadn't had time to fall in love with her.

"Jamie?"

She looked at him. "I can't do that, Nick."

His jaw stiffened, and his eyes became dark. "Because of Holt?" he asked, his words clipped and precise.

Jamie saw the change come over him. It had been so subtle in the car, but the Nick Santoni she was looking at now was the man Max had tried to warn her about.

"It's a known fact, Jamie: You're Max Holt's girl."

"His girl?"

"His woman. But I want you. I can offer you the kind of life you always wanted."

Jamie stared openly.

"I have made it my business to find out about you. I know what you desire the most," he added in the gentlest of voices. "I will make all your dreams come true, Jamie."

Jamie was almost in awe. Nick Santoni was good. Damn good. He knew how to draw people in, seduce them, practically hypnotize them. She could see how many women could be lured in by him.

"You don't have to carry the world on your shoulders anymore, Jamie. I'll be there."

"What about Max?"

"You hold his life in your hands. If you go with me, I will see that nothing happens to him. If you don't, all bets are off."

Max studied the wires carefully. Santoni had spent a ton of money on his inside security system, and although it was state-of-the-art and the best available on the current market, Max knew the system well because he'd used it as a baseline to design his own. The only difference: Max's design would not be available to the consumer for another couple of years. He did not feel at all guilty when he was able to disarm Nick's in less than a minute. The blue laser lights disappeared, and Max pushed through the double doors. He passed through an office with several computers. He'd definitely want to take a look at them, but he had other things on his mind, including finding Dave Anderson. Max walked into the next room, flipped on a light switch, and gave a low whistle when he found himself staring at an entire arsenal of weapons.

"Well, well," he said.

"What's going on, Max?" Muffin asked.

"I found Santoni's playroom." Max looked about the room. He spied a wooden box the size of a coffin. Taking a deep breath, he walked over to it and carefully lifted the lid. Dave Anderson lay inside, wrists and ankles tied together. He opened his eyes.

"I'm dying, Max. They put me in here so I could bleed to death. I'm pretty sure the dog hit a major artery, because I can feel my lifeblood draining from me."

"Where did the dog bite you?"

"Inside my right thigh. Nick's thug called him off because he obviously didn't want to kill me right away. He wanted me to die slowly. I'm surprised I'm still alive."

Max saw blood on Dave's pants. "Lay still, Dave." He pulled out a pocketknife and made a slit in Dave's slacks. He pulled back the material. "It's a nasty bite," he said. "You need medical attention, but you're not likely to die."

"You're just saying that."

"I'm telling you the truth."

Max punched a button on his cell phone. "Muffin, I found Dave. I need to get him to the hospital."

"I'm going to lose my leg, aren't I?" Dave said.

"You're not going to lose your leg, for Pete's sake," Max said. "Now be still so I can cut your bindings." He sawed through them with his knife and pulled Dave up so the man was sitting.

"I'm light-headed from losing half my blood," Dave said.

"Do you think you can walk?"

"*Walk?*" he repeated as if the thought were merely ludicrous. "Are you kidding?"

"I'll help you," Max said. "Muffin, can you get us out of here?"

"I can try," she said.

Jamie sat on the bed in Nick's guest room and pondered her next move. She'd been sent there to rest. And to make up her mind as to what she was going to do with regard to Nick's invitation to leave with him.

Invitation, her foot!

Fleas had his head propped on her knees. She could tell he was as anxious as she was. And she had thought him dumb. She leaned over and pressed her cheek against the top of his head.

"If only I could talk to Max," she whispered so softly that it was little more than a thought. She glanced around. It did not surprise her to find there was no telephone in the room. She desperately needed to talk to Max, warn him. Although Nick had promised no harm would come to Max, she knew Nick's men would shoot him if he came near the property.

Jamie realized she wasn't thinking straight. She had not slept in hours. She felt wired. Too much had happened in such a short period of time; her mind and body were still trying to adjust. "Lie down, boy," she told Fleas. He did as he was told, propping his head on his paws. He looked sad.

Jamie suddenly realized she was shivering. She hadn't quite grown accustomed to the cool mountain nights, and Nick obviously kept the air-conditioning low. She noted the quilt on a nearby chair and draped it across her shoulders. Her eyes burned. Finally, unable to fight the exhaustion, she curled up on the bed. Fleas scooted closer, as if he felt by doing so he could protect her. Jamie stroked his ear. If only she could close her eyes for five minutes. Just five minutes.

Max pulled up to the emergency entrance. "Stay put," he told Dave. "I'm going to get a wheelchair."

"Just ask for a body bag," Dave said.

Max ignored him and climbed from the car. He hurried inside.

"Oh, damn," Dave muttered.

"What is it *now*?" Muffin asked.

"I hope they take me right in. I don't like being around sick people. All those germs."

"You know what I don't understand?" Muffin said. "I don't understand why Max puts up with you. You're the biggest pain in the ass I've ever met. Now why don't you stop sniveling and cut us all a little slack?"

Max and an orderly were back in a matter of minutes. Max opened the passenger door. "Dave, this is Carter. He's going to help you inside, and the doctor is going to take you right in."

"Thank God. Where are you going?"

"I need to call Jamie."

Dave nodded and allowed them to help him into the wheelchair. "Don't worry about me, Max," he said, offering a tight smile. "I'll be all right. Just make sure Jamie's OK."

Max arched one brow but climbed into his car. Muffin was waiting.

"I've already tried Jamie twice," she said. "She's not answering her cell phone."

"Dammit," Max said. "She probably forgot to turn it on again."

"You probably scared the crap out of her when you called and told her to leave the cabin."

"OK, try paging her at Wal-Mart." He chuckled. "If she doesn't answer, tell them to try the menswear section. She might be looking for a new victim."

"I'm going to pretend you didn't say that."

Max waited.

"She didn't respond to the page," Muffin said when she came back on. "They paged her twice. I told them it was an emergency, so they're still trying. I'm on hold."

Max rubbed his hand across his forehead. "Answer the page, Jamie," he muttered under his breath.

"Still nothing," Muffin said.

He sighed. "Tell me this isn't happening."

Max drove on. "Damned if it's not one thing after another." He waited. "Muffin?"

"She's not in the store, Max."

"Shit! Where would she be at this hour of the morning?"

"Maybe she met her friend Michael. I know she likes talking to him."

Max pondered it. "I can't believe she'd go off with him at this hour."

"Maybe Jamie was afraid to be alone."

He was silent for a moment. "What do you know about this guy? This Michael?"

"They met at Wal-Mart, had breakfast a couple of times, and then went to dinner. I know he drives a Jaguar because Jamie said it was really nice."

"Wonder where they went for breakfast?"

"I don't know the name of it, but it's not far from Wal-Mart."

"Shit." Max pulled from the hospital parking lot. He made good time for a truck that was on its last legs.

He drove until he spotted the Wal-Mart store. At the light he took a right. He pulled into the first restaurant he saw. "Wish me luck," he told Muffin as he climbed from the truck.

A blast of cold air hit him as he stepped inside the restaurant. The lights were blinding, and the place smelled of coffee and bacon grease. A tired-looking waitress handed him a menu.

"Long night?" he asked her.

"Yeah. I'm filling in for somebody. Not used to these late hours. You want coffee?"

"Please."

She returned a moment later with a steaming mug and set it before him. "What'll it be?"

"This is fine."

"You're either out late or up early," she said.

"A little of both, I guess," Max told her. "Actually, I'm looking for somebody."

"Yeah?"

"I'll bet you could help me. I'll bet you know most of the customers who come in here."

She shrugged. "I work the breakfast and lunch shift."

"I'm curious about a guy named Michael. He drives a Jaguar. You know him?"

"Depends on who's asking and why."

Max raised his hand, exposing a $100 bill. "I think he's seeing my girlfriend. It's over between us, but I'd like to know. Pride and all that."

"Pretty blonde?"

"Yep."

The waitress reached for the money. "Sorry, I don't get involved in Mr. Juliano's personal affairs." She walked away.

Max sat there for a moment, his expression frozen in place. He stood slowly and made for the door. Muffin was waiting when he climbed inside the truck.

"That was quick. What'd you find out?"

Max opened his mouth to speak, but the words didn't come. He cleared his throat. "It's bad," he whispered.

"Max? What is it?"

"I know why Nick Santoni has been playing games with us. He wanted Jamie."

"Max, what are you talking about?"

"Nick Santoni has Jamie."

SEVENTEEN

Jamie opened her eyes and discovered she'd slept almost three hours. She bolted upright, blinked several times, tried to clear her head. She got up and walked into the adjoining bathroom. She almost didn't recognize the woman in the mirror. Fatigue had painted dark shadows beneath her eyes, and she looked pale.

"If I live through this I'm going to have to start taking better care of myself," she muttered.

She turned on the cold water and splashed it on her face, but when she reached for a towel, she found none. Her face dripping, she opened the drawer beside the sink. It contained unopened bottles of shampoos, lotions, soaps, and toothbrushes. For overnight guests, she thought. Odd that a man like Nick Santoni would think of something like that. No, it probably was the work of a housekeeper.

Jamie opened the cabinet door and reached for a towel. Beneath the stack she saw a slender white telephone. She pulled it out, not at all surprised to find it there.

Nick had known she would find it. He knew she would try to contact Max. Whether he knew she would have suspected as much she could only guess. The only thing Jamie knew for certain was that she had to protect Max at any cost.

Any cost.

The phone jack was easy to find. Jamie plugged in the telephone and dialed Max's cell number. He answered on the first ring.

"It's me," she said.

"Jesus Christ, Jamie, where are you?"

Had Jamie not been listening for the soft click on her end, she would not have heard it. Nor did she miss the relief in Max's voice. "I can't give you that information, Max. I only have a second to talk."

"Jamie, listen to me. Michael Juliano is Nick Santoni."

"I know."

"Is he there?"

"Not at the moment. Max, I've decided to go away with Nick. He wants to make a fresh start."

Silence. Finally, he spoke. "I see."

"I knew you would."

"Are you sure about this, Jamie? Do you know what you're getting into?"

"Nick wants to make a fresh start."

"So what the hell do you want from me?" Max's voice was terse.

"I'm asking you to back off. Give Nick and me this chance."

"You want me to just forget everything, walk away, and let you screw up your life? The man almost killed us. Dammit, Jamie, I thought you were smarter than this."

"I'm not screwing up my life, and even if I were, it's none of your business."

"What about us?"

"There is no us, Max. How many times have I told

you? Back off." Jamie hung up the telephone and returned it to Nick's hiding place. She was pretty certain
Max was with the program; he was good at reading
between the lines.

Someone knocked at the door. She stood and crossed
the room. She found one of Santoni's men holding a
tray of food and a small pot of coffee.

"Mr. Santoni thought you might want a snack."

Jamie stepped back, and he carried the tray inside
and placed it on a round table beside the chair. "Thank
you," she said. "Is the fog lifting?"

He did little more than look her way. "Mr. Santoni
will be in shortly," was all he said before he closed the
door behind him.

Jamie ignored the small wedge of Brie and fruit and
delicate finger sandwiches, instead reaching for the
silver coffee server. The china was delicate—white,
edged with gold. A linen napkin with Nick's initials
covered a small basket of croissants with various jams
and jellies.

Fleas thumped his tail, an expectant look on his
face.

"OK, come here." Jamie fed him three finger sandwiches before she turned to her coffee. She barely
had time to finish her cup before someone knocked.
"Come in."

Nick Santoni stepped in and closed the door behind
him. Fleas walked closer to Jamie and propped his
chin on her lap. Nick chuckled. "I'm glad you were
able to rest." He glanced at the tray. "Did you eat or did
you feed it to the dog?"

"I could use a cigarette," Jamie said, ignoring his
question.

Nick pulled open the drawer in the bedside table

and produced her brand of cigarettes, a gold lighter, and a crystal ashtray, which he set on the table. He opened the cigarette pack, offered her one, and lit it for her. Fleas's eyes followed his every move.

"It's OK, boy," Nick said, although he didn't reach out and pet Fleas as he usually did.

"You obviously planned for my visit," Jamie said, inhaling the smoke. It burned her lungs, and she realized she was going to have to either get used to smoking again or give it up altogether. Neither sounded particularly appealing at the moment.

Nick sat on the edge of the bed. "Yes. And for longer than you think. At first all I could think of was getting even with Holt. Until I found out about you." He glanced at the pack of cigarettes. "I know you sometimes smoke when you're upset, although you gave it up some time ago."

"You know a lot about me, Nick."

"Yes."

"Why did you check me out?"

"I was curious. I figured you must be pretty special to capture Maximillian Holt's attention."

"I'm hardly the first woman Max has taken a second look at."

"True. But you've certainly managed to hold his interest, haven't you?"

Jamie met his gaze, a question in her eyes. "You find me appealing because Max likes me?"

He smiled. "Perhaps in the beginning. Now that I know you personally I can't help but like you."

Jamie watched as he reached for the coffee server, refilled her cup, and added the amount of cream and sugar she liked. Then, with hands that appeared too large to grip the dainty handle, he offered it to her.

She sipped as he watched.

"I need to know your decision," he said quietly.

She returned the cup to its saucer. "I'm coming with you."

"Do I sense regret in your voice?"

Jamie could feel his eyes boring into her. She raised her head and met his gaze. "Don't push it, Nick."

He stood. "We leave at dawn. The fog should have lifted by then."

"What do you think?" Muffin asked Max.

"I think Nick knows his eggs are fried, as Jamie would say."

"Could you put that into words that a brilliant computer like me can understand?"

"His time is up. He's planning to leave the country. He'll probably use the local airstrip to get out of Sweet Pea."

"I just heard back from Jersey. Leo Santoni was one pissed mother when I woke him."

"Not my problem. What'd he say?"

"He'll cooperate."

Max nodded. "I guess we're going to have to call in the big guns. Call Quantico and find out where Helms is. Tell him I'll need backup. He'll probably have to send someone local. Also, tell him if he wants Santoni, we play by my rules."

"You're such a hard-ass."

"Where Jamie's life is concerned you're damn right."

Rudy Marconi was waiting for Nick when the man stepped out of the bedroom. They didn't speak until they were inside Nick's office on the other side of the house.

"We couldn't trace the call," Rudy said, "and Holt hasn't returned to the cabin. We've got the place surrounded, but there has been no sign of him."

Nick began packing his briefcase. "I want him found, Rudy."

"I've never let you down before."

Nick regarded him. "Don't let this be the first. I won't rest until Holt is dead." He closed the briefcase. "Oh, that damn bloodhound has to go, too."

Two hours later Jamie followed Nick outside and into a waiting Hummer. The man called Rudy loaded Fleas and several pieces of luggage into the back.

"Good thing I'm traveling light," Jamie muttered, noting her dog barely had room to move around.

Nick chuckled. "You'll have plenty of time for shopping later."

Rudy and a man named Victor whom Jamie had seen scouring the premises climbed into the front seat. Nick opened the door to the backseat so Jamie could get in. He slid in beside her. They pulled up to the gate, Rudy said a few words, and it slid open for them.

"It'll take us about thirty minutes to reach the landing strip," Rudy said.

"Sounds good." Nick put his hand on Jamie's lap. She didn't move it. Fleas propped his head on her shoulder as though offering support. He obviously sensed a problem; he hadn't left her side all night. "You OK, boy?"

He nudged her chin in response.

"Lie down," Jamie said, not wanting the dog to do anything that might annoy Nick. Fleas sank to the floor.

"He seems agitated," Nick said, patting Jamie's knee. "I wonder if he misses the truck?"

"I think it has more to do with the big guns your boys are carrying."

Nick didn't reply.

Jamie saw they were going down the mountain. They had almost reached the foothills when they came upon a number of cars stopped in front of them. Ahead they saw blue lights flashing.

Nick frowned. "What's going on up there?"

"Looks like some kind of accident," Rudy said.

Victor opened his door. "I'll check it out." He climbed out and hurried down the road.

"Where are we going?" Jamie asked.

"To an airstrip."

"And after that?"

Nick smiled. "It's a surprise. You'll love it."

Jamie thought of her newspaper and the little town in which she'd been born and raised. She wondered if she would ever see Vera again. "Will I be able to write to my friends?" she asked.

"Darling, we will make new friends. You'll be so busy you won't have time to think of your old ones."

"Really?" she said, trying not to sound sarcastic. "Well, you just saved me a shit load of money on Christmas cards and postage."

Victor returned. "It's bad, Boss. Three cars involved, several people hurt. The cops are waiting for an ambulance."

"Did they give any indication how long it would take?"

"Said they were trying to hurry things along, but there's glass everywhere."

Nick leaned his head against the seat. "Call the pilot and inform him we're going to be late."

In the distance, Jamie could hear the wail of a siren. She leaned against the door and closed her eyes, but her thoughts never stilled. Her door was locked. She assumed there was a master lock by the driver's side, which meant she was not going to be able to unlock her door on her own. Nevertheless, as the siren grew louder, Jamie began to hope.

The ambulance arrived, and the siren died. Victor opened his door and headed toward the scene once more. He returned a few minutes later. "They're loading people into the ambulance now. Shouldn't take much longer."

Jamie's heart pounded loudly in her chest as the sirens whined out once more. The ambulance was obviously rushing its victims to the hospital. The car inched its way closer to the scene. When they were less than 100 feet away, Jamie sighed expansively.

"Are you OK?" Nick asked as though sensing a shift in her mood.

"I'm wondering if we're going to sit here forever, that's all."

Nick smiled. "You're an impatient woman."

"Would somebody turn on the radio?"

Rudy glanced over his shoulder at Nick, who nodded his OK.

"See if you can find a good country-western station," Jamie said.

Nick looked surprised. "I would never have suspected you liked that kind of music."

"Yes sir," Jamie said. "I like it fast and loud."

Nick chuckled as a Patsy Cline song came on. Fleas stood in the back and let out a growl.

"Turn it up," Jamie said.

Rudy shrugged and turned it up.

Fleas began to bark.

Nick turned. "What's wrong with him?"

"Maybe he has to go to the bathroom," Jamie said.

"Bad timing, boy," Nick replied.

Fleas became more agitated. He tried to climb over the seat toward Jamie.

"Down, boy!" Nick shouted. The dog snapped at him. "What the hell?"

"He's nervous," Jamie said. "The music will calm him down. Turn it louder."

Rudy did as he was told, and the car was suddenly flooded with loud music.

Fleas snarled and bit Nick. Suddenly the dog was all over him. "Let me out of the damn car!" Nick shouted.

Rudy instantly hit the automatic lock. Jamie opened her door, whistled for Fleas, and ran as fast as she could toward the sheriff's cars. She heard Nick shout her name, but she kept running.

One of the deputies looked up and frowned at the sight of her. His name tag read: *Higgins.* "What's wrong, miss?"

"Listen to me!" Jamie cried. "My name is Jane, and I'm wanted by the police for killing Harlan Rawlins."

He frowned. "What?"

"I'm Jane!" Jamie cried. "You've seen me on the news. I killed Harlan Rawlins. I'm pretty sure there's a reward for my capture. Something like one hundred grand."

The deputy frowned. "I haven't heard of any reward. Lady, are you crazy?"

Jamie was only vaguely aware that Nick had walked up beside her. He suddenly, and without warning, burst into laughter. "Honey, that is *not* funny."

The deputy looked surprised to see Nick. He glanced around, then stepped closer. "I didn't see your car back there, Mr., um, Juliano," he whispered. "Is everything OK?"

"Fine, Bill. I'm afraid my girlfriend has had too much to drink. How much longer are we going to have to wait? We have a plane to catch."

"I'll clear the way immediately."

Jamie gaped at the man.

"Your hand is bleeding, Nick," Rudy said once Nick and Jamie were inside the car.

"It's nothing. Just give me something to wrap around it."

Victor passed him a clean handkerchief.

"What do you want me to do with the dog?" Rudy asked.

"Kill him." Nick looked at Jamie. "Use the same knife you used on Rawlins."

Detective Pete Sills reached for the telephone and mumbled into it. He looked at the clock on his nightstand. Six-thirty in the morning.

"Detective Sills, my name is Helms, and I'm with the FBI. Could you spare me a few minutes of your time? It has to do with the Rawlins case."

Sills sat up and rubbed his eyes. "How can I help you?"

"I think maybe I can help you."

"No-o-o-o!" Jamie screamed. She lunged across Nick's lap and half-fell from the car. Fleas rushed over to her even as Rudy reached for him. "Don't kill him!" Jamie cried, pounding Rudy's thighs with her fists, even as Nick tried to pull her back into the car. "For God's sake, Nick, please don't kill him. Please, oh God, please!" She burst into tears.

"Hold it," Nick said to the man.

Rudy paused, knife in hand.

"The dog is dangerous," Nick told Jamie. "Look what he did to my hand."

Jamie saw the blood soaking into the handkerchief. "It's my fault," she said, sobbing against him. "Fleas goes berserk at the sound of country music. I know it sounds crazy, but it's true. You won't have any more trouble with him. I promise." She looked up. Nick's eyes were hard. "Nick, I swear to God I'll do anything."

Nick didn't seem to be listening.

"If you kill the dog you may as well kill me, because I'm not going to cooperate."

Nick sighed. "The dog comes with us," he said. "Keep the radio off." As Rudy loaded the dog in the back once more, Nick looked at Jamie. "This is your first and last warning: One false move and the dog dies."

Sweet Pea's airport was no more than a length of asphalt beside a small building. A twin-engine aircraft waited, lights flashing on each wing, the stairs lowered and ready for boarding.

The pilot and co-pilot wore crisp uniforms and nodded at the group as they assisted Nick's men in loading the luggage. Nick helped Jamie out of the Hummer as the pilot waited at the bottom of the steps. Fleas sidled up to Jamie.

"Jamie, I'm afraid we can't take the dog," Nick said.

She blinked at him. "You promised."

"It's not really up to me."

"Bullshit. You make all the rules."

"I can't risk taking the animal on board an aircraft. Not after what happened earlier."

"I've already explained—"

"Rudy will see that Fleas has a good home."

"I'm not going without him, Nick."

"Don't be difficult, Jamie. I have enough to worry about at the moment. I'll buy you a new dog when we get to where we're going. You can have as many pets as you like."

"I don't want a new dog."

Rudy stepped up to Nick. "We've got trouble." He nodded toward the road that led to the airport.

Jamie turned in the direction they were staring. She sucked in her breath at the sight of her truck bouncing along the road, Max at the wheel.

Nick looked at Jamie. "How did he find out?"

"You're asking me?"

"You spoke with him earlier."

"And you heard every word of my conversation. I never mentioned we were going to the airport, he figured it out for himself. I think you underestimate Max."

"Get on the plane."

"Not without my dog."

Nick slapped her hard. "Either you get on the plane now or I order Rudy to shoot him."

Jamie tasted blood. "I don't take orders from you!" she shouted. "I'm not one of your *boys*. You shoot my dog and you'd better be prepared to shoot me, because I'm going to do my best to kill you with my bare hands. I will *not* get on that plane without my dog, you got that?"

"What the hell do you want me to do about Holt?"

Rudy asked as Max turned onto the road leading to the landing strip.

"Kill him and the dog both."

Jamie almost choked on her anger. She grabbed Nick by the collar. "Leave them out of this, do you hear me? I said I'd cooperate, but you have to keep your part of the bargain. Nick, I'm telling you, you do not want to piss me off."

He almost looked amused. "Are you trying to frighten me, Jamie?"

"No, I'm just telling you what a bitch I can be. You leave my dog behind and you're going to regret the day you climbed in an airplane with me. And from the way you talk, we're going to be in the air a long time. Think about it."

Max parked the truck close by and climbed out. He looked at Jamie, noting the blood on her lip. "You know, Nick, I didn't like you before, but I like you even less now. I don't have much respect for a man who would strike a woman."

"You act as if that matters to me, Mr. Holt," Nick said. "You're as good as dead. Why should your opinion of me matter?"

"You plan to shoot an unarmed man in front of your new girlfriend? She doesn't like you to begin with; why risk alienating her further?"

Nick merely smiled.

"Your egg is fried, Nick."

"Meaning?"

"The jig is up."

"Not exactly." With lightning speed Nick pulled Jamie against him and put a gun to her head.

Jamie felt as though her heart would literally take flight from her chest. Damn her and her mouth. "Nick,

I was sort of exaggerating about how nasty I was going to act on the plane. Why can't we just leave Fleas with Max and get going?"

"She's lying, Nick," Max said. "You don't do things her way and she turns into Satan's daughter."

"You two obviously think this is funny," Nick said. "Max, tell me: How would you like to watch my man Rudy cut Jamie like he did Harlan? Would you find that funny? I think her death would be harder on you than your own."

"Damn," Max said. "You just implicated yourself in Harlan Rawlins's murder."

"We both know he was already dead. The fool was popping pills like they were candy."

"You were his supplier; you knew exactly what you were doing. Some pills just don't mix, and you knew that."

"You're right. Harlan overdosed, but I just wanted to leave my mark on him, and Rudy is so good with a knife."

"I wouldn't pull that trigger if I were you," Max said. He nodded toward the airplane, where an elderly gentleman stood at the door of the craft.

Nick turned and froze. "What the hell?"

The pilot assisted the man down the steps. Once the men had cleared them, the pilot stepped aside and the other man crossed the short distance to where they were standing.

"Hello, Nicholas."

"Uncle Leo, what the hell are you doing here?"

Rudy and his partner lowered their rifles and stepped back.

"I see you've managed to dig your hole deeper. Give me the gun, Nicholas."

He gave a short laugh. "Are you kidding? Do you know who these people are?"

"Yes. And do you know what will happen to the Santoni family if you kill Max Holt and Miss Swift?" He didn't wait for Nick's response. "It's time for you to come home. This is the last time I'm going to ask nicely."

"Are you out of your mind, old man?"

"Give me the gun, Nicky. Don't dishonor me in front of these people."

Nick seemed to ponder it. He started to lower the gun, then jerked it back and aimed it in the direction of his uncle. He pulled the trigger, and the man jerked as the bullet hit him square in the chest. Jamie screamed as Leo Santoni fell to the tarmac, but not before she saw Nick and his men aim their guns in Max's direction.

"It's your turn, Holt," Nick said. He'd barely gotten the words out of his mouth before more shots were fired. Jamie watched in horror as Nick and Rudy crumpled to the ground. Where the hell were the shots coming from?

Max reached for her, and the two pilots cleared the steps, each of them armed. Jamie went willingly into Max's arms. From the corner of her eye she saw Nick move. He raised his gun and aimed in her direction. In a split second Max was in front of her, and Fleas pounced on Nick. His gun went off, and the animal howled and went down. Another shot was fired at Nick's head and he fell back.

Jamie screamed and buried her face against Max's chest, not wanting to see any more bloodshed. Finally, she broke free from Max and ran to her dog. "Fleas, no!" she screamed. "Please don't die. Please don't die."

Max was beside her in seconds. "He's going to be OK, Jamie."

"He's not going to make it," she said, choking back a sob. "He took a bullet for me. He's going to die out here with a bunch of mobsters." She kissed the dog on the top of the head. "He looks so sad, Max. He knows he's dying. I was such a bad master, and he knew it. He probably took the bullet on purpose."

"He always looks sad, Jamie, and he is not likely to die from a wounded tail."

"What?" Jamie looked up.

"The bullet nicked his tail, babe, that's all."

Jamie rose and quickly surveyed the damage. Obviously, a bullet had indeed nicked Fleas's tail about six inches up from the tip. "Is that all? Jeez, there's not even that much blood. Good grief, what a sissy!"

"I'm sure it still hurts like hell," Max said.

As if acting on cue, Fleas moaned.

One of the pilots dropped to his knees beside them. "Are you two OK?"

Max nodded. "Yeah."

"How's the mutt?"

Max chuckled. "I believe he'll live."

"The others are dead. I've already phoned headquarters."

"Who are you?" Jamie blurted.

"Agent Decker with the FBI, ma'am. You sure you're OK?"

"I'm having a nervous breakdown, and I skinned my knee. Other than that—"

"You don't know how long we've waited to get Santoni off the streets, but he was always one step ahead of us."

Jamie stared at Max. "Why was Leo Santoni on the plane?"

"I called him," Max said. "He was trying to convince Nick to come home before he did more damage to the family. I told him I'd hand over Nick in exchange for our safety. I didn't mention I was contacting the FBI. I feel bad that it ended this way."

"Don't," Agent Decker said. "Leo might look old and frail, but there was a time he was as bad as his nephew." The man glanced at Nick, sprawled on the tarmac. "I don't think he would have fared any better with the Santoni family." He gave a satisfied sigh. "We've already picked up Tom Bennett for questioning; we're going to find out who all was on Santoni's payroll."

Jamie refused to look in the dead men's direction. That didn't mean she was sorry they were dead, though. "There's a sheriff's deputy," Jamie said. "I think he may have been working for Santoni. His name is Bill Higgins."

Decker jotted it down. Finally, he offered Max his hand. "Mr. Holt, you managed to help us get two of the most powerful men in the Santoni family off the street. Once we seize their property and their computers we'll be able to learn more about the operation."

"You may not be able to break the code," Max said. "I've been trying."

"Helms said we could count on you for assistance."

"Yeah, he would say that. By the way, I have another job for you guys. I want you to pick up the man who heads up my mergers and acquisitions, pronto. I want a full investigation. I strongly suspect he's involved in this somehow."

"Right away, Mr. Holt."

Jamie shot a startled look in Max's direction. "What about Dave? Is he?"

"I spoke with him earlier. They stitched him up; he's fine."

Fleas, obviously having come to the conclusion he was no longer the center of attention, stood and shook, his big ears flapping in the light breeze. Finally, he sat down and started licking his wounded tail. As though discovering it wasn't as bad as he'd thought, he began licking his privates.

Jamie grimaced. "I *hate* when he does that!"

Decker patted the dog on the head. "Headquarters is sending people right away, Mr. Holt. In five minutes this place will be crawling with cops, probably a couple of local reporters. It would be best if you and Miss Swift weren't here when they arrived."

Jamie looked at Max.

He met her gaze. "You know how I hate publicity."

"What about my story?"

"Jamie, we have to talk."

"No, Max, I'm not going to back down this time. I specifically came here for my story." Then she remembered Rudy had taken her notepad. "Oh, damn."

"What is it?" Max asked. "Lost your notes?"

Epilogue

Max began at the nape of her neck, nuzzling the little indentation at the top of her spine, then running his tongue downward, touching each vertebra as he went. Jamie shivered and buried her face against the feather pillow. Max's big hands skimmed her hips, slightly rough against her smooth skin. He trailed his fingers down one thigh, behind one knee, down her calf.

Finally, he coaxed her onto her back.

And studied her.

Her face was lovely, her cheeks heightened a dusty rose that hinted at her own arousal. Her blond hair was rich and glowing, the color of ripened wheat, wisps framing her face, loose tendrils brushing against gently sloping shoulders. Her skin seemed to glow.

She was perfect in every way. Each curve, each swell, looked as though a master artist had sculpted it.

Jamie's eyes fluttered open as Max scooted upward on the bed and covered her mouth with his. It was the kind of kiss that women only dreamed of, the kind they could sink their hearts into. Max parted her lips with his tongue and tasted her. Jamie felt a ripple of pleasure as his hand cupped one breast.

Jamie opened her eyes and stared at the ceiling. Morning. She felt the coarse sheet beneath her; the smell of pine trees and a bloodhound that was in dire need of a bath had replaced the scent of lavender. "Aw, shit," she muttered.

At the foot of the bed, Fleas rolled over and looked at her. He had obviously sneaked up on the bed during the night.

"OK," she said, "so I was dreaming about sex again. With Max," she added. "It happens all the time." She sat up, and her hair tumbled into her face. Her sleep shirt was wrinkled, and she needed to find her toothbrush. Why couldn't she be as gorgeous as she was in her dreams?

"Welcome to the real world, Jamie Swift," she muttered.

Dave did not look happy when Max and Jamie entered his hospital room. He was wearing a dark frown and a surgical mask.

"What's wrong?" Max asked.

"What's wrong?" Dave echoed, his voice muffled from the mask. He pulled it down. "I'm in a hospital surrounded by illness and disease and you ask me what's wrong? Not only that, I'm risking my life being here. Do you have any idea the number of people who are killed each year in hospitals simply because a doctor or nurse makes an error? I'd have a better chance on an open battlefield."

"How long are they keeping you?" Jamie asked.

"Another day at least. They're giving me antibiotics to fight off an infection, but they don't think I should be treated for rabies because, well, because—"

"Yeah?" Max said.

"I'm not exhibiting any symptoms." He suddenly laughed. "And believe me, I've checked."

Max and Jamie laughed with him.

"I don't know how you guys managed to put up with me," Dave said, still chuckling. "You probably need a vacation. *I* need a vacation from myself."

"My private plane is at your disposal," Max said. He reached into his pocket for his business card. "I've listed a number on the back. Call this person when you're ready to check out of this hotel." He paused. "I'd like to see you back at work in a couple of weeks."

Dave took the card. He raised his eyes to Max's, and they exchanged smiles. "Hey, man, I'm really glad we got Santoni."

An hour later, Max pulled into the parking lot of a small Catholic church. "Why are we stopping here?" Jamie asked.

"I have an appointment with a priest. You want to get hitched while we're here?"

Jamie rolled her eyes. "What's this really about?"

"I'll be right back."

Jamie watched him go. "Muffin?"

"I'm here."

"Why is Max meeting with a priest?"

"He's making an anonymous donation to the community. You didn't hear it from me."

Max rejoined Jamie a few minutes later.

"You never fail to amaze me," she said once he'd climbed into the truck and started the engine.

"Oh, yeah?" He looked at her.

"Yeah."

"Does that mean we're going to have hot steamy sex when we get back to the cabin?"

Jamie felt her face grow hot. Well, OK, that wasn't the only body part that warmed at his words. "I, um, well—"

"Easy for you to say," Max teased.

Max was in the process of packing his belongings when Jamie hung up after talking to Vera. She frowned at him.

"What'd I do this time?"

"You bought me a car. A red Mustang," she added. "Vera just told me."

"I felt bad because your other car got shot up by Santoni's hit man. I didn't want you to be without transportation while it's in the shop."

"What am I supposed to do with two cars and a truck? My driveway isn't big enough."

"That truck is on its last legs."

"That truck will be running long after your so-called Maxmobile gives out, Max. Besides, I have to keep it for Fleas. I'll park it in the backyard and grow flowers around it."

They were interrupted by a knock on the door. "That's probably the guy with the trailer."

"I don't believe this," Max said once they were on the road. "I have seen a lot of dumb things in my day, but I've never seen anything as dumb as this."

"I agree," Muffin said. "It's pretty dumb."

"It doesn't look that dumb," Jamie muttered, although she was careful to stay low in the seat so those in traffic couldn't see her.

Max glanced her way. "You don't think we look strange driving a worthless pickup truck and pulling a two-million-dollar car?"

Muffin grunted. "It's one hundred and fifty feet long, Max. I believe it's called a yacht."

Max tossed Jamie a lazy smile. "We could just hop on and go, just the two of us and—"

"Along with a crew of about twenty," Muffin interrupted.

"You and me, Swifty. Lots of sun, blue sky, and water."

Jamie peered over him from the top of her sunglasses. "You and me on a yacht in the middle of the ocean? That sounds more dangerous than anything we've been through so far. Bad idea, Max."

He smiled. "Jamie, Jamie, Jamie. We're a long way from home, and I can't drive over forty miles per hour in this heap. I'll have plenty of time to wear you down."

"Just so Fleas can ride in the back of the truck with us?" Muffin added. "I hope my laptop friend at MIT doesn't hear about this. I'll never be able to live it down."

"Do you have any better suggestions?" Jamie asked. "We didn't have time to get Muffin reinstalled in your car, which is why you refused to let me go back to Beaumont in my truck."

Max grinned. "That's not the only reason, Swifty. I knew you couldn't bear the thought of leaving me."

Jamie ignored him, despite the gentle pull in her stomach. Max only had to look at her to send her thoughts into a wild frenzy. She glanced over her shoulder at Fleas, who was sitting on a feather mattress and gnawing on a foot-long rawhide bone. "I think he survived the trauma well."

"What trauma?" Muffin said. "Nothing happened. We weren't involved in finding Santoni, remember? You guys need to read the newspaper. The FBI shot and killed two mob figures at a small airstrip, and, acting on a hunch, they broke into an auto salvage company owned by one Thomas Peter Bennetti, aka Tom Bennett, and found a small arsenal. Not only that, they've managed to break through the firewall on the computer. That part wasn't in the newspaper; I found out on my own. So what it boils down to is once again we solved the case and someone else gets the credit."

Max grunted. "The FBI won't be able to decipher Santoni's codes."

"Oh, listen to Mr. Genius," Muffin said. "He couldn't break the code, so he doesn't think anyone else can."

"I could have broken it if I'd had more time," Max said. He sighed. "What we need now is a nice vacation. What do you think, Swifty? I've got this nice boat."